VIRAGO
MODERN CLASSICS
641

Joan Aiken (1924–2004) was born in Rye, Sussex. She was the daughter of the American poet Conrad Aiken, and her stepfather was English writer Martin Armstrong. For both Joan and her sister, novelist Jane Aiken Hodge, writing was in their blood.

Joan Aiken wrote over a hundred books and is recognised as one of the classic children's authors of the twentieth century. Amanda Craig, in *The Times*, wrote, 'She was a consummate story-teller, one that each generation discovers anew', and Philip Pullman said, 'Joan Aiken's invention seemed inexhaustible, her high spirits a blessing, her sheer storytelling zest a phenomenon. She was a literary treasure, and her books will continue to delight for many years to come.'

She wrote her first novel, *The Kingdom and the Cave*, when she was just seventeen years old, and the story collection *The Serial Garden*, featuring the magical Armitage Family, spans her entire writing career, from her earliest published short story, 'Yes, But Today is Tuesday' to the stories she wr[illegible] ›oks are *The Wolves of Willoughby Chase* chronicles and the *Arabel's Raven* series. Joan Aiken received the Edgar Allan Poe Award in the United States as well as the Guardian Award for Fiction. She was decorated with an MBE for her services to children's books.

THE SERIAL GARDEN

The Complete Armitage Family Stories

Joan Aiken

Illustrated by Peter Bailey

Foreword by Lizza Aiken

virago

VIRAGO

This edition published in Great Britain in 2015 by Virago Press

1 3 5 7 9 10 8 6 4 2

'Yes, But Today is Tuesday', 'The Frozen Cuckoo', 'Sweet Singeing in the Choir', 'The Ghostly Governess', 'Harriet's Birthday Present' and 'Dragon Monday' previously published in *All You've Ever Wanted*, Cape, 1953
'Armitage, Armitage, Fly Away Home', 'Rocket Full of Pie', 'Tea at Ravensburgh' and 'Dolls' House to Let, Mod. Con.' previously published in *More Than You Bargained For*, Cape, 1955
'Prelude', 'The Land of Trees and Heroes', 'Harriet's Hairloom', 'The Stolen Quince Tree', 'The Apple of Trouble' and 'The Serial Garden' previously published in *Armitage, Armitage, Fly Away Home*, Doubleday, 1968
'Broomsticks and Sardines' previously published in *A Small Pinch of Weather*, Cape, 1969
'Mrs Nutti's Fireplace' previously published in *A Harp of Fishbones*, Cape, 1972
'The Looking-Glass Tree' previously published in *The Faithless Lollybird*, Cape, 1977
'Miss Hooting's Legacy' previously published in *Up the Chimney Down*, Cape, 1984
'Milo's New Word' previously published in *Mooncake*, Hodder, 1998
'Kitty Snickersnee', 'Goblin Music', 'The Chinese Dragon', 'Don't Go Fishing on Witches' Day' previously published in *The Serial Garden: The Complete Armitage Family Stories*, Big Mouth House, 2008

A CIP catalogue record for this book is available from the British Library.

ISBN 978-0-349-00585-0

Typeset in Goudy by M Rules
Printed and bound in Great Britain by
Clays Ltd, St Ives plc

Papers used by Virago are from well-managed forests and other responsible sources.

FSC
www.fsc.org
MIX
Paper from responsible sources
FSC® C104740

Virago
An imprint of
Little, Brown Book Group
Carmelite House
50 Victoria Embankment
London EC4Y 0DZ

An Hachette UK Company
www.hachette.co.uk

www.virago.co.uk

CONTENTS

THE STORY OF THE ARMITAGE FAMILY

My mother, Joan Aiken, grew up in a little village in the Sussex countryside at a time that now seems quite magical to us – her family's cottage didn't have electricity so they lit oil lamps and candles at night, and their water came from the well in the garden. No one had a car, so anything that couldn't be bought from local farms or made at home was fetched by a carrier with a horse and cart from the nearest town. Joan didn't go to school until she was twelve, but was taught at home by her mother, and from the age of five she hungrily devoured the enormous number of books in the house belonging to her stepfather, Martin Armstrong, who was a writer. Her older brother and sister were away at boarding school and, until her smaller brother was born, her best friends were books.

Joan began making up stories to keep her little brother amused on walks on the Sussex Downs near their home, putting in all the best bits from the books she read – fairy tales or Greek myths and legends – and mixing in people they knew from the village. She added their own adventures too, only instead of the Armstrong family, they became the Armitages, with Mark and Harriet based on their much admired older brother and sister. Gradually she introduced all sorts of other characters, including some terrible visiting relatives, a menagerie of magical beasts and many dreadful old fairy ladies (never called witches!).

In the late 1930s, when Joan was a teenager, the BBC invited her stepfather to write for their Children's Hour programme, and he wrote a series about a family and their extraordinary talking pets, which became an enormous success. Influenced by him, Joan sent the first Armitage story to the BBC – 'Yes, But Today is Tuesday' – and to her delight and amazement it was accepted and broadcast. Over the next sixty years until the end of her life, she often returned to the Armitage family, writing more about their adventures in her childhood village. She said that the stories always came out of the blue, in a terrific and wonderful urge to get themselves written.

Joan wrote more than one hundred books, the most famous being *The Wolves of Willoughby Chase* series of novels, but she always said writing stories was her favourite thing, and whenever a new story collection came out, there would be more about the Armitages and their magical life. She later wrote the Prelude, revealing how Mrs Armitage found a magic stone and wished for her family to have an enchanted life, with the promise of living 'Happily Ever After'. One Armitage story stands out as unforgettable for many readers, but it nearly breaks this promise: 'The Serial

Garden' – Mark's cereal packet 'cut-out' garden that comes to life – has a very surprising ending. Joan had so many letters about this story that she felt she had to return to it and offer some hint of a happier outcome for poor Mr Johansen and his lost princess. Mr Johansen reappears in two more stories, but although Joan did now offer hope for a solution she said she could not undo what had happened before.

Towards the end of her life Joan wrote the last few Armitage stories including one about Milo, the baby brother who had inspired the stories in the first place, and sent them off to be collected together for the first time in one special book. She wanted it to be called *The Serial Garden, The Armitage Family Stories* to tell all those readers patiently waiting for their happy ending that finally they might find what they were looking for – and here it is!

Lizza Aiken 2015

PRELUDE

Once upon a time two people met, fell in love, and got married. Their names were Mr and Mrs Armitage. While they were on their honeymoon, staying at a farm near the Sussex coast, they often spent whole days on the beach, which at that point was reached by a path over a high shingle ridge. The sea was beautifully empty, the weather was beautifully warm, and the beach was beautifully peaceful.

One hot, sleepy afternoon the Armitages had been bathing and were lying on the shingle afterwards, sunning themselves, when Mrs Armitage said,

'Darling, are you awake?'

Her husband snored, and then said, 'Eh? Whatsay, darling?'

'This business of living happily ever after,' she said rather thoughtfully, 'it sounds all right but – well – what do we actually do with ourselves all the time?'

'Oh,' Mr Armitage said yawning. ''Spose I go to the office every day and you look after the house and cook dinner – that sort of thing?'

'I see. You don't think,' she said doubtfully, 'that sounds a little *dull*?'

'Dull? Certainly not.' He went back to sleep again. But his wife turned restlessly onto her stomach and scooped with her fingers among the smooth, rattling brown and yellow and white and grey pebbles, which were all warm and smelled of salt.

Presently she exclaimed, 'Oh!'

'Whassamarrer?' Mr Armitage mumbled.

'I've found a stone with a hole.' She held up her finger with the stone fitting neatly over it – a round white chalk-stone with a hole in the middle.

''Markable,' said her husband without opening his eyes.

'When I was little,' Mrs Armitage said, 'I used to call those wishing-stones.'

'Mmm.'

She rolled onto her back again and admired the white stone fitting so snugly on her finger.

'I wish we'll live in a beautiful house in a beautiful village with a big garden and a field and at least one ghost,' she said sleepily.

'That's Uncle Cuthbert's house,' her husband said. 'He's just left it to me. Meant to tell you.'

'And I wish we'll have two children called Mark and Harriet with cheerful energetic natures who will never mope or sulk or get bored. And I hope lots of interesting and unusual things will happen to them. It would be nice if they had a fairy godmother, for instance,' she went on dreamily.

'Here, hold on!' muttered her husband.

'And a few magic wishes. And a phoenix or something out of the ordinary for a pet.'

'Whoa, wait a minute! Be a bit distracting, wouldn't it, all those things going on? Never know what to expect next! And what would the neighbours think?'

'Bother the neighbours! Well,' she allowed, 'we could have a special day for interesting and unusual things to happen – say, Mondays. But not *always* Mondays, and not *only* Mondays, or that would get a bit dull too.'

'You don't really believe in that stone, do you?' Mr Armitage said anxiously.

'Only half.'

'Well how about taking it off, now, and throwing it in the sea, before you wish for anything else?'

But the stone would not come off her finger.

When they had pushed and pulled and tugged until her finger was beginning to be a bit sore, Mrs Armitage said, 'We'd better go back to the farm. Mrs Tulliver will get it off with soap, or butter. And you're getting as red as a lobster.'

When they reached the top of the shingle ridge, Mrs Armitage turned round and looked at the wide expanse of peaceful, silky, grey-blue sea.

'It's beautiful,' she sighed, 'very beautiful. But it would be nice to see something come out of it, once in a way. Like the sea-serpent.'

No sooner had she spoken those words than a huge, green, gnarled, shining, horny head came poking out of the sea. It was all covered with weeds and bumps and barnacles, like the bottom of some old, old ship. And it was followed

by miles and miles and *miles* of body, and it stared at them with two pale, oysterish eyes and opened a mouth as large as Wookey Hole.

With great presence of mind Mrs Armitage said, 'Not today, thank you. Sorry you've been troubled. Down, sir! Heel. Go home now, good serpent, I've got nothing for you.'

With a sad, wailing hoot, like a ship's siren, the monster submerged again.

'For heaven's sake!' said Mr Armitage. 'The sooner we get that stone off your finger, the better it will be.'

They walked on quite fast across the four fields between

the beach and the farm. Every now and then Mrs Armitage opened her mouth to speak, and whenever she did so, Mr Armitage kindly but firmly clapped his hand over it to stop her.

Outside the farm they met four-year-old Vicky Tulliver, swinging on the gate and singing one of the songs she was always making up:

'Two white ducks and
Two white hens
Two white turkeys sitting on a fence—'

'Do you know where your Mummy is?' Mr Armitage asked.

Vicky stopped singing long enough to say, 'In the kitchen,' so the Armitages went there and Mrs Tulliver gave them a knob of beautiful fresh butter to loosen the stone. But it still wouldn't come off. So they tried soap and water, olive oil, tractor oil, clotted cream, and neat's foot oil. And still the stone would not come off.

'Deary me, what can we try next?' said Mrs Tulliver. 'Your poor finger's all red and swole.'

'Oh, goodness, I wish it would come off,' sighed Mrs Armitage. And then, of course, she felt it loosen its hold at once. And just before she slipped it off, she breathed one last request. 'Dear stone, please don't let me ever be bored with living happily ever after.'

'Well!' said Mrs Tulliver, looking at the stone. 'Did you ever, then! Vicky, you've got the littlest fingers, 'spose you take and drop that stone in the well, afore it sticks on any other body the same way.'

So Vicky took the white stone and hung it on her tiny forefinger, where it dangled loosely, and she went out to the well singing,

'Two white heifers
Two white goats
Two white sheep an'
Two white shoats
Two white geese an'
Two white ponies
Two white puppies
Two white coneys
Two white ducks an'
Two white hens
Two white turkeys
Sitting on the fence—
Two white kittens
Sitting in the sun
I wish I had 'em
Every one!'

And with that she tossed the white stone in the well.

'Deary me,' said Mrs Tulliver, looking out the kitchen window into the farmyard. 'Snow in July, then?'

But of course it wasn't snow. It was all the white creatures Vicky had wished for, pecking and fluttering and frisking and flapping and mooing. Mr Tulliver was quite astonished when he came home from haymaking, and as for Vicky, she thought it was her birthday and Easter and Christmas and August Bank Holiday all rolled into one.

But Mr and Mrs Armitage packed their cases and caught a train and went home to Uncle Cuthbert's house, where they settled down to begin living happily ever after.

And they were never, never bored . . .

YES, BUT TODAY IS TUESDAY

Monday was the day on which unusual things were allowed, and even expected to happen at the Armitage house. It was on a Monday, for instance, that two knights of the Round Table came and had a combat on the lawn, because they insisted that nowhere else was flat enough. And on another Monday two albatrosses nested on the roof, laid three eggs, knocked off most of the tiles, and then deserted the nest; Agnes, the cook, made the eggs into an omelette but it tasted too strongly of fish to be considered a success. And on another Monday, all the potatoes in a sack in the larder turned into the most beautiful Venetian glass apples, and Mrs Epis, who came in two days a week to help with the cleaning, sold them to a rag-and-bone man for a shilling. So the Armitages were quite prepared for surprises on a Monday and, if by any chance the parents had gone out during the day, they were apt to open the front door rather cautiously on their return, in case a dromedary should charge at them, which had happened on a particularly notable Monday before Christmas. Then they would go very quietly and carefully into the sitting-room, and sit down, and fortify themselves with sherry before Mark and Harriet came in and told them precisely *what* had happened since breakfast time.

You will see, therefore, that this story is all the more remarkable because it happened on a Tuesday.

It began at breakfast time, when Mark came into the dining-room and announced that there was a unicorn in the garden.

'Nonsense,' said his father. 'Today is Tuesday.'

'I can't help it,' said Mark. 'Just you go and look. It's standing out among the peonies, and it's a beauty, I can tell you.'

Harriet started to her feet, but Mrs Armitage was firm. 'Finish your shredded wheat first, Harriet. After all, today *is* Tuesday.'

So Harriet very unwillingly finished her shredded wheat and gulped down her coffee, and then she rushed into the garden. There, sure enough, knee-deep in the great clump of peonies at the end of the lawn stood a unicorn, looking about rather inquiringly. It was a most lovely creature – snow-white all over, with shining green eyes and a twisted mother-of-pearl horn in the middle of its forehead. Harriet noticed with interest that this horn and the creature's hoofs had a sort of greenish gleam to them, as if they were slightly transparent and lit up from within. The unicorn seemed quite pleased to see Harriet, and she rubbed its velvety nose for a minute or two. Then it turned away and took a large mouthful of peony blossoms. But almost at once it spat them out again and looked at her reproachfully with its lustrous green eyes.

Harriet reflected. Then she saw Mark coming out, and went towards him. 'I think it's hungry,' she remarked. 'What do you suppose unicorns like to eat?'

'Do you think perhaps honeycomb?' Mark suggested. So they went secretly to the larder by the back door and took a large honeycomb out on a platter. Mark held it to the unicorn, first rolling up his sleeves so that the creature should not dribble honey onto him. It sniffed the honey in a cautious manner, and finally crunched it up in two mouthfuls and looked pleased.

'Now, do you suppose,' said Harriet, 'that it would like a drink of milk?' And she fetched it some milk in a blue bowl. The unicorn lapped it up gratefully.

'I think it must have been travelling all night, don't you?' said Mark. 'Look, it's got burrs all tangled up in its tail. I'll comb them out.'

At this moment their father came out into the garden for his after-breakfast stroll. At the sight of the unicorn he paused, stared at it, and finally remarked:

'Nonsense. Today is *Tuesday*. It must have got left over from last night. It was very careless of you not to have noticed it, Harriet.' The unicorn looked at him amiably and began to wash itself like a cat. Mark went off to hunt for a large comb.

'Do you think we could ride it?' Harriet asked her father.

'Not at the moment,' he answered, as the unicorn

achieved a particularly graceful twist, and began licking the middle of its back. 'If you ask me, I should think it would be like riding the sea-serpent. But, of course, you're welcome to try, when it has finished washing.'

Mrs Epis came out into the garden.

'There's a policeman at the door,' she said, 'and Mrs Armitage says will you come and deal with him, sir, please.'

'A policeman,' Harriet observed to herself. 'They don't usually come on a Tuesday.' She followed her father to the front door.

This policeman was different from the usual one. Harriet could not remember ever seeing him before. He looked at the piece of paper in his hand and said,

'I have an inquiry to make about a unicorn. Is it true that you are keeping one without a licence?'

'I don't know about keeping it,' said Mr Armitage. 'There's certainly one in the garden, but it's only just arrived. We hadn't really decided to keep it yet. I must say, you're very prompt about looking us up.'

'Please let's pay the licence and keep it,' whispered Harriet very urgently.

'Well, how much is this precious licence, before we go any further?' asked Mr Armitage.

The policeman consulted his piece of paper again. 'Ten thousand gold pieces,' he read out.

'But that's absurd. Today is Tuesday!' exclaimed Mr Armitage. 'Besides, we haven't got that in the house. As a matter of fact I doubt if we've got so much as one gold piece in the house.'

Harriet did not wait to hear what happened after that. She went out to the unicorn with two large tears in her eyes.

'Why do you have to have such an enormous licence?' she asked it. 'You might have known we couldn't keep you.'

A large green drop of water the size of a plum dropped down on her hand. It was the unicorn's tear.

Mark came across the lawn with a comb. Harriet felt too sad to tell him that they couldn't afford the unicorn. She watched him begin slowly and carefully combing the long tail. The unicorn looked round to see what was happening, and then gave an approving grunt and stood very upright and still.

'Good heavens!' said Mark. 'Look what's fallen out of its tail! A gold piece! And here's another!' At every sweep of the comb, gold pieces tumbled out onto the grass, and soon there was a considerable pile of them.

'They'll do for the licence!' exclaimed Harriet. 'Quick, Mark, go on combing. We want ten thousand of them. Here are Father and the policeman coming to inspect it.' She began feverishly counting the coins and sorting them into heaps of ten.

'It's going to take a terrible time,' she remarked. 'We might as well ask the policeman to check them.'

The two men seemed rather astonished to see what was going on. Harriet had a feeling that the policeman was not altogether pleased. However, he knelt down and began helping to count out the coins. Just as Agnes came out to tell the children that their eleven o'clock bread-and-dripping was on the kitchen table, they finished the counting. The policeman gave Mr Armitage a receipt and took himself off with the money in a bag over his shoulder. And Mr Armitage looked at his watch and exclaimed that it was high time he did some work, and went indoors.

Mark and Harriet sat on the lawn, munching their bread-and-dripping and looking at the unicorn, which was smelling a rose with evident satisfaction.

'I wonder if it ought to be shod?' murmured Mark, looking at its greenish hoofs. 'If we're going to ride it, I mean.' They went over and examined the hoofs at close quarters. They looked rather worn and sore.

'I don't suppose it's used to stones and hard road like ours,' said Harriet. 'You can see it's a foreign animal by the surprised look it has on its face all the time.'

Mark agreed. 'Would you like to be shod?' he asked the creature. It nodded intelligently. 'Well, if that isn't good enough, I don't know what is.' They made a halter out of a green dressing-gown cord of Harriet's, and led the unicorn down to the forge, where Mr Ellis, the blacksmith, was leaning against a wall in the sun, reading the paper.

'Please, will you shoe our unicorn for us?' asked Harriet.

'What, you two again!' exclaimed Mr Ellis. 'I thought today was Tuesday. First it's dromedaries, then unicorns. Thank 'eavens they've got 'oofs of a normal shape. Well, you lead 'im in, Master Mark. I'm not pining to have that there spike of his sticking into me breakfast.'

The unicorn was beautifully shod, with light, small silvery shoes, and seemed very pleased with them.

'How much will that be?' Harriet asked.

'I'll have to look up in my list, if you'll excuse me,' said Mr Ellis. 'I can't remember what it is offhand, for a unicorn. Cor', you won't 'alf have a time at the Toll Bridge at Potter's End, if you ever takes 'im that way.' He went into the back of the forge, where the great bellows were, and found a grubby list. 'Quagga, reindeer – no – farther on we want,' and he ran his finger down to the end and started up. 'Zebra, yak, wildebeest, waterbuck, unicorn. Twelve pieces of gold, please, Miss Harriet.' Fortunately Mark had put the comb in his pocket, so there was no difficulty about combing twelve pieces out of the unicorn's tail. Then they started back home, fairly slowly, giving him time to get accustomed to the feel of his new shoes. He lifted his feet gingerly at first, as if they felt heavy, but soon he seemed to be used to them.

Back on the lawn he became quite lively, and pranced about, kicking up his heels.

'We haven't thought of a name for him,' said Harriet. 'What about Candleberry?'

'Why not?' said Mark. ' . . . and *now* I am going to ride him.'

The unicorn took very kindly to having riders on his back, except for an absent-minded habit of tossing his head, which on one occasion nearly impaled Harriet on his horn. They noticed that when he galloped he could remain off the ground for quite long stretches at a time.

'He can very nearly fly,' said Harriet.

'Perhaps the air where he comes from is thicker,' suggested Mark ingeniously. 'Like the difference between salt and fresh water, you know.'

And then, just as they were deciding to rig up a jump and see how high he would go, they saw a little old man in a red cloak standing on the lawn, watching them. Candleberry stood stock still and shivered all over, as if his skin had suddenly gone goosey.

'Good morning,' Harriet said politely. 'Do you want to speak to Mr Armitage?'

But the little man had his eyes fixed on Candleberry. 'How dare you steal one of my unicorns?' he said fiercely.

'I like that!' exclaimed Mark. 'It came of its own accord. We never stole it.'

'You will return it at once, or it will be the worse for you.'

'After we've paid for its licence too,' chimed in Harriet. 'I never heard such cheek. We shouldn't dream of returning it. Obviously it ran away from you because it was unhappy. You can't have treated it properly.'

'What!' the old man almost shrieked. 'You accuse *me* of not knowing how to treat a unicorn!' He seemed nearly bursting with rage. 'If you won't give it back, I'll make you. I'll cast a spell over it.'

'Hold on,' said Harriet. 'We've had it shod. You haven't any power over it any more.' Even she knew that.

At these words a terrible look crossed over the old man's face.

'You'll discover what it is to interfere with me,' he said ominously, and struck his staff on the ground. Mark and Harriet with one accord grabbed hold of Candleberry's bridle. The whole place became pitch dark, and thunder rolled dreadfully overhead. A great wind whistled through the trees. Candleberry stamped and shivered. Then the gale caught up all three of them, and they were whisked through the air. 'Hang on to the bridle,' shrieked Mark in Harriet's ear. 'I can see the sea coming,' she shrieked back. Indeed, down below them, and coming nearer every minute, was a raging sea with black waves as big as houses.

When the storm burst, Mr and Mrs Armitage were inside the house.

'I hope the children have the sense to shelter somewhere,' said Mrs Armitage. Her husband looked out at the weather and gave a yelp of dismay.

'All my young peas and beans! They'll be blown as flat as pancakes!' he cried in agony, and rushed out into the garden. But as he went out, the wind dropped and the sun shone again. Mr Armitage walked over the lawn, his eyes starting in horror from his head. For all about the garden were one hundred unicorns!

He went back into the house in a state of collapse and told his wife. 'My garden will be trampled to pieces,' he moaned. 'How will we ever get rid of them?'

'Perhaps Mark and Harriet will have some ideas,' suggested Mrs Armitage. But Mark and Harriet were nowhere to be found. Mrs Epis was having hysterics in the kitchen. 'It's not decent,' was all she could say. She had come upon the unicorns unexpectedly, as she was hanging some teacloths on the line.

Agnes, oddly enough, was the one who had a practical idea.

'If you please, sir,' she said, 'I think my dad wouldn't mind three or four of those to use as plough horses. Someone told me that once you've got them trained, they're very cheap to feed.'

So her father, Mr Monks, came along, looked over the herd, and picked out five likely ones as farm horses. 'And thank you kindly,' he said.

'You don't know anyone else who'd be glad of a few, do you?' asked Mr Armitage hopefully. 'As you can see, we've got rather more than we know what to do with.'

'I wouldn't be surprised but what old Farmer Meads could take some in. I'll ask him,' Mr Monks volunteered. 'And there's old Gilbert the carter, and I believe as how someone said the milkman was looking for a new pony.'

'Do ask them all,' said Mr Armitage desperately. 'And look – stick this up on the village notice-board as you go past.' He hastily scribbled a notice which he handed to Mr Monks:

Unicorns given away. Quiet to ride or drive.

The rest of the day the Armitages were fully occupied in giving away unicorns to all applicants. 'It's worse than trying to get rid of a family of kittens,' said Mrs Armitage. 'And if they don't turn out well, we shall have to move away from the village. Oh, there's the artist who lives up on Pennington Hill. I'm sure he'd like a unicorn to carry his paints around for him.'

All day there was no sign of Mark or Harriet, and the parents began to worry. 'If it were Monday, now, it would be all right,' they said, 'but where can they be?'

Late in the evening, after they had disposed of the last unicorn to the baker's boy, and he had gone rejoicing along to Mr Ellis (who was nearly at his wits' end by this time) to have it shod, Mark and Harriet trailed in, looking exhausted but content.

'Where *have* you been? And what *have* you done to your clothes?' Mrs Armitage asked them.

'It wasn't our fault,' Harriet said drowsily. 'We were bewitched. We were blown over the sea, and we fell in. We would have been drowned, only a submarine rose up under us and took us into Brighton.'

'And why didn't you come straight off, pray?'

'Well, we had to earn some money for our bus fares. They won't take unicorn gold in Brighton, I don't know why. So we organized a show with Candleberry on the beach and earned an awful lot. And then we had a huge tea, and Mark caught the bus, and I followed along by the side on Candleberry. He's terribly fast. He's asleep in the greenhouse now. We thought that would be a good place for him. What's the matter with the garden? It looks trampled.'

Harriet's voice was trailing away with sleep.

'You two,' said Mrs Armitage, 'are going straight to bed.'

'But we *always* stay up to supper on Mondays,' complained Mark in the middle of a vast yawn.

'Yes,' said his father, 'but today, as it happens, is Tuesday.'

BROOMSTICKS AND SARDINES

'Oh, bother,' said Mrs Armitage, looking over her coffee-cup at the little heap of sixpences on the sideboard, 'the children have forgotten to take their lunch money to school. You could go that way to the office and leave it, couldn't you, darling?'

The house still reverberated from the slam of the front door, but the children were out of sight, as Mr Armitage gloomily ascertained.

'I hate going to that place,' he said. 'Miss Croot makes me feel so small, and all the little tots look at me.'

'Nonsense, dear. And anyway, why shouldn't they?' Mrs Armitage returned in a marked manner to the *Stitch Woman and Home Beautifier's Journal*, so her husband, with the sigh of a martyr, put on his hat, tucked *The Times* and his umbrella under his arm, and picked up the money. He dropped a kiss on his wife's brow, and in his turn went out, but without slamming the door, into the October day. Instead of going down the cobbled hill towards his office, he turned left up the little passageway which led to Mrs Croot's kindergarten, which Mark and Harriet attended. It was a small studio building standing beside a large garden which lay behind the Armitage garden; Harriet and Mark often wished they could go to school by climbing over the fence. Fortunately, the children were not allowed to play in the studio garden, or, as the Armitage parents often said to each other, shuddering, they would hear their children's voices all day long instead of only morning and evening.

Mr Armitage tapped on the studio door but nobody answered his knock. There was a dead hush inside, and he mentally took his hat off to Miss Croot for her disciplinary powers. Becoming impatient at length, however, he went in, through the lobby where the boots and raincoats lived. The inner doorway was closed, and when he went through it, he stood still in astonishment.

The studio room was quite small, but the little pink and blue and green desks had been shoved back against the walls to make more space. The children were all sitting cross-legged on the floor, quiet as mice, in a ring round the old-fashioned green porcelain stove with its black chimney-pipe which stood on a kind of iron step in the middle of the room. There was a jam cauldron simmering in the middle of the stove, and Miss Croot, an exceedingly tall lady with teeth like fence-posts and a great many bangles, was stirring the cauldron and dropping in all sorts of odds and ends.

Mr Armitage distinctly heard her recite:

'*Eye of newt and toe of frog . . .*'

And then he said: 'Ahem,' and, stepping forward, gave

her the little stack of warm sixpences which he had been holding in his hand all this time.

'My children forgot their lunch money,' he remarked.

'Oh, thank you, Mr Er,' Miss Croot gratefully if absently replied. '*How* kind. I do like to get it on Mondays. Now a pinch of vervain, Pamela, from the tin on my desk please.'

A smug little girl with a fringe brought her the pinch.

'I hope, ma'am, that *that* isn't the children's lunch,' said Mr Armitage, gazing distastefully into the brew. He saw his own children looking at him pityingly from the other side of the circle, plainly hoping that he wasn't going to disgrace them.

'Oh dear, no,' replied Miss Croot vaguely. 'This is just our usual transformation mixture. There, it's just going to boil.' She dropped in one of the sixpences and it instantly became a pink moth and fluttered across to the window.

'Well, I must be on my way,' muttered Mr Armitage. 'Close in here, isn't it.'

He stepped carefully back through the seated children to the doorway, noticing as he did so some very odd-looking maps on the walls, a tray of sand marked in hexagons and pentagons, a stack of miniature broomsticks, coloured beads arranged on the floor in concentric circles, and a lot of little Plasticine dolls, very realistically made.

At intervals throughout the day, Mr Armitage thought rather uneasily about Miss Croot's kindergarten, and when he was drinking his sherry that evening, he mentioned the matter to his wife.

'Where are the children now, by the way?' he said.

'In the garden, sweeping leaves with their brooms. They made the brooms themselves, with raffia.'

In fact he could see Mark and Harriet hopping about in the autumn dusk. They had become bored with sweeping and were riding on the brooms like horses. As Mr Armitage watched, Mark shouted 'Abracadabra,' and his broomstick lifted itself into the air, carried him a few yards, and then turned over, throwing him into the dahlias.

'Oh, jolly good,' exclaimed Harriet. 'Are you hurt? Watch me now.' Her broomstick carried her into the fuchsia bush, where it stuck, and she had some trouble getting down.

'You see what I mean?' said Mr Armitage to his wife.

'Well, I shouldn't worry about it too much,' she answered comfortably, picking up her tatting. 'I think it's much better for them to get that sort of thing out of their systems when they're small. And then Miss Croot is such a near neighbour; we don't want to offend her. Just think how tiresome it was when the Bradmans lived there and kept dropping all their snails over the fence. At least the children play quietly and keep themselves amused nowadays, and that's *such* a blessing.'

Next evening, however, the children were being far from quiet.

Mr Armitage, in his study, could hear raucous shouts and recriminations going on between Mark and Harriet and the Shepherd children, ancient enemies of theirs in the garden on the other side.

'Sucks to you!'

'Double sucks, with brass knobs on.'

'This is a gun, I've shot you dead. Bang!'

'This is a magic wand, I've turned you into a—'

'*Will* you stop that hideous row,' exclaimed Mr Armitage, bursting out of his French window. A deathly hush fell in the garden. He realized almost at once, though, that the silence was due not so much to his intervention as the fact that where little Richard, Geoffrey, and Moira Shepherd had been, there were now three sheep, which Harriet and Mark were regarding with triumphant satisfaction.

'Did you do that?' said Mr Armitage sharply to his children.

'Well – yes.'

'Change them back at once.'

'We don't know how.'

'Geoffrey – Moira – your mother says it's bedtime.' Mr Shepherd came out of his greenhouse with a pair of secateurs.

'I say, Shepherd, I'm terribly sorry – my children have changed yours into sheep. And now they say they don't know how to change them back.'

'Oh, don't apologize, old chap. As a matter of fact, I think it's a pretty good show. Some peace and quiet will be a wonderful change, and I shan't have to mow the lawn.' He shouted indoors with the liveliest pleasure,

'I say, Minnie! Our kids have been turned into sheep, so you won't have to put them to bed. Dig out a long frock and we'll go to the Harvest Ball.'

A shriek of delight greeted his words.

'All the same, it was a disgraceful thing to do,' said Mr Armitage severely, escorting his children indoors. 'How long will it last?'

'Oh, only till midnight – like Cinderella's coach, you know,' replied Harriet carelessly.

'It would be rather fun if *we* went to the Harvest Ball,' remarked Mr Armitage, in whom the sight of the carefree Shepherd parents had awakened unaccustomed longings. 'Agnes could look after the children, couldn't she?'

'Yes, but I've nothing fit to wear!' exclaimed his wife. 'Why didn't you think of it sooner?'

'Well, dash it all, can't the kids fix you up with something? Not that I approve of this business, in fact I'm going to put a stop to it, but in the meantime . . .'

Harriet and Mark were delighted to oblige and soon provided their mother with a very palatial crinoline of silver lamé.

'Doesn't look very warm,' commented her husband. 'Remember the Assembly Rooms are always as cold as the tomb. Better wear something woolly underneath.'

Mrs Armitage created a sensation at the ball, and was so sought-after that her husband hardly saw her the whole evening. All of a sudden, as he was enjoying a quiet game of whist with the McAlisters, a terrible thought struck him. 'What's the time, Charles?'

'Just on twelve, old man. Time we were toddling. I say, what's up?'

Mr Armitage had fled from the table and was frantically searching the ballroom for his wife. At last he saw her, right across on the other side.

'Mary!' he shouted. 'You must come home at once.' 'Why? What? Is it the children . . . ?' She was threading her way towards him when the clock began to strike. Mr Armitage started and shut his eyes. A roar of applause broke out, and he opened his eyes to see his wife looking down at herself in surprise. She was wearing a scarlet silk ski-suit. Everyone crowded around her, patting her on the back, and saying that it was the neatest trick they'd seen since the pantomime, and how had she done it? She was given a prize of a hundred cigarettes and a bridge marker. 'I had the ski-suit on underneath,' she explained on the way home. 'So as to keep warm, you see. There was plenty of room for it under the crinoline. And what a mercy I did . . .'

'All this has got to stop,' pronounced Mr Armitage next morning. 'It's Guy Fawkes in a couple of weeks, and can't you imagine what it'll be like? Children flying around on broomsticks and being hit by rockets, and outsize fireworks made by methods that I'd rather not go into – it just won't do, I tell you.'

'*Je crois que vous faites une montagne d'une colline – une colline de . . .*'

'*Une taupinière*,' supplied Harriet kindly. 'And you can call father '*tu*,' you know.'

Mark looked sulkily into his porridge and said, 'Well, we've got to learn what Miss Croot teaches us, haven't we?'

'I shall go round and have a word with Miss Croot.'

But as a result of his word with Miss Croot, from which Mr Armitage emerged red and flustered, while she remained imperturbably calm and gracious, such very large snails began to march in an endless procession over the fence from Miss Croot's garden into the Armitage rosebed that Mrs

Armitage felt obliged to go round to the school and smooth things over.

'My husband always says a great deal more than he means, you know,' she apologized.

'Not at all,' replied Miss Croot affably. 'As a matter of fact, I am closing down at Christmas in any case, for I have had a most flattering offer to go as an instructress to the young king of Siam.'

'Thank goodness for *that*,' remarked Mr Armitage. 'I should think she'd do well there. But it's a long time till Christmas.'

'At any rate, the snails have stopped coming,' said his wife placidly.

Mr Armitage issued an edict to the children.

'I can't control what you do in school, but understand if you do any more of these tricks, there will be *no* Christmas tree, *no* Christmas party, *no* stockings, and *no* pantomime.'

'Yes, we understand,' said Harriet sadly.

Mrs Armitage, too, looked rather sad. She had been thinking what a help the children's gifts would be over the shopping; not perhaps with clothes, as nobody wanted a wardrobe that vanished at midnight, but food! Still, would there be very much nourishment in a joint of mutton that abandoned its eaters in the middle of the night; certainly not! It was all for the best.

Mark and Harriet faithfully, if crossly, obeyed their father's edict, and there were no further transformations in the Armitage family circle. But the ban did not, of course, apply to the little Shepherds. Richard, Geoffrey and Moira were not very intelligent children, and it had taken some time for Miss Croot's teaching to sink into them, but when it did, they were naturally anxious to retaliate for being turned into sheep. Mark and Harriet hardly ever succeeded in reaching school in their natural shape; but whether they arrived as ravens, spiders, frogs, or pterodactyls, Miss Croot always changed them back again with sarcastic politeness. Everyone became very bored with the little Shepherds and their unchanging joke.

Guy Fawkes came and went with no serious casualties, except for a few broken arms and legs and cases of concussion among the children of the neighbourhood, and Mrs Armitage began making plans for her Christmas Party.

'We'll let the children stay up really late this year, shall we? You must admit they've been very good. And you'll dress up as Father Christmas, won't you?'

Her husband groaned, but said that he would.

'I've had such a bright idea. We'll have the children playing Sardines in the dark; they always love that; then you can put on your costume and sack of toys and get into the hiding-place with them and gradually reveal who you are. Don't you think that's clever?'

Mr Armitage groaned again. He was always sceptical about his wife's good ideas, and this one seemed to him particularly open to mischance. But she looked so pleading that he finally agreed.

'I must make a list of people to ask,' she went on. 'The Shepherds, and the McAlisters, and their children, and Miss Croot, of course—'

'*How* I wish we'd never heard of that woman's school,' said her husband crossly.

Miss Croot was delighted when Mark and Harriet gave her the invitation.

'I'll tell you what would be fun, children,' she said brightly. 'At the end of the evening, I'll wave my wand and change you all into dear little fairies, and you can give a performance of that Dance of the Silver Bells that you've been practising. Your parents *will* be surprised. And I shall be the Fairy Queen. I'll compose a little poem for the occasion:

'Now, dear parents, you shall see
What your girls and boys can be
Lo, my magic wand I raise
And change them into elves and fays . . .

or something along those lines.'

And she retired to her desk in the throes of composition, leaving the children to get on with copying their runes on their own.

'I think she's got a cheek,' whispered Mark indignantly. 'After all, it's our party, not hers.'

'Never mind, it won't take long,' said Harriet, who was rather fond of the Dance of the Silver Bells and secretly relished the thought of herself as a fairy.

The party went with a swing; from the first game of Hunt the Slipper, the first carol, the first sight of Mrs Armitage's wonderful supper with all her specialities, the turkey vol-au-vent and Arabian fruit salad.

'Now how about a game of Sardines?' Mrs Armitage called out, finding with astonishment that it was half-past eleven and that none of her guests could eat another crumb.

The lights were turned out.

'Please, we'd rather not play this game. We're a bit nervous,' twittered the Shepherd children, approaching their hostess. She looked at them crossly – really they *were* faddy children. 'Very well, you sit by the fire here till it's time for the Tree.' As she left them, she noticed that they seemed to be drawing pictures in the ashes with their fingers, messy little beasts.

She went to help her husband into his cloak and beard.

'Everyone is in the cupboard under the stairs,' she said. 'Harriet hid first, and I told her to go there. I should give them another minute.'

'Who's that wandering about upstairs?'

'Oh, that's Miss Croot. Her bun came down, and she went up to fix it. Don't wait for her – there you are, you're done. Off with you.'

Father Christmas shouldered his sack and went along to the stair cupboard.

'Well,' he exclaimed, in as jovial a whisper as he could manage, stepping into the thick and dusty dark, 'I bet you can't guess who's come in this time.' Gosh, I do feel a fool, he thought.

Silence greeted his words.

'Is there anybody here?' he asked in surprise, and began feeling about in the blackness.

Mrs Armitage, standing by the main switch, was

disconcerted to hear shriek upon shriek coming from the cupboard. She threw on the light and her husband came reeling out, his beard all awry, parcels falling from his sack in all directions.

'Fish!' he gasped. 'The whole cupboard's full of great, wriggling fish.'

It was at this moment that Miss Croot appeared in full fig as the Fairy Queen, and began to recite:

'Now, dear parents, you shall see
What your girls and boys can be . . .'

A somewhat shamefaced procession of large silver fish appeared from the cupboard and began wriggling about on their tails.

'Oh dear,' said Miss Croot, taken aback. 'This wasn't what I—'

'D.T.s,' moaned Mr Armitage. 'I've got D.T.s.' Then his gaze became fixed on Miss Croot in her regalia, and he roared at her:

'Did you do this, woman? Then out of my house you go, neck and crop.'

'Mr Armitage!' exclaimed Miss Croot, drawing herself up, stiff with rage, and she would certainly have turned him into a toad, had not an interruption come from the little Shepherds, who danced round them in a ring, chanting:

'Tee hee, it was us, it was us! Sucks to the Armitages!'

Luckily, at that moment, the clock struck twelve, the fish changed back into human form, and by a rapid circulation of fruit-cup, cherry ciderette, and the rescued parcels, Mrs Armitage was able to avert disaster.

'Well, dear friends, I shall say goodbye to you now,' fluted Miss Croot, after ten minutes or so.

'Thank goodness,' muttered Mr Armitage.

'I'm off to my new post in Siam, but I shall often think with regret of the little charges left behind, and I hope, dears, that you will all keep up the accomplishments that you have learned from me.' ('They'd better not,' growled her host.) 'And that *you*, pets,' (here she bent a severe look on the little Shepherds) 'will learn some better manners. *Au revoir* to all, and *joyeux noël*.'

At these words, the carpet beneath her feet suddenly rose and floated out of the window.

'My carpet!' cried Mr Armitage. 'My beautiful Persian carpet!'

But then they saw that the (admittedly worn) Persian carpet had been replaced by a priceless Aubusson, which, unlike Miss Croot's other gifts, did not vanish away at midnight.

All the same, it took Mr Armitage a long time to get used to it. He hated new furniture.

DOLLS' HOUSE TO LET, MOD. CON.

The family were at breakfast when the front-door bell rang, and Harriet went to see who it was.

'It's old Mrs Perrow,' she said returning. 'She says can she speak to you, Mother?'

'Oh dear,' said Mrs Armitage sadly. 'What can she want?'

She left her bacon and went into the front hall. The rest of the family watched the bacon sympathetically as it gradually went cold on her plate while they listened to a shrill stream of complaints going on and on, punctuated occasionally by a soothing murmur from Mrs Armitage.

'Wretched woman,' said Mr Armitage crossly. 'She must be telling all her family troubles back to Adam, by the sound of it. Mark, put your mother's plate in the hot-cupboard.'

Mark had just done this when his mother came back looking indignant.

'It really is too bad, poor things,' she said sitting down. 'That miserable Mr Beezeley has turned them out of Rose

Cottage on some flimsy excuse – the real reason is that he wants to do it up and let it to a rich American. So the Perrows have nowhere to live.'

'What an old scoundrel,' exclaimed Mr Armitage. 'All the same, I don't see that there's much we can do about it.'

'I said they could live in our loft till they found somewhere else.'

'You did *what?*'

'Said they could live in the loft. I don't know if they'll be able to climb in, though. Children, you'd better go and see if you can rig up a ladder for them.'

Mark and Harriet ran off, leaving their father to fume and simmer while his wife placidly went on with her breakfast.

The loft was over the kitchen, but it was approached from outside, by a door over the kitchen window. Harriet and Mark used it as a playroom and always climbed up by means of the toolshed roof, but grown-ups used a ladder when they entered it.

'Will the Perrows be able to use the ladder?' said Harriet doubtfully. 'The rungs are rather far apart.'

'No, I've had a better idea – Father's new trellis. We'll take a length of that. It's still all stacked by the back door.'

The trellis was ideal for the job, being made of strong metal criss-crossed in two-inch squares. They leaned a section over the kitchen window, fastened the top securely with staples to the doorsill of the loft, and jammed the bottom firmly with stones.

'That should take their weight,' said Mark. 'After all, they're not heavy. Here they come.'

The Perrow family were peculiar in that none of them was more than six inches high. Ernie Perrow and his wife were cousins and lived with his old mother and their nine children. There had always been some Perrows in the village, but no one knew exactly why they were so small. There were various theories about it. Some people thought that a Perrow ancestor had been frightened by Stevenson's *Rocket* when he was young, and had never grown any more. Others said that it was a curse laid on the family by someone who had suffered from their bad temper, or that the Perrows always gave their children juniper wine instead of milk to keep them small.

Whatever the cause of their small size, they were very proud of it, and seldom married outside the family. They were a hard-working, self-respecting clan, rather dour and surly, earning their living mostly by rat-catching, chimney-sweeping, drain-clearing, and other occupations in which their smallness was useful. The women did marvellous embroidery.

They had always owned Rose Cottage, portioning it off, one or two rooms to each family. But Ernie's father, old Mrs Perrow's husband, had been a waster and had been obliged to sell the cottage to Farmer Beezeley's father, who had let him stay on in it and pay rent. The present Beezeley was not so accommodating, and had been trying to get them out for a long time.

Harriet and Mark watched with interest as the Perrows made their way up the path to the loft. Lily and Ernie were each pushing barrows loaded with household belongings, and a trail of minute children followed, some of them only an inch or so high. Harriet began to wonder how the children would manage to climb up the trellis, but they scrambled up like monkeys, while Ernie was rigging a pulley to take the furniture. At the end of the procession came old Mrs Perrow carrying a bluebottle in a cage and keeping up a shrill incessant grumble.

'What I mean to say, fine place to expect us to live, I'm sure. Full of cobwebs, no chimney – where's Lily going to put her oil stove? We shall all be stunk out with paraffin.'

Harriet was enraptured with the oil stove, which the resourceful Ernie had made out of biscuit tins and medicine glasses. She rushed off to call her father to come and see it. Unfortunately he arrived just as the stove, dangling at the end of the rope, swung inward and cracked a pane of the kitchen window. Mr Armitage growled and retired again. He decided to soothe himself by watering his tomatoes, but had only just begun when he was startled by tiny but piercing shrieks; he found a small Perrow in a pram the size of an eggshell (and in fact made from one) in the shade of one of his tomato plants. He had just copiously sprinkled it with Liquifert. He hurried off in a rage, tripped over a long line of washing which had been strung between two hollyhocks, and had to replace twenty nappies the size of postage stamps fastened with clothes-pegs made from split matches bound with fuse wire.

He strode indoors to find his wife.

'This arrangement won't do,' he thundered. 'I'll go and see that miserable Beezeley myself. I cannot have my garden used in this manner. I'm sure to tread on one of those children sooner or later.'

Mrs Armitage ruefully looked at a little Perrow sobbing over the fragments of a doll's tea-set made from corn husks which she had trodden on before she saw it.

'They do seem to spread,' she agreed.

They heard frantic yells from the garden and saw two more children slide down from a cloche and run off, pursued by Ernie with a hairbrush.

'You touch any of these things and I'll tan you,' he shouted.

'It's no use, though,' Mrs Armitage said. 'Ernie and Lily do their best, but they can't be in nine places at once.'

Her husband clapped on his hat and rushed off to Beezeley's farm. He met Mr Beezeley himself, just outside the gate of Rose Cottage.

'Now look here, Beezeley,' he shouted. 'What right have you to turn those Perrows out of Rose Cottage? They paid their rent, didn't they? You can't do things like that.'

'Oh yes, I can, Mr Armitage,' Beezeley replied smoothly. 'Rose Cottage belongs to me, and it's supposed to be an agricultural labourer's cottage intended for men working on my farm. Perrow never did a hand's turn for me. He was all over the village.'

'Indeed,' said Mr Armitage dangerously, 'and who is the agricultural labourer that you have put in, may I ask?'

He turned to look at a huge Packard which stood outside the gate of Rose Cottage.

'Here he comes now,' replied Mr Beezeley agreeably. 'Meet my new farm worker, Mr Dunk R. Spoggin.'

'Well, well!' said that gentleman, strolling towards them. He wore a silk checked shirt, diamond tiepin, and red and white saddle shoes. 'I sure am pleased to meet another new neighbour. Quaint little rural spot you live in here, Mr Er. I aim to wake it up a little.'

'Mr Spoggin is going to work on my farm for a year,' explained Mr Beezeley. 'He has invented a new all-purpose agricultural machine which he wishes to try out, and my farm is going to be the testing ground. You can see them putting it up over there.'

Indeed, a small army of men in blue jeans were putting together something the size of a factory on the big meadow behind Beezeley's farm.

'It ploughs, harrows, sows, manures, hoes, applies artificial heat, sprinkles with D.D.T., reaps, threshes, and grinds,' Mr Spoggin informed them. 'It raises a crop in three days and has it harvested and out of the way in another three. Three days later, the field is ready for a second crop. We should get sixty crops off that field of yours, Mr Beezeley, in the course of the next year.'

Mr Armitage looked incredulous. Dunk R. Spoggin drew himself up.

'You don't believe me, eh? Let me tell you I am *the* Dunk R. Spoggin, maker of the Spoggin Combine, the Spoggin Diesel Dam Dredger, the Spoggin Potato Clamper, the Spoggin Gloucester Old Spot Scratcher, and the Spoggin Gilt-Edged Pig Palace. I could buy out Henry Ford any time, *if* I wanted to. Have a cigar.' He held out a two-foot one.

Mr Armitage accepted, and turned to find that Mr Beezeley had strolled away to inspect the new machine.

'Won't you find it rather confined in Rose Cottage? Surely it is smaller than the sort of thing you are used to?' he asked.

Mr Spoggin smiled expansively.

'Why no, I just love your quaint little old houses. This one is genuine Tooder, I understand. Mr Beezeley wanted to lease it to me, but I said straight out, "No, Mr Beezeley, I am a buying man. I'll give you twenty thousand for it, take it or leave it."'

'Twenty thousand *pounds*?'

'Pounds, yes, sir.'

'And did he take it?'

'He did, and a cheaper property I've never bought. I felt downright mean, and nearly clapped another twenty on top of the first.'

Mr Armitage came home to lunch very thoughtful, and told his wife about their new neighbour.

'No hope of getting the Perrows back if he's bought the place,' he said. 'I'm afraid we're fixed with them for life.'

After lunch Mrs Armitage said: 'Children, if you're going into Bunstable this afternoon, could you get me some embroidery silks? I don't seem to have as many as I thought I had.'

'I know where they are,' thought Harriet, who had seen all the little Perrow girls with beautiful new hair ribbons and sashes.

'And some napkin rings in Woolworth's, please. All those seem to have gone, too.'

A loud cry outside the window startled them, and Mark got there in time to see the butcher's boy trip on the path and scatter chops all over the pansies. The object that had tripped him appeared to be a napkin ring, which was being bowled by a small Perrow boy.

'Right, napkin rings and embroidery silks,' he said. 'That all? Coming, Harriet?'

Harriet always preferred the right-hand side of the Bunstable High Street, because the left side was all taken up with banks, house agents, coal merchants, and building societies, none of which have interesting shop windows. Today, however, her eye was caught as she cycled slowly along by a notice in a house agent's window, and giving a shout to Mark, who was in front, she jumped off and went to investigate.

TO LET: DOLLS' HOUSE 4FT. HIGH. MOD. CON.
DESIRABLE RESIDENCE, NEWLY DECORATED
SEEN BY ARRANGEMENT   INQUIRE WITHIN

Harriet and Mark ran inside and saw a shady, seedy, young man picking his nails behind a deal desk. On a table at the back of the room was an elegant Queen Anne house with steps up to a pillared porch and bow windows.

'Oh,' breathed Harriet, all eyes. Mark was brisker.

'We wish to inquire about the dolls' house,' he said.

'Yes, sir. A delightful family residence. Two recep., three bed, kitchen, bath, usual offices. Calor gas lighting and heating installed by last tenant, who vacated suddenly. Do you wish to have an order to view?'

'Can't we just *view* it?' asked Harriet, gazing covetously through a bow window at one of the two recep.

'Oh dear, no, madam. It's all locked up. The keys are obtainable from the owner.'

'Where does the owner live?'

'The address is Mrs Maria Nightshade, Cobweb Corner, Dead Man's Lane, Blackwood.'

Harriet and Mark burst into tea full of enthusiasm. 'We've found a house for the Perrows,' they cried. Their parents looked sceptical.

'Old Mrs Nightshade? I seem to know the name. Isn't she a witch?'

'Very likely,' Harriet said. 'She lives in a dark little den full of pots and jars with a black cat and an owl. But the dolls' house is *lovely*, just think how pleased the Perrows will be.'

They were having their tea in the kitchen, and at that moment an outburst of thuds and angry screeches reminded them that the Perrows were just overhead.

'It will certainly be nice for them to have a separate room for old Mrs Perrow,' Mrs Armitage agreed. 'I always think it's a mistake to live with your mother-in-law.'

She took the lid off the jam jar and found a small Perrow girl inside, having a peaceful feast and coated from head to foot in raspberry.

'Oh dear. Harriet, put Elsie on this saucer – I should pick her up with sugar tongs – and take her to her mother. Really, it's just like the evacuees all over again.'

Harriet did as she was requested, holding Elsie under the tap on the way in spite of howls.

'*There* she is, the wicked little thing,' exclaimed Lily. 'I'm sorry, miss, I'm sure, but really they're that active it's a job to keep up with them all.'

She was putting them to bed, so Harriet postponed telling her about the house and ran back to the tea-table, where Mark was explaining that they had paid a quarter's rent in advance.

'And they are bringing the house out tomorrow.'

'Where are they going to put it? Not in my garden, I beg.'

'No, no, Miss Rogers said it could go at the end of her field.'

'What's the rent?'

Harriet and Mark looked a little guilty.

'It's three packets of birthday candles a week – the pink, white and blue ones.'

'Funny sort of rent,' remarked her father suspiciously.

'Well, you see, she can't get them herself. People won't sell them to her in case she makes wax images, you know, and sticks pins in them.'

'She'll be able to make plenty now,' Mr Armitage said drily. 'However, far be it from me to interfere in any arrangement which rids us of the Perrows.'

An aniseed ball thudded against the window and cracked it. The Perrow boys were playing hockey with pencil hockey sticks from Woolworth's which Mark had generously but thoughtlessly given them.

'That's the eighth window,' said Mrs Armitage resignedly.

Next day the Perrows moved out amidst universal rejoicing. Harriet and Mark went along to Miss Rogers's field to hear cries of delight at the sight of the beautiful house, but the Perrow enthusiasm was very lukewarm.

'Just look at all those big windows to clean,' said Lily gloomily. 'And Calor gas. Where am I going to put my oil stove? These old-fashioned houses are always draughty, too.'

'Don't you take any notice of her, miss. She's pining for the cottage and that's the truth,' Ernie apologized.

They seemed to settle in comfortably enough though, old Mrs Perrow taking the best front room, and Harriet and Mark presently strolled away to see how Mr Beezeley's new cultivator was getting on. It now covered the entire hundred-acre field and looked like the Crystal Palace. Through the glass walls nothing could be seen but machinery, with Mr Dunk R. Spoggin darting among the cogs and belts.

They saw Mr Beezeley and said good morning to him rather coldly.

'Morning, morning, young people,' he replied. 'Bitter weather for the time of year, isn't it. My rheumaticks are terrible bad.'

Indeed he was walking with great difficulty, almost doubled up.

'You'll be glad to hear that the Perrows have found a suitable house,' Harriet said shortly. 'They've rented Mrs Nightshade's dolls' house.'

'Old Mrs Nightshade over at Blackwood?' said Mr Beezeley, bursting into hearty laughter. 'I sold her a couple of hens that had the henbane once. She's never forgiven me; I bet she'd do me a bad turn if she could. But all's fair in love and farming, *I* say. Ugh, this rheumatism is fairly crippling me.'

The children left him and went home.

'Gosh,' said Harriet, 'do you suppose Mrs Nightshade is giving him rheumatism?'

'Well, he jolly well deserves it. I hope she ties him in knots.'

When they arrived home they were dismayed to hear Mrs Perrow's shrill, complaining voice in the kitchen.

'What I mean to say, it's a fine thing, first to turn us out of our house, then have to live in a loft, all cobwebs though kindly meant I daresay, not what we're used to, and then when we move into the new house what do we find?'

'Well, what *do* you find?' said Mrs Armitage patiently.

'Nothing won't stay put!' cried Mrs Perrow. She had climbed onto a chair and was standing on it, quivering with indignation. 'You put down the kettle and it flies across and sticks on the wall. There's all Lily's bottled elderberries fallen down and broken and the daisy wine full of ashes that blew out of the fire by themselves, and young Sid's got a black eye from the mustard, and the bedroom door slammed and knocked baby down the stairs, and the dishes fall off the dresser all the time, it won't do, Mrs Armitage, it really won't do.'

'Oh dear,' Mrs Armitage said sympathetically, 'it sounds as if you have a poltergeist.'

'Can't say about that, mum, but it's not good enough for me and Ernie and Lily, and that's a fact. We'd sooner live in your house loft, though it's not what we're used to, but stay in that house we cannot and will not.'

Mrs Armitage gazed at her in despair.

Just at that moment, they all heard an extraordinary noise from the direction of Beezeley's farm, a sort of whistling which rose to a roar.

'What can be going on?' exclaimed Harriet. 'Let's go and see. I bet it's the new cultivator.'

They all ran out, leaving Mrs Perrow to continue her complaints to an empty kitchen. A strange sight met their eyes as they reached the new cultivator. It was swaying from side to side, shuddering and groaning as if at any moment it might leave the ground and take off into the air. Mr Spoggin was rushing about in great agitation with an oilcan. Mr Beezeley was there too, but did not seem to be taking much notice; he was standing hunched up, looking very miserable and groaning from time to time.

'Look!' said Mark, 'there's corn sprouting through the walls.'

Wheat ears of an enormous size were pushing their way out between the panes of glass, and through the windows they could see that the whole inside was a tangled mass of stalks which continuously writhed and pushed upwards.

'It's cursed,' cried poor Mr Spoggin frantically. 'None of my other machines has done this. Someone's put a hoodoo on it.'

As he spoke there was a shattering explosion. Bits of broken glass and ears of corn the size of vegetable marrows filled the air. Fortunately the spectators were all blown backwards across several fields by the blast, and came to rest, breathless but unhurt, in Miss Rogers's field outside the dolls' house.

'Well, that certainly is the end,' said Mr Spoggin, struggling to his feet. 'Never again do I try any experiments in your country. There must be something peculiar about the soil. I'm going straight back to the U.S.A. by the next boat.' He paused, with his mouth open and his eyes bulging.

'That dolls' house! Am I dreaming, or is it real?'

'Oh, it's real, right enough,' they assured him gloomily as a saucepan and two little Perrows, inextricably entangled, rolled screaming and kicking down the front steps.

'I must add it to my collection. I have the largest collection of dolls' houses in five continents, including a real Eskimo child's dolls' igloo, made out of genuine snow. I definitely must have that house.'

'That's a fine thing,' shrieked Mrs Perrow, who had come up behind him in time to hear this. 'And where do we live, I should like to know?'

Mr Spoggin was visibly startled but recovered himself quickly and bowed to her.

'I'll make you a present of my place, ma'am,' he said. 'It's a poky little hole, I only paid twenty thousand pounds for it, but such as it is, it's yours. Just up the road, Rose Cottage is the name. Here are the title deeds.' He pulled them out of his pocket.

'We'll take you to see the agent,' Harriet said quickly. 'The dolls' house doesn't belong to the Perrows, and I don't know if the owner will want to sell. I fancy she prefers letting it.'

'She'll sell,' said Mr Spoggin confidently. 'Where's Tin Lizzie?'

He found his Packard roosting in a nearby hawthorn tree and whirled them off to the agent, who received them warily. He was evidently used to complaints from tenants.

'If you want your quarter's rent back, I'm afraid it's out of the question,' he said at once. 'It's been used already.'

'I want to buy that dolls' house,' shouted Mr Spoggin. 'Name your figure.'

'I should warn you that it's haunted,' Harriet muttered. 'There's a poltergeist in it.'

'Haunted?' said Mr Spoggin, his eyes like stars. 'A haunted dolls' house! It'll be the gem of the whole collection.' He was in ecstasies.

'I don't know if my client wishes to sell,' said the agent repressively.

'I'll give you forty thousand pounds for it, not a penny more, so it's no use acting cagey in the hope that I'll put my price up, I shan't,' said Mr Spoggin. 'You can take it or leave it.'

The agent took it.

Mr Spoggin took them home and carried off the dolls' house then and there in Tin Lizzie, having telephoned the *Queen Mary* to wait for him. He left the remains of the cultivator.

Mr Beezeley was not seen for some hours after the explosion, but finally turned up in a bed of stinging-nettles, which had cured his rheumatism but left him much chastened. He spent a lot of time wandering round the deep hole which was all that was left of the hundred-acre field, and finally sold his farm and left the neighbourhood.

As the children came down to breakfast next morning they heard the grumbling voice of old Mrs Perrow in the porch:

'It's all very well, Mrs Armitage, but what I mean to say is, Rose Cottage is not what we've been used to. Cooking on that old oil stove of Lily's after Calor gas and a bathroom and all, say what you like, it's not the same thing, and what I mean to say—'

THE FROZEN CUCKOO

There was a good deal of trouble at breakfast. To begin with, Mr Armitage was late, and that made Mrs Armitage cross, as she always liked to have the meal over quickly on Mondays, so that the dining-room could be turned out. Then she began reading her letters, and suddenly inquired:

'What is the date today?'

'The second,' said Harriet.

'I thought so. Then that means she is coming today. How very inconsiderate.'

'Who is coming today?'

'Your cousin Sarah.'

'Oh no!' said Mark and Harriet together, in deep dismay.

It is dreadful to have to say it of anybody, but their cousin Sarah was really a horrible girl. The only thing she seemed to enjoy was playing practical jokes, which she did the whole time. Nobody minds an occasional joke, but an endless course of sand in the brown-sugar bowl, grease on the stairs, and plastic spiders on the pillowcases soon becomes tiresome.

'It'll be apple-pie beds, apple-pie beds all the way,' said Mark gloomily. 'Can't you put her off?'

'No, Aunt Rachel has to go into the hospital for an operation, so I'm afraid you'll just have to bear with her. She's coming at lunch-time.'

Here Mr Armitage arrived, and sat down rubbing his hands and saying: 'The Christmas roses will be out any minute now.'

'Your bacon's cold,' said his wife crossly. 'Here are your letters.'

He opened a long, important-looking one which had a lot of printed headings on it, and instantly began to puff and blow with rage.

'Evicted? Requisitioned? What's this? Notice to quit forthwith before 11 A.M., December the second. Who the dickens is this from?'

'Good gracious, my dear,' said his wife, 'what have you got there?'

'It's from the Board of Incantation,' he replied, throwing the letter to her. 'They've requisitioned this house, if you please, to make a seminary for young magicians, and we have notice to quit immediately.'

'A. Whizzard,' murmured Mrs Armitage, looking at the signature. 'Wasn't that the name of the man whose book you were so rude about in your review?'

'Yes, of course. I knew the name seemed familiar. A shockingly bad book on spells and runes.'

'Oh dear,' sighed Mrs Armitage. 'I do wish you'd learn to be more tactful. Now we have to find somewhere else to live, and just before Christmas, too. It really is too bad.'

'Do we really have to be out by eleven o'clock?' asked Mark, who, with Harriet, had been listening round-eyed.

'I shall contest it,' said his father. 'It's the most monstrous tyranny. They needn't think they can ride over me roughshod.'

However, Mrs Armitage, who was a quiet but practical person, at once sent Harriet along the village to ask if they could borrow the house of Mrs Foster, who was going off to the south of France, while they looked around for somewhere else to live. Then with the help of Agnes and Mrs Epis she packed up all their clothes and put them in the car. Mr Armitage refused to leave with the rest of the family, and remained behind to tackle the invaders.

At eleven o'clock sharp several men who looked like builders' labourers arrived. They rode on rather battered, paint-stained old broomsticks, and carried hammers, saws, and large sheets of beaverboard.

'Morning, guv'nor,' said one who seemed to be the foreman, advancing up the front steps.

Mr Armitage stood in the way with his arms folded. 'I protest against this unseemly intrusion!' he cried. 'It is entirely contrary to the British constitution.'

'Ah,' said the foreman, waving a screwdriver at him in a pitying manner, 'you're cuckoo.' At once Mr Armitage vanished, and in his place a large bird flapped in a dazed manner round the front door.

Just then an enormous, sleek black car rolled silently up to the gate, and a tall, sleek, dark man stepped out and came up the steps, swinging an elegant umbrella.

'Excellent, Wantage, excellent. I see you have arrived,' he said, glancing about. 'I trust you have had no trouble?'

'Only a little, sir,' said the foreman respectfully, indicating the bird, which let out a hoarse and indignant 'cuckoo!'

'Dear me,' said the sleek gentleman. 'Can this be my unfortunate friend, Mr Armitage? Such a pleasant person – perhaps just a *little* hot-tempered, just a *little* unkind in his reviews? However, it would certainly be equally unkind to wrest him from his old home; we must find some accommodation for him. Hawkins!' The chauffeur's head looked out from the car. 'Bring the case, will you.'

A large glass dome was brought, of the kind which is placed over skeleton clocks, with the hours and minutes marked on one side.

'There,' said the gentleman, tucking Mr Armitage under one arm. 'Now, in the study, perhaps? On one's desk, for inspiration. When I place the bird in position, Hawkins, pray cover him with the case. Thank you. A most tasteful ornament, I flatter myself, and perhaps in time we may even teach him to announce the hours.'

'Your father's being a long time,' said Mrs Armitage rather anxiously to the children. 'I do hope he isn't getting into trouble.'

'Oh, I don't suppose it's worth expecting him before lunch,' said Mark. 'He'll argue with everybody and then probably go for a walk and start drafting a letter to *The Times*.'

So they sat down to lunch in Mrs Foster's house, but just

as they were raising the first bites to their mouths, Harriet gave a little squeak and said:

'Goodness! We've forgotten all about Sarah! She'll arrive at the house and won't know what's happened to us.'

'Oh, she's sure to see Father somewhere around, and he'll bring her along,' Mark pointed out. 'I wouldn't worry. We can go along afterwards and see, if they don't turn up soon.'

At this moment Sarah was walking onwards to her doom. She found the front door of the Armitage house open, and nobody about. This seemed to her a good moment to plant some of her practical jokes, so she opened her suitcase and stole into the dining-room. The long table was already set for tea. There were thirteen places, which puzzled her, but she supposed her aunt and uncle must be giving a party. Some plates of sandwiches and cakes covered with damp napkins were standing on a side table, so she doctored them with sneezing powder, and placed fizz-bangs in some of the teacups.

She was surprised to see that the rooms had been split in two by partitions of beaverboard, and wondered where the family was, and what was going on. Hearing some hammering upstairs, she decided to tiptoe up and surprise them. Feeling around in her suitcase again, she dug out her water pistol, and charged it from a jug which stood on the sideboard. Then she went softly up the stairs.

The door facing the top of the stairs was open, and she stole through it. This was Mr Armitage's study, which Mr Whizzard had decided should be his private office. Just now, however, he was out having his lunch, and the room was empty. Sarah went to work at once. She laid a few thumbtacks carefully on what she supposed to be her uncle's chair, and was just attaching a neat contrivance to the telephone, when there came an interruption. The huge black cat, Walrus, who had stayed behind when the family left, had strolled into the study after Sarah and was taking a deep interest in the dejected-looking cuckoo sitting under the glass dome. While Sarah was busy laying the thumbtacks, he leapt onto the desk, and after a moment's reflection, knocked the glass case off the desk with one sweep of his powerful paw.

'Sarah!' cried Mr Armitage in terror. 'Save me from this murdering beast!'

Completely startled, thinking that her uncle must have come in unheard while her back was turned, Sarah spun around and let fly with her water pistol. The jet caught the unfortunate bird in mid-air, and at once (for the weather was very cold) he turned to a solid block of ice, and fell to the ground with a heavy thud. The cat pounced at once, but his teeth simply grated on the ice, and he sprang back with a hiss of dismay.

At that moment Mr Whizzard returned from lunch.

'Dear me!' he said peevishly. 'What is all this? Cats? Little girls? And who has been meddling with my cuckoo?' But when he saw Mr Armitage's frozen condition, he began to laugh uncontrollably.

'Warlock! Warlock! Come in and look at this,' he shouted, and another man came in, wearing a mortarboard and magician's gown.

'The lads have just arrived in the dragon-bus,' he said. 'I told them to go straight in to tea, as the workmen haven't quite finished dividing up the classrooms. What have you got there?'

'Poor Armitage has become quite seized up,' said Mr Whizzard. 'If we had a deep-freeze—'

Before he could finish, several young student-magicians dashed into the room, with cries of complaint. They were all sneezing.

'Really it's too bad, when we're all tired from our journey! Sneezing powder in everything and tea all over the floor. A joke's a joke, but this is going too far. Someone ought to get the sack for this.'

'What is the matter, my lads?' inquired Mr Whizzard.

'Someone's been playing a lot of rotten practical jokes.'

Sarah quailed and would gladly have slipped away, but she was jammed in a corner. She tried to squeeze past the desk, but one of the drawers was open and caught her suitcase. A small bomb fell out and exploded on the carpet, amid yelps of terror from the students.

'Seize that child,' commanded Mr Whizzard. Two of them unwillingly did so, and stood her before him. He cast his eye over the diabolical contents of her suitcase, and then the label attracted his attention.

'Armitage. Ah, just so, this is plainly an attempt at sabotage from the evicted family. They shall pay dearly for it. Nightshade, fetch an electric heater, will you? There's one in the front hall.'

While they were waiting, Mr Whizzard sat down in his

chair, but shot up again at once, with a murderous look at Sarah.

'Good. Now place the bird before it, in this pencil tray, so as not to dampen the carpet. The cat sits at hand on this chair, ready for when the thawing process commences. It should not be long, I fancy. Now my young friends, you may return to your interrupted meal, and as for you,' with a savage glance at Sarah, 'a little solitary confinement will do you no harm, while I reflect on how to dispose of you.'

Sarah was dragged away and locked into a beaverboard cell, which had once been part of Harriet's bedroom.

'Now I think we deserve a quiet cup of tea, after all this excitement,' said Mr Whizzard to Mr Warlock, when they were left alone. 'We can sip it as we watch poor Mr Armitage melt. I'll ring down to the kitchen.' He lifted the telephone, and instantly a flood of ink poured into his ear.

Meanwhile, Mark and Harriet had decided to come in search of their father and cousin.

'It might be wise not to go in the front way, don't you think?' said Harriet. 'After all, it's rather odd that we haven't heard *something* of them by now. I feel there must have been some trouble.'

So they went stealthily round through the shrubbery and climbed up the wisteria to Harriet's window. The first thing they saw when they looked in was Sarah, pacing up and down in a distracted manner.

'Good gracious—' Harriet began, but Sarah made frantic gestures to silence her. They climbed in as quietly as they could. 'Thank heaven you've come,' she whispered. 'Uncle

Armitage is being roasted to death in the study, or else eaten by Walrus. You must rescue him at once.' They listened in horror, as she explained the position, and then hurriedly climbed out again. Sarah was no climber, so she hung out anxiously watching them, and thinking of the many times her uncle had given her half-crowns and pats on the head.

Harriet ran to the back door, where the cat's tin plate still lay, and began to rattle it, calling 'Walrus, Walrus, Walrus! Dinner! Walrus! Fish!'

Mark climbed along the wisteria to the study window, to wait for the result of this move.

He saw the cat Walrus, who was still sitting on the chair, attentively watching the melting process, suddenly prick up his ears and look towards the door. Then, as Harriet's voice came faintly again, he shot out of it and disappeared.

'Confound that animal!' exclaimed Mr Whizzard. 'Catch him, Warlock!' They both ran out of the door, looking to right and left. Mark wasted no time. He clambered through the window, grabbed the cuckoo, and was out again before the two men returned, frustrated and angry.

'Good heavens, now the bird's gone,' cried Mr Warlock. 'What a fool you were to leave the window open. It must have flown out.'

'Impossible! This is more of that wretched child's doing. I'm going along to see her, right away.'

He burst in on Sarah, looking so ferocious that she instinctively caught up the first weapon she could see, to defend herself. It was a screwdriver, left lying on the floor by one of the workmen.

'What have you done with the cuckoo?' Mr Whizzard demanded.

'I haven't touched it,' Sarah truthfully replied.

'Nonsense. Do you deny that you enticed the cat away by black arts, and then kidnapped the cuckoo?' He approached her threateningly.

Sarah retreated as far as she could and clutched the screwdriver. 'You're crackers,' she said. 'I tell you I haven't—' Her mouth dropped open in astonishment. For where Mr Whizzard had been standing there was nothing but a large white cardboard box, containing red and blue paper fireworks of the kind that you pull at parties; they were decorated with silver moons and stars. At this moment Mark and Harriet came climbing back through the window.

Downstairs in the dining-room the young wizards, having cleared away tea, were enjoying a singsong.

> '*Ha ha ha, he he he* [they sang],
> *Little broom stick, how I love thee.*'

They were interrupted by Mr Warlock.

'Have any of you boys seen Mr Whizzard?' he inquired. 'He went to interview the young female prisoner, and I haven't seen him since.'

'No sir, he hasn't been in here,' the eldest one said. 'Won't you come and play for us, Mr Warlock? You do play so beautifully.'

'Well, just for five minutes, if you insist.' They began to sing again.

> *'Necromancers come away, come away, come come*
> *away,*
> *This is wizard's holiday,'*

when suddenly they were aware of the three children, Mark, Harriet, and Sarah, standing inside the door, holding the red-and-blue crackers in their hands.

'What is the meaning of this?' said Mr Warlock severely. 'You are trespassing on private property.'

'Yes,' said Mark. '*Our* property. This is our house, and we would like you to get out of it at once.'

'Vacate it,' whispered Harriet.

'Vacate it at once.'

'We shall do no such thing.'

'Very well then. Do you know what we have here?' He held up one of the crackers. 'Your Mr Whizzard. And if you don't get out – vacate – at once, we shall *pull* them. So you'd better hurry up.'

The wizards looked at each other in consternation, and then, slowly at first, but with gathering speed, began to put their things together and take them out to the dragon-coach. The children watched them, holding the crackers firmly.

'And you must take down all that beaverboard partitioning,' said Harriet. 'I don't know *what* Mummy would say if she saw it.'

'The workmen have all gone home.'

'Then you must manage on your own.'

The house began to resound with amateurish bangs and squeaks. 'Ow, Nightshade, you clumsy clot, you dropped that board on my toe.' 'Well, get out of the way then, you nitwit necromancer.'

At last it was all done, and at the front gate the children handed over the twelve red-and-blue parts of Mr Whizzard.

'And it's more than you deserve,' said Harriet, 'seeing how you were going to treat our poor Pa.'

'We should also like that screwdriver, with which I perceive you have armed yourself, or we shall not be able to restore our director to his proper shape,' said Mr Warlock coldly.

'Oh, dear me, no. You're nuts if you think we're going to let you get away with that,' said Sarah. 'We shall want it in case of any further trouble. Besides, what about poor uncle – oh dear—' she stopped in dismay. For Mr Warlock had disappeared, and his place had been taken by a sack of coconuts.

'Oh, never mind,' said Harriet. 'You didn't mean to do it. Here, do for goodness' sake hurry up and go.' She shoved the sack into the arms of Nightshade, and bundled him into the coach, which slowly rolled off. 'We must simply dash along to Mrs Foster's. I'm sure Mummy will be worrying.'

They burst in on Mrs Armitage with their story. 'And where is your father?' she asked immediately.

'Oh goodness.' Mark looked guilty. 'I'd forgotten all about him.' He carefully extracted the half-stifled cuckoo from his trouser pocket.

'Out with the screwdriver, Sarah.'

Sarah obediently pointed it at him and said 'You're Uncle' and he was restored to himself once more, but looking much rumpled and tattered. He glared at them all.

'I must say, that's a respectful way to treat your father. Carried in your trouser pocket, indeed!'

'Well, I hope this will cure you once and for all of writing those unkind reviews,' said Mrs Armitage coldly. 'Now we have all the trouble of moving back again, and just when I was beginning to feel settled.'

'And talking of cures,' said Mr Armitage, turning on his niece, 'we won't say anything *this* time, seeing it's all turned out for the best, but if ever I catch you playing any of your practical jokes again—'

'Oh, I never, never will,' Sarah assured him. 'I thought people enjoyed them.'

'Not in this family,' said Mark.

SWEET SINGEING IN THE CHOIR

'Daddy, have we really got a fairy godmother?' asked Harriet, dropping her basket full of holly leaves in a corner of the room and coming over to the fire, where tea was laid on a little table.

'Possibly, possibly,' he replied, without coming out of his evening paper.

'No, but really?' she persisted. 'A rather silly-looking lady, with popping eyes and a lot of necklaces?'

'Oh, yes, now I remember,' said Mr Armitage, putting down his paper and starting to laugh. 'She was the one who dropped you in the font. Your mother never took to her much. And right after the christening she tried to interest me in a scheme for supplying old fairy ladies with needlework patterns.'

'Goodness, can't they make their own?'

'Apparently not. Yes, of course, she was going to give you each a wish for your christening presents, but your mother pointed out that if you had it, then you'd only wish for your lunch and it might be better to wait for a few years.'

'Yes, well, that's just it,' exclaimed Mark. 'We met her just now in Farthing Wood, and she offered us a wish each, so we said could we think it over and tell her tomorrow; you know how it is on the spur of the moment, you can never think of anything sensible.'

'Very prudent of you,' murmured his father. 'Try not to wish for anything that needs *upkeep*, will you, like race horses or aeroplanes. You know what the price of petrol is now.'

Here Mrs Armitage came in and started pouring tea.

'Children, I'm afraid I've a disappointing message for you from Mr Pontwell. He says he's very sorry but he doesn't think he *can* have you in the carol choir.'

'Not have us in the choir? But Mr Willingdon always did.'

'Well, I suppose Mr Pontwell is more particular about voices. He says he wants the singing to be especially good this year. And you know I don't mean to be unkind, but you can neither of you sing in tune at all.'

'Yes, the other day,' agreed Mr Armitage, 'I wondered who could possibly be sawing wood in the bathroom, only to find—'

'Oh, he is a mean man,' said Harriet, taking no notice. '*Nobody* ever minds about keeping in tune in carols. And I do love carol-singing too. Oh, why did Mr Willingdon have to go and get made a canon?'

'Couldn't we go along with them and keep quiet?' suggested Mark.

'No, I thought of that, but he said, "You know how

effervescent Mark and Harriet are, there's no knowing what they'd do." I think he's afraid of you.'

'Well, I think that's most unkind of him. We'll just have to go out by ourselves, that's all.'

'No, no,' said Harriet, 'don't you see what we can do? What about our fairy godmother and the wishes?'

Next day, as arranged, they met the popeyed lady in Farthing Wood.

'Well, dears,' she beamed at them. 'Thought of a good wish?'

'Yes, please,' said Mark. 'We'd both like to have simply wonderful voices – to sing with, I mean.'

The lady looked a little blank. '*Voices?* Are you sure you wouldn't like a nice box of chocolates each? Or a pony?'

'No, thank you very much. We have a unicorn already, you see. But we really do need good voices so that we can get into the carol choir.'

'Well,' she said doubtfully. 'That's a rather difficult wish. I don't think I could manage it for you *permanently*. But perhaps for a week or two, I *might* be able to manage it—'

'Oh, please do try.' They both looked at her imploringly.

'Very well, dears, since it means such a lot to you.' She shut her eyes and clenched her fists with an appearance of terrific concentration. The children waited breathlessly.

'Now, then,' she said after a moment or two, 'try to sing a few notes.'

They were rather embarrassed and looked at each other for encouragement.

'What shall we sing? "Good King Wenceslas?"' They sang

the first few lines rather timidly and were much disconcerted by the notes that boomed out – Harriet's voice had become a terrific contralto which would not have disgraced a twelve-stone prima donna, and Mark's was a deep and reverend bass.

'I say, I hate to seem ungrateful, but couldn't we be soprano and treble – it would be more natural, don't you think?'

'Perhaps you are right, pettie,' said the lady, and closed her eyes again, looking a shade martyred.

'Oh dear, we are giving her a lot of trouble,' Harriet thought.

This time the result was more satisfactory, and they thanked her with heartfelt gratitude.

'How long will it last?' asked Mark.

'Thirteen days. You will find that it wears off at midnight.'

'Like Cinderella,' said Harriet, nodding.

'So remember not to give a performance just at that time. Well, dears, I am *so* pleased to have met you again, and please remember me to your dear mamma.'

'Oh yes, she said do drop in to tea whenever you are passing. Goodbye, and thank you *so* much – you *are* kind—'

When they had left her, they dashed straight to the vicarage and inquired for Mr Pontwell, but were told that he was round at the church.

The new vicar was a red-faced, rather pompous-looking man. He seemed slightly embarrassed at meeting Mark and Harriet.

'Oh – er, hullo, my dear children. What can I do for you?'

'Well, sir, it's about our being in the carol choir,' Mark plunged.

Mr Pontwell frowned. 'Dear me, I thought I had made that perfectly plain to your dear mother. I am afraid I cannot see my way—'

'No, but,' said Harriet, 'we feel sure that you are acting under a wrong impression of our voices. You probably heard us on some occasion when Mark had a cold, and I was, um, suffering from my laryngitis, and of course you had quite a mistaken idea of what we could do. We just want you to be *very* kind and hear us again.'

'Well really, my dear children, I don't think that is the case, and there hardly seems much point in reopening the question – however, if you insist—'

'Oh, we do insist,' agreed Mark. 'What shall we sing, Harriet, "Oh, for the Wings of a Dove"?'

They were much more confident this time, and opened their mouths to their widest extent.

> '*Oh, for the weengs, for the weengs of a dove –*
> Far *away, far away would I rove*.'

When Mr Pontwell heard their exquisite treble voices soaring about among the rafters of the church, his eyes nearly popped out of his head, and he sat down suddenly in a nearby pew.

'Good gracious,' he said, 'I had no idea – of course, you

were quite right to come. My *dear* children – gracious me, what an extraordinary thing. I had quite thought – but there, it only shows how mistaken one can be. You will indeed be an addition to the choir.'

He went on saying things like this as they walked through the churchyard.

'You will come to the practices on Wednesdays and Saturdays, will you?'

'Of course,' said Harriet anxiously, 'and when are we going out singing?'

'Monday evening, the nineteenth.' Mark and Harriet did some rapid calculation. Monday the nineteenth would be the last day of their thirteen days, which seemed cutting it rather fine.

'I suppose it couldn't *possibly* be any earlier?' said Harriet. 'You see, rather odd things sometimes happen to our family on Mondays – rather *unaccountable* things – and it would be so awful if we were late or prevented from coming or anything.' She was thinking of the day when their home had suddenly turned into a castle on the Rhine for twelve hours.

'No, my dear, I'm afraid the date cannot be changed, as I have already made several arrangements for the evening, including a visit of the choir to Gramercy Chase. Sir Leicester will be *most* interested to hear you sing, so I do trust that you will not let any of these – er – unaccountable things happen during the day, *or* while you are out with the choir.' He looked at them sternly.

*

'So you're really in the choir?' said Mr Armitage that evening. 'And going to Gramercy Chase. Well, well, it's a good thing it will be dark.'

'Why?'

'It's the most hideous house between here and Birmingham. Sir Leicester always says he wishes he had a good excuse to pull it down. It was entirely rebuilt, you know, in nineteenth-century gothic, except for the haunted terrace.'

'Haunted?' said Harriet. 'Oh, good. What by? That's where we're going to sing.'

'Oh, some bird, called King William's Raven (don't ask me why), who only appears to foretell bad tidings to the house of Gramercy. The last time was just before the current baronet was killed at Waterloo. He flies above the terrace lighting torches in the brackets – of course, they've put in electric lighting now, so I don't know how he'd manage—'

Harriet and Mark had a somewhat difficult time at the choir practices, as all their village friends were only too familiar with their usual voices, and they had to face a considerable amount of chaff and a lot of astonishment at this sudden development of flute-like tones.

'Been keeping quiet all these years, eh? Didn't want to waste yourself on us, I suppose?'

'Ah,' said Ruby, the blacksmith's daughter, 'they've heard as how Mr Pontwell's going to have a recording made on Monday night.'

In fact, there was a general rumour going round that Mr

Pontwell had something special up his sleeve, and that was why he was so particular about the singers and the practices; though whether he was having the singing recorded, or royalty was going to be there, or some great impresario was staying at Gramercy Chase to hear them, was not known.

Mr Pontwell made a particular point of asking them to wear tidy dark clothes and rubber-soled shoes so that they should not squeak on people's gravel.

'What a fusser he is,' Mark complained to Harriet.

'Never mind,' she replied. 'At least we're going to be *there*.'

Nothing untoward happened to Mark and Harriet on Monday the nineteenth. Indeed the day was suspiciously quiet, and they both of them became slightly anxious as evening approached. However they got safely away from home and met the other carol-singers in the vicarage at eight o'clock, as had been arranged. The vicar was handing out torches and carol books.

'Now, are we all assembled? Excellent, excellent. I suggest we start off with a good rousing "*Adeste Fideles*" outside the church, just to get our lungs in, then through the village as far as Little Foldings (should take a couple of hours), where Mrs Noakes has very kindly promised us hot drinks, and Sir Leicester is sending the station wagon to collect us all there. We are expected at Gramercy Chase round about eleven o'clock.'

As they were starting on their first carol, Mark felt a cold nose pushed down his neck, and turned his head to look into the reproachful green eyes of Candleberry, their unicorn.

'Goodness! I thought you were shut up for the night. Go home, bad unicorn,' he said crossly, but Candleberry shook his head.

'Dear me, is that a *unicorn*?' said Mr Pontwell at the end of '*Adeste Fideles*'. 'He shouldn't really be here, you know.'

'I'm very sorry,' said Mark. 'I can't think how he got out. But he's extremely well trained. He won't interrupt, and he could carry anyone who got tired.'

'Very well,' said Mr Pontwell. 'He certainly makes a picturesque addition. But if there's the least sign of trouble, mind, you'll have to take him home.'

However, there was no trouble, though they had so many requests for encores that they arrived at Little Foldings very much behind schedule and had to gulp down their drinks and hurry out to the station wagon, which sped away through the dark across Gramercy Wold, with the unicorn easily keeping pace beside it. Even so, they arrived at the Chase well after half-past eleven.

Sir Leicester welcomed them, and hurried them at once round to the terrace where they were to sing. Mark and Harriet tried to get a look at the hideousness of the house as they walked past it, but only received a general impression of a lot of pinnacles and gargoyles. The terrace was enormous – at least half a mile long and twenty yards wide, extending to a low wall, which was topped by a series of lamp-posts, now fitted with electric lamps.

The singers, hot and panting from their hurry, flung down

coats and mufflers on the wall, and clustered together opposite the orangery door, where they were to sing. As they were finding their places for the first carol, there was a prodigious clattering of hoofs, and Candleberry arrived, galloping down the terrace like a Grand National winner. Mark went to meet him and quiet him down. When he returned, he muttered to Harriet:

'Now I know what all the fuss was about. There are some blokes over there in the shade with a television camera. That's why Mr Pontwell's been taking such a lot of trouble.'

'Well, do keep an eye on Candleberry,' she muttered back. 'Oh, look, here comes Mr Pontwell. Thank goodness, now we can start before I get nervous.'

They were halfway through their first carol when Mark noticed that Candleberry seemed very uneasy; he was shivering, stamping his feet, and looking over his shoulder a great deal. Mark himself glanced rather fearfully down the long, dark expanse of terrace.

At the same time, Harriet heard something in her ear that sounded like a ratchet screwdriver being painstakingly worked into granite. She turned her head to listen and realized that it was Mark singing. She caught hold of his hand and tapped his watch.

'Hey,' she whispered under cover of the singing, 'it's midnight and we've lost our voices. Better pipe low. Bang goes our chance of charming thousands of listeners.'

Mr Pontwell was energetically conducting 'The Holly and the Ivy' when an unpleasant scent invaded his nostrils. He sniffed again – yes, it was the smell of burning clothes.

Could it be that dratted unicorn, with its incandescent horn? Had it set fire to somebody's cap? He glanced about angrily, and then saw a flame leap up on the terrace wall.

'I say,' called a voice through the singing, 'someone's set fire to our coats!'

In fact, the pile of coats and scarves was now blazing up in a positive bonfire.

Instantly there was a clamour of angry voices, and the singing died away.

'Ladies – gentlemen – my dear friends,' cried Mr Pontwell in anguish, 'please – the evening will be ruined—'

'It's that perishing unicorn,' someone exclaimed furiously. '—Never ought to have been allowed to come—'

But at that moment Candleberry came galloping in hot pursuit of something that was flying along the terrace carrying a light. As they passed through the illumination of the bonfire this was seen to be an enormous dark bird carrying a lighted candle, the flame of which streamed over its shoulder.

'Good heavens,' cried Sir Leicester, who had gone very pale, 'it's the family raven.'

'Please, my dear singers,' implored Mr Pontwell, who thought of nothing but his performance, 'let us have a little order. What do a few coats and scarves matter? Or a little natural fauna? Let me hear a nice spirited rendering of "We Three Kings".'

But at that moment a man dashed towards them from the television camera, crying: 'Bring that unicorn back. It's miraculous! A real unicorn chasing a ghostly raven – good

lord, this will be the television scoop of the century! Stand back, will you? Who owns the unicorn? You, sir? Can you get him to come this way?'

Mark called Candleberry, and the unicorn galloped back, driving the raven in front of him. It was still crossly looking for something to light with its candle. It had been foiled by the electric lamps and had had to fall back on the heap of coats. At last with a croak of decision it swooped down and set fire to somebody's carol book.

'Stop it, stop it,' shrieked Mr Pontwell, but the TV expert at the same moment shouted 'Hold it, hold it. Stand aside, you others. Hold out your books. This is wonderful, wonderful!'

Only Mr Pontwell was not pleased with the evening's work. Everyone else was warmed and exhilarated by the fire and informed that their fees as television performers would amply cover the loss of coats and carol books. Sir Leicester himself seemed to have disappeared, but his chauffeur drove the choir back, cheerful and chattering, at about three in the morning.

'Poor man,' said Harriet to Mark, 'I expect he's worrying about what dreadful doom is going to fall on the House of Gramercy. After all, it's not so funny for him.'

At breakfast next morning the telephone rang. Mr Armitage answered it, and after listening for a few minutes, began to laugh.

'It was Sir Leicester,' he said, returning to the table. 'He's had his dreadful doom. The architect's report on Gramercy Chase has come in, and he's learned that the whole place is riddled with dry rot. It's all got to come down. He's simply delighted. He rang up to ask if I knew of a comfortable cottage for sale.'

ARMITAGE, ARMITAGE, FLY AWAY HOME

'What's all this?' said Mr Armitage, coming down one morning to find the dining-room littered with collecting boxes and trays full of blue paper cornflowers.

'Cornflower day,' said Mrs Armitage.

'So I had inferred,' replied her husband patiently. 'But what's it in aid of?' He peered at some posters lying half unrolled on the floor, which showed a sweet, pathetic old face under a steeple-crowned hat.

'It's to raise money for a bazaar.'

'Yes?'

'And the bazaar is to raise money for a progressive whist drive which is to raise money for a garden fête.'

'So far, so good,' said Mr Armitage, stepping over his daughter, Harriet, who was counting cornflowers, and helping himself to porridge. 'And what's the garden fête in aid of?'

'The S.A.D.O.F.L., of course.'

'And that is?'

'The Society for the Aid of Distressed Old Fairy Ladies.'

'Do you expect to raise much for them?'

'Oh, yes,' said Mrs Armitage confidently. 'Last year we made a terrible lot for the N.S.P.C.M. – enough to provide a warm swimming bath for rheumatic mermaids *and* a beach canteen serving them with hot soup and fish rolls throughout the winter months.'

'Most praiseworthy.' Mr Armitage shuddered a little at the thought of the fish rolls and hurriedly took some bacon.

'So we expect to be able to do something of the sort this year. There's a slight difference of opinion on the committee, unfortunately; some people want a free dispensary for magical ingredients – eye of newt and toe of frog, you know, and belladonna and so forth; but some committee members think that ought to come under the National Health Service anyway, and that we should write to our Member of Parliament about it.'

'So what do they want?'

'A mobile library of magical reference books and free replacements of worn-out wands.'

'Well, it all sounds very fine,' said Mr Armitage, gulping down the last of his coffee and preparing to rush off, for this was his office day, 'provided you think these people *deserve* to be helped.'

'Oh, yes, darling, poor old things! Have you finished counting those out, Harriet? Here come the other helpers, and we must be off.'

The flower sellers were beginning to crowd the front hall. Mrs Armitage gave each of them a set of one tray, a collection box, and a poster. She took the last set herself and, with Harriet, started off along her beat, between the post office and the green.

At first all went excellently. Heads were shaken and sighs heaved over the plight of the poor, resourceless old fairy ladies in want of comforts. Money flowed in, the tin box became heavier and heavier, until by eleven o'clock it was nearly full.

They were approaching a small cottage, set back from the road among apple trees. It was called The Bat's Nest, and in it lived old Mr Grogan, with his housekeeper, old Miss Hooting. Mr Grogan made dolls' furniture. He was stone deaf and hardly talked to anyone except Miss Hooting, who had a very shrill voice which he could just hear. If anyone wanted dolls' furniture, they came and told Miss Hooting their requirements: the size, period, design, and materials wanted. She would pass the information on to Mr Grogan, and in due course the article would arrive, very beautifully made. Harriet had a Queen Anne walnut chest of drawers with brass handles, of his workmanship, and also a rosewood grand piano, its tiny keys made from spillikins, which really played. Miss Hooting, as well as looking after Mr Grogan, kept what was thought to be a hen-battery and sold the eggs. She also made hats and did weaving.

'I do admire Miss Hooting,' people often said.

When Harriet and her mother came up to the cottage, they saw Miss Hooting walking down the garden path to the battery-shed, and as they knew it would be useless to apply to Mr Grogan, they went round to intercept her.

'Good morning,' she said in her creaking voice. 'Would you like to see me feed my birds?'

'Oh, yes, please,' said Harriet.

'What do you give them?' inquired Mrs Armitage.

'Pellets,' replied Miss Hooting, opening a bin that contained tiny whitish balls and shovelling some of them into two buckets. 'Now they are tipped into these containers, so, and I pull the rope to raise them to roof level. Now we can go inside.'

As she opened the door into the battery, which was dark, pandemonium broke loose.

'Those don't sound like hens,' said Mrs Armitage, puzzled.

'Hens? Who said they were hens?' There was a squawking and a screeching, a hooting and a snoring.

'I'll have to switch on the light,' said Miss Hooting, and did so. The birds immediately became quiet in their little cages and sat watching her with great round eyes.

'Goodness,' said Mrs Armitage in surprise. 'They're owls. Do you sell the eggs?'

'Yes, to the United Sorcerer's Supply Stores. They collect the eggs once every six months or so – owls' eggs don't have to be very fresh.'

She pulled the two pellet containers through the hatches, and the visitors saw that the containers ran on wheels along two little overhead railways. When they were pushed, they trundled the whole length of the battery, tipping off a portion of food into each owl's cage. The owls bounced up and down with excitement, but kept quiet.

'Now,' said Miss Hooting, dusting her hands, 'you are collecting, are you not? For some worthy cause, no doubt, but I haven't got my spectacles or my purse, so we must go indoors and I will also show you the bit of weaving I am engaged on.'

They followed her back to the house and into a front room that smelled strongly of raffia, wool, artificial flowers and basket canes, all of which were lying about in large quantities by a large loom.

'Oh,' said Harriet in admiration, 'what lovely stuff!' The piece of cloth on the loom was not at all the sort of handwoven stuff she had expected to see. It was a thick, rich-looking red velvet with a black and gold design woven through it.

'It's for a cloak,' explained Miss Hooting carelessly, coming back with her bag and glasses. 'There's the hat to match.' She nodded at a black steeple-crowned one lying beside the bunch of red ribbons that was to trim it. 'Now what is it you are collecting in aid of?'

'The S.A.D.O.F.L.,' said Mrs Armitage. 'For helping old fairy ladies of various kinds. When they're old, they often get a bit past their work, and we ought to do a bit for them. This is going to a fund for replacing worn-out wands and things of that sort. Gracious, is something the matter?'

Miss Hooting had gone perfectly pale with rage.

'The impertinence!' she exclaimed. 'The barefaced, unparalleled effrontery of coming here and saying that to me! I suppose you did it as a deliberate insult.'

'No, indeed,' said Mrs Armitage, much bewildered. 'I certainly had no such intention.'

'Fiddlestick! I suppose you'll say next you didn't *know* I was a retired enchantress (fairy lady, indeed). I am not in the least distressed, I'll have you know. I have my pension, my salary from Mr Grogan, besides what I make from my owls and handicrafts. I am hard-working and self-respecting, and there are plenty more like me who won't say thank you for your charity. The door is behind you. *Good* morning.'

Unfortunately, at that moment Mr Grogan came downstairs, having heard Miss Hooting's voice raised in rage. He rather liked Mrs Armitage and Harriet, so he said good morning to them and asked Miss Hooting what they had come for.

'Impertinence!' she screeched.

'Yes, I dare say, but what sort of furniture?'

'*Not* furniture. They are collecting for a most offensive cause.'

'Chest of drawers? Yes, I can do a chest of drawers, but what period?'

'*Not* a chest of drawers, an appeal.'

'Made of deal? Never touch the stuff.'

Harriet and Mrs Armitage felt that if they did not leave, Miss Hooting might do something drastic – she was casting meaningful looks at a tall black stick leaning against the mantelpiece. If it was a wand, they thought it would be prudent not to chance the possibility of its not yet being worn out, so, nodding and smiling at Mr Grogan, they escaped.

When the contents of the various collecting boxes were

added together, the total sum was found to be quite a handsome one, though several of the collectors had had unfortunate experiences, like that of the Armitages, with innocent-seeming old ladies.

Mr Armitage shook his head when he heard about it.

'I should leave the whole affair alone if I were you,' he said. 'Buy a grand piano for the Ladies' Social Club, or a machine gun for the Boy Scouts, or something harmless. It's always better to collect for a charity that's a long way off, in Africa or somewhere like that, if you must. These old fairy ladies are devilish touchy and independent, and there's sure to be trouble.'

He was an obliging man, however, and he consented to say a few words to open the bazaar which was due to follow in three weeks, because he said he might not make such a hash of it as the vicar.

Everyone was working early and late making things for the stalls – cakes, embroidered milk-bottle covers, tea-cosy cases, jam-pot containers, bags to put dusters in and bags to put those bags in, dolls with crinolines to put over the coal-scuttle, and crocheted chocolate-bar containers. There was also to be a jumble stall, and all the village flocked to the bazaar in the hope of picking up cheaply the clothes of the children next door which they had been despising and condemning as unsuitable for the past year.

Mr Armitage stood on the platform to say his opening words, supported by his wife and the members of the committee.

'Good afternoon, ladies and gentlemen,' he began,

spurred on to rashness by several cups of very strong tea that he had just drunk. 'We are all assembled here to enjoy ourselves (I hope) and to raise money for all the poor old distressed fairy ladies living round about. Well now, let's give the poor old things a big hand and buy everything in sight, however nasty or useless it appears to be—'

Here he paused with his mouth open, for several old ladies near the front of the hall were standing up and looking at him in a very unfriendly way. Old Mrs Lomax was pointing her stick at him.

'Hush, man, hush,' she croaked:

'By the magic of this wand,
Be a tadpole in a pond.'

Nothing happened.

'*You're* no use,' said old Mrs Lockspith acidly. 'You're one of the ones they need to help, evidently.' She pointed a long Malacca cane at the speechless Mr Armitage, and exclaimed:

'Powers of witchcraft in this cane,
Turn him into a drop of rain.'

Nothing happened.

'Here, this is ludicrous,' said Miss Hooting furiously. 'It's my turn. You ladies are a disgrace to the profession.' She grabbed her own black staff, levelled it at the platform and recited:

'Enough of useless spells and wasted words,
Turn Armitage and wife to ladybirds.'

There was a hush as the people in the audience craned over one another's shoulders to see if the spell had worked this time, and then a spontaneous burst of applause. Miss Hooting bowed haughtily and left the hall.

On the platform, the remaining committee members gazed at one another blankly across a gap. Then the vicar, peering longsightedly at the floor, remarked: 'Ah! What a fortunate thing that I have my collecting box with me.'

He took it from his pocket, tipped out a hummingbird hawk moth, and placed in the box the two ladybirds, who were dazedly crawling about the floor.

'Perhaps I ought to take charge of those,' suggested Harriet, coming up. 'They'll want to go home, I expect.' Secretly, she was a little afraid that the vicar, who was notoriously absent-minded, might forget that there was anything special about the ladybirds and add them to his collection.

She and Mark left the bazaar (which went on swimmingly after such an eventful start and netted two hundred pounds) and took their parents home. They put the ladybirds in a shoebox with some biscuit crumbs and drops of hot sweet tea (for shock) and sat down to discuss the situation.

'Perhaps it's the sort of spell that will wear off in due course,' said Harriet.

'Not if I know Miss Hooting, and I somehow feel it

wouldn't be much use going to her and begging her to take it off,' said her brother.

Harriet grinned. 'I've got an idea,' she said. 'But let's wait till tomorrow. After all, it's rather nice and peaceful like this.'

Agnes and Mrs Epis happened to be on holiday that week, so, with nobody at all to bother them, Mark and Harriet had a beautiful evening: they played mah-jongg till ten and listened to records till midnight.

After next day's breakfast (at which they felt it necessary to eat twice as much as usual and open a pot of strawberry jam to fortify them in their orphaned state), they went and looked into the shoebox.

Much to their surprise they were greeted with a stream of shrill and indignant expostulation. Apparently Mr and Mrs Armitage had recovered the use of their voices. The children were scolded for the uncomfortable bedding they had provided and for not bringing breakfast sooner.

'Now, Mark,' said Mr Armitage. 'I have a most important conference at my office today – there's a meeting of the World Organization of Agricultural Producers being held there, and I'm the chairman. So you'll have to take me. Go and put on some presentable clothes, find a nice airy matchbox with some cotton wool in it, and you can catch the nine-eighteen. And bring the file of papers on my dressing table.'

Mark went off rather gloomily to obey. He had had the best intentions of trying to recover his parents from ladybirdhood, but he had agreed with Harriet that a few days' freedom from grown-ups would be a pleasant change. Now it seemed that they were going to be more parent-ridden than ever.

'Harriet,' Mrs Armitage was saying. 'You'll have to carry me on my National Savings round, and this afternoon I'm going to tea with Mrs Mildew, so you'll have to take me there. Just give my back a spot of polish, will you?'

Harriet complied, thinking regretfully of the day she had planned, riding the unicorn and spring-cleaning her doll's house.

The nine-eighteen was crowded that morning, but when Mark's fellow passengers observed that a tiny voice was speaking to Mark from his breast pocket, they moved well away from him, and at the next stop they all got out.

When Mark and his father reached the office, Miss Choop, the secretary, was sitting on her desk polishing her nails.

'Hello, sonny,' she said condescendingly. 'You're in town early. Your pa's not in yet. Was he at a party last night?'

'Choop!' barked Mr Armitage, so threateningly that she jumped, and the bottle of nail polish rolled across the floor. 'Get off that desk and lay out the agendas for the W.O.A.P. meeting.'

'Where is he?' she said fearfully. 'I thought I heard his voice, but it was sort of shrill and far away. He's – he's not *haunting* me, is he? I swear I never meant to upset the card index.'

'It's all right – he's in here,' said Mark comfortingly. 'He's been turned into a ladybird. You hurry up and get those things laid out in the Board Room – I can hear people coming.'

Members of the World Organization of Agricultural Producers were coming up the stairs, talking in a lot of different languages.

'And where is our esteemed chairman?' Mr Svendsen, a tall Swedish farmer, asked Miss Choop.

'He's there,' she replied tremulously, indicating the matchbox. Mr Svendsen raised his eyebrows. They all filed into the Board Room, and Mark took his father's place holding the matchbox. Miss Choop supplied him with an amplifier.

'Order, gentlemen,' said Mr Armitage shrilly from his perch. 'I call upon the secretary to read the minutes from the last meeting.'

Several of the delegates turned pale and asked each other if it was ventriloquism. A Latin-American delegate fainted dead away.

Mr Armitage was a very efficient chairman and bustled his meeting through several motions without giving the startled delegates any time for argument.

'Item Six,' he said. 'Spraying crops of underdeveloped territories from helicopters. Ah, yes, we have received tenders from two different firms manufacturing insecticides, one British, one Russian. Both their prices are about the same, so it remains to see which of their products is the more effective.'

Heated discussion broke out. It seemed that this was a matter about which the delegates felt very strongly. They shouted in their different languages, gesticulated, and jumped up and down. As far as Mark could make out, the opposing groups were evenly matched.

'There are representatives of the two firms outside with samples of insect powders which they wish to demonstrate,' said Miss Choop. 'Shall I ask them in?'

'I hope that will not be necessary,' said Mr Armitage hurriedly. 'We'll have a vote.'

The voting was exactly even.

'As chairman, I have a casting vote,' said Mr Armitage. 'Being British, I naturally give it to the Br—'

'I demand to have a trial of these powders,' cried the Russian delegate. Mr Armitage was obliged to give in.

Two young men in white coats came in carrying tins of powder, sprays, and little cages of assorted insects.

'This powder produced by my firm,' said the first of them, 'is guaranteed to destroy any insect life within five hundred cubic metres.'

'Six hundred cubic metres,' cried the second, putting down his little cage on the table near Mr Armitage's matchbox. A particularly enormous spider gazed yearningly at Mr Armitage through the bars. His nerve broke.

'I – I've changed my mind,' Mr Armitage declared. 'I think the Osnovskov powder is undoubtedly the better, and it is also a halfpenny a ton cheaper. I am going to give my casting vote in favour of it.'

Both the young men looked greatly disappointed at losing the opportunity to demonstrate their products. The Russian delegate beamed. 'Come out to lunch with me,' he said. 'I shall carry you most carefully, and you shall have a thimbleful of vodka and one grain of caviar.'

'Mark, you wait here till I come back,' his father instructed him.

Mr Armitage arrived home in good spirits, singing the 'Volga Boat Song', but his children were most dispirited.

'I've had an awful day,' said Harriet to Mark after supper. 'National Savings all morning, and that tea with Mrs Mildew! Somebody had brought a baby, and it kept grabbing Mother and trying to swallow her!'

'We must certainly get them changed back somehow. What was that idea of yours?'

Harriet jumped up. 'I thought we'd go and see Mrs Lomax,' she said. 'Come on – we'll shut the parents in their shoebox and put them in the meat safe so they won't come to any harm.'

Mark followed her doubtfully. 'I don't see that Mrs Lomax is likely to help,' he argued. 'She wanted to change Father into a tadpole.'

'Yes, but that was before Miss Hooting called her a disgrace to the profession. Think how touchy they are.'

Dusk was falling when they reached Cobweb Corner, Mrs Lomax's bungalow. While they were still at the bottom of the garden, they could hear angry voices, and when they came nearer, they saw Miss Hooting and Mrs Lomax at opposite sides of the path.

'And if you think I'm going to pay you twenty guineas for that cloak, you're greatly mistaken,' Mrs Lomax was saying furiously. 'Who do you think you are, Dior? The hem is five inches off the ground, I shall look a sight. And the hat is too small. I shan't give you a penny more than fifteen. Disgrace to the profession, indeed.'

Miss Hooting turned, her face as black as thunder, and swept past the children without noticing them.

Mrs Lomax pointed a walking stick after her and shouted: 'Be a woodlouse,' but nothing happened, and she went inside and slammed the door.

Harriet firmly rang the bell, and when the door flew open again, she looked (with some courage) into Mrs Lomax's furious face.

'Mrs Lomax,' she said. 'I know you're not very fond of my family, but I think we might strike a bargain. We want our parents back again, and I expect you'd like a new wand, wouldn't you? That one doesn't seem to be much good. Unfortunately the committee has decided that it's not safe to hand out new wands, so they're all being sent back to the United Sorcerer's Supply Stores and there's going to be a free library instead. But I know where they are now, and I expect I could borrow one – just for half an hour or so – if you'd promise to turn our parents back into human beings for us.'

Mrs Lomax looked much more friendly.

'I think that might be arranged,' she said. 'One can't be too careful over one's associates, and I find I have been quite mistaken in my estimate of Miss Hooting's character. If I can repair any harm she has done to your dear parents, I shall be delighted.'

'You stay here and talk to her and see she doesn't change her mind,' hissed Harriet to Mark. So he chatted politely to

Mrs Lomax and looked at her collection of lizards, while Harriet dashed off to the vicar and begged for the loan of one of the wands which he had stored until they could be dispatched back to London. 'Just for half an hour,' she pleaded. 'While we get Mother and Father changed back. You can't think how we miss them.'

'Very well,' he agreed. 'But please take care. Once in the wrong hands—'

Harriet ran triumphantly back with a heavy ebony stick. 'That should do,' said Mrs Lomax, looking at it professionally, and she recited:

> 'O *Stick, well-seasoned, elegant and sage,*
> *Change ladybird and wife to Armitage.*

'That should do the trick for you.' Then she went on, rather hastily:

> '*All fairy ladies, from tonight,*
> *Turn into owls – and serve them right!*'

A confused sound of screeching came from the trees. Several owls brushed past them.

'Oh, dear,' Harriet said doubtfully, 'I don't think the vicar would like—'

A blue flash wriggled up the stick to Mrs Lomax's hand, she shrank, her eyes became enormous, and all of a sudden she flew off into the trees, crying: 'Tu-whit! Tu-whoo!'

'She's turned herself into one, too,' said Mark. 'She

shouldn't have said *all*. Oh, well, let's take the wand back to the vicar.'

When they reached home, they found their parents completely restored, but still in the meat safe, very cramped and indignant.

'What were you doing out so late, anyway?' asked Mr Armitage.

The number of owls about the village was found to have greatly increased, and as a good many old ladies had mysteriously vanished, the proceeds of the progressive whist drive and the garden fête were used to buy a cannon to put in the school playground.

THE GHOSTLY GOVERNESS

The house stood a little way above the town, on the side of a hill. The front windows looked out on a great bare expanse of downs, stretching into the distance. From the pantry, and the bathroom, and the window halfway up the stairs, you could see down the river valley to Lynchbourne, the smoky port two miles away, and beyond its roofs, masts and funnels was the silver line of the sea.

The children approved of the house at once; it was old and full of unexpected corners, with a smell of polished floors and lavender and old carpets. The family had taken it furnished for August.

'I asked the agent and he said we could use the piano,' said Mrs Armitage, 'so you'll be able to keep up with your practising.'

But Mark and Harriet made secret faces at each other. They preferred the idea of hide-and-seek in the unexplored cupboards or picnics on the downs, or taking a boat down the river to the sea. They also explored the town – it was hardly more than a village – below the house. The thing they liked best was a cottage down by the river. The paths in its gardens were all paved with oyster shells, and there were two great carved dolphins on either side of the door.

'I wonder who lives there,' said Mark. 'I bet they've got some lovely things inside.'

But the cottage seemed to be unoccupied. The windows were all closed and curtained, and no smoke came from the chimney. They found out that it belonged to an admiral, so it seemed probable that he was at sea.

By the end of a week they felt as if they had been there all their lives. Every day they asked if they could take out a picnic lunch, and the Armitage parents declared that they had never known such peace; they hardly saw the children from breakfast till supper-time.

'But I'm glad to find that you're keeping up your practising,' said Mrs Armitage. 'I heard you playing that little German tune – what is it? – "*Du Lieber Augustin*" – very nicely the other evening.'

'Oh, yes,' said Harriet, and looked blank. The conversation turned on other things. Afterwards when she compared notes with Mark they agreed that neither of them had ever played '*Du Lieber Augustin*'.

'Do you suppose Father might have?'

'He never plays anything but Bach and Beethoven.'

'Well, someone must have played it, because I was humming it this morning, so I must have heard it somewhere.'

'Maybe it was on the wireless. Let's take our bikes down to Lynchbourne and see if there's a new ship in.'

They forgot about the incident, but later Harriet had

cause to remember it. She woke in the night very thirsty, and found that her glass was empty. Coming back from the bathroom, she thought she heard a noise downstairs and paused. Could someone be playing the piano at half past one in the morning? Harriet was not at all timid, and she resolved to go and see. She stole down the stairs in her slippers. Yes, there it was again – a faint thread of melody. She pushed the drawing-room door open and looked in.

The moon was setting and threw long stripes of light across the floor and the polished lid of the grand piano. There was nobody in the room. But as Harriet stood in the doorway she heard faint tinkling music which sounded more like a cottage piano than a Bechstein, and after a moment a quavering old voice was lifted in song:

'*Ach, du lieber Augustin, Weib ist hin, Gold ist hin,*
Ach, du lieber Augustin, alles ist hin.'

The piano keys were moving up and down by themselves. Harriet ought to have been terribly frightened, but she was not. The quavering voice sounded too harmless. She stood in fascination, watching the keys move and wondering how long it would go on, and if, perhaps, she were dreaming.

Presently the music stopped, and there was a sound of the stool being pushed back. Harriet took a step backwards. On the edge of the patch of moonlight she saw a little, frail old woman, dressed in a long grey skirt, white starched blouse, and a grey shawl over her shoulders.

'Ah,' she said in a brisk but kind voice, 'you don't know me yet, child, I am your new governess. Come, come, where are your manners? I should see a nice curtsy.'

'How do you do,' said Harriet, curtsying automatically.

'I hope we shall get along very well,' the old lady continued. 'Strict but kind is my motto, and *always* ladylike behaviour. If you want an example of *that,* you have only to look up to our dear queen, who is such a pattern of all the virtues.'

'Yes,' said Harriet absently, looking at her enormous cameo brooch, velvet neckband and elastic-sided boots.

The governess reminded her of the old yellow photographs in her grandmother's house.

'But now, child,' said the old lady, 'you must be going for your afternoon rest. It is nearly two o'clock. Later we shall begin to know each other better. By the way, I have not yet told you my name. It is Miss Allison. Now run along, and don't let me find you chattering to your brother during the rest hour.'

'No, Miss Allison,' said Harriet mechanically, and such was the governess's spell over her that she turned round and did indeed go straight back to bed and sleep.

Next morning at breakfast Harriet was silent, as if stunned. However, her father and brother talked all the time, and her silence was not noticed.

Later, when she and Mark were sitting in a quarry, eating the eleven o'clock instalment of their lunch (chocolate and buns), Mark said:

'What's happened to you? Toothache?'

'No. Mark,' Harriet said, 'do you remember the other day when Mother said something about my practising "*Lieber Augustin*", and I hadn't, and we thought it must have been the wireless?'

'Yes.'

'Well, I think we've got a ghost in the house.' And she told him the story of her last night's adventure.

Odd events were not uncommon in the Armitage family, so Mark did not, as many brothers would have done, say, 'Rats, you're trying to pull my leg.' He sat reflecting for a while. Then he said: 'What did you say her name was?'

'Miss Allison.'

'And she was dressed in a sort of Victorian costume?'

'Yes. I don't know what sort of time exactly – it might be anything from 1840 to 1900 I should think,' said Harriet vaguely, 'but, oh yes, she did say something about looking up to our dear queen as a pattern of propriety. It sounded like Queen Victoria.'

'I do hope we see her again,' said Mark. 'It sounds as if her day and night were the exact opposite of ours, if she told you to go and rest at two in the morning.'

Harriet agreed with this. 'And another thing,' she said, 'I believe she's only visible in the complete dark. Because at first she was sitting in the moonlight playing the piano – at least I suppose she was – and I couldn't see her at all till she stepped out of the light into the darkness.'

'Well, well, we'll have to start picketing her. I suppose she gets up when it gets dark.'

'Nonsense,' said Harriet, 'that wouldn't be till after ten. You never heard of a governess getting up at ten, did you? No, I bet she gets up in the *light*, just as we get up in the dark in winter.'

'Anyway we'll have to have one of us watching for her at night,' Mark went on. 'We'll have to do it in shifts and get some sleep in the daytime. We'd better start now.'

'Let's have lunch first.'

So they ate their picnic and then dutifully lay back on the springy turf and closed their eyes. But it was not a great success, for one or the other of them kept bouncing up with brilliant ideas on ghost-governesses. They agreed that it would be best if they both watched together the first night in case she turned out not to be the mild inoffensive creature that she had appeared to Harriet. They also agreed to take pencils and notebooks with them, in case she took advantage of her governess-hood and started teaching. Besides, they might learn something interesting.

At last they did achieve an intermittent doze, in the hot sun and the silence, and lay there for a couple of hours. Then they picked an enormous basketful of cowslips and started home for a late tea.

That night they listened carefully until the parents had gone to bed, and then slipped downstairs into the drawing-room. As before, the moonlight lay across the floor, but much farther round. Everything was silent, and all they could hear was their own breathing. Harriet began to have a dreadful feeling of disappointment.

'Perhaps she won't come again,' she whispered gloomily.

'Nonsense,' said Mark, 'we've hardly been here any time. If your feet are cold, sit in the armchair and tuck them under you.'

Harriet thought this a good idea. They sat on, and now they could hear the grandfather clock ticking in the hall, and the lonely lowing of a cow somewhere below in the valley.

All of a sudden a quiet voice said: 'Ah! Children! There you are. I've been looking for you everywhere. This, Harriet, is your brother Mark, I presume?'

Harriet's heart gave a violent jump, and then began beating very quickly. Miss Allison was standing, as she had been yesterday, on the edge of a pool of moonlight. She held a ruler in her hand and looked benevolent, but just slightly impatient.

Harriet got up and curtsied, and then she introduced Mark, who was standing with his mouth open, but otherwise looked fairly collected.

'Now we will go to the schoolroom,' said the governess, 'and that is where I should like you to wait for me in future. We will only come to the drawing-room for music lessons on Tuesdays and Fridays.'

The children cast anxious glances at each other, but followed her upstairs meekly enough, watching with interest as she twinkled in and out of patches of moonlight in the corridors, and wondering which room she had decided to use as the schoolroom. They found that it was Mark's bedroom, which was very convenient, as Harriet whispered to him.

'Don't whisper, Harriet dear,' said Miss Allison, who had her back turned, 'it's unpardonably rude.' She was doing something which looked like writing on an invisible blackboard. 'There, that's finished. Now, Harriet, will you bring your back-board out of that corner and lie on it. I wish to see you on it for at least half an hour every day, to give you a ladylike and erect deportment.'

Harriet had a look in the corner but saw nothing except Mark's tennis racket and a box of balls.

'I don't see it,' she said unhappily.

'Nonsense, dear. Your left foot is on it at the moment. Try to be observant.'

As Harriet's left foot was resting firmly on the floor, she felt rather injured, but, catching the governess's eye, she hastily stooped, picked up an imaginary back-board with both hands, and carried it to the middle of the room.

'It would help,' she said to herself, 'if I knew what the dratted thing looked like. But I suppose it's as long as I am.'

'Put it down, child. Now lie on it. Flat on your back, arms at your sides, eyes looking at the ceiling.'

Harriet lay down on the floor, looking at Miss Allison doubtfully, and was rewarded by a nod.

'Now Mark,' said the governess briskly, 'I have written on the blackboard a list of Latin prepositions followed by the ablative case. You will occupy yourself in learning them while I write out an exercise for you both. Harriet, you can be trying to think of twenty wildflowers beginning with the letter *l*.'

She sat down at an invisible table and began briskly writing on nothing. Mark looked gloomily at the empty space where the blackboard was supposed to be, and wondered how he could learn a list of words he couldn't see. This adventure, it seemed to him, was a bit too much like real life. He wished Miss Allison was a more conventional ghost with clanking chains.

Harriet gave him a grin, and then, as Miss Allison looked particularly occupied, she whispered:

'A, *ab*, *absque*, *coram*, *de* . . .,'

Mark's face cleared. Of course, now he remembered the words. Thank goodness he had learned them at school. He thought for a moment anxiously of what would happen if they didn't know what she had written on the blackboard, but anyway, that was in the future. No use worrying about it now.

At the end of what was presumably half an hour, Miss Allison turned round.

'Well!' she said. 'Harriet, you may put away your board. Mark, let me hear you recite. You should have it by rote now.'

'A, *ab*, *absque*,' he began.

'Never let me see you recite like that, Mark. Hands behind your back, feet in the first position, head up.' Mark obeyed peevishly.

'Now begin again.'

'A, *ab*, *absque*, *coram*, *de*,
Palam, *clam*, *cum*, *ex* and *e*
Tenus, *sine*, *pro*, *in*, *prae*
Ablative with these we spy.'

'Very good, Mark, though your pronunciation is a little modern,' she said. 'You may open that blue tin and have a caraway biscuit.'

Mark looked about for a blue tin, saw none, and opened an imaginary one.

Harriet did rather badly over her wildflowers beginning with *l*. Half the ones she thought of, such as lady's smock, lady's slipper, lady's tresses, lords and ladies, and all the lesser stitch-worts and lesser chickweeds were disqualified, leaving her with a very poor list. She got no caraway biscuit. However, as Mark's had been imaginary, she did not greatly mind.

After this, they had to do embroidery. It also was totally

imaginary. They held invisible pieces of linen, threaded invisible needles, and sometimes for the fun of the thing stuck them into their fingers and squeaked with imaginary pain. It was all very amusing. It soon appeared that even if they couldn't see their work, Miss Allison could. She kept up a running fire of comment, from which they gathered that Mark's was bad and Harriet's fairly good. This seemed reasonable enough. Mark was rather indignant at being expected to do embroidery, but after a while the governess began to read aloud to them a fascinating book called *Improving Tales*, all about some good children and some bad ones, so he just stuck his needle in and out and listened.

'There,' said Miss Allison finally, 'that will do for today. For your preparation you will both turn to page two hundred in your Latin grammars and learn the list of words beginning:

'*Amnis, axis, caulis, collis,*
Clunis, crinis, fascis, follis—

and you will also each write me a composition entitled "Devotion to Duty".'

'Please,' said Harriet, 'which is our Latin grammar?'

'Why, Crosby, of course. The blue book. Now run along, dears. You will want to get ready for your walk.'

Mark wanted to go to bed, but she gave him such an extremely firm look that he went out with Harriet.

'You'll have to sleep on the sofa in my room,' she whispered, 'and creep back as soon as it's light. I wouldn't dare try to disobey her.'

'Nor me,' he whispered back. 'She looks much firmer than any of the masters at school.'

Luckily it was very warm, and there were some spare blankets in Harriet's room, so he was quite comfortable and slept well.

They were both rather silent and sleepy at breakfast, but afterwards on the river bank they discussed things.

'What are we going to do about those wretched essays?' asked Mark sourly. 'I'm blowed if I write about devotion to duty.'

'Oh, that's all right,' Harriet replied. 'Don't you see, the composition will be just like the embroidery. We'll show up an imaginary one.'

'I don't quite understand that,' said Mark, screwing up his eyes and throwing stones into the mudbank; the tide was rapidly running out.

'Nor do I,' agreed Harriet candidly, 'but I *think* it's something like this: you see, she must have taught hundreds of children when she was alive, and I expect she made them all do embroidery and write about devotion to duty. So when we give her our imaginary things, she thinks about the ones she remembers. See what I mean?'

'Well, almost.'

'No, what *I'm* worried about,' Harriet went on, 'is if she asks us to learn things and recite. Because if we haven't got the books to learn them from – like this wretched Crosby – we're stumped. Have you ever heard of Crosby?'

'No, we use Kennedy in our class.'

'So do we. Well, maybe we could ask to write them down

from memory instead of reciting them. It'll be all right, of course, if she asks us to learn something like *The Ancient Mariner*.'

'I dunno,' said Mark, 'all this sounds a bit too much like work to me.'

'It is a bit. Still, not too many people have learned Latin prepositions from a ghost. That's something.'

'I tell you,' said Mark. 'The attic.'

'What about it?'

'There are hundreds of old boxes there with things in them that belong to the house. I was up there one day looking for secret passages. Maybe if we looked in them we'd find some old lesson books that belonged to the people who were here before.'

'That's an idea. We might find something about Miss Allison too – a diary or something. Let's go now.'

'Anyway,' Harriet pointed out as they walked back to the house, 'if it does get too much of a good thing, we can always just stay in bed and not go to her.'

'All right for you,' said Mark, 'but I expect she's in my room all the time. She'll probably just haul me out of bed at ten o'clock.'

The lunch bell rang as they came up the garden, so they had to put off their search in the attic.

It was a dark, cool room, lit only by green glass tiles in the roof. Harriet sat for a while pensively on a box while Mark rummaged about, turning out with everything little piles of thickish yellow powder smelling of pine needles.

'That's for the moths,' she said. Then she began folding

the things and putting them back as he went on. They were mostly clothes folded in tissue paper, and old rush baskets pressed flat, large women's hats with draggled bunches of feathers, and pairs of kid gloves.

'People wore things like these in the 1914 war,' said Harriet. 'Look, here's a newspaper. January, 1914. This is too modern.'

'Half a sec,' said Mark, 'over here they seem to be older.' He pulled out an enormous flounced ball-dress of fawn-coloured satin; some shawls; a pair of satin slippers; a little woven basket with a lid, containing brightly coloured glass bracelets and necklaces of glass beads; a large flat box full of fans – ivory, with pink flowers, satinwood, and wonderful plumy feathers.

'I wish there were some letters or books or something,' Mark murmured discontentedly. Harriet was exclaiming to herself over the fans before laying them back in the box.

'This one's very heavy,' said Mark, tugging at a chest. The lid came up unwillingly. Underneath was a gorgeous Chinese hanging of silk, folded square. He lifted it out.

'Aha!' A heavy, old-fashioned Bible lay on the tissue paper.

'Harriet, look here!'

Harriet came across and read over her brother's shoulder the inscription in a beautiful copperplate handwriting: 'to my dear daughter Georgiana Lucy Allison from her affectionate Mother, Christmas 1831.'

'Well!' they breathed at each other. Mark flipped through the leaves, but there was nothing else, except for a faded pansy.

'Let's see what else there is in the box.'

Underneath the tissue paper were more books.

'Lesson books,' said Harriet ecstatically. '*Primer of Geography*. Mason's *Manual of Arithmetic*. Look! Here's Crosby's *Latin Grammar Made Easy*.'

Besides the lesson books there were children's books – *Improving Tales for the Young*, *Tales for Little Folks*, *Good Deeds in a Bad World*, *Tales from the Gospel*, and a number of others, all improving. Several of them also had Miss Allison's name in them. Others had children's names – 'John, from his affec. Governess', 'Lucy, from Mamma', and in a large stumbling script, 'Lucy, from Isabel'.

'We'd better take down all the lesson books,' said Harriet. 'They can live on the bookshelf in your room – there's plenty of empty space.'

They had a further search in the other boxes, but found nothing else interesting except some children's clothes – sailor suits, dresses, and pantalets, which Harriet would have liked to try on. 'But they look so fragile,' she said with a sigh, 'I'd probably tear them.' So everything was replaced and they went downstairs, each with an armful of books.

Later that evening, Harriet's mother found her sprawled on the drawing-room sofa looking at a book and then shutting it and muttering to herself.

'You look as if you were learning poetry,' said Mrs Armitage, glancing over her shoulder. 'What, *Latin!* Good heavens, I have got diligent children. Incidentally I wish you'd find another tune to practise on the piano. I find myself singing that *Lieber Augustin* all day long.'

That night, when Harriet went along to Mark's room at about midnight, she found him already at work reciting the principal parts of Latin verbs.

'Mark knows his list of words very well, Harriet. I trust that you will also be able to earn your caraway biscuit,' remarked Miss Allison, and then, while Harriet lay on her imaginary back-board, the governess read them a long, boring chapter about the War of the Roses.

'I generally start my pupils at the *beginning* of history, with William the Conqueror,' explained Miss Allison, 'but your dear mother expressed a wish for you to study this period particularly.'

Afterwards Harriet recited her Latin and also earned a caraway biscuit. Then Harriet and Mark showed Miss Allison their invisible essays on Duty, and Harriet's point was proved. Miss Allison obviously saw them, even if the children didn't, and peevishly pointed out several spelling mistakes.

'Mark, you will write out the word "ceiling" fifty times,' she said. 'That will be all for this morning, dears. Harriet, will you ask Anne to run up with a duster, and I will dust my room myself. And tell her that she forgot to sweep under the bed yesterday, though I reminded her particularly.'

'Mother,' said Mark one morning. 'Can I change my bedroom? I'd much rather sleep in the room next to Harriet.'

'Well, if you do,' said his mother, looking at him acutely, you must promise not to be popping in and out of each other's rooms all night. I thought I heard something last night.' But they gazed at her so innocently that she agreed and said they could change the things over themselves.

'Just as well,' said Mark, when they were carrying sheets along the passage. 'Do you know she hauled me out of bed last night and asked me what I thought I was doing sleeping on the schoolroom sofa?'

'She *is* queer,' Harriet remarked thoughtfully. 'I sometimes wonder if she really *sees* us at all. She obviously doesn't see the same furniture we do, because sometimes she uses tables and chairs that aren't there, and when she talks about our parents, she doesn't mean Mother and Father, because they never said anything to her about the War of the Roses.'

'And there's all this business about Anne and Cook, too. I suppose she sort of sees them all around. Poor old thing,' said Mark, tucking in a lump of blanket, 'I'm getting quite fond of her.'

'You know, I'm sure she has something on her mind,' added Harriet. 'She looks so worried at times, as if she was trying to remember things.'

It soon appeared that the children had something on their minds, too.

'You both of you look dreadfully tired nowadays,' remarked Mrs Armitage. 'You aren't sickening for measles, are you? And don't you think you're overdoing this holiday work a bit? Surely you don't need to do all that Latin and History. The other afternoon when you were asleep on the lawn, Mark, I heard you muttering the dates of the kings of England in your sleep. Take a bit of rest from it. By the way, there's an Admiral Lecacheur coming to tea this afternoon – he lives in that little house on the river you've taken such a fancy to. If you want to get invited to have a look round it, you'd better put in an appearance.'

'Lecacheur?' said Mark vaguely. 'I seem to know the name.'

'Yes, it's the family who lived here before. He's the owner of this house, actually, but he's mostly away, so he prefers to let it and live in the cottage.'

Lecacheur! Of course it was the name written in the lesson books! Mark and Harriet exchanged a swift, excited look.

'Is he an old man?' asked Mark carelessly.

'About sixty, I believe. Now I must fly. I've masses to do. Be good, children.'

'If he's about sixty,' said Harriet, when they were alone, 'he must have been born in 1885. I *wish* we knew when Miss Allison died.'

'Well, we know she was alive in 1831 because of that Bible. I wonder how old she was when she was given that?'

'Say she was about ten,' said Harriet, counting on her fingers, 'that makes her sixty-five when the admiral was born. Well, that's quite possible. She looks more than that. He may easily have known her. We'll have to draw him out, somehow.'

'Maybe, if he knew her, he'd know what it is she worries about,' said Harriet hopefully. 'You know, I believe if we could find out what's on her mind and help her, she'd vanish. That's the sort of thing ghosts do.'

'Well, I'm not sure I'd be sorry,' said Mark, puffing out a deep breath. 'I'd like a night's sleep for once. Remember when we didn't wake up, how cross she was next night? And I've had just about enough Latin verbs. *And* the kings of England.'

Harriet agreed. 'And the parents are beginning to think that there's something funny going on. Father started whistling *Lieber Augustin* the other day, and then he turned and gave me an *awfully* queer look.'

Admiral Lecacheur turned out to be a pleasant man, large, jovial, grey-haired. It was not difficult for the children to get an invitation from him to go and look at his cottage.

As he showed them the stuffed shark and the model ships in bottles, Harriet summoned up the courage to speak.

'Admiral,' she finally said timidly, 'did you ever know a Miss Georgiana Lucy Allison?'

'God bless my soul, yes,' he said, turning round and smiling at her. 'She was our family governess. Is there some stuff of hers still knocking about in the house?'

'Yes, there are some books of hers. And a Bible.'

'Old Allie,' he said reminiscently. 'She was a wonderful old girl. Must have been with our family for fifty years. She taught three generations of us. I was the last!'

'Did she teach you?'

'I remember her very well,' he went on, without noticing the interruption, 'though she died, I suppose, when I was about five. That would be around 1890. But she'd already taught me to read, and some of the multiplication table, and the kings of England. She was great on learning things by heart. Not like the modern education you get now, I daresay. 'Cedric,' she used to say, 'how will you ever get on in life if you don't know these things?' Ah, well. Here I am an admiral, and I daresay if she'd taught me longer, I should have been Admiral of the Fleet. But there! She must have died more than fifty years ago.'

He smiled at their serious faces and said, 'Now here's a thing you ought to like. Just look at the size of that!' And he handed Harriet a shell the size of a dinner plate.

'Well, we still don't know what's on her mind,' said Mark, as they walked homewards.

'No, but we couldn't ask him all at once. Another time we'll jolly well pump him.'

But as things turned out they didn't need to. That night when Mark was reciting the dates of the kings of England, he absent-mindedly followed William and Mary with 'Queen Anne, 1700.'

There was an ominous pause, and Miss Allison suddenly burst into tears.

'Cedric, you wicked boy,' she sobbed, 'will you *never* get it right? How can you expect to be a success in life, if you don't know your dates? And you going into the Navy, too.' She hid her face in her hands, but through them they could hear her say, 'I'm getting so old. How can I die happy if that boy doesn't know the date of Queen Anne? All the others learned it.'

'Please don't cry,' said Mark awkwardly, patting her shoulder. 'It was only a mistake. I do know it. Really I do. It's 1702, isn't it?'

But she went on sobbing 'Cedric! Cedric!' and after a minute Harriet touched his arm and pulled him softly out of the room.

'Let's go to bed,' she whispered. 'We can't do anything about her. And I've got a brilliant idea. Tell you in the morning.'

Next day she dragged him down to Dolphin Cottage. The admiral was surprised to see them. 'What, you again so early? You're just in time to help me syringe my greenfly.'

'Admiral,' said Harriet, fixing her eyes on him earnestly, 'will you tell me something terribly important?'

'What is it,' he said, very much astonished.

'Tell me when Queen Anne came to the throne.'

He burst into a great roar of laughter, slapping his knees. 'Well, I'm blessed; do you know, it's funny you should ask me that, because it's the one date I never have been able to remember. Miss Allison used to get wild about it. "I shan't die happy till you know that date, Cedric," she used to say. But she did die, poor old soul, and I don't know it to this day.'

'Come and sit down,' said Harriet, dragging him to a garden seat. One on each side, she and Mark told him the whole story. When he heard how Miss Allison made their nights a burden, he shouted with laughter.

'That's just like her, bless her,' he exclaimed.

'So you see, it really has got to stop,' Harriet explained. 'We're getting worn out, and I'm sure she is too – after all, she must be about a hundred and twenty, far too old to be teaching. And she's so miserable, poor dear. I think you can help us.'

She told him their plan, and after some hesitation the admiral agreed. 'But if you're pulling my leg,' he threatened, 'you'll never forget it, the pair of you.'

'Now you've got to learn it,' said Harriet. 'Write it on a bit of paper somewhere – here, I'll do it for you. Now stick it up where you'll be able to see it all day. And we'll meet you at the garden gate tonight at midnight.'

'What your parents would say if they caught us—' he exclaimed, but he agreed. The children went home very hopeful.

The meeting came off as arranged. They let him in by the garden door and took him quietly up the back stairs into the schoolroom, where Miss Allison was pacing up and down looking very impatient.

'What time,' she began, and then suddenly she saw who was with them. 'Why, *Cedric*!'

'Allie!' he exclaimed.

'You wicked boy! Where have you been all this time?'

'I'm sorry,' he said meekly, looking more like a small boy than a grey-haired man of sixty.

'Just you tell me one thing,' she said, drawing herself up and giving him a piercing look. 'When did Queen Anne come to the throne?'

The children gazed at him anxiously, but they need not have worried. He had learned his lesson this time.

'Seventeen-two,' he said promptly, and they sighed with relief.

Miss Allison burst into tears of joy.

'I might have known it,' she sobbed. 'My good boy. Why, now you know that, you might even become an admiral, and I can die happy.'

And as they watched her, suddenly, flick! like a candle,

she went out, and there was no one in the room but their three selves.

'Well, I'm blessed,' said the admiral, not for the first time. 'Old Allie.' He walked quietly from the room. Mark saw him down to the garden gate. When he came back, he found Harriet dabbing at her eyes with a handkerchief.

'You know, I'm going to miss her,' she said. 'Oh, well, let's go to bed.'

They never saw Miss Allison again.

ROCKET FULL OF PIE

In heaven's name, what is that?' said Mr Armitage, coming in and finding his wife with a length of scarlet muffler apparently intended for an ostrich dangling from her knitting needles.

'Comforts for the Lifeboatmen,' she told him. 'My Women's Union members are making mufflers for the Shambles Lifeboat crew.'

Mr Armitage carefully picked his way through the tangle and sat down in front of the fire, moving a large model yacht to make room for his feet, and eliciting a cry of protest from Mark, who was sitting by the wireless.

'Careful, Father! The paint's not nearly dry yet.'

'Christmas holidays,' grumbled Mr Armitage. 'How thankful I shall be when they're over. Mark, turn off that awful voice, will you?'

'But it's interesting,' complained Mark, turning it off. 'It was an appeal for more weather ships, and I wanted to find out about them.'

'You will have to find out some other way. I want peace

and quiet,' said his father unsympathetically. 'Lifeboats – weather ships – my family seems to have gone marine crazy.'

'Mummy's going for a sail on Monday,' Harriet told him.

'A sail? In December? For mercy's sake, why?'

'It's the Women's Union Christmas Outing,' Mrs Armitage explained patiently. 'We're having the presentation of the mufflers to the lifeboat crew, and then the club members are being taken for a trip out to the Shambles lighthouse, where we shall have tea. The lighthouse keepers are providing the tea and we are providing the food. I'm one of the hostesses this month, so I shall have to get busy.'

'Make some of your mince pies,' said Mr Armitage. 'That'll fetch 'em. But isn't Monday rather an unwise day for your excursion?'

Monday, in the Armitage family, was a day on which unexpected things were likely to happen – a live Cockatrice had once settled in the garden and eaten up all the vegetables, breathing out fire as he did so, and on another Monday, the Fairy Queen had held At Home on the front lawn, completely preventing any tradesmen from calling for twenty-four hours. The Armitage parents were always relieved when Monday was over, and tried not to embark on any risky venture upon that day if they could help it.

'Can't be avoided this time, I'm afraid,' Mrs Armitage said, sighing. 'It was the only day when all the members could come.'

All that week Mrs Armitage and Harriet were busy making mince pies. Mark, for once, was not helpful.

'He's making another of his model yachts, I suppose,' Harriet said. 'That's why he always comes to meals late with gluey hands.'

'You can come on the trip, as you've been such a help, Harriet,' said her mother. 'But I shan't ask Mark. That'll teach him to cooperate a bit more next time I'm busy.'

Mark did grumble when he heard that he had not been invited. 'I've always wanted to see inside the lighthouse,' he said. But as his protests were unavailing, he soon retired to his den and began sawing away.

'Who is the other hostess and what is she providing?' said Mr Armitage on Saturday, eyeing the growing mountain of mince pies.

'It's Mrs Slabb,' his wife said gloomily.

'Oh dear.'

'She's making some rock cakes. I tried to persuade her that sandwiches would be nice, but she didn't take the hint. She said she reckoned her cakes would fill up the boys' stomachs better.'

'Fill them up? They'll *cement* them up, more likely,' said Mr Armitage. 'Remember the cake she made for the Guess the Weight Competition at last year's Christmas Bazaar – the only person who guessed within a stone was the Strong Man from the Bumstead Circus.'

'Never mind, she's a kind old thing and we can't hurt her feelings,' Mrs Armitage said firmly.

Monday dawned grey and bleak without a breath of wind.

'Looks like snow,' said Mr Armitage, but the barometer stood at 'Set Fair'.

The Women's Union members assembled on the launching ramp punctually at two o'clock for the presentation amid cries of 'Did you remember to lock the back door?' and 'Are the hens shut up?' from the crew, who were mostly their husbands and relatives.

Mrs Armitage made a short speech before unveiling the huge cardboard carton which contained the gift mufflers.

'Thank you kindly one and all,' said the coxswain (his name was Alf Putnam), 'I hereby have pleasure in handing them out to the men, who I'm sure will thoroughly appreciate them – specially as they've seen them being knitted for the last six months. Bert Althorpe!'

Bert stepped forward to receive his muffler and Alf pulled a generous blue length out of the box, which Bert wound round his neck before stepping back again.

'Hey, you've left one end behind – you haven't got it all yet, chum,' someone called out. As Bert pulled, more and more muffler unreeled from the carton. The blue length was followed by a red one, and that by an orange one.

'Oh dear,' exclaimed Mrs Armitage in dismay. 'Can someone have joined them all together? There's been some bad coordination somewhere.'

This, it seemed, was the case. Rods, poles, perches, chains, and furlongs of endless muffler, every colour of the rainbow, were drawn out and lay about the beach and ramp in gorgeous festoons.

'Looks like Christmas all right, don't it,' muttered Bert to Lofty Wainwright.

'Alf, you better stop pulling it out. If you once get lost in that lot, we shan't see you again alive.'

'Maybe we should cut it,' said Alf, mopping his brow.

'You can't do that,' cried a dozen ladies. 'It would all unravel. The ends will have to be stitched up.'

'Well, let's put it out of the way for now,' said Alf rather desperately, 'and get on with the next part of the programme.'

Several people clapped at this.

'Ladies, please take your places in the lifeboat, as indicated to you by Bert, William, and Nobby,' said Alf. 'Fred, you give me a hand with the grub.'

The mince pies had been brought down in two large laundry baskets, covered with clean cloths, and Mrs Slabb had put her cakes in a couple of canvas kit bags which had once belonged to Mr Slabb. When Fred seized one of these he turned pale.

'Blimey!' he said. 'What's in them? Lead piping?'

He and Alf tottered with difficulty to the boat and heaved the sack over the side. When they had put in the second with equal difficulty, Alf muttered to Fred:

'We'd better leave the two baskets behind, accidentally like. Another two of these would sink us. As it is we'll have to move the passengers forrard or we'll be down by the stern.'

So the laundry baskets were left behind on the beach, and the Women's Union were packed further along, amid cries of 'What do you think we are? Sardines? Mind my toe, you big lump! Ooh!'

Harriet, in between Mrs Slabb and Mrs Lightbody, was nearly crushed to death.

The rest of the crew piled in, all except Fred, who was the spare and in any case had said he had more sense than to go joyriding with a passel of females. Alf leaned over the gunwale and pulled the lever and the lifeboat slid majestically down the ramp and into the sea.

Fred, left alone on the beach, dragged the two baskets of mince pies into the shed, noticing as he did so that they were not nearly so heavy as the sacks of cakes, and then began methodically coiling up the length of muffler. There seemed to be roughly a thousand yards of it – nearly a hundred yards for each man. 'Them women,' he muttered to himself. 'Not a stitch of arithmetic in any of 'em.'

When he finished he straightened his back and glanced up at the sky.

'Lumme,' he exclaimed, 'they're going to cop it if they don't look out.'

The clouds were becoming almost as black as ink, and the wind, which had been rising, was now whipping the top of the waves in a very ugly way. A more unpleasant day for an outing could not have been imagined.

Mark, who had just arrived on his bicycle, too late for the launching, gazed in dismay at the lifeboat, which was bouncing uneasily through the sea about halfway between the shore and the lighthouse rock.

'Blowing up for a proper gale,' Fred said to him gloomily.

The passengers in the boat were not at all happy. There were several green faces, and shrieks of dismay were heard as waves occasionally slopped over and soused some of them.

'Never mind, Mum, soon be there and you can cheer yourself up with a nice cuppa,' said Alf to Mrs Lightbody, but Harriet, who had sharp ears, heard him mutter to Nobby: 'Look here, we're getting lower in the water all the time. D'you think we could throw some of these perishing granite buns overboard without anyone seeing?'

He dug an experimental hand into one of the kit bags, pulled out a cake, and tossed it to starboard. A passing gull swooped and deftly caught the cake, staggered in its flight, and fell like a stone beneath the waves. Harriet opened her mouth to gasp with horror, but was relieved to see the gull pop up again in a moment, without the cake but with an expression of extreme astonishment on its face.

'Strewth!' said Nobby, awestruck.

'See what I mean? If we don't jettison those cakes we're going to founder.'

The waves, as large as houses now, towered over the heavily burdened lifeboat, which was settling deeper and deeper between them. Harriet thought they looked like huge black Christmas trees. She watched Alf pick up one of the sacks and stagger towards the side, and then Nobby shouted:

'No, hold it, here we are!'

Another of the large waves, rolling to one side, had revealed the lighthouse just ahead. The three members of its crew were dancing about on a little spur of rock at the foot, anxiously waiting to catch a rope.

'Come on,' they called encouragingly. 'You made it! That's the stuff!' They spoke too soon, however.

As Bert leaned over with the painter, a gigantic wave tipped the lifeboat sideways, and crew, passengers, and cargo were all flung into the sea together as neatly as peas flipped out of a pod. Fortunately they were within a few feet of the rock and all managed to clamber ashore, but they heard the boat slam grindingly on a rock behind them, and turned to see it drift away and then submerge.

'That's that,' said Alf. 'Now how are we going to get back?'

'Oh, Fred will have seen her go down. He'll phone along to Slimehaven and get their boat to come and take us off.'

'Not in this weather they won't. We haven't had a gale like this since '38.'

'Well, don't stand here gossiping,' said Mrs Lightbody tartly. 'Let's get inside and have a warmup, for goodness' sake, and where's that cup of tea? If we don't get some dry clothes on soon they needn't bother to send a boat – they can just float over some coffins.'

The shipwrecked party trooped into the lighthouse, and soon clouds of steam began coming out of its windows as, in turn, members of the Women's Union and lifeboat crew wrapped themselves in blankets and dried themselves in front of the twenty thousand candlepower light. Cups of tea were provided by their kind hosts, but, alas, there was nothing to eat, for Mrs Slabb's cakes had gone down with the boat.

'Better get ready for a hungry Christmas, ladies,' said the

head lighthouse keeper. 'This time of year we're often cut off for two or three weeks if the weather turns nasty.'

Cries of 'Oo-er' and 'Love a duck' greeted this, but he continued: 'We've got supplies of bully beef and biscuits, but they won't go far among ten lifeboatmen and twenty Ladies' Union. It'll be one biscuit and one slice of bully per day till further notice.'

Some of the ladies began to cry, thinking of the turkeys hanging in their larders, and the Christmas puddings all ready for boiling. Mrs Armitage tried to cheer them, but even Harriet felt glum, and her lunch seemed to have been a long time ago. She would have welcomed one of Mrs Slabb's buns.

Just then Alf came in looking puzzled.

'Old Fred's got the rocket apparatus out on the beach,' he said. 'Can't rightly see what he's doing, it's come over so dark, but there's a boy helping him and it looks as if they're trying to send something over.'

Most of the party crowded out onto the rock platform to see what was going on. Over the raging water they could dimly see two figures active on the shore, and presently they saw a flash, though it was impossible to hear the report of the rocket through the gale. But they could soon see a missile hurtling towards them, and amid cries of excitement a large rocket landed a few feet away from where they were standing. Alf went over to it.

'What's in it?' inquired the lighthouse keeper when he staggered back with it in his arms. They all gathered round as he unscrewed the canister.

A large heap of little round golden objects rolled out, from which came a delicious spicy smell, most inviting to the hungry castaways.

'Mince pies! It's Mother's mince pies!' shouted Harriet. 'Three cheers for Fred!'.

There were enough mince pies for everyone, and a few minutes later, a new rocket landed with a second cargo, which was eagerly gathered up and taken inside. Then Fred apparently decided that the light was too bad to risk sending any more, for he and his helper took the firing apparatus back into the shed.

It was not such a miserable party after all which sat munching the mince pies and toasting Fred in mugs of tea. And presently they all went to sleep, wrapped in blankets and packed together on the floor like sardines.

The awakening next morning was not so cheerful, as they were stiff and uncomfortable and, worse still, the storm was raging more fiercely if anything than the day before. After breakfast (one biscuit, washed down with tea), Fred managed to send over two more rocket-loads of pies, but then the gale worsened until it was impossible to see the shore, and the lifeboat crew shook their heads over the chance of any rescue that day.

Mrs Armitage, seeing the Women's Union members looking very glum, organized them into giving the lighthouse a spring cleaning, which it badly needed.

'We'll each scrub twenty steps of the stairs and polish three windows,' she said. 'At least there's one thing we're not short of, and that's water. And there seems to be plenty of soap, too – they are not extravagant with it out here, it's plain.'

The male inhabitants retired outside while this was going on, and waited patiently in the storm rather than be bumped continually with brushes and buckets.

On Wednesday Fred managed to send over the rest of the mince pies, but it was too rough for a rescue. On Thursday, however, which was Christmas Eve, the Slimehaven lifeboat came along the coast, but could not get near the lighthouse because of dangerous lumps of rock which were being flung about by the waves. Several of these pierced the sides of the boat, which were only just patched in time. It was discovered that these lumps were in fact Mrs Slabb's cakes, which the action of salt water and cold air had rendered hard as bullets.

The Slimehaven crew tried several times to get a line to the shore which would pass by the lighthouse, so that provisions could run along it. At first they were unsuccessful, as no ordinary rope could stand the strain of the wind and waves, but finally the marooned group saw them put in to the shore and come out again trailing a cable which, even through the storm, could be seen to consist of sections in different vivid colours.

'Well, I'm blest! They're using our muffler. What a sauce!' exclaimed Mrs Slabb.

'At least it's holding,' said Alf rather sourly.

The Slimehaven boat put out beyond the lighthouse, keeping well clear of it, and then hove to. The crew could be seen feverishly winding away at a winch, and bit by bit the multicoloured line twitched and jerked itself tight, until it was a foot above the waves.

'Look! Look!' cried Harriet. 'Someone's walking out along the rope.'

They all gazed at the point where the line ran up the beach and saw a tiny figure coming slowly but steadily out along the rope. Some of the women could not stand it and went inside, but most of the party watched in fascination, expecting every minute that some extra large wave would knock him from his position.

Harriet saw that it was Mark when he had come about halfway, but she could not make out what he was carrying. It seemed like a model ship, but of no design that she recognized. He was holding it with both hands in front of him and using it to keep his balance.

'I didn't know Mark could tightrope walk,' murmured Mrs Armitage distractedly, without taking her eyes off him.

'Oh yes, we both learned last year from the trapeze artiste at the Bumstead Circus,' Harriet answered absently. 'What's he doing now?'

Mark had come level with them, though he was about twenty yards away to port. He deliberately dropped his little boat onto the water, staggered, nearly missed his balance, recovered it again, and made his way on to the Slimehaven boat, where he was received with clapping and cheers.

'But what's the use of that?' said Mrs Lightbody, puzzled. 'One little toy boat isn't going to help us. It's not worth all that trouble.'

But even as she spoke they saw that all around the little

ship the waves were dying down. Presently the sea near the lighthouse was as calm as a mill-pond, and in scenes of the wildest rejoicing the members of the Women's Union and Shambles crew were rescued from their watery jail, and a Christmas dinner was handed over to their hosts.

'But what was the little ship?' demanded Harriet, and everyone was asking the same question.

'It was a weather ship,' Mark replied. 'You know, there was a radio appeal for more of them, so I thought I'd make one. For calming down the weather, you see.'

'But weather ships are for recording the weather, not for calming it down.'

'Are they? Oh, well, there you are. Father would turn the radio off, so I never did hear about them and I had to guess how to make it. Anyway, I think my sort's more useful,' said Mark. 'I'm going to make some more, but I suppose I'd better make a new lifeboat first.'

HARRIET'S BIRTHDAY PRESENT

'I've been sent home early,' Harriet wrote, 'because they've all got German measles at school, and they don't want any more of us to get them. Isn't it a joke?'

Mark envied her for two days until his mother wrote in some annoyance to say that the first thing Harriet had done when she got home was develop that short but tiresome disease. This meant that Mark would have to stay on at school for four days after term to let her get out of quarantine. He was in the middle of an indignant letter asking her how she could have been so careless when the wire came from his Aunt Hal in London.

'Come here till quarantine over key under flowerpot as usual,' it said.

So Mark tore up his letter, thanked his stars that he had not yet begun to search the small town of Warrington for Harriet's birthday present, and packed himself on the school train with the rest of his friends on Friday morning.

His Aunt Hal's flat was over a garage, which was in itself

delightful. Also you climbed up to it by a flight of steps outside, and there was a balcony, and a marmalade cat called Tomsk.

Hal was in the process of distempering the walls of the three rooms, and they spent an energetic weekend dropping brushfuls of paint over each other and the carpet, only breaking off for large mixed meals and a cinema.

'I've got tickets for *Robin Hood* on Monday evening,' she told him. 'Of course I'm working on Monday. Will you be able to amuse yourself all day?'

'I want to get some lino-cutting tools,' said Mark, 'and there's Harriet's birthday present to shop for. Mother doesn't want me to go down until Tuesday afternoon because of choir practice and the sheets and the fumigating.'

'Okay,' said Hal, 'I'll leave you your lunch, if you like, and meet you at the theatre.'

She had already gone off to work when he got up on Monday morning. He ate his breakfast lying on the floor on his stomach with Tomsk sitting gravely beside him. Aunt Hal had two wonderful books which he always looked at when he came to see her. One of them was about Louis the Eleventh, whom he knew from *Quentin Durward*, and the other was about Napoleon's Moscow campaign. Unfortunately, they were in French, and not very easy, but it was the pictures he looked at them for. These were very strange and exciting. There were three that he always remembered particularly. One of them showed the siege of a castle. The besiegers had put up an enormously tall ladder against the walls and a lot of men had climbed up it. But just when the first ones were getting near the top, the defenders had managed to push the ladder over, and the picture showed it slowly falling backwards, and the horrified faces of the men on it. Another picture was of a man falling through a trap door into an oubliette, and the third was Louis being haunted by all the people he had hanged. Mark spent a lot of time on this book, and then stacked his breakfast things in the kitchen, took the sandwiches that his Aunt Hal had made him, saw that Tomsk had enough milk, and went out.

By lunch-time he had bought his tools, but had not yet decided on Harriet's present. He did not know what he wanted to give her, and felt rather worried. Nothing he saw seemed exactly the thing she would like. He ate his sandwiches in the park, thinking deeply all the time, and then made up his mind to go back to the flat and leave his tools there, as they were heavy and inconvenient. Then he would have a proper hunt for Harriet's present, and if he could still find nothing, there was always next morning.

Tomsk had finished all his milk and wanted some more, so it was just as well he had gone back. He dropped the tools, ate a piece of cake, and went out again into the hazy March sunshine. There was a smell of smoke, and it was very cold, but felt like spring.

This time Mark did not try to go anywhere definite, but just wandered, looking into shop windows, going down streets that looked as if they might lead somewhere interesting, getting on buses and off again (sometimes without paying his fare), and talking to odd people when he felt like it.

He was standing with his hands in his pockets outside the window of a large toyshop when he heard a voice at his elbow.

'Buying geefts, yes?' the voice said softly. 'Here I haf geefts that will nefer break, nefer wear out, recipients nefer tire of heem, yes no?'

Mark looked round and saw a little man sitting on a stool on the pavement with a large box beside him.

'Magic,' the man nodded, 'nefer break, nefer wear out – see?' He held up a very ordinary looking white picnic cup. 'Throw heem on the floor – he never break. Nefer get lost if you watch heem. Water in heem never spilt. Useful – yes no?'

Mark was not very impressed. 'Haven't you anything more exciting than that?' he asked. 'I can get one of these at Woolworth's for sixpence.'

The little man looked hurt, but produced a book whose red and gold cover was splashed all over with horses and dragons and volcanoes.

'Fine book – nefer get tired of heem, nefer lost,' he said.

Mark took the book and opened it.

'But there's nothing inside,' he said disappointedly. The pages were blank.

'Nefer get tired of heem so,' the little man explained.

Mark handed it back, shaking his head.

'Magic elastic – very stretchy,' the man suggested. 'For catapult, yes? Always hit your sparrow, yes no?'

'Where is it?' said Mark, looking about.

'Here,' the little man answered with a broad smile of

triumph. He held out his hands, moving them out and in. 'See how stretchy?'

'I can't see it.'

'Invisible – very fine so,' the man pleaded, but Mark thought that invisible elastic, however stretchy, was not exciting enough for Harriet's birthday present.

'Haven't you anything else?'

The man produced very rapidly a magic lizard which ran about all over the pavement, a bag of invisible (and intangible) toffee, a magic pencil for arithmetic, and a bottle of red mixture guaranteed to turn you into a fox. No antidote was supplied.

'No, thank you,' said Mark politely to all of these.

'Ach,' the little man exclaimed crossly at last, 'fussy you are, yes no? You get on that bus there, he take you where you get a fine present, a lovely present, very classy aha, yes no?'

Mark thought he might as well get on the bus and escape the little man, so he swung himself onto the step, vaguely noticing that it said, 'Kew – extraordinary service.'

'Goodbye – and thank you very much,' he called back. But the little man was laughing very heartily to himself and took no notice.

It was very cold inside the bus, and Mark stared out of the dim window, looking for interesting shops. But there were none, and presently the bus stopped at the gate of Kew Gardens.

'I won't get a present here,' he thought, and decided to go back. But the conductor said, 'All change, please.'

'I want to stay on and go back again,' said Mark.

'Sorry, son – the bus doesn't go back,' the conductor said kindly but firmly, and waited till he got out in the cold. Then the bus trundled off down the road and round the corner.

'Well, I may as well go in, now that I'm here,' Mark said to himself. 'Harriet's present will just have to wait till tomorrow.' He paid at the turnstile and wandered off into the gardens.

The haze was thicker than ever now, and the trees looked spidery and unreal. He moved off across the frosty grass towards the river, and sat on a seat, watching two swans who were wondering whether or not they wanted to fight. To his disappointment they decided not to, and after a few hisses and neck-stretchings, sailed away in different directions. It was too cold to sit still for long, and he turned to his left along a path under dripping beech trees. Then he saw the girl.

She was very tall, and walked swiftly along a path at right angles to his. She wore some sort of dark cape over her head which made her look like a nun, but under this was a glint of red. It was not this which made Mark stare after her, but the thing she carried in her hand.

'I don't know what's the matter with me,' Mark said to himself, 'but I must see what that thing is.'

It glittered and threw off light in a most improbable way, and she carried it carefully in both hands as if it were very precious.

'If I cut across behind those saplings,' thought Mark, 'I ought to meet her somewhere over there.'

He struck across the grass, running when he got behind the trees. When he came out he saw the girl, nearer this time, turning sharply to her right. He took another shortcut, running across flower-beds and behind a long yew hedge, and caught a glimpse of her going towards a gate in the hedge marked Private.

'Oh bother,' thought Mark, 'I expect she lives in one of the gardeners' cottages, and that's where she's going.' For behind the hedge and the gate, he could see chimneys and a curl of grey smoke.

She went through the gate, and he followed her and looked in. A path turned to the right between tall hedges. He saw her dark cape whisk round the corner.

'I don't care,' he said, 'even if it is private. After all, they can't do more than turn me out.' And he slipped in after her.

The path wound about a long way without coming anywhere near the two chimneys. Every now and then it forked, and he had some difficulty in keeping up with the girl. It was like a maze. But at last they passed through another high, barred gate, Mark close behind and going softly now. The girl walked rapidly across a small, cobbled courtyard and into a cottage which had a rainwater barrel outside it and pots of flowers in the windows.

Mark, blind with excitement (he did not know why), followed her into the open door. As he stepped into the dark, a skinny hand shot out from beside him and grabbed him round the throat. He felt himself pulled forward, and resisted with all his might. The hand tightened until stars danced in front of his eyes, and finally everything went black around him.

When he came to, he was lying on a brick kitchen floor. A crow was perched on the window-sill, hunched up, and the girl he had followed was sitting on a chair by the table reading a book with a blue shiny cover on which he could see the words, 'Amalgamated Electrical Companies'. She had taken off her black cape, which was flung over the back of a chair, and was dressed in a long red robe, covered with question marks, exclamation points, semicolons, dollar signs, and so forth. Her hair was as black as the crow's wing, and straight, and her black eyes glittered. She was unmistakably a witch.

'Oh dear,' thought Mark, 'what a fool I was to follow her. I might have known something like this would happen – specially considering it's a Monday.'

He lay still as a mouse and watched her. '"Peel and wash,"' the witch read aloud, '"wrap in brown paper with herbs if liked. Place in oven when thermometer registers 250°. Leave at High until thermometer registers 600° and then turn to Low. Bake for an hour and a half." That seems fairly simple.' She turned the page.

'Wait a minute,' she said, 'this sounds better. "With particularly small ones, it may be found easier not to peel them until they are cooked, when the skin is readily removed. Wrap in brown paper, with herbs in the mouth if liked, and proceed as before, only baking for an hour. Small ones are generally served with redcurrant jelly."' She lifted her eyes from the book and gave Mark a piercing glance.

'Yes, I should definitely say that was a small one,' she murmured, 'and besides, it saves the trouble of peeling it.'

She stood up and came over to Mark.

'Hey, you can't bake me,' said Mark, much alarmed.

'Can't I just, my little cherub,' she answered, smiling sweetly. 'Why do you think I went to all the trouble of enticing you here, if not to wrap you in brown paper, with herbs in the mouth if liked, and place you in my new oven when the thermometer registers 250°?' She picked him up with one muscular hand, and though Mark struggled fiercely, he could not get out of her clutch. She put him on the table, which had a white enamelled top, and cast some sort of rapid spell over him, so that he could not struggle, while she fetched the brown paper and herbs. As she went out of the door, she switched on a large electric stove which glittered with newness. The crow gave a large 'croak' and shuffled sideways along the window-sill.

She came back in a minute with a vast sheet of brown paper and some string, and proceeded to make Mark into a neat parcel, so that he could see nothing at all.

'Drat it,' she said, 'if I haven't forgotten the herbs.' She went over to a cupboard and brought out a paper bag full of strange leaves. Then she untied the bit of string which was around Mark's neck, and pushed away the paper from his face. He could not stop her from stuffing his mouth with the herbs, which tasted most unpleasant. The crow flew across to the table and peered into his mouth with evident interest and approval.

'I can't be bothered to tie him up again,' said the witch.

'I'm too hungry. We've got an hour to wait as it is.' She had a look at the thermometer on the oven door.

'Not near 250°,' she said in disgust, 'what a time it takes. I don't know why I ever bought the thing. Well, I shall just put the creature in now, and use my judgement about the time it takes. We can always poke it with a fork to see if it's tender enough.'

A shiver ran down Mark's spine.

She picked him up and put him in a roasting-pan. 'It says no basting is necessary – that's a comfort,' she muttered, and shoved the pan into the oven. The door shut with a click, and Mark found himself in the dark.

To his surprise, the oven was not hot in the least.

'I know what's happened,' he suddenly thought. 'She's new to this kind of stove and she forgot to turn on both switches. She turned on the oven switch, but she forgot the main one.'

However, this did not comfort him much, for she was bound to remember sooner or later.

Half an hour passed, in which he could hear the witch moving about the kitchen, setting the table and singing to herself something about goats and vervain. Then she opened the oven door.

'Not done yet?' she exclaimed. 'It's as cold as a stone. Something's wrong with the dratted stove.'

The bird gave an angry croak.

'Yes, I know,' she said crossly, 'you always said it was a mistake to get one of these things and you were quite right. Newfangled nonsense. I wish I'd stuck to my good old range.

Switches and thermometers indeed! As for you,' she said, turning furiously to Mark, 'as for you my little seraph, in another five minutes, if this still hasn't hotted, I shall toast you on my toasting-fork in front of the drawing-room fire.' And she fished down from the wall an enormous toasting-fork. Mark shuddered at the sight of it.

The witch shoved him smartly back into the oven and shut the door.

This time he was overcome with despair. He thought of his aunt waiting at the theatre door with the tickets, and how he would not turn up and she would get more and more anxious and telephone the police, and two tears rose in his eyes and trickled slowly backwards down his forehead and into the roots of his hair, where they felt cold and sticky.

There came a knock at the door, and the witch swept across the room and opened it.

'He is here? You haf him all stuffed and trussed, yes no?' asked a voice which Mark recognized as that of the little man with the invisible elastic.

'Yes, I've got him in the oven now,' said the witch. 'Would you like to have a look at him?'

'So the whole thing was a plant,' Mark thought, 'right from the very beginning. What a fool I've been.'

Steps came across the room, and the oven door was flung back.

'There's something wrong with the stove,' the witch said. 'It won't heat up properly. I expect you know what it is.' She pulled the pan out of the oven and dumped it on the table. They both leaned over and prodded Mark.

'See? Not done at all,' she said.

But the little man seemed angry about something.

'You besom,' he said furiously, 'I weel teach you to be lazy. You know I like heem peeled and stuffed and garneeshed. Brown paper and a bunch of herbs in the mouth, indeed!'

'Well, that's what it says in the book,' answered the witch crossly.

'That book is no affair of yours. You haf in your head how I like them cooked. Laziness!'

He was boiling with rage and suddenly gave her a clout on the ear. She flew at him like a tigress and scratched his face. Then they both drew apart, hissing with temper, and began casting spells at each other. Mark could hear them muttering long, formidable words under their breaths, and the sudden little pops as the spells worked. Then, as they became interested and worked up over the quarrel, he found that he could move once more. The witch was using up all her energy, and had none to spare for Mark.

He peered cautiously over the edge of his pan and watched them. It was most instructive. They seemed to observe no rules, but cast spells at each other as quickly as they could get them out, so that in the time it took Mark to blink an eye, he saw the witch grow horns, shrink to half her size, become bright green, turn into a tadpole, and explode in a pink puff of smoke, while the magician became a pool of water, an orange (bad), a marmoset, a piece of string, and finally himself, only with no arms or legs and a kettle instead of a head. Then they both drew a long breath and started again.

Mark soon realized that he was a fool if he did not try to escape now, while nobody was looking at him, and he wriggled feverishly to get his hands from under the piece of string round his waist. Fortunately it did not take long, as the witch, like all women, tied granny knots, which slipped, and he was able to get out from the brown paper and spit the herbs out of his mouth without much difficulty. Then, to his horror, he saw that the crow had noticed him. It flew over to the witch and tried to attract her attention, but at that moment, she turned into a bucket of coal, upside down in mid-air, and he could make no impression on her. Meanwhile, Mark crept out of the pan and across the room to the door.

It was only when he was through it that he realized that it was the wrong door. He found himself in a pitch-dark passage.

However, he could not think of turning back now, and went quickly forward. He came to some steps which went up, and then some more which went down again. At the bottom of these he tripped over an object which lay in the middle of the floor, and fell sprawling. He had an enormous bruise on his forehead, but jumped up and hurried on, absent-mindedly clutching the thing which had tripped him.

Then, to his joy, he saw a crack of light, and found a door which led him out on the other side of the house. He gave one scared glance to see if the witch or the little man were in sight. Neither of them was, and he took to his heels and tore off between the yew hedges.

It was easier to go towards the house than away from it,

and several times he took a wrong turning and found himself back where he had started, which terrified him. But at last, by luck, he made his way out and set off running across the grass without looking behind him.

He pushed his way through the turnstile just in time to see a bus move off, and by making a terrible effort managed to throw himself on it.

'You shouldn't do that,' said the conductor severely, 'you might have been killed.'

'I was in a hurry,' pleaded Mark, and thought lovingly of *Robin Hood*, and his Aunt Hal, and the supper they would eat afterwards, and how next morning he would go present-hunting again. Then, for the first time, he realized that he was still clutching in his hand the thing he had fallen over in the passage.

He looked at it, and his eyes grew large as saucers.

'My goodness,' said the conductor, giving him his ticket, 'you're lucky to have one of these.'

'Yes,' agreed a fat woman across the aisle, 'there's not many little boys has them, or little girls either for that matter.'

And several other people in the bus gave exclamations of astonishment and told him what a lucky young boy he was and how they had always wanted one when they were young.

Mark's heart glowed.

'It's *just* the thing for Harriet's present,' he thought. 'She's always wanted one, and she'll absolutely love it. Maybe she'll lend it to me sometimes too.'

Then, because it was causing almost too much excitement in the bus, he pushed it into his pocket, where it was a rather tight fit.

A sudden thought struck him. The little man had said that he would get a fine present if he went on the Q bus, and he had got one, which just showed that even magicians didn't know what was going to happen. Or perhaps they did know? It was a bit confusing, and Mark slouched back in his seat and watched the misty evening grow darker and darker outside as it slipped past. He wondered how far Harriet had got with their secret house in the willow tree before the German measles struck her down.

He arrived exactly in time for the theatre and enjoyed it so much that he forgot all about his adventure until they were at home, making bacon and eggs. Then he told Aunt Hal about it and showed her the present. She whistled.

'Good gracious,' she said, 'that's better luck than you deserve. What a marvellous one. Harriet will be knocked sideways.'

Mark yawned frightfully, and said he thought he would go to bed. One of the best things about staying with Aunt Hal was that she let you go to bed when you liked, or stay up all night if you preferred.

'I'd better say goodbye now,' she said, 'as I don't suppose you'll be awake when I go off in the morning. Give my love to the family and tell Harriet that she won't get *my* birthday present till the proper day.'

'What is it?' he asked, but she only grinned at him and said, 'Wait and see.'

So Mark had a boiling bath, and, after carefully putting Harriet's wonderful present in the top left-hand drawer, where he would be sure to remember it, he climbed into bed and went to sleep.

DRAGON MONDAY

Mark sat in the train and wished that he could go to sleep. He had been to the dentist and had a local injection, and his cheek still felt most peculiar. He didn't like it at all. So he counted sheep earnestly, but the sheep were obstinate animals, and wouldn't do as they were told, and the train was an extremely rowdy one – he could hear it all the time saying to itself, 'What-did-you-say? Stick-in-the-mud! That's-what-I-said. Stick-in-the-mud!' It was a slow little train, plodding along over the march from Cobchester to Tallant, and, try as Mark would, he could not make it go any faster. He urged it on under his breath and even tried reciting 'Horatius' to it, but it only staggered along more sleepily, and stopped here and there at Ogham, and Nagham, and Liddle Halt, while Mark fumed and looked at his watch.

The fact of the matter was that it was a Monday. That may not mean much to you, but in the Armitage family, it meant a great deal. For on Mondays, very strange things were apt to happen at Wittsuns, the Armitage house, and no one could ever tell what would appear next. One

Monday, for instance, they had had a plague of hippogriffs, and another time, coming home from a walk, Mark and his sister had found the whole place turned into a Pyramid, and their parents changed to mummies – a most inconvenient state of affairs. But luckily it did not last long.

So naturally Mark was in a hurry to get home in case Harriet had been having some amazing adventures while Mr Leacock picked among his teeth. He wandered up and down the carriage, and hung out of the window, and read a magazine which he had already read twice before, and finally settled down and tried to go to sleep again.

This time the sheep were more obedient. They jumped over the stile, but Mark noticed that they found it harder and harder to get over, until they had to creep up one side, foot by foot, and then flock down the other. Were they very old sheep? Or what was it? Then he realized that it was the fault of the stile. It was getting higher and higher, like an elongated ladder, and each sheep had to climb almost out of sight before, with a gasp of relief, it began the descent. Finally the remaining sheep all sat down in a crowd on one side and looked at him reproachfully. The top of the stile was now invisible in the clouds, and it was no longer a stile, but a terribly thick, tangled, barbed-wire fence.

'Well, you certainly can't get over that,' said Mark to the sheep. 'I suppose I'll have to find another way in for you. Come along.'

And he set off, walking along the side of the fence, looking for some sort of gate. When he turned back to see if the sheep were following him, he saw that they were still sitting in a huddled group. Evidently they were waiting till he had found a gate before they took any more exercise. He decided that he did not blame them, and went on.

He was walking along the side of a flat, grey road which stretched away into the distance before and behind him, until both ends were lost in mist. Groundsel and ragwort grew along the edge and a cold wind was blowing. Mark shivered.

'I don't think much of this place,' he said to himself.

However, he pulled up his left sock and walked on, and the dust crept into his shoes. A very small tabby cat came walking towards him, and when it was near gave one plaintive: 'Prrrmp?'

'Well, what are you doing here?' he asked it.

The cat seemed rather doubtful itself, and he picked it up and carried it, quite glad of its warmth, for the wind was colder with every step.

The cat purred, and he talked to it and did not notice until he was nearly there a gate in the fence with a sentry-box beside it.

When a step sounded beside the box, a sentry popped out of it, saluted, and said:

'Good afternoon, sir. Will you go straight in, please?' 'How do you know me?' asked Mark in surprise. 'It's the Mascot,' explained the sentry, pointing to Ibbitts, who was washing his left ear. ''E always goes out 'unting up our pilots. 'E as a wonderful eye for them.'

Mark thought this was rather odd, and would have liked to ask more questions, but the sentry said:

'Will you go straight along now, sir, please? You'll find them waiting for you up by the runway.'

Mark, with Ibbitts perched on his shoulder, walked along the flat, narrow road that led across the field until in the distance he saw the grey-green of an aeroplane hangar.

A crowd of people were standing beside the tarmac runway, where a delightful little aeroplane waited.

When Mark came up to them they all rushed to him and shook him by the hand.

'So glad you were able to come,' said one. 'The plane's perfectly ready for you,' another told him. 'We're really expecting you to go up at once, if you don't mind. It's rather urgent.'

'I'm not very experienced,' said Mark, nervously, but they all pushed him towards the plane, assuring him that the Mascot never picked up an unsuitable person.

He climbed up, and once he was in the cockpit he found that he remembered perfectly how to manage the controls. Ibbitts settled down beside him and tucked his paws in comfortably.

Someone swung the propeller and kicked away the chocks, and he was moving, bumping gently over the ground. Then suddenly he heard a voice yelling:

'Stop!'

The plane slowed down, more or less of its own accord, and he leaned over the side. A couple of men were running along towards him.

'Do you know what you've got to look for?' they shouted breathlessly.

'No!' he answered. 'What does it look like?'

'It's one of those Drumwhistle Dragons,' they told him. 'You'll recognize it easily – retractable undercarriage, red tail, green wings, makes rather a high buzzing noise, and sends out a smokescreen in advance. You can't miss it.'

Mark started once more, and this time took off without interruption. He soared up through a bank of cloud, and then he was in the blazing sunshine, still steadily climbing. He looked out ahead for another plane with a red tail and green wings, but could see nothing, and decided to go northeast and cruise around.

Everything was very quiet for a quarter of an hour. Mark flew, and Ibbitts dozed. But then all at once Ibbitts began to show definite signs of uneasiness, and finally he left the plane altogether, and began to fly round and round it in large circles.

'Ibbitts! Come here at once and don't be silly!' yelled Mark above the roar of the engine.

But Ibbitts evidently saw something ahead, for he was going forward ahead of the plane, craning his neck and staring as if he was tremendously excited.

By and by Mark thought he could see a little puff of cloud far away. He watched it until his eyes were sore, and gradually it grew bigger and bigger, as it came nearer. Ibbitts twittered with excitement and finally came back into the plane, but every few minutes he would leave for a little cruise ahead.

The cloud came extremely near, and then Mark distinguished two red lights gleaming through it.

'I wonder what those are?' he said aloud. There seemed to be no chance of getting a clear view of the Drumwhistle Dragon unless he changed his course, so he began to climb very steeply in the hope of getting above it. The Dragon also climbed, but left its screen behind, bit by bit, until he could see it fairly plainly.

He was very much startled at what he saw, for he had expected a plane something like his own, and this was neither more nor less than an ordinary green-winged dragon, which glared at him with red eyes, and spat out, from time to time, a large mouthful of smoke.

Mark remembered something he had once heard about aerial combat with dragons, so he turned his back and flew away from the creature for a fair distance. When he swung the plane round he saw that the dragon had done the same, and was hovering, waiting till he was ready. Then the two of them hurtled together at a frightful speed. But at the last minute the dragon cheated, for he turned aside and upwards, and spat out a jet of smoke and flame at Mark as he passed.

'The coward!' said Mark indignantly. 'What's the use of having rules if you don't keep to them?'

He flew back, and turned. The dragon was waiting again, this time with a very sinister expression on its face. Its forked tongue was hanging out.

'I believe it's going to do something nasty,' he thought, and wondered what he ought to do. If his plane had a dose of dragon breath at close quarters, it would be all up with him.

When they rushed together again, Mark brought his plane up sharply at the critical moment. As he passed over the dragon, he leaned sideways and emptied the contents of his water flask over the great green scaly back.

There was a frightful explosion, which blew him up about forty feet. When he had control again he looked about, but the dragon was nowhere to be seen. Only some large fragments of what looked like burnt paper were floating slowly downwards.

Mark turned the plane and flew back towards the aerodrome. On the ground people were cheering and waving. He wondered how they knew the result of the battle already, and then he thought that perhaps Ibbitts had flown down and told them. At all events he was nowhere in the plane. The ground came nearer and he felt the wheels touch it slightly. Then suddenly the plane lurched as if something had tripped it. It staggered sideways, and rather deliberately turned over and flung Mark high in the air. It seemed a long time before he met the ground with a bump that dazed him.

He lay where he had fallen for a few minutes, until he knew which was up and which was down. Then he scrambled to his feet and looked about. But the airfield was gone, and he was in the meadow which lay next to the Armitage garden.

He would have thought that he had been dreaming, but for the fact that Ibbitts was sitting gravely beside him, washing his paw. And looking at Ibbitts closely, he saw a black collar round the cat's neck, on which was painted a tiny golden aeroplane.

'Poor Harriet,' said Mark to Ibbitts, 'she will be sorry she's missed this. Still, *she* didn't have to go to the dentist.' He felt his cheek. It had almost recovered its normal shape.

He went into the garden by the back gate, with Ibbitts following him.

Harriet saw him and came running out.

'Do listen—' he began, but she cut him short.

'Oh, *why* weren't you back for tea? We've had such a lovely Monday. Do come and look.'

She dragged Mark down onto the lawn, and he gasped at what he saw. For arranged all round the flower-bed in the centre were twenty-three duchesses, and at the far end was a large swimming pool, entirely filled with pink ice cream.

TEA AT RAVENSBURGH

'Bother,' said Mrs Armitage, reading her mid-morning mail. She took the letter that had annoyed her and went upstairs. Through a closed door came the sound of a typewriter. She tapped on the door and went in. Immediately the typing ceased.

The room she had entered was large and sunny, with a huge dormer window taking up most of one side. It was empty, save for a typing table, portable typewriter and chair, and some shelves of books.

'Oh, Mr Peake,' said Mrs Armitage, 'I'm terribly sorry to disturb you at this hour of the morning, but would you mind if I used the typewriter for five minutes? I must just write a note to Harriet.'

There was an offended silence.

'It's *most* wicked of me, and I won't do it again,' Mrs Armitage went on placatingly, 'but my wretched old Aunt Adelaide has just cabled from the south of France asking me to meet her in London on Saturday, so I shan't be able to go down and take Harriet out from school this weekend. She'll be cross, I'm afraid. Are you sitting in the chair?'

'No, I'm not,' said a voice behind her shoulder. Mrs Armitage jumped. Although she had known him for twenty years, she was never quite used to not knowing where Mr Peake was.

'It's most tiresome,' she said, rattling away at the keys, 'I'd much rather see Harriet, but Aunt Adelaide is so very rich that it would be foolish to offend her.'

'Nevertheless, it seems hard that the little wench should lose her holiday,' said Mr Peake. ''Tis a good child. Last holidays she mended the toes of my carpet slippers until I could not tell where the holes had been.' He stuck out his invisible feet and regarded them with satisfaction.

'Well I know,' agreed Harriet's mother, 'but my husband can't go, he has a meeting of the Grass Growers' Association, and Mark is in quarantine for whooping cough.'

'I shall escort her out,' announced Mr Peake.

Mrs Armitage looked startled.

'Well – that's very sweet of you,' she answered dubiously. 'But are you sure you'll be able to manage?'

'Madam, you forget that I was once an explorer and sailed to the New World. What terrors could a female boarding establishment have for me?'

'In that case, I'll add a PS. to say that you're coming instead. Harriet *will* be excited. And you can take her a spare pair of socks and a pot of gooseberry jam. There.' She flipped her letter out of the machine, quickly addressed an envelope to Miss Armitage, Silverside School, Ham Street, Dorset, and stood up.

'Now perhaps,' said Mr Peake, as she left the room, 'I can get on with my memoirs.' But he said it to himself, for he was a polite man.

Mr Peake was the Armitages' lodger, and if he has not been mentioned before, it is because he was so very quiet and unobtrusive that the family hardly noticed his existence. He had one room, with use of Mrs Armitage's typewriter in the mornings, and he hardly ever came downstairs. He had lived in the house for three hundred years, ever since his death, in fact, and was thought to be writing his autobiography, though as it was invisible no one had read it. He had been a sailor and explorer and a friend of Drake, so there was plenty to write about.

When the Armitage family first moved into the house, they took over Mr Peake from the previous owners. Harriet was a baby at the time, and the nursemaid had left in hysterics next week because one night when Harriet was teething she had come up to the nursery and seen Mr Peake walking to and fro hushing Harriet in his arms; or at least she had seen Harriet, for of course no one saw Mr Peake.

He had always remained very fond of Harriet ever since and used to give her odd little presents which he called fairings or baubles. When she had measles he sat by her bed reading to her for hours and hours. No one had ever known Mr Peake to go to sleep.

Harriet was devoted to Mr Peake, but just the same, she was a little doubtful at the thought of being taken out from school by him. She had not been at Silverside very long, and did not want to get a reputation for peculiarity. It was very disappointing that her mother was obliged to go and meet Aunt Adelaide, as Mrs Armitage always made a good impression – she arrived punctually, wore the right sort of hat, made the right sort of remarks (and not too many of them) when she was taken round the school, and had tea with Harriet at the right places. It was to be hoped that Mr Peake would behave in an equally exemplary manner, but Harriet was afraid that he might seem eccentric to the rest of the school.

On the following Saturday, she hung about in the front hall, hoping to catch him when he arrived. She did not want the difficulty of explaining about an invisible bell-ringer to one of the housemaids. Unfortunately, members of the junior classes were not supposed to loiter in the hall-way and she had to keep pretending to be looking to see if there were any letters for her on the hall table, and then walk briskly up the front stairs and run hurriedly down the back stairs. After one of these descents she was lucky enough to see a pot of gooseberries and a pair of her mother's knitted socks approaching up the front steps, and was just in time to intercept Mr Peake before he rang the bell.

'It is nice to see you,' she said (no one ever remembered to adapt their speech to Mr Peake's peculiarity). 'Let me take that jam from you, and then I have to report that I am going out to my house-mistress and we can be off.'

'I should admire to see a little of this female academy of

learning, if it is convenient,' said her visitor. 'Such things have come in since my day.'

'Oh blow,' thought Harriet. Luckily on a Saturday afternoon she could rely on the place being fairly well deserted, but two tiny juniors squeaked as she showed him around the gymnasium:

'Coo, listen to Harriet Armitage talking to herself. She must be going crackers!'

Harriet swept Mr Peake off to the library before he had half finished gazing at the ropes and the parallel bars.

Talking in the library was normally forbidden but a certain amount of latitude was allowed when visitors were being shown round. Mr Peake took a great interest in the historical section and asked dozens of questions. Harriet noticed with alarm that Madeline Bogg, the Head Girl, who was working for a history examination, was in the next alcove and looking angrily in their direction.

'Harriet, will you stop making all that noise, please. I shall have to give you a hundred lines for talking in here.'

'But I have a visitor with me.'

'Don't talk nonsense, please.'

'Here, give her these lines,' said Mr Peake's voice in her ear. 'Doubtless the subject matter is of no importance? I always travel with some reading material.' And he pulled out a parchment (from his doublet presumably), and passed it to Harriet, who handed it on to Madeline, absently noticing that it seemed to be about ship money. Madeline's jaw dropped.

'Where in the name of goodness did you get this,' she

began. 'It's just the subject I was reading up—' But Harriet quickly dragged Mr Peake away and persuaded him that there was nothing else in the school worth looking at. She reported herself to her house-mistress and they went out into the little town of Ham Street, where Harriet was quickly pounced on by two senior girls coming back from shopping.

'Harriet! What are you doing out by yourself? You know it's not allowed.'

'I'm not by myself, I'm with Mr Peake,' Harriet said miserably.

'Be at ease, the little wench is under my care,' Mr Peake reassured them.

'Mr Peake's had a rather bad cold – that's why you can't see him very well,' Harriet said desperately.

'I can't see him at all,' said Gertrude, the elder girl.

'Perhaps this will certify you of my presence, my fair sceptic.' Mr Peake presented her with a flower, apparently from his buttonhole. It was something like a wild rose but white, with a very sweet scent. They left Gertude and her friend staring at it in perplexity and walked on.

Harriet decided that it would be best if they went to the cinema. It was something of a strain being out with Mr Peake, and she felt that sitting down in the sheltering dark would be a relief. She suggested this plan to him.

'I have never been in one of those places,' he replied, 'but one is never too old to do something new. Let us go by all means.'

When they came to the Paramount, Ham Street's only

cinema, they found that it was showing *The Nineteenth Man*, an 'A' film.

'Two two and three's, please,' said Mr Peake, prompted by Harriet.

'You can't go in without an adult, ducks,' said the cashier, looking through him at Harriet. 'Sorry, it's a smasher, but the manager's just over there.'

'But I've got an adult here – he's in front of me,' explained Harriet rather hopelessly. Mr Peake rapped with his two half-crowns on the cash desk and the cashier let out a shriek which fetched over the manager.

'Two seats in the pit, if you please,' demanded Mr Peake.

'Now, now, none of your nasty ventriloquism tricks here,' he said, scowling at Harriet. 'Go on – hop it, afore I rings your headmistress.'

'This town boasts a river, does it not?' inquired Mr Peake, as they walked once more along the High Street. 'Should we adventure in a boat?'

Harriet privately thought it rather a chilly pursuit for a November afternoon, but perhaps Mr Peake was pining for a taste of his nautical past. She tucked her arm through his, feeling rather sorry for him, and they went down to the boathouse by the bridge, where a few punts and canoes were still being hired out.

'No one under the age of sixteen to go out unaccompanied by an adult,' said the man, pointing inflexibly to a framed copy of the by-laws on a notice board.

'But I *am* accompanied by an adult.'

'One who, moreover, has countless times weathered the Spanish Main,' added Mr Peake. 'Be more polite to your betters, sirrah.'

'Blimey,' said the man, scratching his head. 'Ought to go on the halls, you ought. Run along, now, scram, before I give you in charge.'

'It is an uncourteous city,' said Mr Peake, as they stood irresolutely on the bridge.

'*I* know,' exclaimed Harriet, seeing a bus approaching. 'We'll go and look at Ravensburgh Castle – I've always wanted to.'

They had no trouble on the bus, apart from the conductor's displeasure with the Queen Anne sixpence which Mr Peake absently tendered him (change from rent paid to the last landlord but five, he explained to Harriet). Presently, as the bus filled up, people began to look meaningly at the empty seat next to Harriet, but Mr Peake solved this problem by taking her on his lap. It is a very strange feeling to ride on a ghost's lap in a bus.

Once Mr Peake remarked: 'The horseless carriages in this county are indifferent well sprung,' and the woman on the seat in front of them jumped and looked round at Harriet indignantly.

The sky was clouding when they reached Ravensburgh on its hill, and it was almost cold enough for snow. Harriet shivered and wished that they were allowed to wear duffel coats instead of uniform ones.

'Shall we go up on the ramparts?' Mr Peake inquired. 'I believe one could achieve a view of the sea from them.'

As they were making the circuit of the top they heard shouts from below, and gathered that a uniformed attendant was trying to tell Harriet she should not be up there on her own.

'I fear this is not a very happy outing for you,' said poor Mr Peake.

'Oh no, I'm loving it,' lied Harriet gallantly. As a matter of fact she did feel that to walk in the icy dusk hand in hand with a spectre round the battlements of Ravensburgh was rather a grand thing to do, even though the spectre was such an old friend as Mr Peake. But she would have liked her tea, and wondered what sort of reception they would have if they went into a café.

They came down to a wide room that had once been an upstairs banqueting hall.

'Why, bless my soul,' said Mr Peake, pausing, 'if that isn't – or is it – yes, it is – my old boon companion, Sir Giles Harkness!'

'Where?' asked Harriet, looking all round and seeing nothing.

But Mr Peake had left her side and was exclaiming:

'Giles! My old messmate! How fares it with you?'

'Gregory! Gregory Peake! By my halidome! Well met after three hundred years. What brings you here? You must come and meet my lady – we lodge in the East Tower here. Do you remember that time off Madeira when we were in the pinnace and we saw the three galleons coming up to windward?'

They launched out into a flood of reminiscence.

'Oh dear,' thought Harriet, bored and shivering. 'Now they'll go on for hours; grown-ups always do.'

She tried to climb into one of the embrasures, slipped, stumbled, and turned her ankle rather severely.

'What ails you, lass?' said Mr Peake, turning from his conversation. 'Oh, Giles, this is my little godchild, Mistress Harriet Armitage.'

'Your servant, madam,' said the invisible Sir Giles gravely. 'But there is something amiss? You have injured your foot? My lady shall bind it up straightway.'

Between them the two friends supported Harriet back to the rooms in the East Tower, never for one moment ceasing their flow of chat.

'And do you remember when Francis boarded you in the night and stole all your powder and ball and was away before dawn with none of your men any the wiser? Ah, Frank was a rare one for a jest.'

In the East Tower a lady with a very friendly voice skilfully bound up Harriet's ankle with what felt like a strip of silk.

It was curious to sit among people that one could not see and listen to them talking. Harriet did not think that she should like it for long. She felt inquisitively at the heavy carved arms of her chair, which she could not see either, and wondered if they were made of pale bright new oak.

'Ah, here is our little Hubert,' said Lady Harkness. 'He and the little maid should fadge well together – th'are much of an age.'

As usual on such occasions Harriet took an instantaneous

unreasoning dislike to little Hubert. She was sure that he was a pale, puffy little boy in a ruff and imagined him staring at her with his finger in his mouth.

Comfits were served round, very sweet and chewy, and drinks of Hippocras, which Harriet did not care for. Hubert snatched a bit of Harriet's comfit while his mother was busy pouring out the drinks, and Harriet dealt him what she hoped was a kick on the shin – she heard him squeak.

Then his elder brother Giles came in, a cheerful-sounding boy who told Harriet about his boat, which he kept on the estuary, and invited her to go sailing with him next summer.

'I will if I can,' she promised, wondering if one can go sailing with a ghost. The whole party was becoming more and more dreamlike.

'Mr Peake,' she said, 'I'm afraid we should be going, as I haven't got permission to be out late.' She stood up, and then let out a cry as her ankle gave way under her.

'The wench can't walk on that ankle!' said Sir Giles. 'I'll lend you my mare, Black Peg – she'll have you home like a flash of lightning and find her own way back here again.'

'We are greatly obliged to you,' replied Mr Peake. They left amid cordial invitations to come again.

As far as Harriet could make out, Black Peg had wings; they could not of course be seen, but she could feel feathers. She wondered if the mare was any relation of Pegasus. They covered the distance to Ham Street in ten minutes, though it had taken an hour to come by bus. It was a pity that Black Peg sailed through the school dining-room window. To be deposited by a ghost horse and rider in the middle of a school's Saturday night supper is not the best way to avoid a reputation for peculiarity.

'Harriet,' said the house-mistress coldly. 'Your godfather did not go to see the headmistress, as you should have told him to do before he took you out. And please get rid of that invisible horse and eat your supper.'

Black Peg galloped off through the window again, thinking of spectral oats in her phantom stable no doubt, and Harriet sat down miserably to cold spam and beetroot.

It was all right, though. Miss Drogly pronounced Mr Peake to be a most interesting and delightful man – history was her own subject, and they had had a long chat about the Duke of Medina Sidonia. And Mr Peake gave Harriet a dear little pouncet box with a clove orange in it before leaving, and she hugged him and said it had been a lovely party and promised to starch all his ruffs for him next holidays.

Next week Harriet had a letter from her mother.

'Aunt Adelaide was sorry that she had unintentionally prevented our outing, and asked me to send you this to make amends.'

This was sent under separate cover and turned out to be a small folding helicopter, so Harriet's reputation for being a perfectly ordinary girl with normal healthy interests was quite restored.

THE LAND OF TREES AND HEROES

The children had had whooping cough, rather badly, and although they were now well past the distressing stage of going black in the face, crowing, and having to rush from the room, they were still thin, pale, and cross. Mrs Armitage decided that they had better lose a bit more schooling and go to stay with Grandmother for a change of air. Mark and Harriet received the news listlessly. There seemed to be so many snags and prohibitions about going to Grandmother's.

'You'll have to wear sandals all the time.'

'Why, can't Granny stand noise?' asked Harriet.

'No, it's not that, but the floors are so highly polished; well I remember the time your father broke his leg coming downstairs. And of course you must amuse yourselves and not bother Grandmother. She hasn't much time for children.'

'Wouldn't it be better if we stayed at home?' Mark's tone was glum.

'No; a change is what you need. And we shall all be so

busy here, with this wretched by-election.' Mark's mother showed slight relief, indeed, at the thought that her children would be out of the way at this time; they had been known to upset local arrangements.

Grandmother's house was huge, old, and dark; Mark and Harriet tiptoed about in it like two white mice in a cave. Not that Grandmother was unkind; in her vague way she seemed pleased to see them. But after they had been staying with her for a day or two Mark and Harriet understood better what their mother had meant when she said that Granny hadn't much time for children. The old lady was not exactly busy, but most of the time her attention was very much elsewhere.

'Put away that bayonet, Roger,' she would say absently, 'how many times do I have to tell you that it will rust if you don't give it a rub when you bring it into the tent? And hang up your balaclava and ask that sepoy what he thinks he is doing.'

For Granny was very, very old, and had travelled with Grandfather (dead long ago) all over the world, and seen many battles, from Inkerman to Mafeking. She was also extremely deaf and seemed to understand only about a tenth of what the children said to her as she sat knitting, placid and withdrawn, by the fire that always burned in the great hearth. They got most of their advice and information from Nursie, who was almost as old as Grandmother, but was not deaf and took an active interest in their goings-on.

'Why is there a telephone in the orchard?' Harriet wanted to know.

'Ah there, Miss Harriet, dear. Always asking questions like your father before you. Why should it be there but in case your granny wanted to ring up the orchard, then?'

'But there's nobody to answer – only a lot of apple trees.'

'And if you're going to speak to an apple tree, better ring than walk all that way on foot at her age,' said Nursie, which only muddled Harriet more and didn't explain matters in the least. She went on thinking that it was very odd indeed to see a telephone all by itself among the trees, standing on a little pedestal in the grass, with a dovecote roof over it to keep the rain off.

'And why does Granny keep all those musical things hanging in the trees if she can't hear them?' asked Mark.

'Ee-yolian harps, those are, Master Mark, and the others is wind-bells. And as to why she keeps them there – well, there's sounds as the ear can't hear, isn't there? Bats' squeaks, and that?'

'Yes,' said Mark doubtfully.

'Well, then, maybe your granny can hear those! Now run along, the pair of you, and don't bother me. Play anywhere in the garden, climb any of the trees, but don't break any branches. And don't go climbing the laurel tree or the Silver Lady will get you.'

'Oh, who is the Silver Lady?'

'The Silver Lady? Why, she owns the laurel tree, of course. Climb into her tree and she'll send you to sleep. There's a rhyme about it:

'Sleep in the laurel but for an hour
You'll sleep in the Silver Lady's power.

So mind you keep out of it – nasty dangerous thing.'

The children wanted to hear more about the Silver Lady, but Nursie pushed them crossly out, muttering that Silver Lady or no Silver Lady, she'd got to get her silver polished by lunch-time. They wandered into the garden, shivering and forlorn, telling each other that it wasn't worth starting any game before lunch.

Many of the trees were hung with these strange Aeolian harps, or with the silvery glass bells, and it must have been a sheltered part of the country thereabouts, for only occasionally, when some wandering gust found its way through the trees, did there come a twangling and a sighing from high among the branches. Lying awake and coughing at night, Mark often hoped for a snatch of wind-music to breathe him off to sleep, but, perhaps owing to the immense thickness of the solid old walls, it was seldom that a far-off note whispered against his ear.

At five o'clock every evening Granny took off her hearing aid and settled down in front of the television; at the same time, Nursie removed her thick glasses, without which she could not see more than a couple of yards, and dragged her favourite upright chair close beside the wireless, turned on loud; from that minute on, the two old women were quite lost to the children, who would find their supper of bread-and-milk and beef tea (or bread-and-dripping and cocoa) set out on the kitchen table. The kitchen was one of the nicest rooms of the house: huge, but airy and warm, with a great open range, and here they would eat, read, talk, play a leisurely game of ludo, before taking themselves off to bed.

The nights were bad.

Their rooms were adjoining, and if Mark managed to get off to sleep for half an hour, Harriet was sure to have a shattering burst of coughing and wake him up. Then she would doze off until Mark waked her in his turn. They felt that their coughing shook the house from end to end, but of course Granny never heard them at all, and it took ages before Nursie would come muttering and tutting along in her red flannel dressing gown and give them hot drinks of lemon barley. And sometimes, on account of her shortsightedness and not putting on her glasses in the night-time, she would rub their chests with the lemon barley (very sticky) and give them hot camphorated oil to drink. Still, it was nice to have her exclaiming round them like a cross old ghost, and sometimes she sang them to sleep with old, old nursery rhymes:

'*Intery mintery, cuttery corn,*
Apple seed and apple thorn . . .'

in her quavering, wavering voice which seemed to search all round the corners of the room before finding its note.

'Now, that's enough: you must go to sleep,' she would finally say severely, and at this point the children (Harriet would have come in by now and would be sitting, wrapped in eiderdowns, on Mark's bed) always pleaded:

'Oh, please, "The Land of Trees and Heroes" before you go, please!'

And Nursie would sing:

'In the land of trees and heroes
The tawny owl is king
Who locked the door, who holds the key
Hidden beneath his wing.'

'Tell us some more about the land, Nursie?'

'That's all there is, and it's time you went to sleep anyway.' They never got more than the one verse out of her, which ended on a plaintive, unfinished note, but there was something about the song that made them long to know more. Where was the land? And who the heroes? And why was the key hidden? Nursie wouldn't say.

The children still felt too tired and convalescent to play strenuous games, or go riding, or take long walks; they spent most of their outdoor time slowly and haphazardly exploring Granny's enormous, neglected garden.

One cold, nasty afternoon, rummaging in the summer house at the end of the lawn, they found an old bow with a leather cover and a red velvet guard. There was a target, too, but no arrows.

Mark dragged the target, moulting straw at the seams, out onto the lawn, and said, 'We can easily make some arrows. Never mind about feathers. Hazel's the best wood.'

'Nursie said not to break any branches,' Harriet reminded him doubtfully, but she rubbed her finger up and down the smooth springiness of the bow; it did seem a pity not to use it.

'Oh, she only meant big ones, I expect.'

They couldn't find any hazels, but there was an elder-bush growing by the summer-house with a lot of straight young branches shooting in the thick of it. Mark took out his pen-knife and cut three of these, while Harriet, to be on the safe side, politely asked the elder tree if she minded their taking this liberty. There was no reply; she had hardly expected there would be.

'They're rather light but they'll do for a start, to practise with,' Mark said.

He whittled off the leaves and twigs, and cut a bow-string notch in each wand, while Harriet stood hugging her arms together, watching him.

'Now then!'

Stringing the bow, he carefully fitted one of his arrows and fired, aiming high. The light, pithy arrow soared and began a beautiful curve towards the target, but at that moment a gentle wind sprang up and turned it sideways so that it swerved and landed in the laurel tree.

'Oh, blow!' said Mark. 'That's the first wind there's been this afternoon. Hark at the wind-bells! It would happen just when I shot.'

He ran towards the tree.

'Wait!' shouted Harriet, dashing after him. 'What are you doing?'

'Going to get the arrow!'

'But don't you remember – the Silver Lady!'

'Heavens, I'm not going to stay in the tree an hour! It won't take two twos to nip up and get the arrow down. I can see it from here.'

'Do be careful—' She arrived at the tree just as he swung himself into the first crotch and stood with her hands on the trunk, anxiously looking up after him.

'I can almost reach it now,' he called in a moment, from somewhere up in the thickness of the tree. 'Goodness, there's a cat up here – it seems to be fast asleep! And a whole lot of birds, asleep too. How peculiar.'

'Oh, do hurry up!'

'And here's a satchel.' Mark's voice was muffled now by the thick green leaves among which he was scuffling and flapping. 'Good lord, I say, there's a postman asleep up here – I never saw him climb up, did you? And there's something that looks like a butcher's basket full of chops. This is the oddest tree I've ever been . . . ' His voice trailed away on a tremendous yawn.

'Mark!' shouted Harriet, her voice sharp with anxiety.

No answer.

'Mark!' Twisting her head, she peered up, looking into the dark cave of the tree. And then she saw Mark. He was fourteen or fifteen feet up, curled as comfortably into a fork of the tree as if he were lying in a hammock, and he was fast asleep, his head pillowed on his hand. In the fork above him was a big tabby cat, also fast asleep, and over to the left she could dimly make out a butcher's boy in a striped blue-and-white apron, sleeping wedged in a nest of criss-crossing branches.

Harriet shouted till she was hoarse, and shook the tree till she started herself coughing, but there was no reply from any of the peaceful sleepers.

'Oh, goodness,' she said to herself miserably, 'I knew something like this would happen. Now what had I better do?'

Telling Nursie seemed the first step, and Harriet went indoors. But five o'clock had struck and Nursie was listening to a programme of young artists from the Midlands, and was not to be disturbed. She waved Harriet away with a preoccupied hand.

'If I don't get Mark out of that tree before the hour's up,' Harriet thought, 'we shall never be able to wake him. I wonder if I could drag him out by myself?'

She went back to the tree but decided that it would be too risky, even if she put a ladder against Mark's fork and climbed up it; Mark was much too heavy for her to lift, and if he fell from that height, he might easily break a leg. Besides, something ought to be done about the postman and the butcher's boy, too; goodness knows how long they had been there.

'I know,' she thought. 'I'll go for the doctor.'

Dr Groves lived a little way up the lane. They had been to see him when they first arrived, for a check-over, and had liked him very much.

'He'll be able to help,' Harriet thought.

She ran round to the shed by the stables and got out Nursie's bicycle; this was no time for loitering. Without waiting to ask permission, Harriet sped off down the front path and took the steps at a slither.

Thank goodness it was not a surgery night, and Dr Groves was sitting by his fire, peacefully reading the *Lancet*, when Harriet arrived, panting and gasping, about five minutes later.

'Please will you help me,' she wheezed, trying not to cough. 'Mark's gone to sleep in the laurel tree.'

'Eh, dear, has he now,' said Dr Groves. 'And you want me to help pull him down, is that it?'

'Yes, please. And there are two other people up in the tree, and a cat; I expect they ought to come down, too.'

'Tut, tut.' The doctor sounded more disapproving than surprised. 'And what would they have been doing up there, I wonder?'

'I don't know. One of them's the postman. Oh, do please hurry.'

'I can't hurry much, my lass, on account of my leg. Eh, well, well, now, the postman. We'd been wondering where he'd got to when he vanished last May.'

He pulled himself stiffly to his feet, and Harriet remembered with dismay that he had an artificial leg.

'Should I get somebody else?' she said anxiously. 'Will it be too much for you?'

'No, no, I'll manage very well. Just pass me that stick, will you now, and I'll be with you directly.'

They made slow progress back up the road, and Harriet did rings about the doctor in her impatience to get on.

'Ah, it's a great convenience to me, this leg,' he said imperturbably, as he clanked along. 'Bitten off by a shark, it was, in the days when I was a bold buccaneering sea-doctor, and I fitted myself up with the best cast-iron peg I could lay hands on. I can use it for poking the fire or bowling over a charging tiger – and best of all, when some fussing woman gets a pain in her little finger and fancies sending for the doctor, she thinks again and says to herself: "With his iron leg it'll take him an hour and twenty minutes to get here; it's not worth fetching him out," and that saves me a great, great deal of trouble, I can tell you, for I'm a lazy old man and never do two trips when one will do.'

'Oh, yes, I'm sure it does,' said Harriet, wheeling round him distractedly. 'Are you sure you wouldn't like to ride Nursie's bicycle?'

'No, thank you, my bairn, riding a bicycle's one of the things I can *not* do with this leg. But we're managing very well, very well indeed.'

Dusk was falling as he stumped up Granny's steps, and Harriet looked at her watch and saw with a sinking heart that it had taken them forty-five minutes to do the return journey; Mark must have been in the laurel tree for very nearly an hour.

'Ah, yes, there they are,' Dr Groves said, pulling a torch from his pocket and shining it up into the tree. 'Fast asleep, the three of them. And Pussie Baudrons, too, after birds, nae doubt, the naughty grimalkin. And that's an interesting thing, very interesting indeed, that the laurel tree should have such power. When I was a boy I would always use laurel leaves for putting butterflies to sleep. In a jam jar.'

Without listening to his reflections, which seemed likely to go on for ever, Harriet dashed off and came back with

Granny's aluminium fruit-picking ladder, which she planted firmly against the trunk of the laurel.

Dr Groves had embarked on a learned chat with himself about the medical properties of various plants, so she started up the ladder, saying over her shoulder:

'If I pull them down, Dr Groves, do you think you can catch them?'

'I'll do my best, lass. Feet first is the way, feet first, now. Don't let the poor slumberers fall on their heads or you'd do better to leave them bide where they are.'

The butcher's boy was the nearest, and Harriet tugged him down cautiously, being most careful herself not to get into the tree even for a moment. Dr Groves received the long dangling legs and flopped the boy onto the ground, where he lay limp and sprawling. Harriet dropped his basket of chops (they flew in all directions), had to come down, then, and move her ladder round to the other side in order to reach Mark, who was more of a problem; half lifting, half dragging, she at last managed to get him clear of the branches and lower him to the doctor. He was laid down unceremoniously on the chops while they tackled the postman. He was the most difficult of all, for he was higher up still, and in the end Harriet had to go and get the clothes-line and make a very unseamanlike hitch round his shoulders so that she could let him bumpingly down to the doctor. She herself had to come down from time to time to get a good breath of fresh air, for even when she was safely perched on the ladder she found that the laurel tree made her feel uncommonly sleepy.

'I can't reach the cat, but I'm not going to risk being caught by the Silver Lady for a lot of starlings,' she said descending for the last time. 'What shall we do with them now?'

'Eh well, there's little can be done till I've reflected,' said the doctor, who seemed to be infected by the general somnolence, and was yawning dreadfully. 'We'll just get them indoors safe and snug and then I'll be off home. I'll come up in the morning for a confabulation with your granny. Meanwhile they'll take no harm.'

Using the barrow for the longer stretch of the journey, they carted the slumberers into a sort of garden-room, where they were propped about in canvas swings and deck chairs, and covered with tartan rugs. The rising moon silvered the three inert bundles through the window. Harriet and the doctor stepped out, closing the glass door behind them, and the doctor's peg-legged shadow stretched out, long and fantastic, across the lawn, as he stumped off with a good-night wave.

Harriet turned indoors, feeling rather forlorn. She didn't want any supper, and went straight upstairs to bed. The whole house was as quiet as a stringless harp, and she missed Mark's companionable coughing from next door. Nevertheless, she managed to fall asleep and drifted into some very strange dreams about flying cats, laurel trees full of sharks, and a Silver Lady with a wooden leg. 'You give me back my brother!' shouted Harriet, and at once became aware that she was coughing, and that she was awake.

'Eh, nonny, nonny, what's all this?' said Nursie, materialising beside the bed with her candle and red dressing gown. 'Here you are then, my duck, here's a drink of blackcurrant for that cough.' Harriet obediently swallowed it down. It tasted like permanganate.

'Nursie,' she said miserably, 'we've lost Mark. The Silver Lady's got him – he's asleep and won't wake up.'

'Laws-a-me,' Nursie said sharply, 'he's been up the laurel tree then? All the same they are – tell them not to do a thing and they run straight away and do it. A good sleep'll work wonders for his cough, that's one comfort.'

'But how are we going to wake him? The postman's been asleep since May.'

'As to that,' Nursie answered, 'I couldn't say. The rhyme says:

Those by the silver slumber taken
Only the Tawny Owl can waken.

But I can hear a tawny owl down in the orchard this minute and it takes more than them to waken Master Mark in the normal way, let alone when the Silver Lady's put her finger on him. We'll think about it in the morning, Miss Harriet, dear. Deary me, there's the telephone, drat it, at half past nine of the night.'

The telephone was the children's father ringing up to ask if they were behaving themselves. Nursie told him to hold on while she went and fetched Granny from the television, explaining to her on the way what had happened to Mark.

'That you, Mother? How are you?' shouted Mr Armitage, loud enough to penetrate Granny's deafness.

'I am well, thank you, Geoffrey. The children are looking much better.'

'Behaving all right?'

'There is no need to shout, Geoffrey, I can hear perfectly well over the telephone. Mark is unfortunately in a coma; all the fault of the Silver Lady, you know. Otherwise nothing out of the common has occurred.'

'What? What?' shouted Mr Armitage, becoming very agitated. 'What are you doing about it?'

'Why, my dear boy, there is nothing to be done. It is my bedtime now, goodnight.' And Granny firmly rang off, leaving Mr Armitage in a great state of irritation.

The dying tink of the telephone came to Harriet as she lay wide awake and worrying in a patch of moonlight. Something ought to be done about Mark soon, she was sure; otherwise he might sink so deep into sleep that he could *never* be awakened. And then all their plans for Christmas would be spoiled. Not to mention Easter.

The Tawny Owl, Nursie had said. There was a tawny owl, too, in the rhyme about the land of trees and heroes. Perhaps it was the same one? In any case, the time to find a tawny owl was now, while it was dark and the owls were abroad, not tomorrow morning when they were all fast asleep and hidden away in thickets.

Harriet had by now thought herself wide awake, and she got up silently and began putting on her clothes again. The sound of the telephone had given her an idea. It seemed so wild and odd that she hardly liked to put it to herself in actual thought, but she slipped out of her room, carrying her shoes in her hand, and went downstairs to the little telephone room off the front hall. The house was silent again. Nursie and Granny had gone to bed. Only the faint crackle of coal settling for the night came from the kitchen stove.

Harriet sat looking at the telephone in its little pool of moonlight. How did you ring up an orchard? In the end she dialled 'O'.

For a long, long time she could hear ringing, but no one answered. She almost gave up in despair and put the receiver back, but then she thought she might as well wait a bit longer. At last the ringing stopped, there came a click, and she could hear a far-off sighing, like the wind in the branches.

'Who is there?' she asked, rather nervously.

A whisper answered her. 'Cox's Ooooor-ange Pippin speeeeking . . .' it murmured leafily against her ear. 'To whoooooom did you wish to speeeeeeeeek?'

'May I please speak to the Tawny Owl?' Harriet's heart beat in triumph at this success.

'Hold on, pleasssssss . . .' whispered Cox's Orange, and there was another long pause, a long, long pause, while Harriet heard, down the receiver, the trees in the orchard all turning their branches this way and that against the night sky.

Presently there came a click as if somebody had picked up the receiver.

'I – is that the Tawny Owl?' Harriet asked nervously.

'Who?'

'I asked to speak to the Tawny Owl.'

'To who?'

'You mean to whom,' Harriet was on the point of saying, when she realized that it *was* the Tawny Owl speaking. She explained the trouble they were in, and that he was their only hope. 'Oh, please, sir,' she ended despairingly, 'won't you help us? I'm sure Dr Groves won't have much idea what to do.'

'You will need ammunition,' said the Tawny Owl. 'To wit, a bow and some arrows.'

'I can manage that.' Harriet was much encouraged by his voice – a friendly, brown, furry sort of voice. 'What shall I do with them?'

'Bring them to the laurel tree. Do not delay. I will be there.'

'Oh, *thank* you,' Harriet said gratefully.

'Who?'

'You – oh, I mean whooo,' she replied politely, put the receiver back, and ran tiptoeing to the garden-room, where she had left the bow and the remaining two arrows. Everyone was breathing peacefully, and she went out, making snail-tracks in the moony dew, across the lawn to the laurel tree.

She had not been there a moment when the branches parted and a large pale shape coasted silently down and landed as lightly as a dead leaf on her shoulder. She felt the smoothness of feathers against her cheek.

'Whooo,' the Tawny Owl said gently in her ear. 'The arrows – of what wood are they?'

'Elder.'

'A moody personality. Was permission obtained? It would not do to be rude to her.'

'We – we *asked*,' said Harriet anxiously, 'but she didn't answer.'

'I will inquire anew. Do you procure a bicycle and return hither – be swift. Adieu.'

Quick as she was, the owl had returned to the tree before her.

'Elder is graciously pleased to allow the use of those two. It is a propitious wood. Now! We must go fast. I will sit on your shoulder and instruct you as to the route,' said the Tawny Owl.

He soon found, however, that it was easier if he flew ahead and Harriet followed, for he could go much faster. Whizzing after him down the garden path, Harriet realized that she was not going to have time to dismount for the steps and discovered, without much surprise, halfway down them that she had become airborne and was pedalling briskly after the owl ten feet above the white surface of the road, which streamed away like a nylon ribbon beneath her.

'Where are we going?' she called after him.

'To the Land,' his hoot came faintly back between wingbeats, 'to the Land of Trees and Heroes . . .'

It was a wonderful ride. Harriet would not have minded going on all night, seeing the moon-silvered fields sliding under her feet and breathing the sharp cold scent of the trees when they swooped through the darkness of a wood. But presently she found that they were toiling up a long, cloudy ascent; the Tawny Owl went more slowly, and she herself was glad of Nursie's three-speed. Great cliffs of cloud built up on either side, drifts of loose cloud sometimes obscured the path, and at length they came to a door.

The owl flew up against it and clung, like a woodpecker to the side of a tree, and in a moment or two the door swung open and they passed through.

Harriet often wished afterwards that she had had more time to notice the beauties of that land. It was smooth and rolling – a country like a counterpane of grassy downs and small groves on the hilltops, set with statues that shone white, here and there, against the trees. And strolling on the grass, or lying in the shade, some near, some far, were the heroes. Many of them she recognised at once. There was Hercules, doing his best, with the assistance of two grass snakes, to copy the position of a statue of himself, but the snakes were not being cooperative and he was not managing very well. There was Jason, with only one sandal. There was Prince Hal, galloping about on a fiery horse, with Ivanhoe; Davy Crockett and Robin Hood, having a shooting match; Captain Nemo and Captain Ahab, having a nice chat in the shade. Harriet saw with wonder, not unmixed with envy, that the postman was sitting and chatting with them, a large tabby on his lap; that the butcher's boy was playing bowls with Sir Francis Drake and Sir Walter Raleigh; and that Bellerophon was giving Mark a ride on Pegasus.

'How did they get here?' she asked in astonishment.

'They are dreaming,' the Tawny Owl answered her. She had propped her bicycle against an ilex tree, and the owl was once more sitting on her shoulder. 'But now you must not delay – the Silver Lady will soon be returning, and you must shoot her.'

'I don't much want to shoot anybody,' Harriet said doubtfully.

'She will take no harm from it. And only thus will you have power over her. Watch, now—'

'String your bow,' said Robin Hood, who had strolled up and stood watching with friendly interest. 'Then you'll be ready. Like this—'

Several other heroes gathered round with encouragement and advice as Harriet strung her bow and pointed it at the sky. Bellerophon grounded Pegasus in case of accidents. 'Isn't this a grand place?' Mark shouted to Harriet.

'There she goes!' suddenly came a cry from the watchers, and Harriet saw something silvery and unbelievably swift streak across the sky towards the moon.

'Quick!' the Tawny Owl murmured, 'before she hides. Or you will have to wait for twenty-four hours.'

Harriet shot after the flashing figure.

'Oh!' came a long-drawn cry from the watchers. 'You've shot the moon!'

And so indeed she had. Down it came, tumbling and drifting, like a great silver honesty pod falling through leaves of air. All the shadows rushed upward.

Harriet was appalled. But Ivanhoe, galloping up to

where the moon lay blazing coldly, shouted, 'You've caught her!'

'Make haste!' called Jason.

Harriet ran to the moon. It had fallen on its edge and was standing upright, like a half-crown the size of a nursery table. The arrow, thrust clean through, was still quivering. And on the far side of the moon the Silver Lady struggled angrily to be free. The arrow had caught the bracelet on her wrist, and she was a prisoner, fastened by her hand to the shining disc. She was very beautiful, but her rage was frightening, and Harriet hesitated before approaching her; the air all round her was freezingly cold.

'Don't be afraid,' said the Tawny Owl in her ear, and he called to the lady, 'Mistress, the child has beaten you fairly.'

'Not without your help and counsel,' the Silver Lady replied, giving him a black look. 'Well, child, what is it you want? Quick! Selene is not to be humiliated for long.'

'I – I want you to set my brother free, please,' Harriet said hurriedly. 'And the postman and the butcher's boy.'

'Is that all? You might have asked for kingdoms while you were about it.' And the Silver Lady blew in the direction of Mark, who vanished like a pricked bubble. The postman and the butcher's boy disappeared at the same time. Then, twitching her bracelet free from the arrow, the Silver Lady smiled at Harriet enchantingly and shot upwards like a spark into the Milky Way.

'You must put back the moon,' she called over her shoulder, 'or you will be my next prisoner.'

'Put back the moon!' Harriet stared at it in horror. How was that ever to be done? But Perseus grinned at her reassuringly, tugged it out of the ground, and, leaning backwards, slung it up with a mighty swing of his arm.

Higher and higher the moon soared, and finally steadied, like a kite that feels the pull of the wind, and sailed among its accustomed stars.

'Homeward now,' the Tawny Owl warned Harriet. 'Dawn approaches.'

It was a race home, through the mighty door, down the slopes of paling clouds. The stars were thinning out in the sky as Harriet and the owl covered the last furlong, and the bearings on Nursie's bike were red hot.

'Owl,' said Harriet when they stood again beneath the laurel tree, 'is the tree disenchanted now?'

'Oh, no,' said the owl. 'The tree is Selene's, and will always be hers. Just as the other trees in your grandmother's garden each belong to a different Power. Did you not know? The Elder, the Quince, and the dark-berried Yew . . . ' His voice was trailing away as if he were yawning, and he murmured, 'Adieu,' gave Harriet's ear a little peck just as the sun rose, and flitted silently off to a lilac thicket.

Harriet watched him go with regret. There were so many things she had wanted to ask him.

'There!' Nursie clucked in triumph at breakfast. 'Didn't I say a night's rest would break the spell?'

'No,' said Harriet, but she yawned as she said it, and the clatter of knives and forks drowned her voice anyway. Mark, the postman, and the butcher's boy were eating an enormous breakfast. In the middle of it Dr Groves stumped in and heard their tale with interest and envy.

'Did ye now? Do they now?' he exclaimed at intervals as they all compared notes about the land, and Mark told Harriet how he had been chariot-racing with Phoebus and Boadicea. 'Well, something has cured your cough, lad, whether the sleep or the change of air.'

It had. Mark had not coughed once since he had awakened, though Harriet still had a fit of coughing from time to time.

'It is unfair!' she exclaimed. 'When I had all the trouble of fetching him back.'

They had been arguing about this for some time when

they noticed that the doctor and the postman had left the room, and, glancing out of the window, Harriet saw them cross the lawn to the laurel tree. The ladder was still leaning against it and now, helped by the postman, the doctor hauled himself up by his arms with surprising agility and disappeared into the branches. In a moment the postman followed him.

'Hey!' Harriet shouted, leaning from the window. 'That's dangerous! It's still enchanted . . .'

But they were gone, and when the children ran out and stood under the tree they could hear only contented snores coming from the upper branches.

THE STOLEN QUINCE TREE

Harriet was sitting alone upstairs in the dormer window over the porch. There was an old basket chair and a shelf full of entrancing books: *Jackanapes*, *The Silver Skates*, the *Curdie* books, and many others with thick, glossy old bindings and gold lettering. The afternoon sun shone in and made a pinkish patch on the floor. Harriet felt drowsy and comfortable. The remains of whooping cough were still troublesome and kept her awake at nights; Granny had said that she must rest for at least an hour after lunch, from two to three. She was resting now, while Mark practised archery somewhere in the garden.

Granny had gone to call on Mrs Cheevy, and Nursie was at her weekly Women's Institute meeting, so Harriet was in command. It was nice, she thought, to hear the aged house stretching itself and creaking a little around her; the only thing she did wish was that Granny kept a cat, a comfortable tabby or marmalade to stretch beside her in the patch of sunshine and let out a friendly purr from time to time.

JCars passed occasionally in the lane below Granny's ten

brick front steps, but they never stopped. All Granny's friends were very, very old and exchanged letters with her in crabbed, trembling handwriting, but they never came calling. Now, however, to Harriet's surprise, a large glossy car did draw up outside the white gate, and a lady jumped out of it and came purposefully up the steps, calling back a remark to someone in the car as she did so.

'Oh, bother,' Harriet thought, 'now the bell will ring and I shall have to answer it.'

She waited. The bell rang.

Uncoiling herself with reluctance from the squeaking chair (which had left basket marks all over her legs), she went downstairs, absent-mindedly stepping over the patch of sunshine where the cat ought to have been lying.

The lady was standing outside the glass-paned front door, looking inquisitively about her. She had on a most interesting hat, Harriet noticed, flowerpot-shaped and made of reddish furry material; out from under its brim curled green-and-white tendrils of Busy Lizzie, which then turned round and climbed up the sides of the hat. The lady's pale, smiling eyes peered from underneath this in rather an odd way.

'Well, little girl,' the lady said, and Harriet took an instant dislike to her, 'is your mummy in?'

'She doesn't live here,' Harriet said politely. 'This is my grandmother's house.'

'I *see*,' the lady said. 'Well, may I see *her* then?' She spoke with a hint of impatience.

'I'm afraid everyone is out except me.'

'Oh dear,' said the lady, smiling, 'then I shall have to

explain to you. You see, the fact is that I am Miss Eaves, Wildrose Eaves, and I have been looking everywhere, but *every*where, for a quince tree. Well! I was driving along this lane and I looked up, and I said to myself, "There's my quince tree!" So I came straight up here to ask if I could buy it.'

'Do you mean,' said Harriet doubtfully, 'buy Granny's quince tree? Or do you want to buy some quinces? Because I don't think they'll be ripe for a few days, but we could let you know when we pick them.'

'No, dear,' said Miss Eaves patiently, 'I want to buy the *tree*.'

I'm sure Granny would never think of selling the whole tree,' said Harriet decidedly. 'For one thing, wouldn't it die? And she's very very fond of it, I know—'

'I can see you don't quite understand, dear. I am Wildrose Eaves, *the* Wildrose Eaves, you know.'

Harriet plainly didn't know, so the lady explained that she wrote a very famous column, which appeared in a Sunday paper every week, about gardening. 'And people all over the world, you see, know every inch and corner of my mossy old garden just from reading about it in the *Sunday Tidings*.'

'How nice,' Harriet said.

'Well it *would* have been nice, dear, if there *was* such a garden, but the fact is the whole thing was made up. But now I've had this very tempting offer from an American magazine which wants to come and take pictures of it, so you see I'm quickly putting the whole thing together, my charming old cottage, Shadie Thatch, and the yew hedges and pansy beds, but the one thing I couldn't get hold of was a quince tree, and that's very important because I've mentioned it more than once.'

'Couldn't you say it had died?'

'Oh, no, dear. Nothing in the garden at Shadie Thatch ever dies.'

'Well,' said Harriet, 'I'm afraid it's not at all likely that Granny will want to sell the tree, but I'll tell her about it. Perhaps you could ring her up about teatime?'

'Tell her I'll pay five hundred pounds for the tree – with its quinces on, naturally. That's most important,' said the lady, and she ran down the steps again to her shiny car.

'I never heard such nonsense,' said Granny when she came home and Harriet had made her put on her hearing aid and pay attention to the matter. 'Sell the quince tree! Whatever next? The woman's a fool, and about as shady as her thatch, from the sound of her.'

When the telephone rang, Granny stomped off to give Miss Eaves a piece of her mind. Harriet heard her shouting, 'I wouldn't take five hundred pounds nor yet five thousand. And that's my last word; no, certainly not, I shouldn't dream of it.' And she rang off vigorously.

'Why,' she went on, coming back and picking up her knitting, 'your grandfather planted that tree the year we were married, and I've made quince jam from it for the last fifty years. The impertinence of her! But it's all the same nowadays – people think they can have all the benefits without doing any work for them.'

And then it was time for supper and shortly after that time for Harriet and Mark to go to bed.

The children generally woke early in the morning, and if it was fine, they got up, took biscuits from the pantry, and went out riding. There were two fat, lazy ponies called Dapple and Grey who lived in the paddock at the bottom of the orchard and whose job it was to pull the roller over Granny's wide lawns, wearing felt slippers on their little hoofs. The children were allowed to ride the ponies, and although they could seldom be persuaded out of a jiggling trot, it was a nice thing to do before breakfast. So next morning Harriet and Mark put on their jeans, went down through the orchard, caught the ponies with a bait of sugar, and took them up across the lawn to a side gate leading into the lane.

'We could go to Cloud Bottom,' Mark was saying as they came round the corner of the house. 'We haven't – good heavens, look!'

They both stared in astonishment and horror. For where, yesterday, the quince tree had grown, beautiful with its rusty leaves and golden fruit, this morning there was nothing but a huge, trampled, earthy hole.

'Tyre marks,' said Mark, 'and big ones. Someone's been here with a truck or a big van.'

'The beasts!' exclaimed Harriet. 'That beastly woman! I thought she looked sly. Now what are we going to do?'

'I wonder how long they've been gone?'

'Granny'll be awfully upset when she finds out.'

'It's still jolly early,' said Mark, looking at his watch, 'and they can't have dug it up in the dark. I bet they haven't gone far yet. Let's follow the tracks and see if we can find which way they went. Do you remember where the woman said she lived?'

'Didn't give an address,' Harriet said gloomily.

They mounted and went out into the lane. It was easy to see from the tyre marks and broken bushes where the truck had backed in, and a trail of snapped twigs showed which way it had gone. Luckily the lane was a muddy one, and where it widened, the tread marks showed plainly. The children kicked Dapple and Grey into a sort of amble, their fastest gait, and went on like bloodhounds. They hadn't much idea what they would do if they caught up with the thieves, but they did feel very strongly that the tree must be put back before Granny discovered its loss.

'Remember the time when the black-marketeers stole the holly from the two round bushes?' Mark asked Harriet. 'She was quite ill. Goodness knows what this would do to her.'

'And the time when the little pippin tree died,' Harriet said, nodding. 'I say, look over there!'

The lane curved round a couple of meadows, and across the tops of three hedges they could see what looked like a big removal van, stationary at the edge of a little wood.

'I bet it's them,' said Mark. 'We must make a plan.'

They cut across the fields, skirted the wood, and came out into the lane on the far side of the van. Here there were no tyre marks. 'It's them all right,' pronounced Mark. 'We'd better send the ponies home – they may have seen them when they were taking the tree.'

They dismounted and thumped off Dapple and Grey across the fields in the direction of home.

'Now you must limp,' Mark said.

Harriet picked out two or three good sharp flints from the mud in the lane and put them in her shoes. She never did things by halves. Then they went on towards the van, which was still not moving. They saw two men sitting on the road bank, smoking.

The children walked slowly towards them, Harriet hobbling and clutching Mark's elbow.

'Up early, aren't you?' said one of the men. 'What's the matter? Little girl hurt her foot?'

'I think I've sprained it,' gasped Harriet.

'Could you possibly give us a lift?' said Mark. 'I don't think she ought to walk on it.'

'Where do you live?' asked one of the men.

'Lower Little Finching,' answered Mark, inventing quickly.

'Never heard of it. We're going to Gorsham.'

'Oh, that would be fine. You could put us off at Gorsham crossroads.'

The men finished their cigarettes and stood up, moving slowly towards the van. It was the usual enormously high furniture removal van, and said simply SMITHS REMOVALS AND STORAGE on its side. Mark noticed with suppressed excitement that a couple of rusty leaves were jammed at the bottom of the roll-down steel back.

He wanted to draw Harriet's attention to this but didn't dare.

'Lift the little girl in, Weaver,' said the shorter man. 'I want to check the fuel.'

When he started, he said, 'First garage we see I must stop for juice. Only half a gallon left. All that winching used a lot.'

The other man scowled at him in a silencing way. 'So they've got a winch inside there,' Mark thought, 'run by a belt-drive off the engine.' He had been wondering how they got the tree out of the ground and into the van.

The driver edged his way cautiously along the narrow track which was called Back Lane because it swung out in a semicircle behind the village and then joined the main road again farther along. Just past this road junction was Smalldown Garage, and Ken Clement, who owned it, was a friend; it was Ken who came and mowed Granny's lawn with her crazy, temperamental old motor mower.

'I'll pull in here,' said the driver, when he saw Ken's sign.

'How about a bit of breakfast?' suggested Weaver, noticing that the sign also said Snacks.

'Okay. You want any breakfast, kids?'

'No, thank you,' said Mark, who was afraid that Ken would ruin things by greeting them. 'We've had ours.' He wished it were true.

'Well, we shan't be long. You can stay in the cab if you want.'

Both men jumped out, and the driver called to Ken, who

was hosing down a van, and asked him to fill up the tank. Then they went in at the café door, which was round the side of the garage, out of sight.

'Now,' said Mark to Harriet, 'you must go in and distract their attention. Make a noise, play tunes on the jukebox or something, and don't forget to limp.'

Harriet hobbled off. Her foot was really sore by now; she didn't have to pretend. In the café a fat girl was just giving the men plates of bacon and eggs. Luckily Harriet did not know her.

Harriet bought some chocolate and then limped across and put sixpence into the jukebox which jerked and rumbled once or twice and began to play a rather gloomy song:

'If she bain't a pal to me
What care I whose pal she be?'

'Oh, blimey!' said Weaver. 'I never can hear that song without crying.'

'Why?' asked the other man.

'It reminds me so of the missus.'

'Well, she's at home waiting for yer, isn't she?'

'Yes, that's just what I mean!' Sure enough, his face was all creased sideways, like a cracker that is just going to be pulled, and as the song went on its gloomy way, he fairly burst out boohooing.

'Here, shall I turn the perishing thing off?'

'Oh, no, Fred, don't do that. It's lovely – makes me feel

ever so sad. Put in another sixpence and let's have it again. You don't hear it often nowadays.'

'Lumme,' said Fred, 'there's no accounting for tastes.' But he kindly put in another sixpence and started the tune again when it ended, while Weaver sat happily crying into his eggs.

Harriet went quietly out.

'It's all right,' she said to Mark, who was waiting round the front. 'They're good for another twenty minutes.'

'That should do us; come on quick, Ken's waiting. He filled the tank and we had a look inside (lucky that that twig stuck out, it stopped the lock from engaging properly) and it's our tree all right.'

They ran. Ken was in the cab of the van already, and his son Laurie was in the back; Harriet and Mark piled in with Laurie. As Ken pulled out, his other son Tom ran a tractor across the forecourt with a deafening roar that effectively drowned out the noise of their own departure. It seemed queer to be riding along in a van with a quince tree. A few of the quinces had fallen off, but not so many as might have been expected.

'Must be a very well-sprung van,' Mark said.

'Proper shame, though, to take your Granny's quince tree like that,' Laurie said. 'Why not tell the police?'

'Oh, I expect those men were just hired to do the job. The main thing is to get it back before Granny notices.'

'Ar,' Laurie said, 'it's going to be a rare old fetch-me-round getting her out and back in the ground. Lucky there's this here crane on board.'

They could feel the bumpy, slower progress as Ken edged the van up the lane, and the occasional swish of a branch against the sides. Then he stopped, turned, and backed into Granny's orchard.

Laurie stood up and prepared to jump out. 'Cor,' he said, 'a blooming pusscat. Where did she come from?'

They all noticed the cat for the first time. She was sitting in the quince tree looking at them somewhat balefully – a big tortoise-shell with pale green eyes. Harriet was rather upset to notice also that the red flowerpot hat that had so much attracted her attention to Miss Eaves's head was lying at the foot of the tree.

'Do you think it's her?' she asked apprehensively. 'Miss Eaves? Now I come to think of it she did look as if she might be a witch.'

'If so, why go to the trouble of hiring a van to steal the tree?' Mark answered.

'She couldn't take it across running water.'

'That's true,' Mark said. 'Well, to be on the safe side, we'd better stow her somewhere out of harm's way.'

'I'll take her.' Harriet clasped the cat firmly around its middle and tucked the red hat under her arm. Then she blushed, thinking how unsuitable this treatment was for the dignified Miss Eaves. If it *was* Miss Eaves.

'Still, it was jolly mean to steal Granny's tree,' she said to the cat.

There were lots of unfurnished rooms at the back of Granny's house: apple rooms, onion rooms, tomato rooms, herb rooms, and chutney rooms. Harriet shoved the reluctant cat into an apple room with a saucer of water, shut the door and window carefully, and raced back to the house. It was still very early.

Ken had backed the van right up to the edge of the hole, and they had pulled down a ramp and were now swinging out a movable crane attached to one of the inside walls. The crane's padded clutch was still holding on to the quince tree's trunk, which was all wrapped in felt for protection. Ken got back into the cab and started the engine, and the crane cable tightened and began to throb. The quince tree lurched slightly.

Ken jumped out again. 'You kids get in the back there and push,' he said. 'Laurie, pass this rope round the tree and swing her if she goes askew. I'll work the crane.'

Little by little the tree slid forward along the polished steel floor of the van and began to slither down the ramp. The roots, which had been pressed up against the walls, sprang out straight.

'Handy little gadget that crane is, in a furniture van,' Laurie said, giving the rope a tug and wiping his face with an earthy hand. 'Now we're going to have fun though, getting her back in the hole.'

It wasn't so bad as he feared – the hole was far larger than the tree needed and it was just a case of tumping it up and down to make sure the roots were all comfortable. Then, working like beavers, they piled the earth back into the hole and trampled it down.

'It looks terrible,' Harriet said. 'As if wild bulls had been here.'

'Turf, that's what we want,' said Laurie. 'This here grass'll take a month of Sundays to come back.'

'Turf down by the cricket pavilion,' said his father. 'We was just going to renew the pitch. The club won't begrudge old Mrs Armitage half a load.'

They swung the crane inboard again, hauled down the back (Mark jammed a twig in at the bottom, just as it had been before), and all piled into the cab. Ken hustled the van back down the lane to the garage.

Tom was still exercising his tractor in the forecourt. He gave them a reassuring wave. 'Haven't come out yet,' he shouted.

Sure enough, when Harriet tiptoed to the café window and peered in, the two van men were still drinking tea, and Weaver was crying while he listened to a tune that went:

'Oh, breathe not her name
Or don't breathe it often—'

Later, she often wondered how long it was before they discovered that the tree had gone.

Meanwhile Ken had collected a load of turf from the cricket pitch and took it back in the tractor-trailer. Mark and Harriet rode back with him and helped pack the turfs around the foot of the quince tree, working outwards until they met the unspoiled grass.

'Lucky it was lawn underneath,' Ken said, 'and not rose garden or summat. That wouldn't have been so easy to fake. Now you fetch the ponies and we'll give the turf a good old flattening.'

'We'd better have the quinces picked as quickly as possible,' Harriet remarked as they laced on the ponies' felt slippers and harnessed them to the roller, 'in case Miss Eaves has another try. Once the quinces are off, the tree isn't any use to her.'

'I noticed the telephone linesmen as we were coming through the village from the pavilion,' Mark said. 'I'll ask them to come and help.'

The linesmen always helped Granny pick her fruit, and when they heard Mark's story, they said they would be along with their ladders right away. Ken said he supposed he had better go back and look after the business, and he drove off, waving aside the thanks of Mark and Harriet.

'Never thought she'd look so good,' he shouted. The ponies were shuffling round and round with the roller, and the grass beneath the tree had begun to look as if it had been there all its life. A few leaves and one more quince had fallen.

'Well, us'll make a start,' said the leader of the telephone men.

'I'll just go and tell Granny you're here,' said Harriet. 'It's ten minutes to breakfast time.'

Granny was delighted to hear that the men had begun on the quinces; she said ever since that woman had called, she had been thinking about quince chutney. As soon as breakfast was over, without even going out to look at the tree, she got out a cookery book and a cauldron, told Nursie to make some strong tea with molasses in it for the men, and instructed the children to bring in all the quinces that had been picked.

Soon the house was full of the aromatic scent of Granny's quince, tomato, and onion chutney, and Mark and Harriet were kept busy peeling, chopping, and running to and fro with more supplies, while old Nursie doddered around ordering everyone about and taking the men enormous jam tarts.

'Do you think the tree will be all right?' Harriet said to Mark as they stood watching the last of the quinces come down.

'Oh, I should think so,' he said. 'That's that, now we can let Miss Eaves out. If it *is* Miss Eaves.'

Harriet ran indoors with the last basketful.

'Put them in the quince room, child,' said Granny, stirring away at her pungent brew. 'And then come back and have a good sniff at this steam; it will cure your cough. By the way—'

'Oh!' exclaimed Harriet, stopping on the kitchen hearth. 'How did *she* get here?'

'I was going to ask you that,' said Granny mildly. 'I heard her mewing in the apple room. She's not one of the village cats.'

Miss Eaves was sitting comfortably on the hearthstone, washing her tortoise-shell paw with a pink tongue. If it *was* Miss Eaves. How had she mewed loudly enough to penetrate Granny's deafness, Harriet wondered.

'I've been wanting a cat,' Granny went on. 'Ever since old Opussum went to sleep in the laurel tree, the mice have been getting at the codlins. So I buttered her paws and I shall keep her – unless, of course, anyone turns up to claim her.'

Harriet was rather taken aback, but Miss Eaves looked

uncommonly placid and pleased with herself. An empty sardine saucer stood at one side of the hearth.

After she had had her good sniff at the quince steam (which did indeed cure her cough), Harriet ran off to consult Mark.

'If she's had her paws buttered,' he said gloomily, 'she'll probably never leave of her own accord. We shall have our work cut out to get rid of her.'

And certainly a tactful taking of Miss Eaves to the boundary hedge and dropping her over it did nothing to dislodge her; there were so many windows kept open in Granny's house that Miss Eaves could always get in one or another of them and turn up purring in time for the next meal. Meanwhile, to the children's relief, the quince tree showed no signs of ill effects from its upheaval.

On Nursie's next W.I. afternoon, Granny was making quince honey in the kitchen when Harriet saw the Brushitoff Brush man drive up to the door.

'Do you want any brushes today, Granny?' Harriet shouted through the steam. 'The brush man's here.'

'No, child. Last week we had an onion brush, the week before a tomato brush, and the week before that a tin of apple polish. Nothing this week, tell him, thank you.'

On the way to the front door Harriet found Mark and hissed her plan to him, also borrowing all the money he had, which was sevenpence.

'Granny doesn't want anything, thank you,' she said to the man, 'but may I look at what you've got. I want to buy a – a present.'

The Brushitoff man rapidly undid his suitcase and spread out a most multifarious display of brushes – straight, curved, circular, pliable, nylon, bristle, sponge, and all colours of the rainbow.

'Oh, how lovely,' Harriet said admiringly. 'Gracious, isn't it hard to decide. How much is that one?'

'Three and sixpence, miss.'

'And this?'

'Five and eleven.'

'Oh dear, they do cost a lot, don't they? How much is this little one?'

'Two and six.'

Harriet went on hopefully digging in the suitcase. She tried out a muff brush on her cuff and a pot-plant swab on her finger tip. Finally, after much thought, she purchased a tiny button brush that cost only a shilling. The man collected all the other brushes together and drove off in his van.

'Well,' said Harriet, meeting Mark breathless on the path outside, 'did you do it?'

Mark nodded. 'Took Miss Eaves round out the back door and popped her in the van.'

'Loose?'

'No, I put her in an empty apple-polish carton. She'll get out in half an hour or so.'

'That should be enough,' said Harriet, satisfied.

They hoped they had heard the last of Miss Eaves.

Next morning though, at breakfast, Granny sat looking very puzzled over a letter on lavender-coloured writing paper on which the printed heading 'Wildrose Eaves' nestled among a cluster of forget-me-nots.

'Most extraordinary,' said Granny suspiciously, 'here's some woman writing to thank me for her delightful visit when to the best of my knowledge she's never been near the place. Says how much she's looking forward to another visit. Must be mad – isn't Eaves the name of the person who wanted my quince tree?'

In fact, it soon appeared that Miss Eaves found catching mice in Granny's apple rooms much more to her taste than writing untruthful gardening articles for the *Sunday Tidings*. After three days she was back again, purring beside the kitchen stove, and the children gave up trying to persuade her to go away, though Harriet never really became accustomed to waking up and finding a lady journalist who was also a witch sleeping on the end of her bed.

'Dear me,' Granny said, some weeks after the children had gone back to school, 'there must have been a gale one night recently. That quince tree has blown completely around. The big branch used to be on the south side. And I never heard a thing, not a thing. Just fancy that, puss.'

But Miss Eaves, purring round her ankles, said nothing, and Granny strolled on to look at the medlar tree, murmuring, 'I'm getting very old; very, very old, puss; very, very old.'

THE APPLE OF TROUBLE

It was a black day for the Armitage family when Great-uncle Gavin retired. In fact, as Mark pointed out, Uncle Gavin did not exactly retire; he was pushed. He had been High Commissioner of Mbutam-Mbutaland, which had suddenly decided it needed a High Commissioner no longer but would instead become the Republic of Mbutambuta. So Sir Gavin Armitage, K.C.M.G., O.B.E., D.S.O., and so forth, was suddenly turned loose on the world, and because he had expected to continue living at the High Commissioner's Residence for years to come and had no home of his own, he moved in with the parents of Mark and Harriet.

The first disadvantage was that he had to sleep in the ghost's room. Mr Peake was nice about it; he said he quite understood, and they would probably shake down together very well, he had been used to all sorts of odd company in his three hundred years. But after a few weeks of Great-uncle's keep-fit exercises, coughing, thumping, harrumphing, snoring, and blazing open windows, Mr Peake became quite thin and pale (for a ghost); he migrated through the wall into the room next door, explaining apologetically that he wasn't getting a wink of sleep. Unfortunately the room next door was a bathroom, and though Mark didn't mind, Mr Armitage complained that it gave him the jumps to see a ghostly face suddenly loom up beside his in the mirror when he was shaving, while Harriet and her mother had to take to the downstairs bathroom, which Mr Armitage had built onto the house after Mark's outdoor prize bathroom was destroyed by a pair of feuding Druids. Great-uncle Gavin never noticed Mr Peake at all. Besides, he had other things to think about.

One of his main topics of thought was how disgracefully the children had been brought up. He was horrified at the way they were allowed to live all over the house, instead of being pent up in some upstairs nursery.

'Little gels should be seen and not heard,' he boomed at Harriet, whenever she opened her mouth. To get her out from underfoot during the holidays, he insisted on her enrolling in a domestic science course run by a Professor Grimalkin, who had recently come to live in the village.

As for Mark, he had hardly a minute's peace.

'Bless my soul, boy' – nearly all Great-uncle Gavin's remarks began with this request – 'Bless my soul, what are you doing now? *Reading?* Bless my soul, do you want to grow up a muff?'

'A muff, Great-uncle? What is a muff, exactly?' And Mark pulled out the notebook in which he was keeping a glossary of Great-uncle Gavin.

'A muff, why, a muff is a – a funk, sir, a duffer, a frowst, a tug, a swot, a miserable little sneaking *milksop*!'

Mark was so busy writing down all these words that he forgot to be annoyed.

'You ought to be out of doors, sir, ought to be out playin' footer.'

'But you need twenty-two people for that,' Mark pointed out, 'and there's only Harriet and me. Besides it's summer. And Harriet's a bit of a duffer at French cricket.'

'Don't be impudent, boy! Gad, when I was your age, I'd have been out collectin' birds' eggs.'

'Birds' eggs,' said Mark, scandalized. 'But I'm a subscribing member of the Royal Society for the Protection of Birds.'

'Butterflies, then,' growled his great-uncle.

'I read a book, Great-uncle, that said all the butterflies were being killed by indiscriminate use of pesticides and what's left ought to be carefully preserved.'

Sir Gavin was turning aubergine and seemed likely to explode.

'Boy's a regular sea-lawyer,' he said furiously. 'Grow up into one of those confounded trade-union johnnies. Why don't you go out on your velocipede, then, sir? At your age I was keen as mustard, by gad! Used to ride miles on my penny-farthing, rain or shine.'

'No bike,' said Mark, 'only the unicorn, and he's got a swelled fetlock; we're fomenting it.'

'Unicorn! Never heard such namby-pamby balderdash in me life! Here,' Great-uncle Gavin said, 'what's your weekly allowance when your pater's at home?'

With the disturbed family ghost and the prospect of Uncle Gavin's indefinite stay to depress them, Mr and Mrs Armitage had rather meanly decided that they were in need of three weeks in Madeira, and had left the day before.

'Half a crown a week,' said Mark. 'I've had three weeks in advance.'

'How much does a bike cost nowadays?'

'Oh, I daresay you could pick one up for thirty-five pounds.'

'*What?*' Great-uncle Gavin nearly fell out of his chair, but then, rallying, he pulled seven five-pound notes out of his ample wallet. 'Here, then, boy; this is an advance on your allowance for the next two hundred and eighty weeks. I'll collect it from your governor when he comes home. Cut along, now, and buy a bicycle, an' go for a topping spin and *don't let me see your face again till supper-time.*'

'But I don't want a bicycle,' said Mark.

'Be off, boy, make yourself scarce, don't argue! – On second thoughts, 'spose I'd better come with you, to make sure you don't spend the money on some appallin' book about nature.'

So Great-uncle Gavin stood over Mark while the latter unwillingly and furiously purchased a super-excellent, low-slung bicycle with independent suspension, disc brakes, three-inch tyres, five speeds, and an outboard motor. None of which assets did Mark want in the least, as who would, when they had a perfectly good unicorn to ride?

'Now, be off with you and see how quickly you can get to Brighton and back.'

Day after day thereafter, no sooner had he eaten breakfast than Mark was hounded from the house by his relentless great-uncle and urged to try and better his yesterday's time to Brighton.

'Gosh, he must have led those Mbutam-Mbutas a life,' Mark muttered darkly in the privacy of Harriet's room.

'I suppose he's old and we ought to be patient with him,' Harriet said. She was pounding herbs in a mortar for her domestic science homework.

The trouble was, concluded Mark, gloomily pedalling along one afternoon through a heavy downpour, that during his forty years as a High Commissioner Great-uncle Gavin had acquired the habit of command; it was almost impossible not to obey his orders.

Almost impossible, but not quite. Presently the rain increased to a cloudburst.

'Drat Great-uncle Gavin! I'm not going all the way to Brighton in this,' Mark decided. 'Anyway, why *should* I go to Brighton?'

And he climbed a stile and dashed up a short grassy path to a small church nearby which had a convenient, dry-looking porch. He left his bike on the other side of the stile, for that is another disadvantage of bikes: you can never take them all the way to where you want to go.

The church proved to be chilly and not very interesting, so Mark, who always carried a paperback in his pocket, settled on the porch bench to read until the rain abated. After a while, hearing footsteps, he looked up and saw that a smallish, darkish, foreign-looking man had joined him.

'Nasty afternoon,' Mark said civilly.

'Eh? Yes! Yes, indeed!' The man seemed nervous; he kept glancing over his shoulder down the path.

'Is your bicycle, boy, by wall yonder?' he asked by and by.

'Yes, it is.'

'Is a fine one,' the man said. 'Very fine one. Would go lickety-spit fast, I daresay?'

'An average of twenty miles per hour,' Mark said gloomily.

'Will it? Will it so?'

The little man fell silent, glancing out uneasily once more at the rainy dusk, while Mark strained his eyes to see the print of his book. He noticed that his companion seemed to be shuffling about, taking a pack off his back and rummaging among the contents; presently Mark realized that something was being held out to him. He looked up from the page and saw a golden apple – quite a large one, about the size of a Bramley. On one side the gold had a reddish bloom, as if the sun had ripened it. The other side was paler. Somebody had taken two bites out of the red side; Mark wondered what it had done to their teeth. Near the stalk was a dark brown stain, like a patch of rust.

'Nice, eh?' the little man said, giving the apple to Mark, who nearly dropped it on the floor. It must have weighed at least four pounds.

'Is it real gold all through?' he asked. 'Must be quite valuable.'

'Valuable?' the man said impressively. 'Such apple is beyond price. You, of course, well-educated, familiar with Old Testament tale of Adam and Eve?'

'W-why, yes,' Mark said, stammering a little. 'But you – you don't mean to say *that* apple—?'

'Self same one,' the little man said, nodding his head. 'Original bite marks of Adam and Eve before apple carried out of Eden. Then – see stain? Blood of Abel. Cain killed him for apple. Stain will never wash off.'

'Goodness,' Mark said.

'Not all, however – not all at all! Apple of Discord – golden apple same which began Trojan War – have heard of such?'

'Why yes. But – but you're not telling me—'

'Identical apple,' the little man said proudly. 'Apples of Asgard, too? Heard of? Scandinavian golden apples of perpetual youth, guarded by the goddess Idunn?'

'Yes, but you don't—'

'Such was one of those. Not to mention Apples of Hesperides, stolen by Hercules.'

'Hold on – surely it couldn't have been both?'

'Could,' the little man said. 'Was. William Tell's apple – familiar story? – same apple. Newton – apple fell on head letting in dangerous principle of gravity. This. Atalanta – apple thrown by Venus to stop her winning race. Also, Prince Ahmed's apple—'

'Stop, stop!' said Mark. 'I don't understand how it could possibly be *all* those.' But somehow, as he held the heavy, shining thing in his hand, he did believe the little man's story. There was a peculiar, rather nasty fascination about the apple. It scared him, and yet he wanted it.

'So, see,' the little man said, nodding more than ever, 'worth millions pounds. No lie – millions. And yet I give to you—'

'Now wait a minute—'

'Give in exchange for bicycle, yes? Okay?'

'Well, but – but *why?* Why don't you want the apple?'

'Want bicycle more.' He glanced down the road again, and now Mark guessed.

'Someone's after you – the police? You stole the apple?'

'Not stole, no, no, no! Did swap, like with bicycle, you agree, yes?'

He was already halfway down the path. Hypnotized, Mark watched him climb the stile and mount the bike, wobbling. Suddenly, Mark found his voice and called,

'What did you swap for it?'

'Drink of water – in desert, see?'

'Who's chasing you, then?'

By now the little man was chugging down the road and his last word, indistinct, floated back through the rain, something ending in '—ese'; it might have been Greek for all Mark could make of it.

He put the apple in his pocket, which sagged under the weight, and, since the shower was slackening, walked to the road to flag a lift home in the next truck.

Great-uncle Gavin nearly burst a blood vessel when he learned that Mark had exchanged his new bicycle for an apple, albeit a golden one.

'Did what – merciful providence – an *apple?* – Hesperides?

Eden? Asgard? Never heard such a pack of moonshine in all me born – let's see it, then. Where is it?'

Mark produced the apple and a curious gleam lit up Uncle Gavin's eye.

'Mind,' he said, 'don't believe a word of the feller's tale, but plain that's val'ble; far too val'ble an article to be in *your* hands, boy. Better give it here at once. I'll get Christie's to value it. And of course we must advertise in *The Times* for the chappy who palmed it off on you – highly illegal transaction, I daresay.'

Mark felt curiously relieved to be rid of the apple, as if a load had been lifted from his mind as well as his pocket.

He ran upstairs, whistling. Harriet, as usual, was in her room mixing things in retorts and crucibles. When Uncle Gavin, as in duty bound, asked each evening what she had been learning that day in her domestic science course, she always replied briefly, 'Spelling.' 'Spellin', gel? Rum notion of housekeepin' the johnny seems to have. Still, daresay it keeps you out of mischief.' In fact, as Harriet had confided to Mark, Professor Grimalkin was a retired alchemist who, having failed to find the Philosopher's Stone, was obliged to take in pupils to make ends meet. He was not a very good teacher; his heart wasn't in it. Mark watched Harriet toss a pinch of green powder into a boiling beaker. Half a peach tree shot up, wavered, sagged, and then collapsed. Impatiently Harriet tipped the frothing liquid out of the window and put some more water on to boil.

Then she returned to the window and peered out into the dark.

'Funny,' she said, 'there seem to be some people waiting outside the front door. Can't think why they didn't ring the bell. Could you let them in, Mark? My hands are covered in prussic acid. I expect they're friends of Uncle Gavin's.'

Mark went down and opened the door. Outside, dimly illuminated by light from the porch, he saw three ladies. They seemed to be dressed in old-fashioned clothes, drain-pipe skirts down to their ankles, and cloaks and bonnets rather like those of Salvation Army lasses; the bonnets were perched on thick, lank masses of hair. Mark didn't somehow care for their faces, which resembled those of dogs – but not tame domestic dogs so much as starved, wild, slightly mad dogs; they stared at Mark hungrily.

'Er – I'm so sorry? Did you ring? Have you been waiting long?' he said.

'A long, long time. Since the world-tree was but a seed in darkness. We are the Daughters of the Night,' one of them hollowly replied. She moved forward with a leathery rustle.

'Oh.' Mark noticed that she had bats' wings. He stepped back a little. 'Do you want to see Great-uncle – Sir Gavin Armitage? Won't you come in?'

'Nay. We are the watchers by the threshold. Our place is here.'

'Oh, all right. What name shall I say?'

To this question they replied in a sort of gloomy chant, taking turns to speak.

'We are the avengers of blood.'

'Sisters of the nymph with the apple-bough, Nemesis.'

'We punish the sin of child against parent—'

'Youth against age—'

'Brother against brother—'

'We are the Erinyes, the Kindly Ones—' (But their expressions were far from kindly, Mark thought.)

'Tisiphone—'

'Alecto—'

'And Megaera.'

'And what did you wish to see Sir Gavin about?' Mark knew his great-uncle hated to be disturbed once he was settled in the evening with a glass of port and *The Times*.

'We attend him who holds the apple.'

'There is blood on it – a brother's blood, shed by a brother.'

'It cries for vengeance.'

'Oh, I *see*!' said Mark, beginning to take in the situation. Now he understood why the little man had been so anxious for a bicycle. 'But, look here, dash it all, Uncle Gavin hasn't shed any blood! That was Cain, and it was a long time ago. I don't see why Uncle should be responsible.'

'He holds the apple.'

'He must bear the guilt.'

'The sins of the father are visited on the children.'

'Blood calls for blood.'

Then the three wolfish ladies disconcertingly burst into a sort of hymn, shaking tambourines and beating on them with brass-studded rods which they pulled out from among their draperies:

'We are the daughters
Of darkness and time
We follow the guilty
We punish the crime
Nothing but bloodshed
Will settle old scores
So blood has to flow and
That blood must be yours!'

When they had finished, they fixed their ravenous eyes on Mark again and the one called Alecto said, 'Where is he?'

Mark felt greatly relieved that Uncle Gavin had taken the apple away from him and was, therefore, apparently responsible for its load of guilt, but as this was a mean thought he tried to stifle it. Turning (not that he liked having the ladies behind his back), he went into the sitting-room, where Uncle Gavin was snug by the fire, and said,

'There are some callers asking for you, Great-uncle.'

'God bless my soul, at this time of the evenin'? Who the deuce—'

Great-uncle Gavin crossly stumped out to the porch, saying over his shoulder, 'Why didn't you ask 'em in, boy? Not very polite to leave 'em standing—'

Then he saw the ladies, and his attitude changed. He said sharply,

'Didn't you see the notice on the gate, my good women? It says "No Hawkers or Circulars". I give handsome cheques to charity each year at Christmas and make it a rule never to contribute to door-to-door collections. So be off, if you please!'

'We do not seek money,' Tisiphone hungrily replied.

'Milk-bottle tops, jumble, old gold, it's all the same. Pack of meddlesome old maids – I've no time for you!' snapped Sir Gavin. 'Good night!' And he shut the door smartly in their faces.

'Have to be firm with that sort of customer,' he told Mark. 'Become a thorough nuisance otherwise – tiresome old harpies. Got wind of that golden apple, I daresay – shows what happens when you mix with such people. Shockin' mistake. Take the apple to Christie's tomorrow.

Now, please see I'm not disturbed again.' And he returned to the sitting-room.

Mark looked uneasily at the front door, but it remained shut; evidently the three Kindly Ones were content to wait outside. But there they stayed; when Mark returned to Harriet's room he looked out of the windows and saw them, sombre and immovable, in the shadows outside the porch, evidently prepared to sit out the night.

'Not very nice if they're going to picket our front door from now on,' he remarked gloomily to Harriet. 'Goodness knows what the postman will think. And *I* don't fancy 'em above half. Wonder how we can get rid of them.'

'I've an idea,' Harriet said. 'Professor Grimalkin was talking about them the other day. They are the Furies. But it's awfully hard to shake them off once they're after you. Maybe the postman won't see them. They aren't after *him*.'

'There must be *some* way of getting rid of them,' Mark said glumly.

'There are various things you can do, biting off your finger—'

'Some hope of Uncle Gavin doing that!'

'Or shaving your head.'

'Wouldn't be much use since he's bald as a bean already.'

'You can bathe seven times in running water or take the blood of pigs—'

'He already *does* take a lot of cold baths and we had pork for supper, so plainly that's no go.'

'Well, you can go into exile for a year,' Harriet said.

'I only wish he would.'

'Or build them a grotto, nice and dark, preferably under an ilex tree, and make suitable offerings.'

'Such as what?'

'Anything black, or they rather go for iris flowers. Milk and honey, too. And they can be shot with a bow of horn, but that doesn't seem to be very successful as a rule.'

'Oh, well, let's try the milk-and-honey and something black for now,' Mark said. 'And I'll make a bow of horn tomorrow – I've got Candleberry's last year's horn in my room somewhere.' Candleberry was the unicorn.

Harriet, therefore, collected a black velvet pincushion and a bowl of milk and honey. These she put on the front step, politely wishing the Daughters of Night good evening, to which their only response was a baleful silence.

Next morning the milk and honey were still there. So were the Furies. Evidently they did not intend to be placated so easily. By daylight they were even less attractive, having black claws, bloodshot eyes, and snakes for hair. However, slipping down early to remove the saucer in case the postman tripped over it, Harriet did notice that all the pins had been removed from the pincushion. And eaten? This was encouraging. So was the fact that when the postman arrived with a card from their parents in Madeira – *Having wonderful time, hope you are behaving yourselves* – he walked clean through the Furies without noticing them at all.

'Perhaps they're only visible to relatives of their victims,' Harriet suggested to Mark, who was working on the unicorn horn with emery paper.

'I hope they've taken the pins to stick in Uncle Gavin,' he growled. In default of bicycle exercise Uncle Gavin had made Mark do five hundred press-ups before breakfast and had personally supervised the operation. Mark felt it would be far, far better to shoot Uncle Gavin than the Furies, who, after all, were only doing their duty.

The most annoying thing of all was that, after his initial interview with them, Uncle Gavin seemed not to notice the avenging spirits at all ('He only sees what he chooses to,' Harriet guessed) and walked past them quite as unconcernedly as the postman had. He packed up the golden apple in a cigar box, rang for a taxi, and departed for London. The Furies followed him in a black, muttering group, and were seen no more for several hours; Mark and Harriet heaved sighs of relief. Prematurely, though; at teatime the Furies reappeared, even blacker, muttering still more, and took up their post once more by the front door.

'Lost the old boy somewhere in London,' Mark diagnosed. 'Or perhaps they were chucked out of Christie's.'

The unwanted guests were certainly in a bad mood. This time they were accompanied by a smallish thickset winged serpent or dragon who seemed to be called Ladon. Harriet heard them saying, 'Down, Ladon! Behave yourself, and soon you shall sup on blood.' Ladon, too, seemed to have a snappish disposition, and nearly took off Harriet's hand when she stooped to pat him on returning home from her Domestic Science lesson.

'What a beautiful green his wings are. Is he yours?' she said to the Furies politely.

'He is the guardian of the apple; he but waits for his own,' Tisiphone replied dourly.

Ladon did not share the Furies' scruples about coming indoors; evidently he was used to a warmer climate and found the doorstep too draughty. He followed Harriet into the kitchen and flopped his bulky length in front of the stove, hissing cantankerously at anyone who came near, and greatly discomposing Walrus the cat.

Walrus was not the only one.

'Miss Harriet! Get that nasty beast out of here at once!' exclaimed Mrs Epis, the cook, when she came back from shopping. 'And what those black ladies are doing out on the front doorstep I'm sure *I* don't know; I've two or three times give 'em a hint to be off, but they won't take it.'

Evidently Mrs Epis counted as one of the family or else she had a guilty conscience. Mark and Harriet soon found that visitors to the house who had episodes in their past of which they had cause to be ashamed were apt to notice the Erinyes in a patchy, nervous way and hurry away with uneasy glances behind them, or else break into sudden and embarrassing confessions.

And Ladon was a thorough nuisance. As long as Harriet kept on the fan heater in her room, he would lie in front of it rolling luxuriously on his back and only snapping at anyone who approached him. But at bedtime, when she turned the fan off – for she hated a warm room at night – he became fretful and roamed snarling and clanking about the house. Even Uncle Gavin tripped over him then and blamed the children furiously for leaving what he thought was a rolled-up tent lying in the passage.

'Things can't go on like this,' Mark said despondently.

'We've certainly got to get rid of them all somehow before Mother and Father come home next week,' Harriet agreed. 'And Uncle Gavin's plainly going to be no help at all.'

Uncle Gavin was even more tetchy than usual. Christie's had sent him a letter saying that, in view of the apple's unique historical interest, it was virtually impossible to put a price on it, but in their opinion it was certainly worth well over a million pounds. They would return the apple by the next registered post pending further instructions. And the advertisement which appeared in *The Times* every day, 'Will person who persuaded young boy to exchange valuable new bicycle for metal apple on August 20 please contact Box XXX,' was producing no replies.

'Nor likely to,' said Mark. 'That chap knows when he's well out of trouble.'

When Mark had finished his horn bow, he tried shooting at the Furies with it. The operation was a total failure. The arrows, which he had decided to make out of slivers from a fallow-deer's antler, were curved and flew on a bias, missing the visitors nine times out of ten. If they did hit, they merely passed clean through, and, as Mark told Harriet later, he felt a fool having to pick them up under the malign, snakey-and-bonneted gaze of Alecto, Megaera and Tisiphone.

Harriet, however, came home in good spirits. She pulled out and showed Mark a paper covered with Professor Grimalkin's atrocious handwriting. 'What is it?' he asked.

'Recipe for a friendship philtre. You've heard of a love philtre? This is like that, only milder. I'm going to try it in their milk. Now don't interrupt, while I make it up.'

She put her crucible on to bubble. Mark curled up at the end of her bed and read his bird book, coming out only when Harriet tripped over Ladon and dratted him, or asked Mark's opinion about the professor's handwriting.

'Is this "verdigris" or "verjuice", do you think? And is that "Add sugar" or "Allow to simmer"?'

'It'll be a miracle if the stuff turns out all right,' Mark said pessimistically. 'Anyway, do we *want* the Furies friendly?'

'Of course we do, it'll be a tremendous help. Where was I now? Add bad egg, and brown under grill.'

Finally the potion was finished and put in a cough-mixture bottle. ('It smells awful,' Mark said, sniffing. 'Never mind,' Harriet said, 'how do we know what they like?') A spoonful of the noxious stuff was divided between three bowls of milk, which were placed on the front step, at the feet of the unresponsive Erinyes.

However, after a moment or two they began to snuff the air like bloodhounds on the track of a malefactor, and as Harriet tactfully retired, she had the pleasure of seeing the three of them lapping hungrily at the mixture. So far, at least, the spell had worked. Harriet went hopefully to bed.

Next morning she was awakened by a handful of earth flung at her window. 'Miss Harriet!' It was Agnes on the lawn. 'Miss Harriet, you'll have to make the breakfast yourself. I'm taking a week's holiday and so's Mrs Epis. And things had better be different when we come back or we'll give in our notice; and you can tell your ma it was me broke the Crown Derby teapot and I'm sorry about that, but there's some things that a body can't bear. Now I'm off home.'

Sleepy and mystified, Harriet went to the kitchen to put on the kettle for Great-uncle Gavin's tea. There, to her dismay, she found the Furies, who greeted her with toothy smiles. They were at ease in basket chairs round the stove, with their long skirts turned back so as to toast their skinny legs and feet, which rested on Ladon. Roused by the indoor warmth, the snakes on their heads were in a state of disagreeable squirm and writhe, which Harriet, too, found hard to bear, particularly before breakfast; she quite sympathized with the cook's departure.

'Oh, good morning,' she said, however, stoutly controlling her qualms. 'Would you like some more milk?' She mixed another brew with potion (which was graciously accepted) and took up a tray of breakfast to Great-uncle Gavin, explaining that Mrs Epis had been called away. By the time she returned, Mark was in the kitchen, glumly taking stock of the situation.

'Feel like a boiled egg?' Harriet said.

'I'll do it, thanks. I've had enough of your domestic science.'

They ate their boiled eggs in the garden. But they had only taken a bite or two when they were startled by hysterical screams from the window cleaner, who, having arrived early and started to work on the kitchen window, had looked through the glass and was now on his knees in the flower-bed, confessing to anyone who would listen that he had pinched a diamond brooch from an upstairs bedroom in West Croydon. Before he was pacified, they had also to deal with the electrician who came to mend the fridge and seemed frightfully upset about something he had done to a person called Elsie, as well as a French onion-seller, who dropped eight strings of onions in the back doorway and fled crying, '*Mon Dieu, mon Dieu, mon crime est découvert! Je suis perdu!*'

'This won't do,' said Mark, as he returned from escorting the sobbing electrician to the gate. Exhaustedly mopping his brow, he didn't look where he was going, barked his shins painfully on Ladon, who was stalking the cat, and let out an oath. It went unheard; the Furies, much cheered by their breakfast and a night spent in the snug kitchen, were singing their bloodthirsty hymn *fortissimo*, with much clashing of tambourines. Ladon and the cat seemed all set for a duel to the death; and Great-uncle Gavin was bawling down the stairs for 'less row while a man was breakfastin', dammit!'

'It's all right,' Harriet soothed Mark. 'I knew the potion would work wonders. Now, Your Kindlinesses,' she said to the Erinyes, 'we've got a beautiful grotto ready for you, just the sort of place you like, except I'm sorry there isn't an ilex tree, if you wouldn't mind stepping this way,' and she led them to the coal cellar, which, being peaceful and dark, met with their entire approval.

'I daresay they'll be glad of a nap,' she remarked, shutting the door thankfully on them. 'After all, they've been unusually busy lately.'

'That's all very well,' said Mark. 'They'd better not stay there long. *I'm* the one that fetches the coal. And there's still beastly Ladon to dispose of.'

Ladon, unlike his mistresses, was not tempted by milk containing a friendship potion. His nature remained as intractable as ever. He now had Walrus the cat treed on the banister post at the top of the stairs, and was coiled in a baleful bronze-and-green heap just below, hissing like a pressure cooker.

'Perhaps bone arrows will work on *him*,' said Mark, and dashed to his bedroom.

As he reappeared, a lot of things happened at once.

The postman rang the front-door bell and handed Harriet a letter for Uncle Gavin and a registered parcel labelled GOLD WITH CARE. Ladon made a dart at the cat, who countered with a faster-than-light left hook, all claws extended. It caught the dragon in his gills, and he let out a screech like the whistle of a steam locomotive, which fetched the Furies from their grotto on the double, brass-studded batons out and snakes ready to strike.

At the same moment Mark let fly with his bow and arrow, and Uncle Gavin burst from his bedroom exclaiming, 'I *will* not have this bedlam while I'm digestin' my breakfast!' He received the arrow intended for Ladon full in his slippered heel and gave a yell that quite drowned the noise made by the cat and the dragon.

'Who did that? Who fired that damned thing?' Enraged, hopping, Uncle Gavin pulled out the bone dart. 'What's that cat doin' up there? Why's this confounded reptile in the house? Who are those people down there? *What the devil's going on around here?*'

Harriet gave a shout of joy. 'Look, quick!' she called to the Furies. 'Look at his heel! It's bleeding!' (It was indeed.) 'You said blood had to flow and now it has, so you've done your job and can leave with clean consciences! Quick, Mark, open the parcel and give that wretched dragon his apple and they can *all* leave. Poor Uncle Gavin, is your foot very painful? Mark didn't mean to hit you. I'll bandage it up.'

Mark tore the parcel open and tossed the golden apple to Ladon, who caught it with a snap of his jaws and was gone in a flash through the landing window. (It was shut, but no matter.) At the same moment the Furies, their lust for vengeance appeased by the sight of Uncle Gavin's gore, departed with more dignity by the front door.

Alecto even turned and gave Harriet a ghastly smile. 'Thank you for having us, child,' she said. 'We enjoyed our visit.'

'Don't mention it,' Harriet mechanically replied, and only just stopped herself from adding, 'Come again.'

Then she sat her great-uncle in the kitchen armchair and bathed his heel. The wound, luckily, proved to be no more than a scratch. While she bandaged it, he read his letter and suddenly gave a curious grunt of pleasure and astonishment.

'God bless my soul! They want me back! Would you believe it?'

'Who want you back, Great-uncle?' Harriet asked, tying the ends of the bandage in a knot.

'The Mbutam-Mbutas, bless 'em! They want me to go

and help 'em as Military and Economic Adviser. Well, well, well! Don't know when I've been so pleased.' He gave his nose a tremendous blow and wiped his eyes.

'Oh, Uncle Gavin, how perfectly splendid!' Harriet hugged him. 'When do they want you to go?'

'Three weeks' time. Bless my soul, I'll have a bustle getting me kit ready.'

'Oh, we'll all help like mad. I'll run down the road now and fetch Mrs Epis; I'm sure she'll be glad to come back for such an emergency.'

Mrs Epis had no objection at all, once she was assured the intruders were gone.

Harriet had one startled moment when they got back to the house.

'Uncle Gavin!' she called and ran upstairs. The old gentleman had out his tin tropical trunk and was inspecting a pith helmet. 'Yes, m'dear, what is it?' he said absently.

'The little brown bottle on the kitchen table. Was it – did you—?'

'Oh, that? My cough mixture? Yes, I finished it and threw the bottle away. Why, though, bless my soul – there's my cough mixture! What the deuce have I been an' taken, then, gel? Anything harmful?'

'Oh no, perfectly harmless,' Harriet hastily reassured him. 'Now, you give me anything you want mended and I'll be getting on with it.'

''Pon me soul,' Uncle Gavin said, pulling out a bundle of spotless white ducks and a dress jacket with tremendous epaulettes and fringes, ''pon me soul, I believe I'll miss you young ones when I'm back in the tropics. Come and visit me sometimes, m'dear? Young Mark, too. Where is the young rogue? Ho, ho, can't help laughing when I think how he hit me in the heel. Who'd have thought he had it in him?'

'He's gone apple picking at the farm down the road,' Harriet explained. 'He wants to earn enough to pay back that thirty-five pounds.'

'Good lad, good lad!' Uncle Gavin exclaimed approvingly. 'Not that he need have bothered, mark you.'

And in fact when Mark tried to press the money on Uncle Gavin, he would have none of it.

'No, no, bless your little hearts, split it between you.' He chucked Harriet under the chin and earnestly shook Mark's hand. 'I'd never have thought I'd cotton to young 'uns as I have to you two – 'mazing thing. So you keep the money and buy something pretty to remind you of my visit.'

But Mark and Harriet thought they would remember his visit quite easily without that – especially as the Furies had taken quite a fancy to the coal cellar and frequently came back to occupy it on chilly winter nights.

THE SERIAL GARDEN

'Cold rice pudding for breakfast?' said Mark, looking at it with disfavour.

'Don't be fussy,' said his mother. 'You're the only one who's complaining.' This was unfair, for she and Mark were the only members of the family at table, Harriet having developed measles while staying with a school friend, while Mr Armitage had somehow managed to lock himself in the larder. Mrs Armitage never had anything but toast and marmalade for breakfast anyway.

Mark went on scowling at the chilly-looking pudding. It had come straight out of the fridge, which was not in the larder.

'If you don't like it,' said Mrs Armitage, 'unless you want Daddy to pass you cornflakes through the larder ventilator, flake by flake, you'd better run down to Miss Pride and get a small packet of cereal. She opens at eight; Hickmans doesn't open till nine. It's no use waiting until the blacksmith comes to let your father out; I'm sure he won't be here for hours yet.'

There came a gloomy banging from the direction of the larder, just to remind them that Mr Armitage was alive and suffering in there.

'*You're* all right,' shouted Mark heartlessly as he passed the larder door. 'There's nothing to stop *you* having cornflakes. Oh, I forgot, the milk's in the fridge. Well, have cheese and pickles then. Or treacle tart.'

Even through the zinc grating on the door he could hear his father shudder at the thought of treacle tart and pickles for breakfast. Mr Armitage's imprisonment was his own fault, though; he had sworn that he was going to find out where the mouse had got into the larder if it took him all night, watching and waiting. He had shut himself in, so that no member of the family should come bursting in and disturb his vigil. The larder door had a spring catch that sometimes jammed; it was bad luck that this turned out to be one of the times.

Mark ran across the fields to Miss Pride's shop at Sticks Corner and asked if she had any cornflakes.

'Oh, I don't think I have any left, dear,' Miss Pride said woefully. 'I'll have a look . . . I think I sold the last packet a week ago Tuesday.'

'What about the one in the window?'

'That's a dummy, dear.'

Miss Pride's shop window was full of nasty, dingy old cardboard cartons with nothing inside them, and several empty display stands which had fallen down and never been propped up again. Inside the shop were a few, small, tired-looking tins and jars, which had a worn and scratched appearance as if mice had tried them and given up. Miss Pride herself was small and wan, with yellowish grey hair; she rooted rather hopelessly in a pile of empty boxes. Mark's mother never bought any groceries from Miss Pride's if she could help it, since the day when she had found a label inside the foil wrapping of a cream cheese saying, 'This cheese should be eaten before May 11, 1899.'

'No cornflakes I'm afraid, dear.'

'Any wheat crispies? Puffed corn? Rice nuts?'

'No, dear. Nothing left, only Brekkfast Brikks.'

'Never heard of *them*,' Mark said doubtfully.

'Or I have a jar of Ovo here. You spread it on bread. That's nice for breakfast,' said Miss Pride, with a sudden burst of salesmanship. Mark thought the Ovo looked beastly, like yellow paint, so he took the packet of Brekkfast Brikks. At least it wasn't very big ... On the front of the box was a picture of a fat, repulsive, fair-haired boy, rather like the chubby Augustus, banging on his plate with his spoon.

'They look like tiny doormats,' said Mrs Armitage, as Mark shovelled some Brikks into his bowl.

'They taste like them, too. Gosh,' said Mark, 'I must hurry or I'll be late for school. There's rather a nice cut-out garden on the back of the packet though; don't throw it away when it's empty, Mother. Goodbye, Daddy,' he shouted through the larder door, 'hope Mr Ellis comes soon to let you out.' And he dashed off to catch the school bus.

At breakfast next morning Mark had a huge helping of Brekkfast Brikks and persuaded his father to try them.

'They taste just like esparto grass,' said Mr Armitage fretfully.

'Yes, I know, but do take some more, Daddy. I want to cut out the model garden, it's so lovely.'

'Rather pleasant, I must say. It looks like an eighteenth-century German engraving,' his father agreed. 'It certainly was a stroke of genius putting it on the packet. No one would ever buy these things to eat for pleasure. Pass me the sugar, please. And the cream. And the strawberries.'

It was the half-term holiday, so after breakfast Mark was able to take the empty packet away to the playroom and get on with the job of cutting out the stone walls, the row of little trees, the fountain, the yew arch, the two green lawns, and the tiny clumps of brilliant flowers. He knew better than to 'stick tabs in slots and secure with paste', as the directions suggested; he had made models from packets before and knew they always fell to pieces unless they were firmly bound together with sticky tape.

It was a long, fiddling, pleasurable job.

Nobody interrupted him. Mrs Armitage only cleaned the playroom once every six months or so, when she made a ferocious descent on it and tidied up the tape-recorders, roller skates, meteorological sets, and dismantled railway engines, and threw away countless old magazines, stringless tennis rackets, abandoned paintings, and unsuccessful models. There were always bitter complaints from Mark and Harriet; then they forgot and things piled up again till next time.

As Mark worked, his eye was caught by a verse on the outside of the packet:

Brekkfast Brikks to start the day
Make you fit in every way.
Children bang their plates with glee
At Brekkfast Brikks for lunch and tea!
Brekkfast Brikks for supper too
Give peaceful sleep the whole night through.

'Blimey,' thought Mark, sticking a cedar tree into the middle of the lawn and then bending a stone wall round at the dotted lines A, B, C, and D. 'I wouldn't want anything for breakfast, lunch, tea, and supper, not even Christmas pudding. Certainly not Brekkfast Brikks.'

He propped a clump of gaudy scarlet flowers against the wall and stuck them in place.

The words of the rhyme kept coming into his head as he worked, and presently he found that they went rather well to a tune that was running through his mind, and he began to hum, and then to sing; Mark often did this when he was alone and busy.

'Brekkfast Brikks to sta-art the day,
Ma-ake you fit in every way—

'Blow, where did I put that little bit of sticky tape? Oh, there it is.

'Children bang their pla-ates with glee
At Brekkfast Brikks for lunch and tea

'Slit gate with razor blade, it says, but it'll have to be a penknife.

'Brekkfast Brikks for supper toohoo
Give peaceful sleep the whole night throughoo . . .

'Hullo. That's funny,' said Mark.

It was funny. The openwork iron gate he had just stuck in position now suddenly towered above him. On either side, to right and left, ran the high stone wall, stretching away into foggy distance. Over the top of the wall he could see tall trees, yews and cypresses and others he didn't know.

'Well, that's the neatest trick I ever saw,' said Mark. 'I wonder if the gate will open?'

He chuckled as he tried it, thinking of the larder door. The gate did open, and he went through into the garden.

One of the things that had already struck him as he cut them out was that the flowers were not at all in the right proportions. But they were all the nicer for that. There were huge velvety violets and pansies the size of saucers; the hollyhocks were as big as dinner plates and the turf was sprinkled with enormous daisies. The roses, on the other hand, were miniature, no bigger than cuff buttons. There were real fish in the fountain, bright pink.

'*I* made all this,' thought Mark, strolling along the mossy path to the yew arch. 'Won't Harriet be surprised when she sees it. I wish she could see it now. I wonder what made it come alive like that?'

He passed through the yew arch as he said this and

discovered that on the other side there was nothing but grey, foggy blankness. This, of course, was where his cardboard garden had ended. He turned back through the archway and gazed with pride at a border of huge scarlet tropical flowers that were perhaps supposed to be geraniums but certainly hadn't turned out that way. 'I know! Of course, it was the rhyme, the rhyme on the packet.'

He recited it. Nothing happened. 'Perhaps you have to sing it,' he thought and (feeling a little foolish) he sang it through to the tune that fitted so well. At once, faster than blowing out a match, the garden drew itself together and shrank into its cardboard again, leaving Mark outside.

'What a marvellous hiding place it'll make when I don't want people to come bothering,' he thought. He sang the spell once more, just to make sure that it worked, and there was the high mossy wall, the stately iron gate, and the treetops. He stepped in and looked back. No playroom to be seen, only grey blankness.

At that moment he was startled by a tremendous clanging, the sort of sound the Trump of Doom would make if it was a dinner bell. 'Blow,' he thought, 'I suppose that's lunch.' He sang the spell for the fourth time; immediately he was in the playroom, and the garden was on the floor beside him, and Agnes was still ringing the dinner bell outside the door.

'All right, I heard,' he shouted. 'Just coming.'

He glanced hurriedly over the remains of the packet to see if it bore any mention of the fact that the cut-out garden had magic properties. It did not. He did, however, learn that this was Section Three of the Beautiful Brekkfast Brikk Garden Series, and that Sections One, Two, Four, Five, and Six would be found on other packets. In case of difficulty in obtaining supplies, please write to Frühstücksgeschirr-ziegelsteinindustrie (Great Britain), Lily Road, Shepherds Bush.

'Elevenpence a packet,' Mark murmured to himself, going to lunch with unwashed hands. 'Five elevens are thirty-five. Thirty-five pennies are – no, that's wrong. Fifty-five pence are four-and-sevenpence. Father, if I mow the lawn and carry coal every day for a month, can I have four shillings and sevenpence?'

'You don't want to buy another space gun, do you?' said Mr Armitage looking at him suspiciously. 'Because one is quite enough in this family.'

'No, it's not for a space gun, I swear.'

'Oh, very well.'

'And can I have the four-and-seven now?'

Mr Armitage gave it reluctantly. 'But that lawn has to be like velvet, mind,' he said. 'And if there's any falling off in the coal supply, I shall demand my money back.'

'No, no, there won't be,' Mark promised in reply. As soon as lunch was over, he dashed down to Miss Pride's. Was there a chance that she would have sections One, Two, Four, Five, and Six? He felt certain that no other shop had even heard of Brekkfast Brikks, so she was his only hope, apart from the address in Shepherds Bush.

'Oh, I don't know, I'm sure,' Miss Pride said, sounding very doubtful – and more than a little surprised. 'There might just be a couple on the bottom shelf – yes, here we are.'

They were sections Four and Five, bent and dusty, but intact, Mark saw with relief. 'Don't you suppose you have any more anywhere?' he pleaded.

'I'll look in the cellar but I can't promise. I haven't had deliveries of any of these for a long time. Made by some foreign firm they were; people didn't seem very keen on them,' Miss Pride said aggrievedly. She opened a door revealing a flight of damp stone stairs. Mark followed her down them like a bloodhound on the trail.

The cellar was a fearful confusion of mildewed, tattered, and toppling cartons, some full, some empty. Mark was nearly knocked cold by a shower of pilchards in tins, which he dislodged on to himself from the top of a heap of boxes. At last Miss Pride, with a cry of triumph, unearthed a little cache of Brekkfast Brikks, three packets, which turned out to be the remaining sections, Six, One, and Two.

'There, isn't that a piece of luck now!' she said, looking quite faint with all the excitement. It was indeed rare for Miss Pride to sell as many as five packets of the same thing at one time.

Mark galloped home with his booty and met his father on the porch. Mr Armitage let out a groan of dismay.

'I'd almost rather you'd bought a space gun,' he said. Mark chanted in reply:

'Brekkfast Brikks for supper too
Give peaceful sleep the whole night through.'

'I don't want peaceful sleep,' Mr Armitage said. 'I intend to spend tonight mouse-watching again. I'm tired of finding footprints in the Stilton.'

During the next few days Mark's parents watched anxiously to see, Mr Armitage said, whether Mark would start to sprout esparto grass instead of hair. For he doggedly ate Brekkfast Brikks for lunch, with soup, or sprinkled over his pudding; for tea, with jam, and for supper lightly fried in dripping, not to mention, of course, the immense helpings he had for breakfast with sugar and milk. Mr Armitage for his part soon gave up; he said he wouldn't taste another Brekkfast Brikk even if it were wrapped in an inch-thick layer of *pâté de foie gras*. Mark regretted that Harriet, who was a handy and uncritical eater, was still away, convalescing from her measles with an aunt.

In two days, the second packet was finished (sundial, paved garden, and espaliers). Mark cut it out, fastened it together, and joined it on to Section Three with trembling hands. Would the spell work for this section, too? He sang the rhyme in rather a quavering voice, but luckily the playroom door was shut and there was no one to hear him. Yes! The gate grew again above him, and when he opened it and ran across the lawn through the yew arch, he found himself in a flagged garden full of flowers like huge blue cabbages.

Mark stood hugging himself with satisfaction, and then began to wander about smelling the flowers, which had a spicy perfume most unlike any flower he could think of. Suddenly he pricked up his ears. Had he caught a sound? There! It was like somebody crying and seemed to come from the other side of the hedge. He ran to the next opening and looked through. Nothing: only grey mist and emptiness. But, unless he had imagined it, just before he got there, he thought his eye had caught the flash of white-and-gold draperies swishing past the gateway.

'Do you think Mark's all right?' Mrs Armitage said to her husband next day. 'He seems to be in such a dream all the time.'

'Boy's gone clean off his rocker if you ask me,' grumbled Mr Armitage. 'It's all these doormats he's eating. Can't be good to stuff your insides with mouldy jute. Still I'm bound to say he's cut the lawn very decently and seems to be remembering the coal. I'd better take a day off from the office and drive you over to the shore for a picnic; sea air will do him good.'

Mrs Armitage suggested to Mark that he should slack off on the Brekkfast Brikks, but he was so horrified that she had to abandon the idea. But, she said, he was to run four times round the garden every morning before breakfast. Mark almost said, 'Which garden?' but stopped just in time. He had cut out and completed another large lawn, with a lake and weeping willows, and on the far side of the lake had a tantalizing glimpse of a figure dressed in white and gold who moved away and was lost before he could get there.

After munching his way through the fourth packet, he was able to add on a broad grass walk bordered by curiously clipped trees. At the end of the walk he could see the white-and-gold person, but when he ran to the spot, no one was there – the walk ended in the usual grey mist.

When he had finished and had cut out the fifth packet (an orchard), a terrible thing happened to him. For two days he could not remember the tune that worked the spell. He tried other tunes, but they were no use. He sat in the playroom singing till he was hoarse or silent with despair. Suppose he never remembered it again?

His mother shook her head at him that evening and said he looked as if he needed a dose. 'It's lucky we're going to Shinglemud Bay for the day tomorrow,' she said. 'That ought to do you good.'

'Oh, *blow*. I'd forgotten about that,' Mark said. 'Need I go?'

His mother stared at him in utter astonishment.

But in the middle of the night he remembered the right tune, leapt out of bed in a tremendous hurry, and ran down to the playroom without even waiting to put on his dressing gown and slippers.

The orchard was most wonderful, for instead of mere apples its trees bore oranges, lemons, limes, and all sorts of tropical fruits whose names he did not know, and there were melons and pineapples growing and plantains and avocados. Better still, he saw the lady in her white and gold waiting at the end of an alley and was able to draw near enough to speak to her.

'Who are you?' she asked. She seemed very much astonished at the sight of him.

'My name's Mark Armitage,' he said politely. 'Is this your garden?'

Close to, he saw that she was really very grand indeed.

Her dress was white satin embroidered with pearls, and swept the ground; she had a gold scarf and her hair, dressed high and powdered, was confined in a small gold-and-pearl tiara. Her face was rather plain, pink with a long nose, but she had a kind expression and beautiful grey eyes.

'Indeed it is,' she announced with hauteur. 'I am Princess Sophia Maria Louisa of Saxe-Hoffenpoffen-und-Hamster. What are you doing here, pray?'

'Well,' Mark explained cautiously, 'it seemed to come about through singing a tune.'

'Indeed. That is very interesting. Did the tune, perhaps, go like this?'

The princess hummed a few bars.

'That's it! How did you know?'

'Why, you foolish boy, it was I who put that spell on the garden, to make it come alive when the tune is played or sung.'

'I say!' Mark was full of admiration. 'Can you do spells as well as being a princess?'

She drew herself up. 'Naturally! At the court of Saxe-Hoffenpoffen, where I was educated, all princesses were taught a little magic, not so much as to be vulgar, just enough to get out of social difficulties.'

'Jolly useful,' Mark said. 'How did you work the spell for the garden, then?'

'Why, you see' (the princess was obviously delighted to have somebody to talk to; she sat on a stone seat and patted it, inviting Mark to do likewise), 'I had the misfortune to fall in love with Herr Rudolf, the Court Kapellmeister, who taught me music. Oh, he was so kind and handsome! And he was most talented, but my father, of course, would not hear of my marrying him because he was only a common person.'

'So what did you do?'

'I arranged to vanish, of course. Rudi had given me a beautiful book with many pictures of gardens. My father kept strict watch to see I did not run away, so I used to slip between the pages of the book when I wanted to be alone. Then, when we decided to marry, I asked my maid to take the book to Rudi. And I sent him a note telling him to play the tune when he received the book. But I believe that spiteful Gertrud must have played me false and never taken the book, for more than fifty years have now passed and I have been here all alone, waiting in the garden, and Rudi has never come. Oh, Rudi, Rudi,' she exclaimed, wringing her hands and crying a little, 'where can you be? It is so long – so long!'

'Fifty years,' Mark said kindly, reckoning that must make her nearly seventy. 'I must say you don't look it.'

'Of course I do not, dumbhead. For me, I make it that time does not touch me. But tell me, how did you know the tune that works the spell? It was taught me by my dear Rudi.'

'I'm not sure where I picked it up,' Mark confessed. 'For all I know it may be one of the Top Ten. I'll have to ask my music teacher, he's sure to know. Perhaps he'll have heard of your Rudolf, too.'

Privately Mark feared that Rudolf might very well have died by now, but he did not like to depress Princess Sophia

Maria by such a suggestion, so he bade her a polite good night, promising to come back as soon as he could with another section of the garden and any news he could pick up.

He planned to go and see Mr Johansen, his music teacher, next morning, but he had forgotten the family trip to the beach. There was just time to scribble a hasty post-card to the British office of Frühstücksgeschirrziegelsteinindustrie, asking if they could inform him from what source they had obtained the pictures used on the packets of Brekkfast Brikks. Then Mr Armitage drove his wife and son to Shinglemud Bay, gloomily prophesying wet weather.

In fact, the weather turned out fine, and Mark found it quite restful to swim and play beach cricket and eat ham sandwiches and lie in the sun. For he had been struck by a horrid thought: suppose he should forget the tune again while he was inside the garden – would he be stuck there, like Father in the larder? It was a lovely place to go and wander at will, but somehow he didn't fancy spending the next fifty years there with Princess Sophia Maria. Would she oblige him by singing the spell if he forgot it, or would she be too keen on company to let him go? He was not inclined to take any chances.

It was late when they arrived home, too late, Mark thought, to disturb Mr Johansen, who was elderly and kept early hours. Mark ate a huge helping of Brekkfast Brikks for supper – he was dying to finish Section Six – but did not visit the garden that night.

Next morning's breakfast (Brikks with hot milk, for a

change) finished the last packet – and just as well, for the larder mouse, which Mr Armitage still had not caught, was discovered to have nibbled the bottom left-hand corner of the packet, slightly damaging an ornamental grotto in a grove of lime trees. Rather worried about this, Mark decided to make up the last section straight away, in case the magic had been affected. By now he was becoming very skilled at the tiny fiddling task of cutting out the little tabs and slipping them into the little slots; the job did not take long to finish. Mark attached Section Six to Section Five and then, drawing a deep breath, sang the incantation once more. With immense relief he watched the mossy wall and rusty gate grow out of the playroom floor; all was well.

He raced across the lawn, round the lake, along the avenue, through the orchard, and into the lime grove. The scent of the lime flowers was sweeter than a cake baking.

Princess Sophia Maria came towards him from the grotto, looking slightly put out.

'Good morning!' she greeted Mark. 'Do you bring me any news?'

'I haven't been to see my music teacher yet,' Mark confessed. 'I was a bit anxious because there was a hole—'

'Ach, yes, a hole in the grotto! I have just been looking. Some wild beast must have made its way in, and I am afraid it may come again. See, it has made tracks like those of a big bear.' She showed him some enormous footprints in the soft sand of the grotto floor. Mark stopped up the hole with prickly branches and promised to bring a dog when he next came, though he felt fairly sure the mouse would not return.

'I can borrow a dog from my teacher – he has plenty. I'll be back in an hour or so – see you then,' he said.

'*Auf Wiedersehen*, my dear young friend.'

Mark ran along the village street to Mr Johansen's house, Houndshaven Cottage. He knew better than to knock at the door, because Mr Johansen would be either practising his violin or out in the barn at the back, and in any case the sound of barking was generally loud enough to drown any noise short of gunfire.

Besides giving music lessons at Mark's school, Mr Johansen kept a guest house for dogs whose owners were abroad or on holiday. He was extremely kind to the guests and did his best to make them feel at home in every way, finding out from their owners what were their favourite foods, and letting them sleep on his own bed, turn about. He spent all his spare time with them, talking to them and playing either his violin or long-playing records of domestic sounds likely to appeal to the canine fancy – such as knives being sharpened, cars starting up, and children playing ball games.

Mark could hear Mr Johansen playing Brahms' lullaby in the barn, so he went out there; the music was making some of the more susceptible inmates feel homesick: howls, sympathetic moans, and long, shuddering sighs came from the numerous comfortably carpeted cubicles all the way down the barn.

Mr Johansen reached the end of the piece as Mark entered. He put down his fiddle and smiled welcomingly.

'*Ach*, how *gut*! It is the young Mark.'

'Hullo, sir.'

'You know,' confided Mr Johansen, 'I play to many audiences in my life all over the world, but never anywhere do I get such a response as from zese dear doggies – it is really remarkable. But come in, come into ze house and have some coffee cake.'

Mr Johansen was a gentle, white-haired elderly man; he walked slowly with a slight stoop and had a kindly, sad face with large dark eyes. He looked rather like some sort of dog himself, Mark always thought, perhaps a collie or a long-haired dachshund.

'Sir,' Mark said, 'if I whistle a tune to you, can you write it down for me?'

'Why, yes, I shall be most happy,' Mr Johansen said, pouring coffee for both of them.

So Mark whistled his tune once more; as he came to the end, he was surprised to see the music master's eyes fill with tears, which slowly began to trickle down his thin cheeks.

'It recalls my youth, zat piece,' he explained, wiping the tears away and rapidly scribbling crotchets and minims on a piece of music paper. 'Many times I am whistling it myself – it is wissout doubt from me you learn it – but always it is reminding me of how happy I was long ago when I wrote it.'

'You *wrote* that tune?' Mark said, much excited.

'Why, yes. What is so strange in zat? Many, many tunes haf I written.'

'Well—' Mark said, 'I won't tell you just yet in case I'm mistaken – I'll have to see somebody else first. Do you mind if I dash off right away? Oh, and might I borrow a dog – preferably a good ratter?'

'In zat case, better have my dear Lotta – alzough she is so old, she is ze best of zem all,' Mr Johansen said proudly. Lotta was his own dog, an enormous shaggy lumbering animal with a tail like a palm tree and feet the size of electric polishers; she was reputed to be of incalculable age; Mr Johansen called her his strudel-hound. She knew Mark well and came along with him quite biddably, though it was rather like leading a mammoth.

Luckily his mother, refreshed by her day at the sea, was heavily engaged with Agnes the maid in spring cleaning. Furniture was being shoved about, and everyone was too busy to notice Mark and Lotta slip into the playroom.

A letter addressed to Mark lay among the clutter on the table; he opened and read it while Lotta foraged happily among the piles of magazines and tennis nets and cricket bats and rusting electronic equipment, managing to upset several things and increase the general state of hugger-mugger in the room.

Dear Sir, (the letter said – it was from Messrs Digit, Digit & Rule, a firm of chartered accountants) – We are in receipt of your inquiry as to the source of pictures on packets of Brekkfast Brikks. We are pleased to inform you that these were reproduced from the illustrations of a little-known 18th-century German work, *Steinbergen's Gartenbuch*. Unfortunately the only known remaining copy of this book was burnt in the disastrous fire which destroyed the factory and premises of Messrs Frühstücksgeschirrziegelsteinindustrie two months ago. The firm has now gone into liquidation and we are winding up their effects. Yours faithfully, P. J. Zero, Gen. Sec.

'*Steinbergen's Gartenbuch*,' Mark thought. 'That must have been the book that Princess Sophia Maria used for the spell – probably the same copy. Oh, well, since it's burned, it's lucky the pictures were reproduced on the Brekkfast Brikks packets. Come on, Lotta, let's go and find a nice princess then. Good girl! Rats! Chase 'em!'

He sang the spell and Lotta, all enthusiasm, followed him into the garden.

They did not have to go far before they saw the princess – she was sitting sunning herself on the rim of the fountain. But what happened then was unexpected. Lotta let out the most extraordinary cry – whine, bark, and howl all in one – and hurled herself towards the princess like a rocket.

'Hey! Look out! Lotta! *Heel*!' Mark shouted in alarm. But Lotta, with her great paws on the princess's shoulders, had about a yard of salmon-pink tongue out, and was washing the princess's face all over with frantic affection.

The princess was just as excited. 'Lotta. Lotta! She knows me, it's dear Lotta, it must be! Where did you get her?' she cried to Mark, hugging the enormous dog, whose tail was going round faster than a turbo prop.

'Why, she belongs to my music master, Mr Johansen, and it's he who made up the tune,' Mark said.

The princess turned quite white and had to sit down on the fountain's rim again.

'*Johansen?* Rudolf Johansen? My Rudi! At last! After all these years! Oh, run, run, and fetch him immediately, please! Immediately!'

Mark hesitated just a moment.

'Please make haste!' she besought him. 'Why do you wait?'

'It's only – well, you won't be surprised if he's quite *old*, will you? Remember he hasn't been in a garden keeping young like you.'

'All that will change,' the princess said confidently. 'He has only to eat the fruit of the garden. Why, look at Lotta – when she was a puppy, for a joke I gave her a fig from this tree, and you can see she is a puppy still, though she must be older than any other dog in the world! Oh, please hurry to bring Rudi here.'

'Why don't you come with me to his house?'

'That would not be correct etiquette,' she said with dignity. 'After all, I *am* royal.'

'Okay,' Mark said. 'I'll fetch him. Hope he doesn't think I'm crackers.'

'Give him this.' The princess took off a locket on a gold chain. It had a miniature of a romantically handsome young man with dark curling hair. 'My Rudi,' she explained fondly. Mark could just trace a faint resemblance to Mr Johansen.

He took the locket and hurried away. At the gate something made him look back: the princess and Lotta were sitting at the edge of the fountain, side by side. The princess had an arm round Lotta's neck; with the other hand she waved to him, just a little.

'Hurry!' she called again.

Mark made his way out of the house, through the spring-cleaning chaos, and flew down the village to Houndshaven Cottage. Mr Johansen was in the house this time, boiling up a noisome mass of meat and bones for the dogs' dinner. Mark said nothing at all, just handed him the locket. He took one look at it and staggered, putting his hand to his heart; anxiously, Mark led him to a chair.

'Are you all right, sir?'

'Yes, yes! It was only ze shock. Where did you get ziss, my boy?'

So Mark told him.

Surprisingly, Mr Johansen did not find anything odd about the story; he nodded his head several times as Mark related the various points.

'Yes, yes, her letter, I have it still' – he pulled out a worn little scrap of paper – 'but ze *Gartenbuch* it reached me never. Zat wicked Gertrud must haf sold it to some bookseller who sold it to Frühstücksgeschirrziegelsteinindustrie. And so she has been waiting all ziss time! My poor little Sophie!'

'Are you strong enough to come to her now?' Mark asked.

'*Natürlich!* But first we must give ze dogs zeir dinner; zey must not go hungry.'

So they fed the dogs, which was a long job as there were at least sixty and each had a different diet, including some very odd preferences like Swiss roll spread with Marmite and yeast pills wrapped in slices of caramel. Privately, Mark thought the dogs were a bit spoiled, but Mr Johansen was very careful to see that each visitor had just what it fancied.

'After all, zey are not mine! Must I not take good care of zem?'

At least two hours had gone by before the last willow-pattern plate was licked clean, and they were free to go. Mark made rings around Mr Johansen all the way up the village; the music master limped quietly along, smiling a little; from time to time he said, 'Gently, my friend. We do not run a race. Remember I am an old man.'

That was just what Mark did remember. He longed to see Mr Johansen young and happy once more.

The chaos in the Armitage house had changed its location: the front hall was now clean, tidy, and damp; the rumpus of vacuuming had shifted to the playroom. With a black hollow of apprehension in his middle, Mark ran through the open door and stopped, aghast. All the toys, tools, weapons, boxes, magazines, and bits of machinery had been rammed into the cupboards; the floor where his garden had been laid out was bare. Mrs Armitage was in the playroom taking down the curtains.

'*Mother!* Where's my Brekkfast Brikks garden?'

'Oh, darling, you didn't want it, did you? It was all dusty, I thought you'd finished it. I'm afraid I've burned it in the furnace. Really, you *must* try not to let this room get into such a clutter, it's perfectly disgraceful. Why, hullo, Mr Johansen, I'm afraid you've called at the worst possible moment. But I'm sure you'll understand how it is at spring-cleaning time.'

She rolled up her bundle of curtains, glancing worriedly at Mr Johansen; he looked rather odd, she thought. But he gave her his tired, gentle smile, and said,

'Why, yes, Mrs Armitage, I understand, I understand very well. Come, Mark. We have no business here, you can see.'

Speechlessly, Mark followed him. What was there to say?

'Never mind,' Mrs Armitage called after Mark. 'The Rice Nuts pack has a helicopter on it.'

Every week in *The Times* newspaper you will see this advertisement:

BREKKFAST BRIKKS PACKETS.
£100 offered for any in good condition,
whether empty or full.

So if you have any, you know where to send them.

But Mark is growing anxious; none have come in yet, and every day Mr Johansen seems a little thinner and more elderly. Besides, what will the princess be thinking?

HARRIET'S HAIRLOOM

'Oh, Mother,' Harriet said, as she did every year, 'can't I open my birthday presents at breakfast?'

'Certainly not! You know perfectly well that you weren't born till half past four. You get your birthday presents at tea-time, not before.'

'We could change the custom now that we're in our teens,' Harriet suggested cunningly. 'You know you hate having to get up at half past two in the morning for Mark's presents.'

But Mark objected strongly to any change, and Mrs Armitage added, 'In any case, don't forget that as it's your thirteenth birthday, you have to be shown into the Closed Room; there'd never be time to do that before school. Go and collect your schoolbooks now, and, Mark, wash the soot from behind your ears; if you must hunt for Lady Anne's pearls in the chimney, I wish you'd clean up before coming to breakfast.'

'You'd be as pleased as anyone else if I found them,' Mark answered.

Later, as he and Harriet walked to the school bus, Mark said, 'I think it's a rotten swindle that only girls in the family are allowed to go inside the Closed Room when they get to be thirteen. Suppose there's a monster like at Glamis, what'll you do?'

'Tame it,' Harriet said promptly. 'I shall feed it on bread-and-milk and lettuce.'

'That's hedgehogs, dope! Suppose it has huge teeth and tentacles and a poisonous sting three yards long?'

'Shut up! Anyway I don't suppose it is a monster. It would have starved long ago. It's probably just some mouldering old great-aunt in her coffin or something boring like that.'

Still, it was nice to have a Closed Room in the family, Harriet reflected, and she sat in the bus happily speculating about what it might contain – jewels, perhaps, rubies as big as tomatoes; or King Arthur's sword, Excalibur, left with the Armitage family for safekeeping when he went off to Avalon; or the Welsh bard, Taliesin, fallen asleep in the middle of a poem; or a cockatrice; or the vanished crew of the *Marie Celeste*, playing cards and singing shanties . . .

Harriet was still in a dreamy state when school began. The first lesson was Geography with old Mr Gubbins, so there was no need to pay attention; she sat trying to think of suitable pet names for cockatrices until she heard a muffled sobbing on her left.

' . . . is of course the Cathay of the ancients,' Mr Gubbins was rambling on. 'Marco Polo in his travels . . . '

Harriet looked cautiously around and saw that her best

friend and left-hand neighbour, Desiree, or Dizzry as everyone called her, was crying bitterly, hunched over the inkwell on her desk so that the tears ran into it.

Dizzry was the daughter of Ernie Perrow, the village chimney-sweep; the peculiarity of the Perrow family was that none of them ever grew to be more than six inches high. Instead of sitting at her desk in the usual way, Dizzry sat on top of it, at a small table and chair that Mark had obligingly made for her out of matchboxes.

'What's the matter?' whispered Harriet. 'Here, don't cry into the ink – you'll make it weaker than it is already. Haven't you a handkerchief?'

She pulled sewing things out of her own desk, snipped a shred off the corner of a tablecloth she was embroidering, and passed it to Dizzry, who gulped, nodded, took a deep breath, and wiped her eyes on it.

'What's the matter?' Harriet asked again.

'It was what Mr Gubbins said that started me off,' Dizzry muttered. 'Talking about Cathay. Our Min always used to say she'd a fancy to go to Cathay. She'd got it muddled up with *café*. She thought she'd get cake and raspberryade and ice cream there.'

'Well, so what?' said Harriet, who saw nothing to cry about in that.

'Haven't you heard? We've lost her – we've lost our Min!'

'Oh, my goodness! You mean she's died?'

'No, not *died*. Just lost. Nobody's seen her since yesterday breakfast time!'

Harriet privately thought this ought to have been rather

a relief for the family but was too polite to say so. Min, the youngest of the Perrow children, was a perfect little fiend, always in trouble of one kind or another. When not engaged in entering sweet jars in the village shop and stealing Butter Kernels or Quince Drops, she was probably worming her way through keyholes and listening to people's secrets, or hitching a free lift round the houses in the postman's pocket and jabbing him with a darning needle as a reward for the ride, or sculling about the pond on Farmer Beezeley's ducks and driving them frantic by tickling them under their wings, or galloping down the street on somebody's furious collie, or climbing into the vicar's TV and frightening him half to death by shouting, 'Time is short!' through the screen. She frequently ran fearful risks but seemed to have a charmed life. Everybody in the village heartily detested Min Perrow, but her older brothers and sisters were devoted to her and rather proud of her exploits.

Poor Dizzry continued to cry, on and off, for the rest of the day. Harriet tried to console her but it seemed horridly probable that Min had at last gone too far and been swallowed by a cow or drowned in a sump or rolled into a Swiss roll at the bakery while stealing jam – so many ill fates might easily have befallen her that it was hard to guess the likeliest.

'I'll help you hunt for her this evening,' Harriet promised, however, 'and so will Mark. As soon as my birthday tea's finished.'

Dizzry came home with Harriet for the birthday tea and was a little cheered by the cake, made in the shape of a penguin with blackcurrant icing and an orange beak, and by Harriet's presents, which included a do-it-yourself water-divining kit from Mark (a hazel twig and a bucket of water), an electronic guitar that could sing as well as play, a little pocket computer for working out sums, and from the children's fairy godmother a tube of endless toothpaste. Harriet was not particularly grateful for this last; the thought of toothpaste supplied for the rest of her life left her unmoved.

'I'd rather have an endless supply of liquorice,' she said crossly. 'Probably I won't have any teeth left by the time I'm ninety; what use will toothpaste be then?'

Her presents from Dizzry were by far the nicest: a pink-and-orange necklace of spindleberries, beautifully carved, and a starling named Alastair whom Dizzry had trained to take messages, answer the telephone or the front door, and carry home small quantities of shopping. (At first Harriet was a little anxious about Walrus the cat's reactions to this new member of the household, and indeed Walrus was somewhat aggressive, but Harriet found she had no need to worry: Alastair had also been trained to defend himself against cats, and Walrus soon learned to keep his paws to himself.)

'Now,' said Mrs Armitage rather nervously when the presents had been admired, 'I'd better show Harriet the Closed Room.'

Mr Armitage hurriedly retired to his study while Mark, controlling some natural feelings of envy, kindly said he would help Dizzry hunt for Min, and carried her off to inspect all the reapers and binders in Mr Beezeley's farmyard.

Harriet and Mrs Armitage went up to the attic, and Mrs Armitage paused before a cobweb-shrouded door and pulled a rusty key out of her pocket.

'Now you must say, "I, Harriet Armitage, solemnly swear not to reveal the secret of this room to any other soul in the world."'

'But when I grow up and have a daughter,' objected Harriet, 'won't I have to tell her, just as Great-Aunt Charlotte told you and you're telling me?'

'Well, yes, I suppose so,' Mrs Armitage said uncertainly. 'I'd rather forgotten how the oath went, to tell you the truth.'

'Why do we have to promise not to tell?'

'To be honest, I haven't the faintest idea.'

'Let's skip that bit – there doesn't seem much point to it – and just go in,' Harriet suggested. So they opened the door (it was very stiff, for it had been shut at least fifteen years) and went in.

The attic was dim, lit only through a patch of green glass tiles in the roof; it was quite empty except for a small, dusty loom, made of black wood with a stool to match.

'A loom?' said Harriet, very disappointed. 'Is *that* all?'

'It isn't an ordinary loom,' her mother corrected her. 'It's a hairloom. For weaving human hair.'

'Who wants to weave human hair? What can you make?'

'I suppose you make a human-hair mat. You must only use hair that's never been cut since birth.'

'Haven't you tried?'

'Oh, my dear, I never seemed to get a chance. By the time your father's Aunt Charlotte showed me the loom everyone was wearing their hair short; you couldn't get a piece long enough to weave for love or money. And then you children came along – somehow I never found time.'

'Well, *I* jolly well shall,' Harriet said. 'I'll try and get hold of some hair. I wonder if Miss Pring would let me have hers? I bet it's never been cut – she must have yards. Maybe you can make a cloak of invisibility, or the sort that turns swans into humans.'

Harriet was so pleased with this notion that only as they went downstairs did she think to ask, 'How did the loom get into the family?'

'I'm a bit vague about that,' Mrs Armitage admitted. 'I believe it belonged to a Greek ancestress that one of the crusading Armitages married and brought back to England. She's the one your middle name Penelope is after.'

Without paying much attention, Harriet went off to find Mark and Dizzry. Her father said they had gone along to the church, so she followed, pausing at the post office to ask elderly Miss Pring, the postmistress, if she would sell her long grey hair to be woven into a rug.

'It would look so pretty,' Harriet coaxed. 'I could dye some of it pink or blue.'

Miss Pring was not keen.

'Sell my hair? Cut it off? The idea! *Dye* it? What impertinence! Get along with you, saucebox!'

So Harriet had to abandon that scheme, but she stuck a

postcard on the notice board: HUMAN HAIR REQUIRED, UNCUT; BEST PRICES PAID, and posted another to the local paper. Then she joined Mark and Dizzry, who were searching the church organ pipes for Min, but without success.

Harriet had met several other members of the Perrow family on her way: Ernie, Min's father, driving an old doll's pushchair that he had fitted with an engine and turned into a convertible like a Model T Ford; old Gran Perrow, stomping along and gloomily shouting 'Min!' down all the drainholes; and Sid, one of the boys, riding a bike made from cocoa tins and poking out nests from the hedges with a bamboo stick in case Min had been abducted.

When it was too dark to go on searching, Harriet and Mark left Dizzry at Rose Cottage, where the Perrows lived. 'We'll go looking tomorrow!' they called. And Harriet said, 'Don't worry too much.'

'I expect she'll be all right wherever she is,' Mark said. 'I'd back Min against a mad bull any day.'

As they walked home he asked Harriet, 'What about the Closed Room, then? Any monsters?'

'No, very dull, just a hairloom.'

'I say, you shouldn't tell me, should you?'

'It's all right – we agreed to skip the promise to keep it secret.'

'What a letdown,' Mark said. 'Who wants an old loom?' They arrived home to trouble. Their father was complaining, as he did every day, about soot on the carpets and black tidemarks on the bathroom basin and towels.

'Well, if you don't *want* me to find Lady Anne's necklace—' Mark said aggrievedly. 'If it was worth a thousand pounds when she lost it in 1660, think what it would fetch now.'

'Why in heaven's name would it be up the *chimney*? Stop arguing and go to bed. And brush your teeth!'

'I'll lend you some of my toothpaste,' Harriet said.

'Just the same,' Mark grumbled, brushing his teeth with yards of toothpaste so that the foam stood out on either side of his face like Dundreary whiskers and flew all over the bathroom, 'Ernie Perrow definitely told me that his great-great-great-grandfather, Oliver Perrow, had a row with Lady Anne Armitage because she ticked him off for catching field mice in her orchard; Oliver was the village sweep, and her pearls vanished after that; Ernie thinks old Oliver stuck them in the chimney to teach her a lesson, and then he died, eaten by a fox before he had a chance to tell anyone. But Ernie's sure that's where the pearls are.'

'Perhaps Min's up there looking for them too.'

'Not her! She'd never do anything as useful as that.'

Harriet had asked Alastair the starling to call her at seven; in fact, she was raised at half past six by loud bangs on the front door.

'For heaven's sake, somebody tell that maniac to go away!' shouted Mr Armitage from under his pillow.

Harriet flung on a dressing gown and ran downstairs. What was her surprise to find at the door a little old man in a white duffel coat with the hood up. He carried a very large parcel wrapped in sacking. Harriet found the sharp look he gave her curiously disconcerting.

'Would it be Miss Armitage now, the young lady who put the advertisement in the paper then?'

'About hair?' Harriet said eagerly. 'Yes, I did. Have you got some, Mr—?'

'Mr Thomas Jones the Druid, I am. Beautiful hair I have then, look you – finer than any lady's in the land. Only see now till I get this old parcel undone!' And he dumped the bundle down at her feet and started unknotting the cords. Harriet helped. When the last half-hitch twanged apart, a great springy mass of hair came boiling out. It was soft and fine, dazzlingly white, with just a few strands of black, and smelled slightly of tobacco.

'There, now, indeed to goodness! Did you ever see finer?'

'But,' said Harriet, 'has it ever been cut short?' She very much hoped that it had not; it seemed impossible that they would ever be able to parcel it up again.

'Never has a scissor blade been laid to it, till I cut it all off last night,' the old man declared.

Harriet wondered whose it was; something slightly malicious and self-satisfied about the old man's grin as he said 'I cut it all off' prevented her from asking.

'Er – how much do you want for it?' she inquired cautiously.

'Well, indeed,' he said. 'It would be hard to put a price on such beautiful hair, whatever.'

At this moment there came an interruption. A large van drew up in front of the Armitage house. On its sides iridescent bubbles were painted, and, in rainbow colours, the words SUGDEN'S SOAP.

A uniformed driver jumped out, consulting a piece of paper.

'Mr Mark Armitage lives here?' he asked Harriet. She nodded.

'Will he take delivery of one bathroom, complete with shower, tub, footbath, deluxe basin, steel-and-enamel hairdryer, and a six years' supply of Sugden's Soap?'

'I suppose so,' Harriet said doubtfully. 'You're sure there's no mistake?'

The delivery note certainly had Mark's name and address on it.

'Mark!' Harriet yelled up the stairs, forgetting it was still only seven a.m. 'Did you order a bathroom? Because it's come.'

'Merciful goodness!' groaned the voice of Mr Armitage. 'Has *no* one any consideration for my hours of rest?'

Mark came running down, looking slightly embarrassed.

'Darn it,' he said as he signed the delivery note, 'I never expected I'd get a *bathroom*; I was hoping for the free cruise to Saposoa.'

'Where shall we put it, guv?' said the driver, who was plainly longing to go away and get some breakfast at the nearest truck-driver's pull-up.

Mark looked about him vaguely. At this moment Mr Armitage came downstairs in pyjamas and a very troublesome frame of mind.

'Bathrooms? Bathrooms?' he said. 'You've bought a bathroom? What the blazes did you want to go and get a bathroom for? Isn't the one we have good enough for you, pray? You leave it dirty enough. Who's going to pay for this? And why has nobody put the kettle on?'

'I won it,' Mark explained, blushing. 'It was the second prize in the Sugden's Soap competition. In the *Radio Times*, you know.'

'What did you have to do?' Harriet asked.

'Ten uses for soap in correct order of importance.'

'I bet *washing* came right at the bottom,' growled his father. 'Greased stairs and fake soft centres in chocolates are more your mark.'

'Anyway he won!' Harriet pointed out. 'Was that all you had to do?'

'You had to write a couplet too.'

'What was yours?'

Mark blushed even pinker. 'Rose or White or Heliotrope, Where there's life there's Sugden's Soap.'

'Come on now,' said the truck driver patiently. 'We don't want to be here all day, do we? Where shall we put it, guv? In the garden?'

'Certainly not,' snapped Mr Armitage. He was proud of his garden.

'How about in the field?' suggested Harriet diplomatically. 'Then Mark and I can wash in it, and you needn't be upset by soot on the towels.'

'That's true,' her father said, brightening a little. 'All right, stick it in the field. And now will somebody *please* put on a kettle and make a cup of tea, is that too much to ask?'

And he stomped back to bed, leaving Mark and the driver to organize the erection of the bathroom in the field beside the house. Harriet put a kettle on the stove and went back to Mr Jones the Druid, who was sunning himself on the front porch.

'Have you decided what you want for your hair?' she asked.

'Oh,' he said. 'That is a grand new bathroom you have with you! Lucky that is, indeed. Now I am thinking I do not want any money at all for my fine bundle of hair, but only to strike a bargain with you.'

'Very well,' Harriet said cautiously.

'No bathroom I have at my place, see? Hard it is to wash the old beard, and chilly of a winter morning in the stream. But if you and your brother, that I can see is a kindhearted obliging young gentleman, would let me come and give it a bit of a lather now and again in *your* bathroom—'

'Why, yes, of course,' Harriet said. 'I'm sure Mark won't mind at all.'

'So it shall be, then. Handy that will be, indeed. Terrible deal of the old beard there is, look you, and grubby she do get.'

With that he undid his duffel coat and pulled back the hood. All around his head and wound about his body like an Indian sari was a prodigiously long white beard that he proceeded to untwine until it trailed on the ground. It was similar to the white hair in the bundle, but not so clean.

'Is that somebody's beard, then?' Harriet asked, pointing to the bundle.

'My twin brother, Dai Jones the Bard. Bathroom he has by him, the lucky old *cythryblwr*! But soon I will be getting a bigger one. Made a will, my dad did, see, leaving all of his money to the one of us who has the longest and whitest beard on our ninetieth birthday; that falls tomorrow on Midsummer Day. So I crept into his house last night and cut his beard off while he slept; hard he'll find it now to grow another beard in time. All Dada's money I will be getting, he, he, he!'

Mr Jones the Druid chuckled maliciously.

Harriet could not help thinking he was rather a wicked old man, but a bargain was a bargain, so she picked up the bundle of beard, with difficulty, and was about to say goodbye when he stopped her.

'Weaving the hair into a mat, you would be, isn't it?' he said wheedlingly. 'There is a fine bath mat it would make! Towels and curtains there are in the grand new bathroom of yours but no bath mat – pity that is, indeed.' He gave her a cunning look out of the corner of his eyes, but Harriet would not commit herself.

'Come along this evening, then, I will, for a good old wash-up before my birthday,' Mr Jones said. He wound himself in his beard again and went off with many nods and bows. Harriet ran to the field to see how the bathroom was getting on. Mark had it nearly finished. True enough, there was no bath mat. It struck Harriet that Mr Jones's suggestion was not a bad one.

'I'll start weaving a mat as soon as we've had another thorough hunt for Min Perrow,' she said. 'Saturday, thank goodness, no school.'

However, during breakfast (which was late, owing to various events) Ernie Perrow drove along in the pushchair with Lily and Dizzry to show the Armitages an air-letter which had arrived from the British Consul in Cathay.

Dear Sir or Madam,

Kindly make earliest arrangements to send passage money back to England for your daughter Hermione who has had herself posted here, stowed away in a box of Health Biscuits. Please forward without delay fare and expenses totalling £1,093.7s.1d.

A postscript, scrawled by Min, read: 'Dun it at larst! Nuts to silly old postmun!'

'Oh, what shall we do?' wept Mrs Perrow. 'A thousand pounds! How can we ever find it?'

While the grown-ups discussed ways and means to raise the money, Mark went back to his daily search for Lady Anne's pearls, and Harriet took the woebegone Dizzry up to the attic, hoping to distract her by a look at the hairloom.

Dizzry was delighted with it. 'Do let's do some weaving!' she said. 'I like weaving better than anything.'

So Harriet lugged in the great bundle of beard, and they set up the loom. Dizzry was an expert weaver. She had been making beautiful scarves for years on a child's toy loom. She could nip to and fro with the shuttle almost faster than Harriet's eyes could follow. By teatime they had woven a handsome thick white mat with the words 'Bath Ma' across the middle (there had not been quite enough black for the final T).

'Anyway you can see what it's meant to be,' Harriet said. They took the new mat and spread it in their elegant bathroom.

'Tell you what,' Mark said, 'we'd better hide the bath and basin plugs when Min gets back or she'll climb in and drown herself.'

'Oh, I do wonder what Dad and Mum are doing about getting her back,' sighed Dizzry, who was sitting on a sponge. She wiped her eyes on a corner of Harriet's cloth.

'Let's go along to your house,' Harriet said, 'and find out.'

There was an atmosphere of deep gloom in the Perrow household. Ernie had arranged to sell his Model T pushchair, the apple of his eye, to the Motor Museum at Beaulieu.

'A thousand pounds they say they'll give for it,' he said miserably. 'With that and what I've saved from the chimney sweeping, we can just about pay the fare. Won't I half clobber young Min when I get her back, the little varmint!'

'Mrs Perrow,' Harriet said, 'may Dizzry come and spend the evening at our house, as Mother and Daddy are going to a dance? And have a bath in our new bathroom? Mother says it's all right, and I'll take great care of her.'

'Oh, very well, if your ma doesn't mind,' sighed Mrs Perrow. 'I'm so distracted I hardly know if I'm coming or going. Don't forget your wash things, Diz, and the bathsalts.'

Harriet was enchanted with the bathsalts, no bigger than hundreds-and-thousands. On Midsummer Eve the Armitage children were allowed to stay up as late as they liked. Mark, a single-minded boy, said he intended to go on hunting for

Lady Anne's necklace in the chimney. The girls had their baths and then went up to Harriet's room with a bagful of apples and the gramophone, intending to have a good gossip.

At half past eleven, Harriet, happening to glance out of the window, saw a light in the field.

'That must be Mr Jones,' she said. 'I'd forgotten he was coming to shampoo his beard. It's not Mark, I can still hear him bumping around in the chimney.' There was indeed an excited banging to be heard from the chimney-breast, but it was as nothing compared with the terrible racket that suddenly broke out in the field. They heard shouts and cries of rage, thuds, crashes, and the tinkle of smashed glass.

'Heavens, what can be going on?' cried Harriet. She flung up the sash and prepared to climb out of the window.

'Wait for me!' cried Dizzry.

'Here, jump into my pocket. Hold tight!'

Harriet slid down the wisteria and dashed across the garden. A moment later they arrived at the bathroom door and witnessed a wild scene.

Evidently, Mr Jones the Druid had finished washing his beard and had been about to leave when he saw his doom waiting for him outside the door in the form of another, very angry old man who was trying to batter his way in.

'It must be his brother!' Harriet whispered. 'Mr Jones the Bard!'

The second old man had no beard, only a ragged white frill cut short round his chin. He was shouting:

'Wait until I catch you, you *hocsdwr*, you *herwhaliwr*, you *ffrawddunio*, you wicked old *llechwr*! A snake would think shame to spit on you! Cutting off your brother's beard, indeed! Just let me get at you and I'll trim you to spillikins, I'll shave your beard round your eyebrows!' And he beat on the door with a huge pair of shears. A pane of glass fell in and broke on the bathroom's tiles; then the whole door gave way.

Dizzry left Harriet's pocket and swarmed up onto her head to see what was happening. They heard a fearful bellow from inside the bathroom, a stamping and crashing, fierce grunts, the hiss of the shower, and more breaking glass.

'Hey!' Harriet shouted. 'Stop wrecking our bathroom!'

No answer. The sound of battle went on.

Then the bathroom window flew open and Jones the Druid shot out, all tangled in his beard, which was snowy white now, but still damp. He had the bath mat rolled up under his arm. As soon as he was out, he flung it down, leapt upon it, and shouted, 'Take me out of here!'

The mat took off vertically and hovered, about seven feet up, while Jones the Druid began hauling in his damp beard, hand over hand.

'Come back!' Harriet cried. 'You've got no right to go off with our bath mat.'

Jones the Bard came roaring out of the window, waving his shears.

'Come back, *ystraffaldiach*! Will you come down off there and let me mince you into macaroni? Oh, you wicked old weasel, I'll trim your beard shorter than an earwig's toenails!'

He made a grab for the bath mat, but it was just out of reach.

'He, he, he!' cackled Jones the Druid up above. 'You

didn't know your fine beard would make up so nice into a flying carpet, did you, brother? Has to be woven on a hair-loom on Midsummer Eve, and then it'll carry you faster than the Aberdovey Flyer.'

'Just let me get at you, *rheibiwr*!' snarled Jones the Bard, making another vain grab.

But Dizzry, who was now jumping up and down on top of Harriet's head, made a tremendous spring, grabbed hold of a trailing strand of Jones the Druid's beard, and hauled herself up onto a corner of the flying bath mat.

'O dammo!' gasped the Druid at the sight of her. He was so taken aback that he lost his balance, staggered, and fell headlong on top of his brother. There was a windmill of confusion of arms and legs, all swamped by the foaming mass of beard. Then Jones the Bard grabbed his shears with a shout of triumph and began chopping away great swags of white hair.

Harriet, however, paid no attention to these goings-on.

'Dizzry!' she shouted, cupping her hands round her mouth. 'It's a wishing-mat. Make it take you—'

Dizzry nodded. She needed no telling. 'Take me to Cathay!' she cried, and the mat soared away through the milky air of Midsummer Night.

At this moment Mark came running across the field.

'Oh, Mark,' Harriet burst out. 'Look what those old fiends have done to our bathroom! It's ruined! They ought to be made to pay for it.'

Mark glanced through the broken window. The place was certainly a shambles: bath and basin were both smashed, the sponge rack was wrapped round the hairdryer, the towels were trodden into a soggy pulp, and the curtains were in ribbons.

The Jones brothers were in equally bad shape. Jones the Bard was kneeling on Jones the Druid's stomach; he had managed to trim every shred off his brother's head, but he himself was as bald as a coot. Both had black eyes and swollen lips.

'Oh well,' Mark said. 'They seem to have trouble of their own. I bet neither of them comes into that legacy now. And I never did care much for washing anyway. Look, here comes Dizzry back.'

The bath mat swooped to a three-point landing; Dizzry and Min rolled off it, laughing and crying.

'You wicked, wicked, bad little girl,' Dizzry cried, shaking and hugging her sister at the same time. 'Don't you ever dare do such a thing again!'

'Now I will take my own property which is my lawful beard,' said Mr Jones the Bard, and he jumped off his brother's stomach onto the mat and addressed it in a flood of Welsh, which it evidently understood, for it rose in the air and flew off in a westerly direction. Mr Jones the Druid slunk away across the field looking, Dizzry said, as hangdog as a cat that has fallen into the milk.

'Now we've lost our bath mat,' Harriet sighed.

'I'll help you make another,' Dizzry said, 'there's plenty of hair lying about. And at least we've got Min back.'

'Was it nice in Cathay, Min?' Mark asked.

'Smashing. I had rice cake and cherry ice and Coca-Cola.'

At this point Mr and Mrs Armitage returned from their dance and kindly drove Dizzry and Min home to break the joyful news to their parents. Harriet and Mark had a try at putting the bathroom back to rights, but it was really past hope.

'I must say, trouble certainly haunts this household,' remarked Mr Armitage, when he came back and found them at it. 'Hurry up and get to bed, you two. Do you realize it's four o'clock on Midsummer Morning? Oh, Lord, I suppose now we'll have to go back to the old regime of sooty footmarks all over the bathroom.'

'Certainly not,' said Mark. 'I'd forgotten to tell you. I found Lady Anne's pearls.'

He pulled them out and dangled them: a soot-black, six-foot double strand of pearls as big as cobnuts, probably worth a king's ransom.

'Won't Ernie Perrow be pleased to know they really were in the chimney?' he said.

'Oh, go to bed!' snapped his father. 'I'm fed up with hearing about the Perrows.'

MRS NUTTI'S FIREPLACE

Mark, who wished to get rid of the space gun his great-uncle had sent him, and acquire something more useful, had brought home a copy of *Exchange and Mart*.

'"Princess-type boiler fireplace exchanged for gent's bicycle,"' he read aloud consideringly.

'But we don't want a fireplace,' Harriet pointed out. 'And we haven't a bicycle.'

'Or there's five gross jazz-coloured balloons, a tiger's head, and two whale teeth. Offered in exchange for go-kart or griffin's eggs.'

'The balloons would be nice.' Harriet swallowed her last bite of cake – they were having a Friday tea – and came to hang over his shoulder. 'If we had a go-kart.'

'"Sale or exchange road-breaker tools interested arc welder, spray plant, w.h.y. Buyer collects." I do wonder w.h.y.? They seem queer things to collect.'

'"Pocket Gym, judo suit, height increaser, neck developer, strength course, weights and Dynamic Tension course." *That* seems a bargain. Only three pounds.'

'No height increasers in this family, thanks,' said Mr Armitage, without looking up from his evening paper. 'Or weight increasers. Kindly remember the house is three hundred years old.'

'"A hundredweight of green garnishing in ten-inch sections, de-rinder and sausage-spooling machinery"; they might come in handy for Christmas decorations,' Harriet said thoughtfully.

'"One million toys at 65p per 100, including Woo-Woos, Jumping Shrimp, et cetera."'

'Mother wouldn't like the Jumping Shrimp.'

'I would not,' agreed Mrs Armitage, pouring herself another cup of tea.

'*Gosh*! "7 in. span baboon spider with ½ in. fangs, £5."'

'*No*.'

'I don't really want it,' Harriet said hastily. 'But – listen – "2½-year-old Himalayan bears, only £42" – oh, Mother, they'd be lovely. "Or would exchange griffin's eggs." What a pity we haven't any of those. Lots of people seem to want them.'

'*Forty-two pounds?* You can't be serious. Besides, it would be too warm for Himalayan bears here.'

'"Various rattlesnakes, 6ft Mangrove snake, £8."'

'Shall we get away from this section?' Mr Armitage suggested, lowering his paper. 'Anyway, isn't it time for your music lesson, Mark?'

'Yes, in just a minute. Here's something that might interest Mr Johansen,' Mark said. '"Would exchange room in town for room in country; pleasant outlook required. View by appointment." Mr Johansen was saying only last week that he wished he had a bedsit in London so that he could go to concerts and not always have to miss the last movement to catch the ten-fifteen. I'll take this along to show him.'

'Bring it back, though,' said Harriet, who did not want to lose track of the Himalayan bears.

Mark was very fond of Mr Johansen, his music teacher, a sad, gentle man who, as well as teaching the piano and violin, had for many years run a dogs' weekend guest house. Lately, however, he had given up the dogs because he said he was growing too old to exercise them properly. When young, he had been in love with a German princess who had been lost to him by an unfortunate bit of amateur magic. He had never married. Everybody in the village liked him very much.

'Look, Mr Johansen,' said Mark, before settling down to his five-finger exercises. 'You were saying only the other day that it was a pity not to use your spare room; here's somebody wanting to exchange a room in town for one in the country. Don't you think that would do for you?'

'Ach, so?' Mr Johansen carefully scanned the advertisement. 'Why yes, ziss might certainly be useful. I wvonder wvere ziss room is? I will write off to ze box number.' He made a note of it.

A week passed. Harriet, who had developed a passionate wish for a Himalayan bear, was hardly seen; she spent every evening making very beautiful dolls' furniture out of egg-shells, plastic egg-boxes, yoghurt pots, snail shells, and shampoo containers; when she had a hamper full of furniture, she hoped to sell it all to a London toyshop for the price of a bear. She had not mentioned this plan to Mrs Armitage, who thought that a cat and a unicorn were sufficient pets for one family.

'Candleberry's lovely to ride on,' Harriet said to Mark, 'but you can't bring him indoors. And Walrus is always out catching mice. A bear would be cosy.'

Mark was in the middle of his lesson with Mr Johansen the following week when there came a brisk peal at the front-door bell. The music master opened the door and let in an uncommon-looking old lady, very short, very wrinkled, rather like a tortoise with a disagreeable expression, wearing rimless glasses and a raincoat and sou'-wester which might have been made of alligator-skin. She limped, and walked with a stick, and carried a carpet-bag which seemed to be quite heavy.

'Answer to advertisement,' she said in a businesslike manner. 'Name, Mrs Nutti. Room in town exchange room in country. Which room? This one?'

She stumped into the music-room. Mark twirled around on his music-stool to look at her.

'No, no. Upstairs,' said Mr Johansen. 'Ziss way, if you please.'

'Good. Upstairs better. Much better. Better outlook. Air fresher. Burglars not so likely. Can't do with burglars – Well, show way, then!'

Mr Johansen went ahead, she followed; Mark came, too.

The music teacher's house was really a bungalow, and the

spare room was really an attic-loft, with sloping ceilings. But it had big dormer windows with a pleasant view of fields and woods; Mr Johansen had painted the walls (or ceiling) sky blue, so that you could imagine you were out on the roof, rather than inside a room; there was blue linoleum on the floor, an old-fashioned bed with brass knobs and a patchwork quilt, and an even older-fashioned washstand with a jug and basin covered in pink roses.

'Very nice,' said Mrs Nutti, looking round. 'Very nice view. Take it for three months. Beginning now.'

'But wait,' objected Mark, seeing that Mr Johansen was rather dazed by this rapid dealing. '*He* hasn't seen *your* room yet. And shouldn't you exchange references or something? I'm sure people always do that.'

'References?' snapped Mrs Nutti. 'No point. Not exchanging references – exchanging rooms! You'll find my room satisfactory. Excellent room. Show now.'

She snapped her fingers. Mark and Mr Johansen both lost their balance, as people do in a fairground trick room with a tilting floor, and fell heavily.

Mark thought as he fell,

'That's funny, I'd have said there was lino on this floor, not carpet.'

'*Donnerwetter!*' gasped Mr Johansen (Mark had fallen on top of him). They clambered to their feet, rather embarrassed.

'It is zose heavy lorries,' the music master began explaining apologetically. 'Zey do shake ze house so when zey pass; but it is not so very often—'

Then he stopped, staring about him in bewilderment, for Mrs Nutti was nowhere to be seen.

Nor, for that matter, was the brass-headed bed, the patchwork quilt, the washstand with jug and roses, the blue ceiling—

'Gosh,' said Mark. He crossed to one of two high, lattice casement windows, treading noiselessly on the thick carpet, which was intricately patterned in red, blue, rose-colour, black, and gold. '*Gosh*, Mr Johansen, do come and look out.'

The music master joined him at the window and they gazed together into a city filled with dusk, whose lights were beginning to twinkle out under a deep-blue clear sky with a few matching stars. Below them, a street ran downhill to a wide river or canal; a number of slender towers, crowned with onion-shaped domes, rose in every direction; there were masts of ships on the water and the cries of gulls could be heard.

Immediately below there was a small cobbled square and, on the opposite side of it, a café with tables set under a big leafy tree which had lights strung from its branches. A group of men with odd instruments – long curving pipes, bulb-shaped drums, outsized Jews' harps – were playing a plaintive tune, while another man went around among the tables, holding out a wooden bowl.

'I do not understand,' muttered Mr Johansen. 'Wvat has happened? Wvere are we? Wvere is Mrs Nutti? Wvere is my *room*?'

'Why, don't you see, sir?' said Mark, who, more accustomed to this kind of thing, was beginning to guess what had happened. 'This must be Mrs Nutti's room that she said she'd show you. I thought she meant in London, but of course in the advertisement it didn't actually say London it just said 'room in town' – I wonder what town this is?'

'But – ach, *Himmel* – zen wvere *is* my room?'

'Well, I suppose Mrs Nutti has got it. This seems quite a nice room, though, don't you think?'

Mr Johansen gazed about it rather wildly, pushing long thin hands through his white hair until the strands were all standing on end and he looked like a gibbon.

Mrs Nutti's room was furnished in a much more stately way than the humble attic bedroom. For a start, there was a massive four-poster bed with crimson damask hangings. The walls, also, were covered with some kind of damask, which made the room rather dark. Two tall black polished cabinets on claw feet stood against the wall facing the windows. A lamp in a boat-shaped gilt container hung suspended by a chain from the ceiling and threw a dim light. A velvet curtain, held back by a tasselled cord, partly covered the doorway; a small organ stood to the right of the door. Strangest of all, opposite the doorway there was a fireplace with a large heavy pair of polished metal andirons and a massive white marble mantelpiece which appeared to have suffered from some accident. The right side of the mantel was supported by a large carved marble heraldic beast with a collar round its neck, but the beast that should have supported the left-hand side was missing; it had apparently been dragged out of the wall, like a decoration from an iced cake, leaving nothing but a jagged hole.

'*That's* a bit of a mess,' Mark said. 'I do think Mrs Nutti should have put it right for you before she lent you her room. It's rather a shame; the monster on the other side is awfully nice. A kind of furry eagle.'

'A griffin,' corrected Mr Johansen absently. 'Ze legs, you see, are zose of a lion. Head, zat of an eagle, also wvings. But wvere *is* zis Mrs Nutti?'

'Wherever she is, she's left her carpet-bag behind,' said Mark, picking it off the floor. 'Blimey, what a weight. Hey, Mrs Nutti? Are you downstairs?'

He put the bag down again, walked through the open door, and stuck his head back through again to say, 'She really has done a neat job, Mr Johansen, it's still your landing outside.'

Bemusedly, Mr Johansen followed him out and discovered that, as Mark had said, the transformation of the loft-room went no farther than the door; outside were Mr Johansen's tidy bare landing, his coconut-matted stairs, and his prints of Alpine flora.

They went down, expecting to find Mrs Nutti in the music-room. But she had gone.

'Back to wherever she came from, I suppose,' Mark said.

'Taking my room wizz her,' Mr Johansen murmured plaintively.

'But really, sir, hers is quite a nice room, don't you think? And it has a smashing view. I know it's not London, which is what you wanted, but maybe they have concerts in this town, too. Where do you suppose it is?'

'How should I know?' said poor Mr Johansen, twisting his hair some more.

'Do let's go back upstairs and have another look.' But by the time they had gone back, full dark had fallen on the town outside the window of the new room, and not much could be seen except a wide prospect of twinkling lights. They could hear music from across the square, and smell delicious smells of herbs and grilled meat.

'We'll have to come back in daylight,' Mark suggested. 'Tell you one thing, though, this place must be east of England; it gets dark sooner.'

'Zat is so,' agreed Mr Johansen. 'In any case, I suppose zose towers are minarets; zis town is perhaps in Turkey or Persia.'

'What's Turkish music like, is it nice? Shall we have a wander round the streets and ask where the place is?'

Mr Johansen was somewhat hesitant about this; it took Mark a while to persuade him.

But now they came up against a difficulty: they could see the town, but there seemed to be no way of getting into it. If they went downstairs and out through Mr Johansen's front door, they merely found themselves in his ordinary garden, walking between neat rows of Canterbury bells towards the commonplace village street.

'We'll have to jump out of the window,' Mark said. But it was a very much higher drop from Mrs Nutti's window – and onto a cobbled street at that – than from Mr Johansen's attic. Mr Johansen demurred.

'Never should I be able to face your dear muzzer if you

wvere to break your leg. Besides, how should we get back?' Mark had not considered this problem.

'I'll bring our fruit-ladder from home tomorrow morning,' he said. 'Perhaps I'd better be off now; Mother gets worried if I'm more than three-quarters of an hour late for supper, and thinks I've fallen in a river or something.'

Harriet was greatly interested in the story of Mr Johansen's room-exchange.

'I wonder *why* Mrs Nutti wanted to swap?' she pondered, and made Mark tell her over and over the few not particularly enlightening things the old lady had said.

'She seemed worried about burglars? And part of the fireplace was missing? Perhaps burglars had gone off with it?'

'You'd hardly think anyone would pinch half a fireplace,' Mark objected. 'Still, it was gone, that's true. Maybe she wanted to make sure no one could go off with the other half.'

'What was in the carpet-bag she left behind? Did you look? Do you think she left it by mistake or on purpose?'

'I didn't look. It was jolly heavy, whatever it was. Maybe she got fed up with carrying it about.'

'When you go down tomorrow, I'm coming too,' Harriet said firmly.

'Good, then you can help carry the ladder.'

Taking the ladder was a waste of time, however, as they soon discovered. They leaned it up against the front of the house, so that its narrow top was wedged firmly against what appeared to be the window of Mr Johansen's attic.

Then they rang the door-bell and the music master let them in.

'Is the room still there, sir? Has Mrs Nutti been back? Did she fetch her bag? Can you still see the city?'

'Ja – ja – ze room is still zere, and ze bag also. But Frau Nutti has not returned. You wvish to see it?' he asked Harriet kindly.

'Oh yes, please!'

Mark and Harriet ran eagerly upstairs, Mr Johansen following more slowly.

'There!' said Mark with pride, pointing to the view.

'Coo!' breathed Harriet, taking it all in.

It was blazing daylight now, and obviously hot, hot weather, most unlike the grey, chilly June day they had left behind downstairs. Dogs lay panting in the shade under the big tree. Men in caps like chopped-off cones sat sipping coffee and cool drinks. Boats with coloured sails plied to and fro across the river.

'What a gorgeous place,' said Harriet. 'Do let's go down. *Oh* – where's the ladder?'

'Not there,' said Mark sadly.

'What a swindle. I've an idea though – next time we come, we'll bring a rope. Then we can tie it to the window-catch and climb down.'

Mark cheered up at this practical plan. 'It's bad luck about your concerts, though, sir; still, I suppose it's only for three months.'

'Is no matter. I can listen to zose men across ze square; zeir music is most uncommon. Also, I have ze organ to play on.'

He sat down at the little organ, fiddled around with

bellows and pedals, and suddenly produced a short, sweet, powerful snatch of melody.

'Oh, do go on!' cried Harriet, as he stopped.

But he, looking round, said, 'Wvat wvas zat noise?'

A kind of crack or tap had come from the other side of the four-poster. Harriet ran round.

'It sounded like an electric bulb going. Oh, is this Mrs Nutti's bag? Heavens, it's heavy – whatever can there be in it?'

Harriet parted the flaps of the bag, which was not fastened, and began lifting out masses of empty paper bags, crumpled old magazines, newspapers, tissues, paper napkins, and other wadding.

'What a lot of junk. There's something hard and heavy right at the bottom though – quite big, too. Oh, it's an egg.'

Mr Johansen got up from the organ-stool and came to look over their shoulders at the contents of the carpet-bag.

An egg it certainly was, and no common egg either. It was a good deal bigger than a rugby ball; it might just have fitted into the oval kind of washing-up bowl. It was plain white, but veined over with faint greenish-blue lines. Egg-shaped.

'How queer that Mrs Nutti should have forgotten about it—' Harriet was beginning, when the sound came from the egg again – crack!

'It's hatching!'

At this, Mr Johansen suddenly became very upset.

'No, no, zis I cannot have. Zis is too much! Her room, yes, I do not object, provided she take goot care of my room,

I wvill do ze same for hers. But to have care of an egg, no, no, zat is ze outside, *das tut mir zehr leid*, I am not an incubator! Ze doggies I haf give up, because I can no longer take sufficient care—'

'I'll hatch it, I'll look after it!' said Harriet eagerly. 'I've hatched lots of owls' eggs, I'll put it in our airing-cupboard, I'll look after it carefully, Mr Johansen. I'm sure Mother won't mind. Oh, do you suppose it could be a roc?'

'Not big enough,' said Mark.

Mr Johansen looked doubtful and distressed. 'Suppose Frau Nutti come back? It is, after all, her egg?'

'Then you tell her to come up the road to us,' Mark said. 'My sister really knows a lot about eggs, sir, she's an expert chick-raiser.'

'In zat case, best to get it home before it hatches quite out, *nicht wahr*?'

This proved a difficult task. The carpet-bag was so heavy that it took them all their united strength to get it down the stairs.

'And you said Mrs Nutti was a little old lady?' said Harriet, scarlet with effort. 'How can she ever have carried it all the way from—'

'All the way from wherever she came from?'

'Well, *we* certainly can't carry it from here to home. Mr Johansen, could we possibly borrow your wheelbarrow?'

'*Jawohl*, yes indeed,' said Mr Johansen, only too glad to be rid of the responsibility of the egg before it hatched. They balanced the fruit-ladder across the barrow and put the carpet-bag on top of the ladder, and so set off for home. Mr

Johansen watched them anxiously until they were out of sight; then he started upstairs, going slowly at first but faster and faster. He entered Mrs Nutti's room, sat down at the organ, and was soon lost, deaf, and regardless of anything but the beautiful music he was making.

When Harriet and Mark reached the Armitage house and unloaded the carpet-bag, they were disconcerted to find that the egg's weight had bent the ladder into a V like a hockey-stick.

'Oh dear,' Harriet said. 'I'm afraid Father's not going to be very pleased.'

Luckily their parents were out, so they were able to manhandle the egg upstairs without interference. A cast-iron cannonball would not have been much harder to deal with.

'What kind of bird can it possibly be?' panted Harriet.

Mark had a theory, but he wasn't going to commit himself just yet.

'Maybe it comes from some planet where the atmosphere is less dense. Anyway, whatever it is, it seemed to enjoy Mr Johansen's music. Perhaps we ought to play to it, to help it hatch.'

'No organ, though; it'll have to be satisfied with recorders.'

The egg took longer to hatch than they had expected; perhaps the recorder music was not so stimulating. A couple of weeks went by. Occasional cracking noises came from the airing-cupboard, but Harriet had carefully swathed the egg in winter blankets, so that it was not visible; Mrs Armitage said absently, 'I do hope the immersion heater isn't going to blow up again,' but she was busy making strawberry jam and did not investigate the noises. 'Why have you children taken to playing your recorders on the upstairs landing all day long? Can't you find anything better to do?'

'Rehearsing for the fête,' Harriet said promptly.

'It seems a funny place to rehearse.'

'Well, it's warm, you see – just by the airing-cupboard.'

At last the egg burst.

'Good God, what's that?' said Mr Armitage, rushing in from the garden, where he had been thinning out lettuces.

'Oh my gracious, do you think someone's planted a bomb on us?' exclaimed his wife, dropping a pot of jam on the kitchen floor.

'More likely something those children have been up to,' said their loving father.

Mark and Harriet had been eating their elevenses – apples and cheese – in the playroom.

At the tremendous bang they looked at each other with instantaneous comprehension of what had happened, and raced upstairs.

'Heavens! The smell!' gasped Harriet.

It was very strong.

'Sulphur,' said Mark knowledgeably.

There was a good deal of mess about, too. The airing-cupboard door was a splintered wreck, and the floor and the walls for some distance round were splashed with yellow goo, like egg-yolk, only more so. Several windows were cracked.

A tangle of damp and soggy blankets and towels on the

upstairs landing made it difficult to get to the airing-cupboard.

Mr and Mrs Armitage arrived.

'What *happened*?' cried Mrs Armitage.

'Harriet put an egg to hatch in the airing-cupboard,' Mark explained.

'An egg? What kind of an egg, would you be so kind as to explain?'

'Well, we don't know yet – someone left it with Mr Johansen, you see, and he didn't feel quite equal to the worry—'

'Oh, delightful,' said Mr Armitage. 'So he just passed it on to us. Mr Johansen is an excellent music teacher but I really—'

'Listen!' said Harriet.

From the sodden mass of household linens still inside the cupboard came a plaintive sound.

It was a little like the call of a curlew – a kind of thin, bubbling, rising, sorrowful cry.

'It's the chick!' exclaimed Harriet joyfully, and she began pulling out pillowcases and tablecloths. Out with them came the lower half of Mrs Nutti's egg, and, still crouched in it, filling it and bulging over the broken edges, they saw a bedraggled, crumpled, damp, dejected creature that seemed all bony joints and big eyes and limp, horny claws.

'Well – it's rather a poppet,' Harriet said, after a pause. Mr Armitage stared at it and made a thoughtful comment. 'I'm not one for rash statements, but I don't think I *ever*, in all my born days, laid eyes on an uglier, scrawnier, soggier, more repulsive-looking chick. In the north country they'd call it a bare golly. What's it supposed to be, tell me that?'

'And for this hideous monster,' wailed Mrs Armitage, 'all our sheets and blankets and tablecloths and the best monogrammed towels have to be ruined?'

'Honestly, Ma, don't worry,' Harriet said. 'Mark and I will take everything down to the coin-op dry-clean after lunch, I promise. I must just give the chick a rinse first, and set him on the playroom radiator to dry. You'll see, when he's cleaned up and fluffed out he'll look quite different.'

'He can look a whole lot different and still be as ugly as sin,' prophesied Mr Armitage.

'And what's he going to eat?' demanded Mrs Armitage, as Harriet lifted up the chick, eggshell and all, and carried him away, staggering under his weight, to the playroom, calling to Mark over her shoulder as she did so to fetch a bucket of water and some soapless shampoo.

While they were cleaning and disinfecting the sheets and blankets at the laundrette (it took three trips and the whole afternoon and all their next month's allowance) Mark said to Harriet, 'Now do you know what the chick is?'

'No, but he's a very queer shape, I must say. His back end isn't a bit like a bird, and he's got a funny, straggly tail with a tassel at the end. How big do you think he's likely to grow?'

'I should think he's about a fifth of his full size now.'

'How do you reckon that?'

'I think he's a griffin-chick.'

'A griffin?' said Harriet, dismayed. 'Are you sure?'

'Well, he's just like the one carved on Mrs Nutti's mantelpiece.'

'Oh my goodness,' Harriet said sadly. 'If only we'd known when he was in the egg, we could have exchanged him for a Himalayan bear.'

'No, we couldn't,' said Mark primly. 'He's not ours to swap. He's Mrs Nutti's. I suppose she sent him to the country to hatch out.'

'Well, *I* think it was very neglectful of her to go off and just *leave* him.'

When they finally tottered home with the last piles of

clean laundry ('Honestly,' grumbled Mark, 'we shall have biceps like boa-constrictors after all the lifting we've done lately.'), Harriet's disappointment over the loss of the Himalayan bear was greatly reduced.

'Oh, I say!' she exclaimed, lifting a fold of newspaper in the laundry basket, which they'd left propped against the warm radiator. 'Do look! He's dried off and he's *furry*!'

At the sound of her voice, the griffin chick woke up, sleepily uncurled, and staggered out from among the crumpled newspapers.

His appearance was now quite different. The dark, damp tendrils all over his back, sides, and legs were fluffed out into soft, grey fur, like that of a soft, grey-haired Persian cat. His stumpy little wings and head were covered with pale grey eiderdown. His beak, brown before, had turned red, and it was wide open.

'Gleep. Gleep. Thrackle, thrackle, thrackle. Gleep. GLEEP!'

'Oh heavens, he's starving! Just a minute, furry, hang on a tick, and we'll get you something to eat. Do you suppose he'll eat bread-and-milk?'

'We can try,' said Mark.

Bread-and-milk went down splendidly, when dolloped into the gaping red beak with a dessert spoon. One basinful was not enough, nor were two, nor were seven. But after the ninth bowlful, the baby griffin gave a great happy yawn, closed his beacon eyes simultaneously, clambered onto the lap of Harriet, who was kneeling on the floor beside him, tucked his head under a wing (from where it immediately slipped out again as the wing was not nearly big enough to cover it) and fell asleep.

After about three minutes, Harriet said,

'It's like having a cart-horse on one's lap. I'll have to shift him.'

Struggling like a coal-heaver, she shifted the chick onto the hearthrug. He did not even blink.

Harriet and Mark sat thoughtfully regarding their new acquisition.

'He's going to be expensive to feed,' Mark said.

This proved an understatement.

After three weeks, Mrs Armitage said, 'Look, I don't want to seem mean, and I must admit your Furry does look better now that he isn't so bony and goose-pimply, but – thirty-six bowls of bread-and-milk a day!'

'Yes, it is a lot,' agreed Harriet sadly.

'Maybe Mr Johansen could contribute towards his support?'

'Oh, no, he's awfully hard up,' Mark said. 'I'll pay for the bread and Harriet can pay for the milk. I've some money saved from apple-picking.'

'That still leaves the sugar and raisins.'

Harriet decided that she would have to dispose of her dolls' furniture.

Unfortunately, that was the day when Furry, tired of his newspaper nest, looked round for somewhere new to roost, and noticed the wicker hamper in which Harriet stored her finished products. He flapped his little wings, jumped up on top, turned round two or three times, digging his claws into the wicker, until he was comfortable, stuck his head under his wing (where it now fitted better; his wings were growing fast), and went to sleep. Slowly the hamper sagged beneath his weight; by the time Harriet found him it was completely flattened, like a wafer-ice that has been left in the sun.

'Oh, *Furry*! *Look* what you've done!'

'Gleep,' replied the baby griffin mournfully, stretching out first one hind leg and then the other.

He was hungry again.

'It's no use blaming him,' Harriet said, inspecting her ruined work. 'He just doesn't know his own weight.'

The next night was a chilly one, and in the middle of it, Furry, becoming fretful and shivery and lonesome, clambered onto Harriet's bed for warmth and company. Harriet, fast asleep, began to have strange dreams of avalanches and earthquakes; by the morning, three legs of her bed had buckled under Furry's weight; Furry and Harriet were huddled in a heap down at the southwest corner.

'It's queer,' said Mark, 'considering how fast he's putting on weight, that he doesn't grow very much bigger.'

'He's more condensed than we are,' Harriet said.

'Condensed!' said Mrs Armitage. 'From now on, that creature has got to live out of doors. Any day now, he'll go right through the floorboards. And your father says the same.'

'Oh, Mother!'

'It's no use looking at me like that. Look at the playroom floor! It's sagging, and dented all over with claw marks. It looks like Southend Beach.'

'I suppose he'll have to roost in the woodshed,' Harriet said sadly.

They fetched a load of hay and made him a snug nest. While he was investigating it, and burying himself up to his beak, they crept indoors and went to bed, feeling like the parents of Hansel and Gretel.

Next morning Furry was up on the woodshed roof, gleeping anxiously. The woodshed had tilted over at a forty-five degree angle.

'Oh, Furry! How did you ever get up there?'

'He must have flown,' said Mark.

'But he can't fly!'

'He was bound to start soon; his wings are nearly full grown. And proper feathers are sprouting all over them, and on his head, too.'

If Furry had flown up to the roof of the shed, however, he showed no signs of remembering how to set about flying down again. He teetered about on the sloping roof, gleeping more and more desperately. At last, just in time, he managed to fly a few hasty, panic-stricken flaps, and coasted to earth as the shed collapsed behind him.

'You *clever* baby,' said Harriet, giving him a hug to show that nobody blamed him.

'Thrackle, thrackle. Gleep, cooroocooroo, gleep.' Furry leaned lovingly against Harriet. She managed to leap aside just before he flattened her; he now weighed as much as a well-nourished grizzly.

Harriet and Mark were extremely busy. In order to earn Furry's keep, they had taken jobs, delivering papers, selling petrol at the garage, and washing up at the Two-Door Café, but they were in a constant state of anxiety all the time as to what he might be doing while they were away from home.

'Do you think we ought to mention to Mr Johansen that it's rather difficult with Furry?' Harriet suggested one day. 'It isn't that I'm not *fond* of him—'

'It's rather difficult to get him to pay attention these days; Mr Johansen, I mean.'

Indeed, the music master seemed to be in a dream most of the time.

'Never haf I played such an instrument, never!' he declared. When he was not playing Mrs Nutti's organ, he was leaning out of the spare-room window, gazing at the view, listening to the music across the square, rapt in a kind of trance. Mark was a little worried about him.

'Honestly, sir, don't you think you ought to get out for a bit of fresh air sometimes?'

'But you see, I have ze feeling zat from zis window I might someday see my lost Sophie.'

'But even if you did, we still don't know how to get into the town.'

Their experiment with rope had proved a failure. The rope had simply disappeared, as fast as they paid it out of the window. Nor was it possible to attract the attention of the people down below and persuade them to fetch a ladder (which had been another of Harriet's suggestions). Neither shouts nor waves had the slightest effect. And Mr Johansen had vetoed any notion of either Mark or Harriet climbing out.

'For you might disappear like ze rope, and zen what should I tell your dear muzzer?'

'So even if you did see your lost Sophie from the window, it wouldn't do you much good; it would be more of a worry than anything else,' Mark said with ruthless practicality.

'Ach – who knows – who knows?' sighed Mr Johansen.

Several more weeks passed. Furry, measured by Mark, was now nearly as big as the marble griffin under the mantelpiece.

Then, one evening, when Mark was in the midst of his piano lesson, Harriet burst in.

'Oh – Mr Johansen – I'm terribly sorry to interrupt – but it's Furry! He's flown up on top of the water-tower, and he's dreadfully scared, and gleeping away like mad, and I'm so afraid he might damage the tower! *Do* come, Mark, and see if you can talk him down, you're the one he trusts most. I've brought a pail of bread-and-milk.'

They ran outside, Mr Johansen following. It was the first time he had been out for days.

The village water-tower stood a couple of fields away from the music master's bungalow. It was a large metal cylinder supported on four metal legs, which looked slender to support the weight of who knows how many thousand gallons of water, but were apparently equal to the job. It did not, however, seem likely that they were equal to supporting a full-grown griffin as well, particularly since he was running back and forth on top of the cylinder, gleeping distractedly, opening and shutting his wings, leaning to look over the edge, and then jumping back with a tremendous clatter and scrape of toenails on galvanized iron.

'*Furry*!' shouted Mark. 'Keep calm! Keep calm!'

'Gleep! Thrackle, thrackle, thrackle.'

'Shut your wings and stand still,' ordered Mark.

With his eyes starting out as he looked at the awful drop below him, the griffin obeyed.

'Now, Harriet, swing the bucket of bread-and-milk round a bit, so the smell rises up.'

Harriet did so. Some bread-and-milk slopped out on the grass. The sweet and haunting fragrance steamed up through the evening air.

'Gleeeeeep!' A famished wail came from the top of the water-tower.

'You're very silly!' Harriet shouted scoldingly. 'If you hadn't got yourself up there, you could be eating this nice bread-and-milk now.'

'Furry,' called Mark, 'watch me. Are you watching?'

Silence from up above. Then a faint thrackle.

'Right! Now, open your wings.'

Mark had his arms by his sides; he now raised them to shoulder height.

Furry, after a moment or two, hesitantly did the same.

'Now lower them again. Do as I do. Just keep raising and lowering.'

Following Mark's example, Furry did this half a dozen times. The tower shook a bit.

'Right, faster and faster. Faster still! Now – *jump*! KEEP FLAPPING!'

Furry jumped, and forgot to flap; he started falling like a stone.

'Gleep!'

'*Flap*, you fool!'

The onlookers leapt away; just in time, Furry began flapping again, and, when he was within eight feet of the ground, suddenly soared upwards once more.

'*Don't* land on the tower again. Flap with *both* wings – not just one. You're going ROUND AND ROUND,' Mark shouted, cupping hands about his mouth. 'That's better. Don't flap so fast. Slower! Like this!'

He demonstrated.

Furry hurtled past, eyes tight shut, claws clenched, wings nothing but a blur. Then back again. It was like the progress of a balloon with the string taken off.

'Make your strokes *slower*.'

'It's as bad as learning to swim,' Harriet said. 'People get quick and frantic in just the same way. Still, he is doing better now. Just so long as he doesn't hit the tower. Or Mr Johansen's roof.'

Several times Furry had only just cleared the bungalow. At last, more or less in control, he flapped himself down to Mr Johansen's front garden, shaving off all the front hedge on his way, and flattening a bed of Canterbury bells.

Mark and Harriet arrived at top speed, with the half-full bucket slopping between them, and set it down on the path. Furry, gleeping between mouthfuls, began frantically gobbling.

At this rather distracted moment, Mrs Nutti arrived.

'What's this, then, what's this?' she snapped angrily, taking in the scene at a glance. 'Who let him out? Should be *upstairs*, in room, not in garden. Burglars, burglars might come, might see him.'

'Out?' said Harriet. 'He's too heavy to keep indoors these days.'

'All wrong – very bad,' said Mrs Nutti furiously. 'Why did I take room in country? To keep him out of way of griffin collectors. Town full of them. Come along, you!' she bawled at Furry. Before Mark or Harriet could protest, she had snapped a collar on his neck and dragged him indoors up Mr Johansen's staircase.

They ran after her.

'Hey, stop!' shouted Mark. 'What are you doing with him?'

Arriving in the spare room, they found Mrs Nutti struggling to push Furry into the ragged hole under the mantelpiece.

'You don't mean,' gasped Harriet, outraged, 'that you intend him to spend the rest of his life there, holding up that shelf?'

'Why else leave egg here to hatch?' panted Mrs Nutti angrily, dragging on the collar.

But Furry, reared on freedom and bread-and-milk, was too strong for Mrs Nutti.

With a loud snap, the collar parted as he strained away from her, and he shot across the room, breaking one of the bedposts like a stick of celery. The window splintered as he struck it, and then he was out and away, flapping strongly up into the blue, blue star-sprinkled sky over the foreign city.

One gleep came back to them, then a joyful burst of the full, glorious song of an adult griffin.

Then he dwindled to a speck and was gone.

'There!' said Harriet. 'That just serves you right, Mrs Nutti. Why, you haven't looked after him and you expected him to hold up your fireplace!'

She was almost crying with indignation.

Mrs Nutti spoke to no one. With her lips angrily compressed, she snatched up the carpet-bag, cast a furious look round the room, and marched out, pulling the room together behind her as one might drag a counterpane.

By the time they heard the front door slam, they were back in Mr Johansen's attic, with its brass bedstead and patchwork quilt.

Mr Johansen walked slowly to the window and looked out, at the trampled garden and the empty bread-and-milk bucket, which still lay on the path.

'I suppose we'll never see Furry again,' Mark said, clearing his throat.

'Or I, my Sophie,' sighed Mr Johansen.

'Oh, I don't know,' Harriet said. 'I wouldn't be surprised if Furry found his way back sometime. He's awfully fond of us. And I'm *sure* you will find your Sophie someday, Mr Johansen. I really am sure you will.'

'We'll start looking for another room in town for you right away!' Mark called back as they walked out through the battered gate.

'It really is lucky Furry didn't hit the water-tower,' Harriet said. 'I should think it would have taken years of pocket-money to pay for *that* damage. Now – as soon as we've fixed up the airing-cupboard door—'

'—And the fruit-ladder—'

'And the woodshed, and the legs of my bed, and Mr Johansen's front gate – I can start saving up for a Himalayan bear.'

THE LOOKING-GLASS TREE

They were putting up the village fair on the green. It was a long job. The thud-thud of hammers banging in the posts for coconut shies echoed all over the village, along with the cheerful stutter of generating motors hoisting the big roundabout into position. The village green was on quite a steep slope, and the big roundabout had to be propped under its lower side on piles of bricks, an arrangement that Mr Armitage condemned as crazily unsafe. Each year, he earnestly begged his children not to ride on the roundabout. Each year, they pointed out that the fair had been going since 1215 with no particular loss of life. Otherwise, they took no notice of his warnings.

Mr Armitage sat in his downstairs study, trying to work, but the noise distracted him, which was a pity, as he had the house to himself for once. Mrs Armitage was out for the day, visiting a sick cousin; Mark and Harriet were down on the green, watching the fair put itself together.

'During the last year, sugar prices have declined rapidly,' wrote Mr Armitage, trying to ignore the sound of thumping.

Then he realized that what he heard was not the distant hammering but somebody banging on his window. He looked up from the report on sugar he was trying to write and found himself staring into the unattractive face of Miss Pursey.

Miss Pursey had bought the small field next to the Armitage garden six months before. Nobody quite knew how this had happened, as old Mr Fewkes, who previously owned the field, had often said he would never sell it, and if he did so, he would sell it to the Armitages. But then, suddenly, one day, he *had* sold it. 'I dunno what came over me,' he said helplessly to Mr Armitage in the pub, 'seemed as 'ow the young lady 'ad an uncommon argymentative persuading way o' going on at me.' And in less than a week after that, a firm of builders unfamiliar to the Armitages had begun slapping up a bungalow, and in a suspiciously short time after *that*, not more than a month, all was completed and Miss Pursey moved into her house.

It seemed almost certain that Miss Pursey was a witch. The bungalow, although made from pre-cast concrete, was constructed so as to resemble a witch's cottage with a roof made from sections of plastic thatch, fake diamond paning in the windows, and Tudor beams painted on the walls.

'She has roses and hollyhocks painted growing up the walls, too,' reported Harriet, who had been over to watch the builders in action. 'Even the bees were fooled.'

The back of the bungalow, in complete contrast, was painted with a trompe-l'oeil reproduction of a Greek temple, done in such ingenious, deceitful perspective that it was good enough to fool anyone, not only bees, until they were about two feet away; one or two of Mr Fewkes's sheep who wandered into the field through a gap in the hedge were seen trying to push their way among the painted Doric columns and looking puzzled, as only sheep can look, because they were unable to do so.

But Miss Pursey, when she moved in, soon discouraged the sheep. In no time at all, she had a boring, tidy garden laid out, a lot of square beds neatly dug divided by cinder paths.

'She waters her plants with boiling water,' Harriet reported.

She also watered the sheep with boiling water, until they took the hint and retired to their own side of the hedge.

Miss Pursey was not neighbourly. She had such a very discouraging expression on her face while she dug her beds and marked off her seed drills that the Armitages, without even discussing the matter, left her strictly alone.

Mr Armitage was therefore surprised and not best pleased to find her banging on his study window at eleven o'clock on a Monday morning.

Miss Pursey was tall, plump, and brisk in her movements. She was not old – in her mid-twenties perhaps – but extremely plain. She wore her straight black hair in a bun at the back and cut in a no-nonsense fringe in the front. She also wore a miniskirt, which was a mistake, as it left bare most of two large, bulging legs tapering down to small, stubby feet in spike-heeled shoes; the legs looked like two exclamation points: !! supporting a capital O. She had very large black-rimmed glasses – two more O's through which she directed an accusing glare at Mr Armitage as he reluctantly opened the window. He thought that if she had not so obviously been a witch she might have been a gym instructor or a hockey teacher.

'Your cat—' said Miss Pursey angrily, as soon as he had the catch undone.

'How do you do,' said Mr Armitage with great politeness, opening the window to its full extent. 'I believe we have not formally introduced ourselves yet. I am Everard Gilbert Armitage – delighted to meet you, Miss – er?'

'Pearl Pursey,' she said snappishly. 'Your cat, Mr Armitage, is wrecking my tree.'

She turned and pointed.

Mr Armitage, unwillingly stepping out through the window (which was a French one), followed her to the wicket gate in the boundary hedge that separated the Armitage garden from Miss Pursey's field.

Just beyond the hedge, a small tree was growing. And in the branches of the tree, looking very unsuitable – for he was about half its size – but very pleased with himself, was the Armitages' enormously large black cat, Walrus, so called because he wore his top front teeth outside his chin, like a walrus's tusks. The teeth were sticking out now even more than usual as he dangled self-consciously over two branches of the tiny tree, making it sway like a fishing rod with a polar bear balanced on top of it.

Mr Armitage immediately thought of two things.

He remembered that the tree had been growing there

before Miss Pursey arrived, so that in a way it could not be said to be her tree; she certainly had not planted it.

He also remembered that the strip of land immediately beyond the Armitage boundary hedge was in fact a footpath; a right-of-way leading across the fields to the next village. Nobody used it any more, because it was more comfortable to go round by road, which was why the little tree had had a chance to grow up. But actually neither the tree nor the land it grew on belonged to Miss Pursey; they were public property.

However, Mr Armitage didn't believe in crossing his bridges before they were built, preferred peace and quiet, and wanted to get on with his report about sugar. He did not mention any of these things, but merely remarked, 'A cat, ma'am, in law, is counted as a member of the class *ferae naturae*, for whose actions the owners cannot be held responsible.'

'I don't care a twopenny fig for your idiotic law,' snapped Miss Pursey. 'I want that cat removed before it does irreparable damage to my tree.' And she glared at Walrus, who swayed serenely about in the branches of the tiny tree, with his tail stuck out sideways to avoid getting it entangled in a twig.

Mr Armitage said, 'Here, puss, puss!' wondering as he did so why Miss Pursey did not herself remove the cat. He was well within reach, for the tree was only four feet high.

Walrus took no notice of Mr Armitage.

'I'll have to go back to the house and bang on his plate,' Mr Armitage said, and did so. Walrus ate his meals off a tin plate, the sound of which, when banged with a spoon, always fetched him at a gallop, no matter where he was. It was the only time he did gallop. As soon as he heard the banging now, he dropped from the tree like a sack of coal, leaving it wildly swaying, and shot off to the kitchen, where Mr Armitage had to open a can of sardines, because there seemed to be no cat food. 'And don't go up that tree any more,' he admonished Walrus, who took no notice. He was busy flicking sardine oil about with his whiskers.

Miss Pursey did not thank Mr Armitage. She was to be seen in the distance angrily inspecting the little tree for damage.

Mr Armitage shut his study window and went back to work. But at lunch, a cold one assembled by the children from ingredients assembled by Mrs Armitage, there came a furious rapping at the door.

'Your cat,' said Miss Pursey to Harriet, who opened the door, 'is up my tree *again*. Please come and remove it at once.'

Harriet went through the gate in the hedge and lifted Walrus out of the tree. He allowed himself to be lifted, but he looked martyred about it and let his back legs dangle down, always a sign that he was not pleased. 'You see, he remembers that there used to be a chaffinch's nest in the hedge just beside that tree,' Harriet explained.

'I don't care what kind of a nest there was or what he remembers,' Miss Pursey said. 'Don't let this happen again, or I shall be obliged to take drastic action.'

'My goodness!' Harriet said, returning to the lunch table.

'Miss Pursey's got some really awful-looking plaster gnomes in her garden, wheeling little barrows full of skulls. They're enough to give anyone nightmares.'

'And did you notice the plastic toadstools?' said her father.

'The red-and-white-spotted ones?' said Harriet. 'Those aren't plastic. I had a good look at them. They're real. She must have been sowing quick-grow toadstool spores. I've read about those red-and-white ones. On the steppes of Siberia, they are regarded as a great delicacy, and may be sold for three or four reindeer apiece.'

'Well, we are not in Siberia now,' said her father, 'and have no reindeer, thank heaven. Don't eat any of those toadstools; they give you hallucinations.'

'I suppose the Siberians like hallucinations,' Mark said thoughtfully.

In the next few days, a great many more toadstools and other fungi sprouted in Miss Pursey's garden, including *Amanita phalloides*, the death cap, which gives anybody who eats it three or four days of increasingly unpleasant sensations ending in death. Miss Pursey had a full bed of death-caps. She had also stinkhorns, false blushers, sickeners, devil's boletus, and lurid boletus. As well as her fungi, she had several handsome bushes of deadly nightshade, covered with large glossy black berries – enough, as Mr Armitage said, regarding them apprehensively, to poison the whole village. He strongly recommended his children to keep well away from Miss Pursey's garden.

'But we have to keep going in to get Walrus out of the tree,' objected Mark.

Walrus, not an intelligent cat, seemed obsessed by memories of the chaffinch's nest. He spent as much of his time as possible in the little tree, which was developing a permanent list towards the hedge. Mark and Harriet had to make constant rescue dashes, and Harriet worried about the situation. They could not keep guard over Walrus for twenty-four hours a day – after all, they had to go to school, and it seemed likely that any drastic action taken by Miss Pursey would be very drastic indeed.

'I wonder why she doesn't take Walrus out of the tree herself?' said Mark.

'I expect it's because cats are witch animals,' suggested Harriet. 'Probably you aren't allowed to touch somebody else's familiar.'

'But Walrus isn't anyone's familiar.'

'I know, but *she* doesn't know that.'

'She could do something at long distance – lasso him or shoot him.'

'Don't!' shuddered Harriet.

Familiar or unfamiliar, one evening Walrus did not arrive at his usual headlong speed when Harriet banged the tinplate supper gong.

There followed a long, worried wait.

'Oh goodness,' said Harriet with quivering lip, 'I do hope Miss Pursey hasn't done something awful. Do you think we should go round and ask—'

'Half a mo,' said Mark. 'Something's trying to get through the cat flap.'

Something was having a hard struggle.

'Oh!' cried Harriet. 'If that fiend has hurt Walrus—'

She rushed to the door and opened it. At once it was plain why the creature outside had been unable to get in through the cat flap. A full-grown timber wolf bounded past Harriet into the kitchen. He stood about three foot high, weighed about two hundred and fifty pounds, and was covered in a shaggy, greyish-white coat with a splendid ruff about his neck.

Mark and Harriet were disconcerted, but the wolf seemed quite accustomed to his surroundings; he made straight for Walrus's tin plate, and sucked up the small portion of chopped rock salmon that lay upon it with one scoop of his long, supple tongue. Then he looked around for more.

'Oh gosh,' said Harriet, 'has she changed Walrus to this?'

'Looks like it,' said Mark. He approached the wolf with caution and felt under the silvery sweep of ruff. 'Yes! Here's Walrus's flea collar – lucky for him it was the stretch kind.'

'It must be stretched pretty far. Do you think it's too tight for him!'

'Seems okay. We'd better leave it on; I daresay wolves have fleas, too.'

Wolf-Walrus quite plainly thought one small portion of fish quite insufficient and demanded more with one long, lugubrious howl.

'All right – here—' said Harriet, hastily dumping out the rest of the panful. 'I'm afraid he's going to be expensive to feed. Almost as bad as darling Furry.'

Furry had been a griffin who lodged briefly with the

Armitages and required at least forty bowls of bread-and-milk a day, with raisins.

'Very handsome, though,' said Mark, admiringly stroking the muscular shoulders with their tremendous coat of fur as Wolf snuffled down the rest of the fish. 'I quite like the idea of having a wolf.'

Mrs Armitage did not like it when she came into the kitchen to make supper.

'Children! What *have* you got there?'

Wolf, stretched in front of the stove, took up the entire hearthrug.

'Miss Pursey has turned Walrus into a wolf. We'll have to enlarge the cat flap quite a lot,' Harriet said. 'But don't worry – Mark can do it with his fretsaw. I don't know if Wolf will be able to squeeze through the bathroom window.'

Wolf had a try. It was plain that he had not yet grown accustomed to the change in his size. At two in the morning, the Armitages woke to a rending crash, and soon after, Mark was almost suffocated by Wolf's two hundred and fifty pounds spread out across the eiderdown. Next day, it was discovered that the bathroom window frame had been stove in.

And the carpets and table legs soon began to suffer severely.

'I really don't think we can keep him,' Mrs Armitage said. 'Besides, he's much more short-tempered than he used to be. Walrus was always such a placid cat. Perhaps some zoo—'

'Oh, Mother! How *could* you? Why, it's our old Walrus, that we've had ever since he was a kitten—'

'Well, you'll have to approach Miss Pursey. Ask her to change him back. But be tactful – I don't want you changed to owls or weasels.'

'You'd think that Miss Pursey might be glad to change him back, actually,' said Harriet. 'He does quite as much damage in his wolf shape.'

Certainly Walrus no longer tried to climb the little tree. Timber wolves do not climb trees; which was just as well, for two hundred and fifty pounds of wolf-Walrus would have done for the tree completely. But wolves dig a lot; and Miss Pursey was often to be seen throwing furious stones after Walrus, who had just scooped out a large cavity in her hemlock bed, or among her poison ivy.

Mark went round to the bungalow, as he had not yet had conflict with Miss Pursey, and put the case to her politely.

'I expect he's got over his tree habit by now. Walrus has quite a short memory. He's quite a stupid cat. Couldn't you see your way to change him back?'

But Miss Pursey was unapproachable.

'Why should I?' she snapped. 'I have just about lost my patience with your family. You give me nothing but trouble. Get out of my garden and don't let me see you in it again.'

Mark left before she lost any more patience.

'We'll have to think of something else,' he said to Harriet.

'I've had an idea,' she said. 'There's a new stall at the fair this year. Janie Perrow was telling me – it's a magician. Janie says he's marvellous. He can cure all sorts of illnesses and change spring onions into diamonds – I bet he can change a wolf back into a cat. Though it does seem rather a pity,' she added, wrapping an arm around Walrus's huge grey bulk. He snapped at her hand in his sleep. They were sitting on the hearthrug after tea.

'Let's go down to the fair now,' said Mark, jumping up. 'Have you any money?'

'A pound saved from hop-picking.'

'I've got two. Perhaps Father will give us something. A magician might be expensive.'

Mr Armitage was cautious. 'First find out if the chap will do it. Then find out how much it costs. Then I'll see.' He added gloomily, 'It would be more useful if he could find some way of removing Miss Pursey. However, do your best.'

Mark and Harriet ran down to the village fair, which was spread all over the village green. It was called the Slow-Fair, happened once a year, and lasted for two weeks, from six to midnight every night. The stalls and sideshows were all terribly expensive, so Mark and Harriet usually waited until the last night, which was always the gayest and wildest, when pigs and coconuts were being auctioned off, and the fair people, having made a good deal of money, were more inclined to let customers onto the swings and roundabouts at half price, if half price was all they could afford, rather than let them go home with any money left unspent.

The roundabout, perched slantways on the hillside, was a particularly good one, with dragons and cockatrices, griffins, unicorns, hydras, cameleopards, and Tasmanian devils, all painted in brilliant and luminous colours. It made a tremendous noise of bawling music and grinding machinery. Before getting down to business with the magician, Mark and Harriet each had one ride on it; he chose a dragon and she a cockatrice. It really felt like flying as one swung out over the tremendous drop on the lower side.

Close by the roundabout stood a very small stall indeed. It was hardly larger than a horse box and had a sign on top, very brightly painted, illuminated by lightbulbs all around, which said, MAESTRO CAPPODOCCIO, Leech to the Old Man of the Mountains, Tooth Puller to Prester John, Chirurgeon to the Grand Lama, Hakkim to the Bey of Tunis, and his Superb Assistant, Alicia Morgiana, Queen of the Sorceresses. Not to mention Lupus, the Wisest Beast in Christendom.

'This must be our man,' said Mark. 'There doesn't seem to be much going on in his van, though.'

Indeed, the little van, which was on wheels, seemed dark and silent enough. The door was closed. A small window on one side gave out a dim gleam of light.

Harriet stood on tiptoe and peered through the window. 'I can see someone in there sitting on a stool,' she reported. So she went around to the end, climbed up the two steps, and tapped on the door. After a considerable pause, it was slowly pulled back.

Inside stood a pale girl with lanky fair hair and a good many spots. She wore a sagging skirt, a draggled cardigan, trodden-over shoes, and a lot of mascara. She was chewing gum. She hardly looked like the Queen of the Sorceresses.

'Is Maestro Cappodoccio about?' said Harriet.

'I couldn't say, I'm sure,' said the girl, as if she didn't care, either. She had a flat, uninterested voice.

'When will he be back?'

'I couldn't say. He'll be back sometime.'

'Are you his assistant?'

'Yes,' the girl said, shifting her gum from one cheek to the other.

'Well, can you help us?'

'Nah. Not without the professor.'

'Well, can we come in and wait?'

'Suppose so,' said the girl unenthusiastically, and went back to her stool. They edged inside. The van was about five foot by seven – large enough to accommodate four or five people standing, but not much more. At the far end was a stove with a black pot boiling. The walls were lined with shelves containing small pots and jars labelled Ac. Phen., Ol. Euc., Sod. Bic., etc. There were two pull-down bunks. The ceiling was painted with geometrical signs. The girl's stool was the only seat, and she had gone back to reading *Girl's Star Weekly*.

Mark and Harriet each stood facing a wall. Harriet's had the window in it. She discovered with surprise that it was not a window, but a picture. One-way glass? It had certainly been a window from the outside, but now, instead of the fairground, she saw, very far away, a garden with mossy lawns, weeping willows, a fountain, a stone seat—

'Gosh,' murmured Harriet half to herself. 'It isn't a picture. It's real.' She had noticed that the weeping willow was swaying in the breeze.

She jogged Mark's elbow.

'Hey – look at this. It's a real garden – miles and miles away—'

'Sure it's not a TV screen?' murmured Mark, turning around cautiously so as not to knock any of the little pots. But as soon as he studied the framed garden, he went very pale – his eyes almost popped out of his head. '*Harriet!* Do you know what that is?'

'No, what?' she glanced warningly at the girl, but the girl was absorbed in an article about 'Your Stars, Your Makeup, and You.'

'That garden!' hissed Mark. 'It's Mr Johansen's garden. Wait here! I'm going to fetch him right away!'

And without wasting a moment he slipped out of the van and rushed off into the dusk.

Harriet had known immediately what he meant. Mark's music teacher, a kind, sad, white-haired man called Rudolf Johansen, had once, many years before, fallen in love with a German princess whom he had the misfortune to lose through a piece of drawing-room magic. Somewhere, folded up in an enchanted garden inside the pages of a book, the Princess Sophia Maria Louisa of Saxe-Hoffenpoffen-und-Hamster was still waiting for Mr Johansen, but nobody knew where she was or where the book was. It had been lost. But now here, according to Mark, was a picture of her garden – no, the garden itself, Harriet thought – and Mark should know, for he had once cut it all carefully off the sides of six cereal packets and pasted it together, only to have it destroyed during some disastrous spring cleaning.

Harriet gazed at the garden as if it might melt away in front of her eyes.

Far in the distance, she saw a speck of silvery white, which slowly came closer and turned into a tiny, faraway lady, stiffly dressed in a white crinoline, with her powdered hair dragged high on top of her head. Miles away, at the far end of the lawn, she sat herself rather wearily down on a stone seat, laying her hand on the head of a big shaggy dog who sat down on the ground by her feet.

'That must be Princess Sophie! If only Mark can find Mr Johansen, and if only Mr Johansen can remember his tune— For entry to the garden could be achieved only by humming a tune that Mr Johansen himself had made up.

'Hey,' said Alicia, the Queen of the Sorceresses, closing her magazine and standing up. 'I can hear the professor coming, and he's got someone with him. Only one customer allowed at a time. You'd best wait outside.'

'But we were here first,' Harriet protested.

'Can't help that,' said the girl, and jerked her head towards the door. Harriet went out and stood beside the van, in its shadow. She could hear voices and footsteps approaching, for the merry-go-round was temporarily at a standstill. Then, at her feet, she heard the rattle of a chain.

Rather startled, she looked down and saw a large paw extending from under the van.

It looked suspiciously like that of Walrus.

Harriet dropped on her knees. Her eyes were accustomed to the dim light; she found herself staring straight into the face of a large pale grey wolf.

Was it Walrus?

Very cautiously, she held out a hand. 'Are you Walrus?' she whispered.

A low growl answered her.

The voices and footsteps had now arrived outside the van. Harriet heard a man's voice – a dry, gentle, calm voice, rather like that of Mr Garrett, her English master, who liked to recite such long poems that not infrequently he put the whole class to sleep.

'But, madam, I already have a wolf in my act,' he was saying. 'As you can see from my sign. I have Lupus, the Wisest Beast in Christendom, who can tell gold from sham by touch and recognizes all the letters of the Greek alphabet.'

'That's why I thought you'd like to have two.' The other voice was Miss Pursey's – Harriet recognized it at once. 'Two would be better still. You could teach the second one the Russian alphabet – it's a Siberian wolf, actually – and how to tell butter from marge.'

'Why do you wish to dispose of the animal?'

'It's a nuisance in the garden,' said Miss Pursey.

Harriet's blood boiled. 'Oh, the monster!' she thought. 'Not content with turning our poor Walrus into a wolf, she's now arranging to sell him into captivity.'

'I'd have to see the animal before I could come to a decision,' the man – presumably Maestro Cappodoccio – said. 'If you'd like to bring him here, I'll give you my answer.'

'Oh, very well,' said Miss Pursey annoyedly, and her steps receded into the dark again.

The magician went into his van. Harriet followed him at once.

'That woman who just offered you a wolf,' she began in high indignation. 'She's no right to. For a start, it isn't a wolf at all, but our cat, Walrus! And—'

Professor Cappodoccio looked at Harriet attentively. He was a plump, grey-haired man with kind but very compelling brown eyes. She had interrupted him in the act of putting on a black robe over his ordinary grey suit.

'You say the animal is not a wolf—'

At that moment, Mark and Mr Johansen arrived with most unceremonious speed.

'May we come in, sir?' gasped Mark, and instantly did so. He was dragging Mr Johansen by the arm. Both of them were out of breath. 'Look!' panted Mark triumphantly to his music teacher. 'Look – there she is!'

He pointed jerkily to the tiny telescoped garden where the ant-sized Princess Sophie was thoughtfully pulling her large dog's ears.

'*Ach!*' breathed Mr Johansen joyfully. 'Ach, yes! Zat is my Sophie! *Ach, Himmel*, I never zought to see her once more!' He was terribly moved. Tears stood in his eyes. His chest, which was still heaving from the speed of their run, began to heave also with suppressed sobs.

'Can you call out to her, sir?' gulped Mark. 'Attract her attention?'

Mr Johansen shook his head. He was still too out of breath for that. But he handed Mark a tiny silver dog whistle. Mark, still very puffed, blew one short soft note on the whistle. It was quick, but it was enough for the dog in the garden to catch it. Up shot her head – and suddenly she was off at a gallop, careering like the wind along the length of the huge lawn. It was plain that she was barking in wild delight, but she was still so far away that no sound could be heard, until she reached the very edge of the frame, when, faintly, faintly, they could hear a faraway reverberation of tiny barks. She was running this way and that, obviously much puzzled.

And the princess, equally startled, had risen to her feet – was apparently calling to the dog – asking what was the matter.

'Am I to understand, sir,' inquired Professor Cappodoccio with sympathetic interest, 'that you are acquainted with the lady and the dog in my wall hanging? I have long wondered—'

'*Ach* so, zat is no wvall hanging – zat is ze *Garten* of Princess Sophia of Saxe-Hoffenpoffen. *Indeed* I am acqvainted wiz it! In one little minute, I sing a song wvich—'

But in one little minute a whole lot of other things happened, very unexpectedly. Miss Pursey reappeared, looking decidedly ruffled, with a set of parallel scratches on her face; she held both ends of a rope which she had passed under the collar of an equally angry-looking Walrus. Apparently once he had lost his cat form she had more control of him.

Observing that there were several people in the van – though the only one she could see from the step was Mr Johansen – Miss Pursey tied Walrus's rope to the door handle and called out, 'Dr Cappodoccio! Can you come out here a moment?'

At the sound of her loud, peremptory voice, Dr Cappodoccio's assistant, the pale, bored Alicia, reacted with startling speed. She leapt to her feet, dropping the *Girl's Star Weekly*, and darted to the doorway, moving through the group of people as fast as an adder shooting through a patch of dry grass. And her whole appearance changed; the look of languid discontent dropped away, replaced by malevolent purposefulness.

'Well, there!' she exclaimed triumphantly. 'I didn't *think* I could mistake that voice! If it isn't our Playful Pearl, the pride of Beelzebub Training College! Dear old pushy Pearl, the most unpopular girl on the necromantic campus – Pal Pearl who wouldn't ever *dream* of cribbing another student's incantation or pinching someone else's spell tables or borrowing their six-pointed star-calculator and forgetting to return it, oh, *no*!'

She shot her face forward to within an inch of Miss Pursey, who looked somewhat discomposed.

'What about my pyramid that you stole just before final examinations? What did you do with it?' hissed Alicia.

'Pyramid? What pyramid?' riposted Miss Pursey loftily. 'My good girl, I haven't the least idea what you are maundering on about. Just because you did badly in your finals is no excuse for trying to put the blame on others – it's not my fault if you came bottom.'

'No? I've come on quite a bit since then, though,' said Alicia with menace, and she pointed her pale, skinny finger at Miss Pursey. A blue flash wriggled along it, and suddenly a blaze of cobalt fire enveloped Miss Pursey, who emerged from it quite bald and very angry indeed. Her spectacles had melted in the heat and fallen off. She glared at Alicia short-sightedly and extended all her fingers, which spurted white fire.

'Hussy!'

'Jade!'

'Minx!'

'Doxy!'

'Strumpet!'

They lunged at each other, feinting and sidestepping like

fencers. Alicia's cardigan burst into flame, and she tossed it off. A black bat, dislodged from Miss Pursey's handbag, fluttered off with indignant, high-pitched squeaks. Absorbed in their dispute, the two sorceresses, flaming, sparking, making serpentine darts at each other, kept moving towards the big roundabout, which was now whirling around again high above them with its tremendous music, noise and light.

Harriet watched riveted with suspense as the pair, slashing at each other with their white and blue fire, shouting inaudible insults at one another, edged closer and closer under the side of the roundabout. And then finally there came a prodigious blinding flash and crash. The whole merry-go-round keeled over – amid bangs, bumps, sounds of splitting wood, and shrieks of consternation.

Mark, Dr Cappodoccio, and Mr Johansen dashed out of the van; people came rushing from all over the fairground.

And just to add to the general hurly-burly, Walrus and Dr Cappodoccio's wolf, Lupus, had discovered one another and were at each other's throats, snarling, biting, and rolling over and over.

'Walrus! Stop that at *once*! I'm *surprised* at you!' exclaimed Harriet and dragged him away from Lupus, getting considerably scratched in the process. She shut him in the van.

Mark and the two men had rushed to the scene of the accident, and she joined them. Already ambulances, police cars, fire engines, and breakdown trucks were converging from all sides.

Luckily, though there were plenty of black eyes, scrapes and bruises, nobody seemed to be seriously hurt. The injured were given first aid and allowed to go. But, oddly enough, there seemed to be no trace of either Miss Pursey or Alicia.

When all was quiet again, Harriet, Mark and Mr Johansen returned to the magician's van.

The little garden scene was still quietly there on the wall, as if none of this tremendous excitement had been taking place outside. But Princess Sophie and the dog, Lotta, were gone. The garden was empty. The only intimation that any dog had been present was Walrus on the floor below, restored to cat form, hissing angrily, with his tail swelled up like a chimney sweep's brush, as it did when he met any dog.

'I sing ze song,' said Mr Johansen. 'Zey wvill come back, I hope.'

Trembling a little, very carefully, he hummed his tune.

But nothing happened. Nobody came. The garden stayed the same size.

Mr Johansen sang the song again. Still nothing happened.

'I'm afraid,' said Dr Cappodoccio compassionately, 'all that black magic going on outside must have left a concentration of poison in the atmosphere and some destructive vibrations which have upset your spell. *What* a pity!'

'Oh, curse that Miss Pursey!' said Mark furiously. 'It's all her fault. I hope the roundabout squashed her flat.'

'*Poor* Mr Johansen,' said Harriet.

Mr Johansen looked so utterly white, tired, and defeated

that Dr Cappodoccio, evidently a kindhearted man, suggested, 'Why don't you spend the night with me, sir? You can have my assistant's bunk (a most disagreeable, unhelpful girl; I am not at all sorry that she is gone). By tomorrow, when the vibrations have settled, perhaps your spell will work once more.'

Mr Johansen allowed himself to be persuaded. Mark and Harriet went rather dismally home, taking turns to carry Walrus, who was still uttering frightful threats against the Wisest Beast in Christendom.

'I've never known him so aggressive,' Harriet remarked.

'The whole evening was a mess,' Mark muttered bitterly, as they went up to bed.

However, the next morning showed that the evening had not been a total disaster.

It was plain that Miss Pursey had never come home, and in her absence, her house was rapidly collapsing, melting, decaying, and sinking into the ground, like a very old mushroom. Already most of it was gone. Many of the plants in her garden had died; the only thing that still seemed living and healthy was the little tree on the footpath.

And Walrus, after all, was once more their old familiar outsized monster of a fat black cat.

'Though, in a way, we shall rather miss having a wolf,' Harriet said, hugging him. Walrus turned and bit her, quite hard. She gazed at him in astonished reproach.

Halfway through the morning, Dr Cappodoccio's van drew up outside the front door. Mr Johansen climbed out of it and rang the front-door bell.

'Hasn't the spell worked yet, Mr Johansen?' Harriet asked him anxiously as she opened the door.

'Ach, no! Not yet!' he sighed. 'And zo ziss Dr Cappodoccio has very kindly inwited me to go wizz him on his woyages and be his assistant. Zen, wven ze spell comes out clear once more, I wvill be on ze spot.'

'Oh dear,' Mark said sadly. 'We shall miss you, Mr Johansen!'

'Shall you know how to be a magician's assistant?' Harriet asked doubtfully.

'He wvill teach me; is not difficult, he tell me.'

'You'll find it a bit different from giving piano lessons.'

Mark and Harriet accompanied Mr Johansen to the gate. Both were rather dismayed at the thought of the gentle old man abandoning his house and gypsying off in this unexpected manner.

Dr Cappodoccio had left the van and was standing by their garden hedge, gazing at the little tree that Miss Pursey had been so keen to protect. He seemed quite excited about it.

'Do you know that you have a great treasure here?' he said, his brown eyes shining with enthusiasm. 'In three years' time that will be a full-grown Looking-glass Tree.'

'What's a Looking-glass Tree?' asked Harriet.

'Oh, my dear young lady! The Looking-glass Tree is the ninth wonder of the world! It grows but once in a hundred years, takes four years to come to full growth, is found only on waste or common land, has leaves that reflect the sun in unrivalled splendour, flowers of incomparable beauty, fruits that will cure any disease from Bell's Palsy to Housemaid's Knee, its bark is unequalled as an ingredient for distilling spells, potions, simples and compounds. It breathes out a scent that cures deafness and phlebitis for eighty miles around—'

'Really?' said Mark, turning to look at the humble little tree; it might have been an apple or a quince; it seemed to have nothing particularly special about it.

'So *that* was why Miss Pursey bought this bit of land!'

'But if the tree can do all these things in three years' time – will it be able to help Mr Johansen find his princess?'

'Dear me, yes! One leaf – a *third* of a leaf – will give anyone the thing he loves most.'

'What a shame that it can't do it *now*!'

'Never mind – in zree years' time we come back,' said Mr Johansen with his gentle smile, and the two old gentlemen got into their gaily painted van and drove off, with Lupus, the wise wolf, sitting between them. Dr Cappodoccio turned his head to shout, 'Mind you look after the tree!'

'It's going to be a bit of a responsibility,' sighed Harriet.

Miss Pursey never reappeared. Strangely enough, two skeletons were found under the wreckage of the roundabout, but they could not have been those of Miss Pursey and Alicia, Queen of Sorceresses, for they were many thousands of years old; local archaeologists became quite excited about them.

Mr Armitage said: 'I told you that roundabout was unsafe. I always said so.'

The fat cat, Walrus, was never so placid again. Into extreme old age he retained several habits that he had acquired during the time that he was a wolf.

MISS HOOTING'S LEGACY

For weeks before Cousin Elspeth's visit, Mrs Armitage was, as her son Mark put it, 'flapping about like a wet sheet in a bramble bush'.

'What shall we do about the unicorn? Cousin Elspeth doesn't approve of keeping pets.'

'But she can't disapprove of him. He's got an angelic nature – haven't you, Candleberry?'

Harriet patted the unicorn and gave him a lump of sugar. It was a hot day in early October, and the family were having tea in the garden.

'He'll have to board out for a month or two at Coldharbour Farm.' Mrs Armitage made a note on her list. 'And you,' she said to her husband, 'must lay in five cases of Glensporran. Cousin Elspeth will only drink iced tea with whisky in it.'

'Merciful powers! What this visit is going to cost us! How long is the woman going to stay?'

'Why does she have to come?' growled Mark, who had been told to dismantle his home-made nuclear turbine, which was just outside the guest-room window.

'Because she's a poor old thing, and her sister's just died, and she's lonely. Also she's very rich, and if she felt like it, she could easily pay for you and Harriet to go to college, or art school, or something of that sort.'

'But that's *years* ahead!'

'*Someone* has to think ahead in this family,' said Mrs Armitage, writing down *Earl Grey tea, new face-towels* on her list. 'And Harriet, you are not to encourage the cat to come upstairs and sleep on your bed. It would be awful if he got into Cousin Elspeth's room. She writes that she is a very light sleeper—'

'Oh, poor Walrus. Where *can* he sleep, then?'

'In his basket, in the kitchen. And Mark, will you ask Mr Peake to stay out of the guest bathroom for a few months? He's very obliging, but it always takes a long time to get an idea into his head.'

'Well, he *is* three hundred years old, after all,' said Harriet. 'You can't expect a ghost to respond quite as quickly as ordinary people.'

'Darling,' said Mrs Armitage to her husband, 'sometime this week, could you find a few minutes to hang up the new mirror I found at Dowbridges'? It's been down in the cellar for the last two months—'

'Hang it where?' said Mr Armitage, reluctantly coming out of his evening paper.

'In the guest-room, to replace the one that Mark broke when his turbine exploded—'

'I'll do it, if you like,' said Mark, who loved banging in nails. 'After all, it was my fault the other one got broken.'

'And I'll help,' said Harriet, who wanted another look at the new mirror.

She had accompanied her mother to the furniture sale, a couple of months ago, when three linen tablecloths, one wall mirror, ten flowerpots, and a rusty pressure cooker had been knocked down to Mrs Armitage for £12 in the teeth of spirited and urgent bidding from old Miss Hooting, who lived at the other end of the village. For some reason the old lady seemed particularly keen to acquire this lot, though there were several other mirrors in the sale. At £11.99, however, she ceased to wave her umbrella and limped out of the sale hall, scowling, muttering, and casting angry glances at Mrs Armitage. Since then she had twice dropped notes, in black spidery handwriting, through the Armitage letterbox, offering to buy the mirror, first for £12.50, then for £13, but Mrs Armitage, who did not much like Miss Hooting, politely declined to sell.

'I wonder *why* the old girl was so keen to get hold of the glass?' remarked Harriet, holding the jam jar full of nails while Mark tapped exploringly on the wall, hunting for reliable spots. The mirror was quite a big heavy one, about two metres long by one metre wide, and required careful positioning.

'It seems ordinary enough.' Mark glanced at it casually. The glass, plainly quite old, had a faint silvery sheen; the frame, wooden and very worn, was carved with vine leaves and little grinning creatures.

'It doesn't give a very good reflection.' Harriet peered in. 'Makes me look frightful.'

'Oh, I dunno; about the same as usual, I'd say,' remarked her brother. He selected his spot, pressed a nail into the plaster, and gave it one or two quick bangs. 'There. Now another here. Now pass us the glass.'

They heard the doorbell ring as Mark hung up the mirror, and a few minutes later, when they came clattering downstairs with the hammer and nails and the stepladder, they saw their mother on the doorstep, engrossed in a long, earnest conversation with old Mrs Lomax, Miss Hooting's neighbour. Mrs Lomax was not a close friend of the Armitage family, but she had once obligingly restored the Armitage parents to their proper shape when Miss Hooting, in a fit of temper, had changed them into ladybirds.

Odd things frequently happened to the Armitages.

'What did Mrs Lomax want, Ma?' Harriet asked her mother at supper.

Mrs Armitage frowned, looking half worried, half annoyed.

'It's still this business about the mirror,' she said. 'Old Miss Hooting has really set her heart on it, for some reason. Why didn't she just *tell* me so? Now she has got pneumonia, she's quite ill, Mrs Lomax says, and she keeps tossing and turning, and saying she has to have the glass, and if not, she'll put a curse on us by dropping a bent pin down our well. Perhaps, after all, I had better let the poor thing have the glass.'

'Why? You bought it,' said Harriet. 'She could have gone on bidding.'

'Perhaps £11.99 was all she had.'

'There were other glasses that went for less.'

Mr Armitage was inclined to make light of the matter. 'I don't see what dropping a bent pin into the well could do. I expect she's delirious. Wait till she's better; then you'll find the whole thing has died down, very likely.'

Next day, however, the Armitages learned that old Miss Hooting had died in the night.

'And not before it was time,' said Mr Armitage. 'She must have been getting on for a hundred. Anyway, that solves your problem about the mirror.'

'I hope so,' said the wife.

'Now all we have to worry about is Cousin Elspeth. Did you say she takes cubes of frozen tea in her whisky, or frozen whisky in her tea?'

'Either way will do, so long as the tea is Earl Grey . . . '

Cousin Elspeth's arrival coincided with old Miss Hooting's funeral.

The funeral of a witch (or 'old fairy lady' as they were always politely referred to in the Armitages' village, where a great many of them resided) is always a solemn affair, and Miss Hooting, because of her great age and explosive temper, had generally been regarded as the chairwitch of the village community. So the hearse, drawn by four black griffins, and carrying a glass coffin with Miss Hooting in it, looking very severe in her black robes and hat, was followed by a long straggling procession of other old ladies, riding in vehicles of all kinds, from rickety perch phaetons with half the springs gone, to moth-eaten flying carpets and down-at-the-wheel chariots.

Mark and Harriet would very much have liked to attend the ceremony, but were told firmly that, since the family had not been on very good terms with Miss Hooting, they were to stay at home and not intrude. They heard later from their friend Rosie Perrow that there had been a considerable fuss at the graveside because Miss Hooting had left instructions that her coffin was not to be covered over until 1st November, and the vicar had very strong objections to this.

'Specially as the coffin was made of glass,' Rosie reported.

'I suppose he thought kids might come and smash it,' said Mark.

'So they might. Miss Hooting wasn't at all popular.'

Cousin Elspeth, when she arrived, was in a state of high indignation.

'Rickety, ramshackle equipages all along the village street, holding up the traffic! My taxi took twenty-eight minutes to get here, and cost me £9.83! Furthermore, I am accustomed to take my tea at four-thirty precisely, and it is now twelve meenutes past five!'

Cousin Elspeth was a tall, rangy lady, with teeth that Mr Armitage said reminded him of the cliffs of Dover, a voice like a chainsaw, cold, granite-coloured eyes that missed nothing, hair like the English Channel on a grey, choppy day, and an Aberdeen accent as frigid as chopped ice.

In a way, Mark thought, it was a shame that she had just missed Miss Hooting; the two of them might have hit it off.

Tea, with three kinds of scones, two kinds of shortbread, and cubes of frozen Glensporran in her Earl Grey, was just beginning to soothe Cousin Elspeth's ruffled feelings, when there came a peal at the front-door bell.

'Inconseederate!' Cousin Elspeth sniffed again.

The caller proved to be Mr Glibchick, the senior partner in the legal firm of Wright, Wright, Wright, Wright, and Wrong, who had their offices on the village green. All the Wrights and Wrongs had long since passed away, and Mr Glibchick ran the firm with the help of his partner, Mr Wrangle.

'What was it, dear?' inquired Mrs Armitage, when her husband returned, looking rather astonished, from his conversation with the lawyer.

'Just imagine – Miss Hooting has left us something in her will!'

Cousin Elspeth was all ears at once. Making and remaking her own will had been her favourite hobby for years past; and since arriving at the Armitage house she had already subtracted £400 and a writing-desk from Mark's legacy, because he had neglected to pass her the jam, and was deliberating about whether to bequeath a favourite brown mohair stole to Harriet, who had politely inquired after her lumbago.

'Left us a legacy? What – in the name of goodness?' exclaimed Mrs Armitage. 'I thought the poor old thing hadn't two pennies together.'

'Not money. Two mechanical helots, was what Mr Glibchick said.'

'Helots? What are they?'

'Helots were a kind of slave.'

'Fancy Miss Hooting keeping slaves!' Harriet looked horrified. 'I bet she beat them with her umbrella, and made them live on burnt toast-crusts.'

'Little gels should be seen and not hairrd,' remarked Cousin Elspeth, giving Harriet a disapproving glance, and changing her mind about the brown mohair stole.

Next day, the mechanical slaves were delivered by Ernie Perrow in his tractor-trailer.

They proved to be two figures, approximately human in shape, one rather larger than life-size, one rather smaller, constructed out of thin metal piping, with plastic boxes for their chests, containing a lot of electronic gadgetry. Their feet were large, round, and heavy, and they had long, multi-hinged arms, ending in prehensile hands with hooks on the fingers. They had eyes made of electric light-bulbs, and rather vacant expressions. Their names were stencilled on their feet: *Tinthea* and *Nickelas*.

'What gruesome objects!' exclaimed Mrs Armitage. 'For mercy's sake, let's give them to the next jumble-sale; the very sight of them is enough to give me one of my migraines!'

Cousin Elspeth entirely agreed. 'Whit seengulrly reepulsive airrticles!'

But Mark and his father, seeing eye to eye for once, were most anxious to get the mechanical slaves into working order, if possible.

'Besides, it would be very tactless to give them to a sale. Miss Hooting's friends would be sure to get to know.'

'The things are in a horrible condition,' pronounced Mark, after some study of the helots. 'All damp and dirty and rusty; the old girl must have kept them in some dismal outhouse and never oiled them.'

'What makes them go?' inquired Harriet, peering at a damp, tattered little booklet, entitled *Component Identification*, which hung on a chain round Tinthea's neck.

'It seems to be lunar energy,' said her father. 'Which is pretty dicey, if you ask me. I never heard of anything running on lunar energy before. But that seems to be the purpose of those glass plates on the tops of their heads.'

'More to 'em than meets the eye,' agreed Mark, wagging his own head.

As it happened, the month of October was very fine. Hot, sunny days were succeeded by blazing moonlit nights. Tinthea and Nickelas were put in the greenhouse to warm up and dry off. Meanwhile, Mark and his father, each guided by a booklet, spent devoted hours cleaning, drying, oiling, and de-rusting the family's new possessions.

'"Clean glazed areas with water and ammonia solution," it says.'

'"Brush cassette placement with household detergent."'

'Which is the cassette placement?'

'I think it must be that drawer affair in the chest.'

'Chest of drawers,' giggled Harriet.

Tinthea, on whom Mark was working, let out something that sounded like a snort.

'"Keep latched prehensile work/monitor selector function aligners well lubricated with sunflower or cottonseed oil." Which do you think those are?'

'Its hands?' suggested Harriet.

Mr Armitage, doing his best to clean the feet of Nickelas, which were in a shocking state, matted with dirt and old, encrusted furniture polish, accidentally touched a concealed lever in the heel, and Nickelas began to hop about, in a slow, ungainly, but frantic way, like a toad in a bed of thistles. The helot's hand, convulsively opening and shutting, grasped the handle of Mr Armitage's metal tool-box, picked up the box, and swung it at its owner's head. Mr Armitage just managed to save himself from a cracked skull by falling over sideways into a tray of flowerpots. Nickelas then clumsily but effectively smashed eight greenhouse panes with the end of the tool-box, using it like a sledge-hammer, before Mark, ducking low, managed to grab the helot's leg and flick down the switch.

'Oh, I see, *that's* how they work!' Harriet pressed Tinthea's switch.

'Don't, idiot!' shouted Mark, but it was too late. Tinthea picked up a bucket of dirty, soapy water and dashed it into Harriet's face just before Mr Armitage, with great presence of mind, hooked the helot's feet from under her with the end of a rake. Tinthea fell flat on the ground, and Mark was able to switch her off.

'We have got to learn to programme them properly before we switch them on. They seem to have charged up quite a lot of lunar energy,' said Mr Armitage, trying to prise Nickelas's steel fingers loose from the handle of the tool-chest.

He read aloud: '"To programme the helots: turn the percept/accept/monitor/selector to zero. If the helot is in multiple cycle, depress the Clear key. The memory will then return to State o½. Bring the memory factor into play by raising shutter of display window, simultaneously depressing locking lever, opening upper assembly carriage masker, sliding drum axle out of tab rack, shifting wheel track chain into B position, and moving preset button to ←→ signal." Is that clear?' said Mr Armitage after a little thought.

'No,' said Mark. 'Do these things have memories then?'

'I think so. I'm not quite sure about that State o½. Maybe they still have some instructions programmed into them by old Miss Hooting. I don't quite see how to get rid of those. Here, it says, "the helot will remember the previous day's instructions and repeat for an indefinite number of operations unless the memory factor is cancelled by opening 'R' slot and simultaneously depressing all function keys." I must say,' said Mr Armitage, suddenly becoming enthusiastic, 'if we could get Nickelas, for instance, to take over all the digging and lawnmowing and carry the dustbin to the street, I should be quite grateful to old Miss Hooting for her legacy, and I'm sorry I ever called her a trouble-making old so-and-so.'

'And maybe we can programme Tinthea to wash dishes and make beds?' Harriet suggested hopefully.

But there was a long way to go before the helots could be set to perform any useful task with the slightest certainty that it would be carried out properly.

Tinthea, programmed to make the beds, showered sunflower oil liberally all over the blankets, and then tore up the sheets into shreds; she finished by scooping handfuls of foam rubber out of the mattresses, and unstringing all the bed-springs. The only bed spared was that of Cousin Elspeth, who always kept her bedroom door locked. Tinthea was unable to get into her room, though she returned to rattle vainly at the door handle all day long.

Nickelas, meanwhile, ran amok with the motor mower, trundling it back and forth across the garden, laying flat all Mrs Armitage's begonias and dahlias in fifteen minutes; Mark was able to lasso him and switch him off just before he began on the sweet peas.

'We'd better get rid of them before they murder us all in our beds,' said Mrs Armitage.

'It seems a shame not to get *some* use out of them,' said Harriet. 'Don't you think we could teach Tinthea to do the cooking?'

But Tinthea's notion of cooking was to pile every article from the refrigerator into the oven, including ice-cubes and Mr Armitage's special film for his Japanese camera. And then Harriet found her supplying buckets of strong Earl Grey tea to Nickelas, who was pouring them over Mr Armitage's cherished asparagus bed.

Instructed to pick blackberries for jam, Nickelas came back with a basket containing enough deadly nightshade berries to poison the entire village. Tinthea, set to polish the stairs, covered them with salad oil; Harriet was just in time to catch Cousin Elspeth as she slid down the last six steps. The results of this were quite advantageous, for Harriet was, on the spot, reappointed to the brown mohair stole in Cousin Elspeth's will (though not informed of the fact), and Cousin Elspeth's lumbago, as it proved subsequently, was cured for ever by the shock of the fall; still, the Armitage household began to feel that the helots were more of a liability than an asset.

But how to dispose of them?

'If I were ye, I'd smesh 'em with a hetchit,' snapped Cousin Elspeth.

'I don't think *that* would be advisable. A witch's legacy, you know, should be treated with caution.'

'A witch! Hech!'

Mr Armitage telephoned the local museum to ask if they would accept the helots; but Mr Muskin, the curator, was away for a month in Tasmania, collecting ethnological curiosities. The nearest National Trust mansion had to refer the possibility of being given two lunar-powered helots to its Acquisitions Board; and the librarian at the village library was quite certain she didn't want them; nor did the Primary School.

For the time being, Tinthea and Nickelas were locked in the cellar. 'They won't pick up much lunar power there,' said Mr Armitage. They could be heard gloomily thumping about from time to time.

'I think they must have learned how to switch each other on,' said Mark.

'It's a bit spooky having them down there,' shivered Harriet. 'I wish Mr Muskin would come back from Tasmania and decide to have them.'

Meanwhile, to everybody's amazement, a most remarkable change was taking place in Cousin Elspeth. This was so noticeable and so wholly unexpected, that it even distracted the family's attention from the uncertainty of having two somewhat unbiddable helots in the cellar.

In fact, as Mr Armitage said to his wife, it was almost impossible to believe the evidence of one's own eyes.

In the course of three weeks Cousin Elspeth's looks and her temper improved daily and visibly. Her cheeks grew pink, her eyes blue, and her face no longer looked like a craggy mountain landscape but became simply handsome and distinguished. She was heard to laugh, several times, and told Mrs Armitage that it didn't matter if the tea wasn't always Earl Grey; she remembered a limerick she had learned in her youth about the old man of Hoy, restored the writing-desk to Mark in her will, and began to leave her bedroom door unlocked.

Curiously enough, after a week or two, it was Mrs Armitage who began to think rather wistfully of the wasted helot manpower lying idle down there in the cellar. She told Mark to fetch Tinthea to help with the job of washing blankets. Which Cousin Elspeth pointed out should be done before the winter.

'After all, as we've got the creatures, we might as well make *some* use of them. Just carrying blankets to and fro, Tinthea can't get up to much mischief. But don't bring Nickelas, I can't stand his big staring eyes.'

So Mark, assisted by Harriet, fetched the smaller helot from the cellar. They were careful not to switch her on until she was in the utility room, and the cellar door locked again on the inert Nickelas.

But Harriet did afterwards recall that Tinthea's bulbous, sightless eyes seemed to watch the process of locking and unlocking very attentively.

For once, however, the smaller helot appeared to be in a cooperative mood, and she hoisted wet blankets out of the washing machine and trundled off with them into the garden, where she hung them on the line without doing anything unprogrammed or uncalled-for, returning three or four times for a new load.

It was bright, blowy autumn weather, the leaves were whirling off the trees, and the blankets dried so quickly that they were ready to put back on the beds after a couple of hours.

'Ech! Bless my soul!' sighed Cousin Elspeth at tea, which was, again, taken in the garden as the weather was so fine. 'This veesit has passed so quickly, it's harrd to realize that it will be November on Thurrsday. I must be thinking of reeturrning to my ain wee naist.'

'Oh, but you mustn't think of leaving before our Hallowe'en party,' said Mrs Armitage quickly. 'We have so much enjoyed having you, Cousin Elspeth, you must make this visit an annual event. It has been a real pleasure.'

'Indeed it has! I've taken a grand fancy to your youngfolk.' Cousin Elspeth beamed benevolently at Mark and Harriet, who were lying on their stomachs on the grass, doing homework between bites of bread and damson jam.

'Where's Tinthea?' Harriet suddenly said to Mark. 'Did you put her away?'

'No, I didn't. Did you?'

Harriet shook her head.

Quietly, she and Mark rose, left the group round the garden table, and went indoors.

'I can hear something upstairs,' said Mark.

A thumping could be heard from the direction of Cousin Elspeth's room.

Harriet armed herself with a broom, Mark picked a walking-stick from the front-door stand, and they hurried up the stairs.

As they entered Cousin Elspeth's room, Tinthea could be seen apparently admiring herself in the large looking-glass. Then, advancing to it with outstretched monitor selection function aligners, she was plainly about to remove it from the wall when Mark, stepping forward, tapped down her main switch with the ferrule of the walking-stick. Tinthea let out what sounded like a cry of rage and spun half-round before she lost her power and became inert with dangling mandibles and vacant receiving panel; but even so it seemed to Harriet that there was a very malevolent expression in her sixty-watt eyes.

'What was *really* queer, though,' Harriet said to her brother, 'was that just before you hooked down her switch, I caught sight of her reflection in the glass, and she looked – well, not like a helot, more like a person. There is something peculiar about that mirror.'

She studied herself in the glass.

'The first time I saw myself in it, I thought I looked horrible. But now I look better—'

Mark eyed his reflection and said, 'Perhaps that's what's been happening to Cousin Elspeth, seeing herself in it every day . . .'

'Of *course*! Aren't you clever! So that's why old Miss Hooting wanted it! But what shall we do about Tinthea?'

'Put her back in the cellar. You take her legs. Don't touch the switch.' Tinthea sagged heavily between them as they carried her back to the cellar. And when she was set down next to Nickelas, it seemed that a warning message flashed between the two pairs of sightless eyes.

The Armitages' Hallowe'en party was always a great success.

This year Mrs Armitage, with Cousin Elspeth and Harriet helping, produced a magnificent feast, including several Scottish delicacies such as haggis and Aberdeen bun; Mark and Harriet organized apple-bobbing, table-turning, and fortune-telling with tea-leaves (large Earl Grey ones), flour, lighted candles, and soot. The guests came dressed as trolls, kelpies, banshees, werewolves, or boggarts, and the sensation of the evening was the pair of helots, Tinthea and Nickelas, who, carefully and lengthily programmed during days of hard work by Mr Armitage, passed round trays of cheese tarts, chestnut crunch fancies, and tiny curried sausages.

'But they're not real, are they?' cried Mrs Pontwell, the vicar's wife. 'I mean – they are Mark and Harriet, cleverly dressed up, aren't they, really?'

When she discovered that the helots were not Mark and Harriet, she gave a slight scream and kept well out of their way for the rest of the evening.

Many of the guests remained, playing charades, until nearly midnight, but Cousin Elspeth, who intended to leave the following morning, retired to bed at half past ten.

'Och! I've just had a grand time,' she said. 'I never thocht I'd enjoy a party so well. But old bones, ye ken, need plainty of rest; I'll e'en take maself of to ma wee bed, for I must be up bricht and airlly the morn.'

Her absence did not diminish the gaiety of the party, and Mrs Armitage was serving cups of hot chocolate with rum in it while everyone sang 'Widecombe Fair', when piercing shrieks were heard from upstairs. Simultaneously, all the lights went out.

'Och, maircy! Mairder! Mairder! Mairder!'

'Sounds as if someone's strangling Cousin Elspeth,' said Mark, starting for the stairs.

'Where did you put the matches?' said Harriet.

There were plenty of candles and matches lying around, but in the confusion, with guests and members of the family bumping about in the dark, it was some time before a rescue party, consisting of Mark, Mr Armitage, and Mr Shepherd from next door, was able to mount the stairs with candles and make their way to Cousin Elspeth's room.

They found that lady sitting up in bed in shawl and nightcap, almost paralytic with indignation.

'A deedy lot you are, upon my worrd! I could have been torrn leemb fra leemb before ye lifted a feenger!'

'But what happened?' said Mr Armitage, looking round in perplexity.

'The mirror's gone!' said Mark.

'Whit happened? Whit *happened*? Yon unco' misshapen stravaiging shilpit monsters of yours cam' glomping intil ma room – bauld as brass! – removed the meerror fra the wall, and glomped off oot again, as calm as Plato! Wheer they have taken it, I dinna speer – nor do I care – but thankful I am this is the last nicht in life I'll pass under *this* roof, and I'll ne'er come back afore death bears me awa', and it's only a wonder I didna die on the spot wi' petrification!' And Cousin Elspeth succumbed to a fit of violent hysterics, needing to be administered to with burnt feathers, sal volatile, brandy, snuff, hot-water bottles, and antiphlogistine poultices.

While this was happening, Mark said to Harriet,

'Where do you suppose the helots have taken the mirror?'

'Back to the cellar? How did they get out?'

By this time, most of the guests had gone. The blown fuse had been mended and the lights restored. Mark and Harriet went down, a little cautiously, to inspect the cellar, but found it empty; the lock had been neatly picked from inside.

As they returned to the hall, the telephone rang. Mark picked up the receiver and heard the vicar's voice.

'Mark, is that you, my boy? I'm afraid those two mechanical monsters of yours are up to something very fishy in the churchyard. I can see them from my study window in the moonlight. Will you ask your father to come along, and tell him I've phoned PC Loiter.'

'Oh, *now* what?' groaned Mr Armitage on hearing this news, but he accompanied his children to the churchyard, which was only a five-minute run along the main street, leaving Mrs Armitage in charge of the stricken Cousin Elspeth.

A large, bright hunter's moon was sailing overhead, and by its light, it was easy to see Nickelas and Tinthea hoisting up Miss Hooting's glass coffin. They had excavated the grave with amazing speed, and now carefully placed the coffin on the grass to one side of it. Then they laid the mirror, reflecting surface down, on top of the coffin.

As the Armitages arrived at one gate, the vicar and PC Loiter came from the vicarage garden.

'Here! What's going on!' shouted PC Loiter, outraged. 'Just you stop that – whatever you're doing! – If you ask me,' he added in an undertone to Mr Pontwell, 'that's what comes from burying these here wit— these old fairy ladies in churchyards along with decent folk.'

'Oh dear me,' said the vicar, 'but we must be broad-minded, you know, and Miss Hooting had been such a long-established member of our community—'

At this moment, Nickelas and Tinthea, taking no notice of PC Loiter's shouts, raised the mirror high above the coffin, holding it like a canopy.

'What's the idea, d'you suppose!' Mark muttered to Harriet.

'So as to get the reflection of Miss Hooting inside the coffin—'

'Ugh!'

The coffin suddenly exploded with the kind of noise that a gas oven makes when somebody has been too slow in lighting the match. The helots fell backwards, letting go of the mirror, which fell and smashed.

A large owl was seen to fly away from where the coffin had been.

PC Loiter, very reluctantly, but encouraged by the presence of Mr Pontwell and Mr Armitage on either side, went forward and inspected the coffin. But there was nothing in it, except a great deal of broken glass. Nor was the body of Miss Hooting ever seen again.

'*I* think it was a plan that went wrong,' said Harriet to Mark. '*I* think she hoped, if she had the mirror, it would make her young and handsome and stop her from dying.'

'So she sent the helots to get it? Maybe,' said Mark.

'What a shame the mirror got smashed. Because, look at Cousin Elspeth!'

Cousin Elspeth, overnight, had gone back to exactly what she had been at the beginning of the visit – sour, dour, hard-featured, and extremely bad-tempered.

'Ye might have provided a drap of Earl Grey for my last breakfast!' she snapped. 'And, as for that disgreeceful occurrence last nicht – aweel, the less said the better!' After which she went on to say a great deal more about it. And, as she left, announced that Mark would certainly not get the writing-desk, nor Harriet the mohair stole, since they were undoubtedly responsible for the goings-on in the night.

'Somehow, I don't see Cousin Elspeth putting us through art school,' mused Harriet, as the taxi rolled away with their cousin along the village street.

'That's a long way off,' said Mark peacefully.

Mr Armitage was on the telephone with Dowbridges, the auctioneers.

'I want you to come and fetch two robots and enter them in your Friday sale. Please send a truck at once; I'd like them out of the house by noon. Yes, *robots*; two lunar-powered robots, in full working order, complete with instruction booklets. Handy for workshop, kitchen, or garden; a really useful pair; you can price the large one at £90 and the small at £50.'

On Friday, Mrs Armitage and Harriet attended the sale, and returned to report with high satisfaction that both helots had been sold to Admiral Lycanthrop.

'*He'll* give them what for, I bet,' said Mark. '*He* won't stand any nonsense from them.'

But, alas, it turned out that the admiral, who was rather

hard of hearing, thought he was bidding for two rowboats, and when he discovered that his purchase consisted instead of two lunar-powered mechanical slaves with awkward dispositions, he returned them, demanding his money back.

The Armitages came down to breakfast on Saturday to find Nickelas and Tinthea standing mute, dogged, and expectant outside the back door …

KITTY SNICKERSNEE

Harriet went once or twice a month to take spinning lessons from old Mrs Holdernesse who lived down the hill. In between the lessons, Harriet collected sheeps' wool from all the local barbed-wire fences, blackthorn thickets, and blackberry clumps, for Mrs Holdernesse to spin. Two weeks' work generally produced a basketful of grey, greasy, lumpy wool, smelling strongly of ammonia, and tangled about with thorns and dried grass and thistly-prickles. Next time Harriet saw the basketful, it would be snowy white, bleached, washed, and dried in the sun, then combed and smoothed and cleaned of all its prickles by rubbing and scraping on a teazel-board. (Teazels were the thistle-heads of tall, spiny plants which grew down in the marshy fields known as the Wildbrooks because they flooded in winter. Teazels seemed to have been invented by Nature specially for the purpose of scratching thorns and lumps of mud out of sheeps' wool.)

Mrs Holdernesse was small and old, with white hair done in a knob on top, small skinny hands, and eyes like triangular chips of blue flint in her pale face. Her hands were amazingly skilful – with one she kept pulling out lumps of wool from the basket, while with the other she twirled and fed it into a quivering strand, which was drawn on to the shoulder of the spinning-wheel, and she kept that spinning round by pedalling with her right foot. And, when the basket of loose tufts was empty, she had a ball, big as her two fists, of strong white crinkly wool, which would be either knitted into sweaters or woven into rugs. Harriet had one of the sweaters. It had been dyed a bright golden yellow with lichen scraped off trees, and was too warm to be worn except in the very coldest weather.

'Sheep know how to keep warm,' said Mrs Holdernesse. 'You never see a sheep shivering.'

While she was spinning or weaving she told Harriet all kinds of interesting facts: how the whole of this country was once deep forest, tall oaks which were all cut down to build ships; and how the inhabitants of Easter Island had done the same thing until there were no trees left on their island, so they could never sail away again . . . how the Romans had brought walnut trees and their own gods to Ancient Britain . . . Harriet listened and learned how to twirl the cluster of wool into a filament, not too thick, not too thin or it would break; if it did break Mrs Holdernesse, with her bony nimble fingers, could twist the two strands together without the least difficulty, but Harriet found it very much harder, and would rub and twist until the strands grew grubby before she made a satisfactory join.

One day Harriet arrived with a much larger basketful

than usual. The wool was particularly filthy and matted; some of it was almost solid with dirt.

'While you are having your lesson I shall put this lot to soak in a bath of foxglove juice,' Mrs Holdernesse decided. 'That will dissolve the mud and dirt. It almost feels as if there is something solid in there, among the wool. Where in the world did you find all this?'

'There's an old shepherd's hut on top of Coldharbour Mount. It blew down in last week's storm and left quite a deep pit underneath. I found all this lot in there. The place hadn't been used for years.'

'Coldharbour Mount? Yes . . . there used to be a lot of stories about that place; the Roman road from the sea runs over the top, so it has been used ever since then, and probably for centuries before that – by smugglers and highwaymen and soldiers on their way to and from wars,' remarked Mrs Holdernesse, settling down again on her spinning-stool and working her wheel into motion. 'Mind that strand, Harriet, it is getting a trifle too thick, fine it down a little. Yes, that is better.'

'Tell me some of the stories about Coldharbour Mount.'

'There used to be a big oak tree where two tracks met.'

'Yes,' said Harriet. 'It is still there. Not far from the ruined hut.'

'It was called the "copt tree".'

'What does "copt" mean?'

'It was an Arabic word, relating to an early religious sect. As recently as a hundred years ago it was thought to be unlucky to pass that tree without leaving an offering.'

'What sort of offering?'

'Oh, anything would be acceptable – a piece of bread, sugar-lump, even a hair off your head. Children who passed that way were thought to be in need of special protection.'

'What kind of protection?'

'They had to wear a magic charm on a neck cord.'

'What kind of magic charm?'

'Your lump of amber would do,' Mrs Holdernesse said smiling. Harriet wore a lump of amber on a silver chain; she had had it last year for a present when her birthday fell during a family trip to Lyme Regis. 'Amber is often used as a charm against witchcraft and the attacks of demons.'

'I take it off at night,' said Harriet thoughtfully. 'Maybe I should keep it on.'

'Not so many demons about nowadays. Perhaps.'

'Do you think there are evil spirits on Coldharbour Mount?'

'There might be a tree goddess called Black Annis,' Mrs Holdernesse said. '—There, that's the end of your wool; shall we go and see how the foxglove bath is working?'

'Who was Black Annis? What did she do?'

'She was a cousin of the Egyptian goddess Sekhet, a lion lady. As Bast, the cat goddess, she was kind and friendly; as Sekhet she was ferocious and demanding. The Romans probably brought her over. There would have been some of her worshippers in the Roman army. Ah,' said Mrs Holdernesse, stirring the muddy wool soup in her copper bath, 'here is something quite solid in the middle of the brew; I shall fish it out with the laundry tongs.'

She did so, flicking aside trailing strands of wet leaves and bracken and grass.

'Why, it's a mask!' exclaimed Harriet.

'So it is. A cat mask. This must certainly be Black Annis. Or one of her descendants.'

'It's very shiny. Do you think it is silver?'

'Yes, I do. Very thin. Very old. You have found something quite valuable, Harriet!'

When the mask was dried, and rubbed with a silver-cloth, it shone brilliantly.

'How old do you think it is?'

'Many centuries,' Mrs Holdernesse said, looking calmly down at the calm cat face. 'It probably came from the north African coast. It would have been used for religious ceremonies – the priest or priestess would wear it.'

'Oh, do put it on, Mrs Holdernesse! Let me see what you look like in it!'

'Thank you, no. Not on any account. And I advise you not to do so, Harriet.'

'Why?' asked Harriet, though she thought she had an idea. There was something about the cat mask which attracted and yet scared and chilled her – she was eager to put it on; she wanted to see what the world would look like, seeing through those eye-slots – and yet she had a shivery feeling that, once she had put the mask on, she might not be able to take it off . . .

'That mask has seen a lot of history.' Mrs Holdernesse

laid the mask on the window-seat leaning against a green cushion. The eye slots, with green behind them, seemed to be watching like cold cat's eyes.

'Do you know any of its history?' Harriet asked, twirling away at her strand of wool.

'I know that in ancient Egypt priests and priestesses wore masks like this for temple ceremonies. Somehow the mask must have made its way to Britain. And I have an idea about its more recent history – well, fairly recent—' Without pausing in her spinning, Mrs Holdernesse picked up a new lump of wool, drew it out into a thread, and joined it to another which had nearly come to an end. She went on: 'About two hundred years ago there was a highwayman in these parts – or rather a highwaywoman. It was said of her that she wore a cat mask so the people she robbed would never be able to recognize her. Coldharbour Mount was one of her favourite haunts.'

'My goodness! This must have been the mask that she used. What was her name?'

'She had various nicknames – Kitty Sickle-claws, and Kitty Snickersnee, and Kitty Sekateur because she had a razor-sharp dagger and used to stab her victims, so that very few of them survived. One can see,' said Mrs Holdernesse, 'a connection with the goddess Sekhet.'

'What happened to her?'

'She had a child – little Jemmy. She used to leave him with a woman who lived in West Burwood, over the hill. But the Bow Street men found out about him. And so when Kitty held up a coach on Coldharbour Mount a voice from

inside called "Drop your weapon or little Jemmy gets a dose of lead down his gullet!" And little Jemmy called out, "Mammy! Mammy!"'

'So what happened?'

'She dropped her weapon and the Bow Street men arrested her.'

'Did she go to prison?'

'No, they hanged her right there and then, from the big oak tree. There was quite a commotion about that, questions asked in Parliament, why hadn't she a proper trial. But the Bow Street men said she was resisting arrest. And she had killed quite a few innocent travellers, so the whole thing blew over. Only there was trouble about the mask.'

'The mask. Why?'

'They couldn't get it off her. So she was buried in it. There is a story – but no more than a piece of local legend – that a hundred years later somebody dug her up – her skeleton – and took the mask off the skull. Whether that is a true tale I don't know . . . '

'What became of little Jemmy?'

'There were questions asked in Parliament about him, too. He certainly died. It is thought that he was accidentally shot in the struggle when Kitty was taken. In any case, who'd want to bring up a highwaywoman's child?'

'It's a sad story,' said Harriet. 'What do you think I should do with the mask?'

'You could give it to the museum in West Burwood.'

'Y-e-s – I suppose I could.'

'Or,' said Mrs Holdernesse, spinning away, 'you could drop it in the dew pond on Coldharbour Mount. Myself, I'd advise that.'

'I would *so like* to try it on.'

'It wants you to do that.'

'Why?'

'That is what it was made for. And it has been dead – empty – inactive – for a long time now. Once it must have been used every day – it was important and powerful—'

'It still feels powerful,' said Harriet, picking up the mask. It was as thin and light as a piece of tinfoil, it had a mellow shine in the light from the window, it looked mild and harmless as a Christmas decoration. There were two slots on each side, behind the cheek pieces.

'I suppose they would have ribbons or strings through those holes, to fasten it on someone's head,' said Harriet. She picked up a discarded length of wool and threaded it through one of the holes. Then she found a second piece and threaded that.

'If I were you,' said Mrs Holdernesse, 'I'd put the mask into this bag and forget about it.'

From a cupboard she took a hand-woven bag, fastened at the mouth by drawstrings. She passed it to Harriet. Very reluctantly Harriet slid the mask into the bag and pulled the cords to gather the neck together. Then she thought about the mask in the bag, cut off from daylight, as it had been for so long in that sodden lump of greasy sheeps' wool.

It was a sad, suffocating, creepy feeling. The mask wanted, badly, to be back in daylight. She knew it did.

'I think it is time you went home, Harriet,' said Mrs Holdernesse, looking at Harriet very straightly. 'And I think it would be a good thing if you left the mask in this house.'

'Oh, no. I want to show it to Mark.'

Harriet picked up the bag with the mask in it.

'It would be much better if you left it here,' said Mrs Holdernesse.

For a mad moment Harriet wondered if Mrs Holdernesse wanted to wear the mask herself. But no, that was impossible. She had said so. What did she want to do with it? Bury it in her garden? Or would she carry it up to the top of Coldharbour Mount and drop it in the dew pond?

'Harriet,' said Mrs Holdernesse, '*whatever* you do, don't put on that mask!'

'Thank you for the lovely spinning lesson, Mrs Holdernesse,' Harriet said politely. 'And I'll see you on Wednesday week.'

She walked out of Mrs Holdernesse's house, carrying the woven bag.

An early, foggy dusk had fallen. There was going to be a sharp frost. Harriet thought about the highway robber, Kitty Sickle-claws, wearing a black cloak, riding a black horse, going softly up the deep chalk lane that led through woods up to the top of Coldharbour Mount. Her silver mask, under the black hood of her cloak, would gleam faintly in the misty light. Did she ever take the mask off? Or was little Jemmy accustomed to a silver, cat-faced mother?

Mark was at home, in the work-room he shared with Harriet, solving something on his computer.

'Look what I found,' said Harriet. She undid the strings of the bag and pulled out the mask, which she laid on Mark's work table.

Two things happened. Mark's computer went wild, throwing jags and flashes all over the screen. And Walrus, the elderly cat, who was sitting by the fire, let out a frightful hiss and catapulted out of the window, which, luckily, was open.

'Blimey!' said Mark. 'What a nasty thing! Wherever did you get it?'

Harriet told him its story. Mark said,

'Mrs Holdernesse is a sensible old bird. If I were you, I'd take her advice. Look at how poor old Walrus acted.'

'Well – I'll see how I feel about it tomorrow.'

'I am sure Dad would say get rid of it.'

The Armitage parents were spending the evening at a London theatre.

Harriet said, 'I would *so* like to put it on. Just for a moment, to see how it feels.'

'You'd be crazy.'

'I suppose so,' said Harriet halfheartedly.

They had supper while the mask watched them from the kitchen dresser. Harriet had leaned it against a bowl of tomatoes. Its eyes were red.

Mark tried to persuade Walrus to come into the house, but he wouldn't be persuaded, despite the fact that it was growing colder and colder.

'Tell you what,' said Mark. 'How about putting the mask into Father's safe for the night. It's obviously very valuable. And just in case you had a sudden mad impulse to put it on – you know you never can remember the combination number. And there's nothing in the safe that can come to harm – only Ma's diamond earrings.'

'She probably wore them to London.'

Harriet was not overenthusiastic about Mark's plan, but she finally allowed him to put the mask back in its bag, and the bag in the safe, which was in Mr Armitage's study. Then Mark and Harriet locked up the house and went to bed.

Harriet had great trouble getting to sleep. She lay thrashing about her bed, longing for the mask. Her head, and particularly her face, felt hot as fire. She imagined how cool the silver shell would feel against her blazing cheeks.

At last she fell into a heavy, feverish slumber. And she began to dream. She dreamed that they were all waiting for her. Who? They were lined up on both sides of the temple – rows and rows of them, all in white, with pleated head-dresses. They were holding torches that poured smoke and flame and gave off a hot, resinous smell.

'I shall be late!' Harriet said. 'I shall be late!'

She hurried out of bed, threw on clothes, pattered down-stairs . . .

She went into Mr Armitage's study, easily dialled the correct combination, opened the safe, took out the hand-woven bag. Then she slipped the mask from the bag and put it on, tying the two strands of wool in a knot behind her head. Without pausing for a moment she unlocked the front door, went out, crossed the garden, and took the lane that led up to Coldharbour Mount.

The night was thick, icy-cold, and starless. Frost scrunched under her feet. Owls flew silently overhead, then let out harsh wailing cries. Foxes yapped in the woods beside the track.

It was a forty-minute run up to the great oak. Harriet never slowed down.

'I'll be late, they are waiting, I'll be late,' she kept muttering.

When she came to the big oak tree she hesitated for the first time, and it was there that Mark, panting, caught up with her. He grabbed her arm.

'Harriet! *Harriet*! What on earth do you think you're doing?'

Then he saw that she was fast asleep. Her eyes were open but unfocused. Ignoring him, she started trying to climb the oak tree.

'Harriet! Wake up! WAKE UP!'

He gripped her wrist and shouted in her ear.

Silently, she wrestled with him.

'Oh, please wake up, Harriet!'

Mrs Holdernesse came hurrying forward from behind the oak tree.

'Ah, Mark! I was afraid that something like this might happen. Could you, very kindly, fetch my spinning-wheel and stool out of my car. While you do that, I will hold Harriet.'

'Shall you be able to?' he said doubtfully. 'She's very strong. Extra strong!'

'I will hold her like this.'

Mrs Holdernesse grabbed Harriet's hair, which was loose, as she had left it when she went to bed. A bunch of hair came out, which Mrs Holdernesse carefully laid at the foot of the oak tree – but she kept a firm hold on the rest.

Harriet was obliged to stand still, with tears streaming out from under the silver mask.

'Poor girl,' said Mrs Holdernesse. Her tone was full of sympathy. 'Finding that mask was a shocking piece of bad luck. But we are trying to help you. Like this!' She took a little pointed quill from a pouch at her belt and suddenly and sharply jabbed it into Harriet's wrist. Harriet let out a cry of indignation, and her eyes flew open.

Mark had come back with the spinning-wheel and stool.

'Mark, can you take the mask off your sister's face?'

'It won't come,' said Mark, panting, after a few minutes' struggle. 'Feels as if it was glued on.'

Mrs Holdernesse had settled on her stool and started the spinning-wheel on its swift circuit. She said,

'Look at the wheel, Harriet, watch the wheel. Keep watching. See how it goes round and round – like the world, like the sun, in a circle. Think of circles.' She sang, suddenly, in a thin, clear voice, 'Cross Patch, Draw the latch, sit by the fire and *spin* – spin – spin – spin – *spin* my lady's wolsey, weave my lady's web—'

The wheel spun and spun. Harriet's eyes, fixed on it, flickered and flickered. Suddenly, with a long, heart-rending sigh, she lifted up her hand and removed the mask from her face. It came away without the least difficulty.

'Take it, Mark,' ordered Mrs Holdernesse, 'and drop it in the dew pond.'

Mark did so. The mask felt hot, like a plate that has been in the oven. Without it, Harriet looked lost, bewildered.

'Good,' said Mrs Holdernesse. 'Now you go and sit in the car while Mark and I pack the stool and wheel into the boot.'

As they did so, Mrs Holdernesse muttered to Mark, 'I shouldn't talk about this to Harriet at all. Just let her go back to bed. Don't mention it tomorrow. It has been like an infection that she caught.'

'Okay,' said Mark.

'You're a good boy . . .'

Mrs Holdernesse drove them rather slowly down the bumpy chalk track and left them at their door. Mark wondered how long she had been up there on Coldharbour Mount waiting for Harriet to arrive.

At the front door they found the cat Walrus, impatient to be let into the house. As soon as Harriet was in bed he jumped up beside her and spread his large black shape across three-quarters of the bed-space.

GOBLIN MUSIC

The Armitage family had been to Cornwall for a week at the end of April. They did this every year, for 30 April was old Miss Thunderhurst's birthday. Miss Thunderhurst lived next door to the Armitages and the celebrations of her birthday grew louder and wilder every year. This year was her hundredth birthday and, as Mr Armitage said, staying at home through the festivities was not to be thought of. So the Armitages went off to their usual rented seaside cottage in the little port of Gwendreavy where, if you wanted to buy a loaf of bread, you had to row across the estuary to South-the-Water on the other side. There was a wonderful secondhand bookshop in South-the-Water; when they were sent across for the bread, Mark and Harriet put in a lot of time browsing there and came back with battered copies of treasures such as *What Katie Knew*, *The Herr of Poynton*, *Eric or Little Women*, *More About Rebecca of Manderley Farm*, and *Simple Peter Rabbit*. The family took their cat, Walrus, along with them on these holidays, and he had a fine time catching fish.

So it was decidedly puzzling, when the family returned

home after a five-hour drive, arriving in the middle of the night, to find a line of muddy cat footprints on the white paint of the front door, leading straight upwards, from the doorstep to the lintel.

'Cats don't walk up vertical walls,' said Mr Armitage indignantly, rummaging for the front door key.

'Here it is,' said his wife, getting it out of her handbag. And she added, 'I *have* seen Walrus bounce upwards off a wall when the jump to the top was a bit more than he reckoned he could manage.'

'Granted, but not *walk up the whole wall*.'

Walrus was sniffing suspiciously at the lowest of the footprints, and he let out a loud and disapproving noise between a hiss and a growl.

'Let's go in,' said Mrs Armitage hastily in case Walrus's challenge received an answer. 'They are only kitten prints. And I'm dying for a cup of tea and bed.'

'I'm surprised to see that marquee still there,' grumbled her husband, carrying bags into the house.

Since Miss Thunderhurst's party had been planned for an extra big one this year, she had rented a marquee for the occasion, and got permission to put it in Farmer Beezeley's field across the road. The car's headlights had caught the great grey-white canvas shape as the Armitages turned into their own driveway.

'So we still have all that nuisance ahead, poles clanking and trucks blocking the road while they take it down,' growled Mr Armitage, as ruffled as Walrus.

'Oh, I expect they'll do that tomorrow while we're still

getting unpacked,' said his wife. 'Here's your tea, dear. I'm going up.'

But when Mrs Armitage was halfway up the stairs, the most amazing noise started up outside the house. It seemed to be piano music played by giants. It was a fugue – the same tune played again and again, overlapping like tiles on a roof, in different keys, some high, some low.

'It's rather terrific,' said Mark, impressed in spite of himself.

'Terrific? It's the most ear-splitting racket I ever heard! At three minutes to one a.m.? Are they out of their flagrant minds? I'm going across to give them what-for!'

'Oh, Gilbert! Do you think that's neighbourly? We don't want to be on bad terms with Miss Thunderhurst.'

'How long does she expect her birthday to last? It's the fourth of May, dammit.'

Mr Armitage strode out of the front door, down the steps, across the road, and Mark followed him, curious to see what instruments produced that astonishing sound.

The door-flaps of the marquee were folded back. A dim glow inside was just enough to show that the big tent was completely packed with people – far more, surely, than even Miss Thunderhurst would have invited to her birthday celebrations – and Miss Thunderhurst knew every soul in the village.

'Where is Miss Thunderhurst? I want to speak to her,' Mr Armitage said to a shortish, stoutish person who met him in the entrance.

'Miss Thunderhurst has long since departed to her own place of residence.'

'Oh, *indeed*! – well, who's in charge here? You are making a devilish rumpus and it has to stop. At once!'

'Oh, no, sir. That is not quite possible.'

'Not possible? I should just about think it *is* possible! You are making an ear-splitting row. It has to stop. At once!'

'No, sir. To make music is our right.'

'*Right?* Who the deuce do you think you are?'

'We are the Niffel people. Our own place of residence – Niffelheim-under-Lyme – has been rendered unfit for occupation. They set light to an opencast coal mine on top of our cave habitation, and the roof collapsed. Luckily there was no loss of life, but many were injured. Much damage. So we appealed to the County Council and they have found us this dwelling for the time. We are sadly cramped but it must serve until we find a more suitable home.'

'Oh! I see! Very well. If the council settled you here, that's different. – I suppose you don't know how long you'll be here? . . . But you must, *immediately*, stop making that atrocious row. People need to sleep.'

'No, sir. To make the music is our right. Is our need.'

'Not at this time of night, dammit!'

'Sir, we are nocturnal people. Earthfolk. Gloam-goblins. Our work is done at night-time. By day we sleep. Dark is our day. Day is our dark. Music is our stay.'

'Who is in charge here? Who is your president – or whatever you have? Your head person?'

'I am the Spokesman. My name is Albrick,' the small man said with dignity. 'Our First Lady – our Sovereign – is the Lady Holdargh.'

'Well, let me speak to her.'

'She is not here at this time. She travels. She seeks a place for us.'

'Oh. Well – won't you, in the meantime, *please* stop making this hideous din!'

'No, sir. That we cannot do. It is our must.' And as Mr Armitage looked at him in incredulous outrage, he repeated with dignity, 'It is our must.'

'Come on, Dad.' Mark plucked his father's arm. 'We can't make a fuss if they are here by permission of the Council. I'll lend you a pair of earplugs.'

Very unwillingly and reluctantly Mr Armitage allowed himself to be led back across the road to his own house. There he was supplied with earplugs by Mark (who used them when practising with his Group) and a sleeping-pill by his wife.

Harriet, during this interval, had opened a tin of sardines for Walrus, who was upset and nervous at the traces of an intruder around his home. Mark and his father came back just as she was about to go out in search of them. Mr Armitage stomped off gloomily upstairs, muttering, 'Niffel people indeed!'

'What's going on?' Harriet asked Mark. 'Couldn't Dad get them to stop?'

'No, he couldn't. They aren't Miss Thunderhurst's guests at all. They are goblins – displaced goblins.'

'Goblins? I've never met a goblin. Who displaced them?'

'A burning coal mine. Coal is burned underground these days to make gas. The goblins were obliged to shift. They didn't seem unfriendly. Their spokesman was quite reasonable. They are nocturnal. They work at night. And they need music to work.'

'I wonder what sort of work they do? Could you see? Were they doing it?'

'No, I couldn't see. There were a whole lot of them in the tent – several hundred at least. All crammed together in a very dim light.'

'Well!' said Harriet. 'Fancy having a group of hardworking goblins across the road. I can't wait to see what they make. I'll go across after breakfast.'

'They'll all be asleep,' her brother pointed out.

'Bother! So they will. But I suppose they start to get active after sunset, about half past seven. I'll go and call on them then. Now I'm off to bed. Come on, Walrus.'

But Walrus was going out, to watch for goblin cats, and, if necessary, beat them up.

The full moon had just worked its way round the corner of the house, and was blazing in at Harriet's bedroom window, throwing a great square of white light across her bedroom wall. Harriet had once sat in a train opposite two women who were evidently sisters in some religious order. They wore black habits and white wimples. They were laughing a great deal and talking to each other nonstop in some foreign language that was full of s's and k's. Harriet could not at all understand what they were saying, but she somehow took a great liking to them and, when she got home, drew a picture of them from memory and hung it up on her bedroom wall. Two or three months later she noticed an interesting phenomenon: when the moon shone on her picture, she could see the two women's hands move about and sometimes catch a little of what they were saying. Now, too, she could partly understand the language, but one of the two women, the spectacled one, had a bad stammer, and Harriet only caught a word here and a word there.

'Refugees – immigrants – l-l-look after them somehow – p-p-poor d-d-dears—'

Tonight the moonlight was fully on the picture, and the two women were deeply engrossed in what they were saying.

'Hardworking – industrious – deserving.'

'No place for them here—'

'Only l-l-lead to t-t-trouble—'

Harriet went and stood in front of the picture. 'Excuse me—' she began politely. Then she realized that she was blocking off the moonlight from the picture and the ladies stopped talking and moving their hands.

'I'm so sorry, I didn't mean to interrupt,' said Harriet, and stepped to one side. But now a cloud had drifted across the moon and the ladies remained silent. Harriet waited for ten minutes, but by the time the cloud had floated away, the moon had moved also, and no longer shone in at the window.

'I'll try again tomorrow,' thought Harriet, and went to bed, for she was tired.

In the morning, as soon as breakfast was over, Mark and Harriet raced across the road to inspect the new occupants of Farmer Beezeley's meadow.

The Gloam Goblins were packing up their work materials and preparing their evening meal. They were evidently smiths and potters. They had portable kilns and forges.

'They seem to use solar heat,' said Mark. 'It's very adaptable of them! If they lived underground up to now they must have changed their habits very quickly.'

'Oh look,' said Harriet. 'There are stalls with things for sale.' The things for sale were lace made of filigree iron, exquisitely fine and light; also iron jewellery, and pottery.– bowls, plates, cups, jugs, also very light and delicate, ornamented with a dark-green and white glazed pattern resembling the foam on a wave crest.

'Ma would like these,' said Harriet. Mrs Armitage collected china and had brought back from Cornwall an enormous blue-and-white platter with a romantic landscape on it which she had found in a junk shop in South-the-Water.

'I'll come back later with some money and buy one of these,' Harriet told the little woman behind the stall, who smiled and nodded.

The goblins were about half the size of humans. Their skin was brown and weather-worn as if at some time they had lived out of doors for centuries. Their faces were rugged, rather plain but friendly and honest-looking. Their manners were somewhat abrupt, as if all they wanted was to be left alone to get on with what they were doing. Mark and Harriet now felt rather embarrassed and apologetic at their plan to inspect the new arrivals like creatures in a zoo. They retreated from the doorway, taking in as quickly and unobtrusively as possible all the activities that were going on: pots of vegetable stew being stirred over small fires, bedding rolls pulled out of sacks and spread on the ground, children's faces being washed in basins of water. There were cats and dogs, too, of a size to match their owners.

'You don't mind us just looking?' Mark said to Albrick, the man who had talked to his father. Albrick was evidently a smith; he was packing up a small anvil and a portable forge and cooling off his tools in a pail of water.

'Very well cannot stop you, can I?' said Albrick gruffly. But he added, 'You are all right. But some folk do more than just look – they want us to go. Where we stopped before here, we needed guards with swords and pistols. And the young ones needed to go out with guards. Folk in this village not bad – but not welcoming. What can we expect?'

'I expect – if it weren't for the music at night—'

'Ah, the music. It is our must.' Albrick glanced towards the interior of the tent and Mark and Harriet, following the direction of his eyes, had a glimpse of a massive structure – a portable organ? – which a party of goblins were wrapping up in layers of thick felt.

'Our must,' Albrick repeated. 'Work and music.'

'Oh!' said Mark. 'Is it an organ? Oh, I'd love to play it. Could I? *Could* I?'

Mark had piano lessons from Professor Johansen in the village and was understood to show promise. He was certainly very keen and practised a great deal.

'You wish to play our keyboard?' Albrick said doubtfully. 'You do nothing foolish?'

'Oh *no*!'

'He does play quite well,' Harriet put in hopefully.

'We see. We see. Not now. I put my child to bed. Goodbye. We talk again.'

Albrick nodded in a dismissive manner and called, 'Dwine! Dwiney! Bedtime!'

'Here, Father!' A small tousle-headed goblin child came rushing towards him followed by a goblin kitten. 'Come, Fryxse!' she called to the cat. But Fryxse was small, wayward, and playful. He clawed and scampered his way up the side of the marquee and disappeared. On his way, no doubt, to go and tease Walrus.

Mark and Harriet strolled along the village street to find how the rest of the neighbours were reacting to having a community of Gloam Goblins deposited on their doorstep.

Mr Budd the blacksmith said, 'They're not bad. Decent enough. The chairperson, that Albrick, he's a sensible chap. Good workman, too. Knows what's what. He comes round to my forge for a chat now and then. There's not much I can tell him about iron.'

'But what about their music?'

Mr Budd gave a half grin, rubbing his bristly jaw.

'Don't worrit me none. I'm deaf, see? All blacksmiths are deaf, 'count of the hammering. I pulls the covers over me head, nights, and sleep through the lot. And little Dwiney, his kid, she'd be in here all evening long, with her cat, if I didn't chase her home to bed. Taken a fair shine to her, I have. Sharp as a tack, she be.'

Mrs Case, at the village shop, was not so enthusiastic.

'Only middling customers, see? Grow a lot of their own stuff, they do, in pots and trays. Vegetarians, like. I will say, they pay up promptly for what they do buy – but at first they wanted to pay in gold coins. "Gold?" I say to them, "I'm not having any of that fancy stuff. You'll have to go and change it at Mr Watson's bank." Which they did, I'm bound to say. A lot of them never heard of a bank before. The music? Drives me up the wall, that do. Shouldn't be allowed.'

'They need it for their work,' Mark said.

'Well, they oughta do their work somewhere else, where they won't drive honest day-biding folk clean barmy. That's what I say! And so do lots of neighbours.'

Half the village shared Mrs Case's feelings. If the newcomers had to make such an ear-splitting row in order to do their work, why then they must move to a place where nobody could hear them. Else why couldn't they alter their habits to fit in with their new neighbours?

Mrs Owlet, a witch, the Chair Person of the Parish Council, threatened to stage a protest about the new arrivals.

'And it will be terribly inconvenient if she does,' worried Mrs Armitage, who was secretary to the Council. 'Last time she protested it was about the plan for a bypass running through Titania Copse; never shall I forget the trouble.'

'The cows were all giving sour milk for eight weeks,' remembered Mr Armitage. '—Mind, she was quite right about the bypass. What is she threatening to do this time?'

'Put up a pillar in the middle of the village green and stand on it till somebody gives way. Like Saint Simeon Stylites.'

'I should think the pillar would collapse. Mrs Owlet must weigh as much as the Statue of Liberty. Ask her round for a drink, and I'll see if I can't persuade her to think of some other form of protest.'

'What in the world can we offer her to drink?'

'She likes low-calorie poison,' Harriet said. 'Sue Case told me her mother orders it specially for Mrs Owlet and they deliver four cases a week.'

'Oh, well, we'd better get some. And some Wolfsbane-flavoured cheese straws.'

'I'll make those,' Harriet offered. 'And little Dwiney Albrick can help.'

Little Dwiney Albrick, that sociable child, had taken a great fancy to the Armitage family and spent a lot of time in their house, unless her father came and fetched her.

'Don't let her be a nuisance to ye, ma'am,' he said to Mrs Armitage.

'No, we're very fond of her, Mr Albrick. Her and that crazy kitten of hers . . .'

The Armitage house contained a room which was simply known as the Top Room. In it were kept all the things that members of the family had acquired in one way or another, but had no plans for just at present: the huge blue-and-white platter that Mrs Armitage had bought in Cornwall; a spinning-wheel for llama's wool that was waiting for Harriet to collect enough wool from Hebdons' Llama Farm; a fishing-rod for when Mr Armitage had a spare day from the office to visit his carp pools; several thousand empty egg-boxes stacked against the wall, which Mark intended to make into a launching-pad for the flint-powered spacecraft that he was in the process of constructing.

Mark spent more time than the rest of the family in this pleasant attic, with its skylight looking out over the village green, and little Dwiney and her kitten liked to come and keep him company. Dwiney was a quiet and untroublesome companion; she drew pictures, using a box of crayons that Harriet had given her, arranged little chips of flint into patterns, and sang to herself in a soft, true little voice while Mark played on the shallow, tinkling old piano that also lived up there.

Dwiney's kitten was something else. It was not that he was badly behaved – after a tendency to tease Walrus had been firmly dealt with by that character – but he was so interested in everything and so inquisitive that it was not safe to leave him unobserved for more than a very few minutes.

On the evening that Mrs Owlet was invited for a drink, Mark was working on his spacecraft and chose to stay upstairs; he was never particularly fond of adult company and he thought Mrs Owlet was an old bore anyway; always carrying on about the human race and their habit of hurting and killing one another.

'Can't we persuade you to try some other form of protest?' suggested Mr Armitage hopefully when the lady guest had been provided with a plateful of Wolfsbane cheese straws and a brimming beaker of low-calorie poison.

'Why, pray?' snapped Mrs Owlet. She was a large, commanding lady; Harriet imagined her on top of an eighty-foot column on the village green and decided that it would be an impressive sight.

'Well – I don't want to discourage you – but those young tearaways on their motorbikes – not from our village, I'm thankful to say, they come over from Trottenworth – I don't like to think what they might get up to if they arrived one evening and saw you on your column – what's it going to be made of, by the way?'

'Fuel containers,' snapped Mrs Owlet, 'threaded together on a ship's mast I purchased from the United Sorcerer's Supply Stores; they are erecting it now, on the green. It will be a most superior addition to the village – I expect photographers from the national press, and our Member of Parliament has been sent an invitation; he has half promised to come down on Sunday – and of course representatives from the National Trust and Downlands Heritage will certainly come – I expect a sculpture award, it will certainly put our village on the map.'

'But it is on the map already,' said Mrs Armitage plaintively. 'We surely don't want a lot of tourists and day-trippers coming and rubbernecking – do we? – and I'm sure the poor goblins don't either. They hate being stared at. It would probably be at times when they would be asleep—'

Mr Armitage saw that their guest was displeased by these remarks, and made haste to change the subject.

'How do you plan to get to the top of the pillar?' he inquired, thinking of cranes and hoists.

Mrs Owlet was affronted.

'To someone with my qualifications that presents no problem at all,' she said shortly. 'I merely levitate. In fact' – she looked at her watch – 'I should be on my way now.'

And, nodding perfunctory thanks, she drained her glass and left the room and the house.

At this moment, upstairs, little Dwiney's kitten, Fryxse, was sitting in the middle of the Top Room, eyeing Mark's massive rampart of egg-boxes stacked against the wall. Mark, at the piano, was playing a tune which he had christened 'Dwiney's Night Song'. He hoped to play it to Mr Albrick, to persuade him to let Mark have a try on the organ.

Dwiney was listening with total attention. When Mark had finished she gave a sigh of pure happiness. 'Oh, that was nice, Mark! Play it again!'

But, at that moment, Fryxse finished his calculations, and sprang to the top of the egg-box mountain, bouncing lightly halfway to give himself extra launching-power.

Mark and his father argued for years afterwards about whether the fact that, by sheer unfortunate accident, one of the egg-boxes was *not* empty but contained six eggs and a use-by label that was five years old made any difference to the ultimate outcome.

There was a thunderous crash, followed by the slithering sound of a torrent of egg-boxes cascading down the attic stairs to the bedroom floor. This was accompanied, simultaneously, by the powerful smell of six five-year-old eggs, which poured through the house like poison gas and caused the Armitage parents to run into the garden in case it *was* poison gas.

Poor Fryxse, the cause of this cataclysm, was terrified, and rushed from the room, down the stairs, and out through the front door, which Mrs Owlet had left open behind her.

'Fryxse! Come back! It's all right! Come *back*!'

Dwiney rushed after him – out the front door, through the garden, across the road – straight into the path of the young tearaways from Trottenworth on their motor-bikes come to laugh at the lady balancing on top of her pillar.

Both Dwiney and her kitten were killed instantly.

That night, when the square of moonlight slipped round the wall to the picture of the two Sisters, Harriet addressed them.

'Please listen! Things are in a very bad way here. The goblins are terribly unhappy. Mrs Owlet is threatening to jump down off her pillar in protest at the goblins being here if they don't leave and go somewhere else. They say they don't care if she does jump. But they have nowhere to go . . .'

A black cloud drifted across the sky and blotted out the picture of the Sisters.

Harriet went unhappily to bed. Since the house still reeked of five-year-old eggs, she packed a lavender-bag under her pillow. But it made very little difference.

Next day was little Dwiney's funeral.

One or two people (including Mrs Owlet from her pillar) raised objections to little Dwiney being buried in the village churchyard, but the vicar responded so fiercely that they soon backed down.

Everybody was at the ceremony except Mrs Owlet. The funeral had been held at twilight so as not to interfere with anybody's habits. The villagers were just coming home from work, the goblins just waking up. A huge mass of flowers had been brought by different people and laid in the corner of the churchyard where the new small grave had been dug for Dwiney and her kitten.

Harriet arrived just as the service was about to begin. An enormous hunter's moon had recently risen and was floating above the churchyard wall, competing with the setting sun. Harriet had been in her bedroom, consulting with the pictured Sisters.

And this time she had obtained a reply.

The vicar, ending his short sad talk by the small grave, said:

'And I'm sure that none of us would wish or expect our good neighbours the goblins to move away from our village now, since they must leave this sad token behind them. We were all fond of little Dwiney – she was like our own child – we would never dream of asking them to leave—'

'Yes, we would!' shouted Mrs Owlet from the top of her pillar. 'If they don't agree to get away from here by the end of this week, I'm going to jump from my pillar! And that will make a heap of trouble for them!'

'So jump, you old bag!' shouted one of the goblins – not Albrick, who was standing wrapped in silence by the grave.

Mrs Owlet jumped.

Her landing was not at all spectacular, for Mark and some of his friends had piled all the empty egg-boxes under the column in a massive, rustling heap which also contained the fragments of Mrs Armitage's blue platter and Harriet's spinning-wheel. And smelled of five-year-old eggs. So the landing was soft, if untidy.

But meanwhile, at the graveside, Harriet had come forward, and was saying, 'I have a message for the goblin people from their Lady Holdargh. She has talked to the two Sisters who live on my bedroom wall, and she wishes to tell you that she has found a good place underground for you all to live, in a cave in southern Tasmania. Plenty of room for all, and there will be no problem about the music. She will be expecting you there tomorrow by E-Travel.'

'Tasmania!' whispered some of the crowd. 'That be a long way sure-lye!'

'Don't worry about little Dwiney's grave, Mr Albrick,' whispered Harriet to the man beside her. 'Mark and I will look after it very carefully, I promise!'

Next day the goblins were gone and there was no trace of them left. The huge tent was clean and tidy as if it had just been put up. Only, on the Armitages' doorstep were two parcels, containing a very beautiful iron lacework necklace and an elegant green-and-white bowl.

Mark said sadly, 'I never did get a chance to play on their organ.' And Harriet sighed as they looked at the last book saved from their Cornish trip – *Elizabeth and Her Secret German Garden* – somehow at the moment she had no wish to read it.

Every year on Dwiney's grave they found a very uncommon flower, a beautiful white star, not like any product of English fields or gardens. '*Actinotus helianthi*,' the vicar said. It could only have come from Tasmania.

THE CHINESE DRAGON

Harriet and her parents were having tea when a robin flew in through the open window and started circling madly around the kitchen at a speed far greater than was safe or sensible.

'Drat that bird!' exclaimed Mrs Armitage. 'It is so intrusive! If I leave the back door open for three minutes he's in, and drinking out of the cat's water bowl. And he has no excuse. I fill the bird bath every day.'

'She may be a hen,' said her husband. 'Female robins look just like the males.'

'"Robins are very pugnacious",' Harriet read, looking them up in the bird book. '"In winter females have separate estates." I wonder why?'

'Never mind its estate,' said Mrs Armitage. 'Show it the door!'

Harriet opened both door and window as wide as they would go, and showed them to the robin, who took not the slightest notice, but did another circuit of the kitchen, then whizzed through the inner door, and made its way to the sitting-room.

'Oh, don't let it go in there, stop it, *stop it*!' wailed Mrs Armitage. 'All my patience cards are laid out on the sewing-table and the patience was beginning to look as if it would come out – there was a blocking queen, but if I could manage to shift her—'

Too late! A loud fluttering, scattering sound from the next room suggested that the robin had found the cards, and disorganised them. Harriet, who had snatched up the tea-cosy and followed the robin, called through the open door:

'Ma, I'm afraid your cards are all over the floor.'

'Oh! That wretched bird! I've never got the Chinese Dragon patience out yet, and I really was beginning to think that I might manage it this time . . . It's supposed to be wonderful good luck if you get it to come out . . .'

'Well, anyway, I've caught the robin. Copped it in the cosy.' Harriet returned to the kitchen with her prize, which she carried tenderly and delicately in both hands. The tea-cosy was a large and handsome one. It had been made as a joint enterprise by Mr Armitage and his daughter from two semicircular bits of blanket left over from a dressing gown Mrs Armitage had made for Mark's birthday. The two pieces of blanket had been blanket-stitched together along the curving edge. Mr Armitage had embroidered three red-and-green tulips in wool on one side, and Harriet had done a rather good scarlet dragon on hers.

(Harriet had been very much into dragons last year, and had done them everywhere, on the fridge door, table napkins, and towels. Now she was into Himalayan bears.)

She walked across the kitchen, stepped outside the back

door, opened the edges of the tea-cosy, and invited the robin to leave.

It was not cooperative.

'It likes being in the cosy. Nice and warm. Reminds it of life in the nest. Or in the egg.'

'Well, shake it out! Get into its head that it is not welcome inside the house! The garden is the place for robins. Cards all over the sitting-room floor . . . I was really certain that I was going to get the Dragon patience out this time—'

'Harriet! Hurry up and eject that bird!' called her father. 'The tea is growing cold in the pot.'

By vigorously shaking the cosy, Harriet finally managed to persuade the robin to fly off into the garden.

'Shut the door, please, to show the bird it's not welcome.'

Harriet did so. The door bell instantly rang.

'That can't be the robin, surely?' Harriet opened the door again. 'But I didn't notice anybody outside—'

A tall, handsomely dressed, grey-haired lady swept past Harriet and into the Armitage kitchen.

'*Good* day to you, dear pipple!' she fluted. 'I have heard such a *lot* about you! I am so delighted to meet you at last! I am Lady Havergal-Nightwood, my husband is Sir James – you are probably aweer that we have just moved into Nightwood Park Hall and of course I lost no time in seeking you out, the virry first thing I must do, I said to dulling Jimbo, my husband, the virry first thing must be to look up those cliver Armitages, I have heard so *mich* about you from all sides – is that tea you have in the pot? How delightful! Yes, jist a cip, if you will, and limon, not milk – yis, I said to

Jimbo, I must get the Armitage family on our list without delay – they must be the virry first!'

'Find a lemon in the fridge, can you?' Mrs Armitage muttered to Harriet. 'And slice it.'

'Nightwood Park Hall,' remarked Mr Armitage politely. 'You'll find it a trifle damp, won't you? Been standing empty for fifteen years, isn't that right? Waiting for some inheritance problem between two brothers to get itself solved?'

'Yis, yis, and it has *bin* solved at last!' cried Lady Havergal-Nightwood radiantly. 'In favour of my dear husband, Jimbo – his brother is thought to be dead – he went to Midigascar and has not returned for sivinteen years. So you may – if you wish – address me as Queen of the Wood! (The title, of course, goes with the house and has done so since the days of the Conqueror.)'

'Really, Your Majesty, how very interesting.'

'Oh, but do call me Piggy!'

'Er – Piggy?'

'Short for Miguerite, dears – my dulling mother was another Mig – all the gairls in the family – back to ten-sixty-six – have been Daisies—'

'Back to the Conqueror, just fancy that,' said Mrs Armitage, handing the visitor a cup of tea with a large chunk of lemon floating in it.

'Thanks, dulling – oh, in fict, way, *way* before the Conqueror! But now, whit I winted to ask you, dulling Mrs Armitage – you are the cliver lady who knows just *iverything* about Silitaire—'

'Silitaire?'

'Patience, dulling, patience – card games for one person, that you play by yoursilf – alas, my dulling Jimbo has no head for card games—'

'Oh, patience, yes – I mostly do Klondike or Napoleon or Streets-and-Alleys or Beleaguered Castle – for relaxation, you know, at times when the children have been extra active – But you wish to learn?'

Mrs Armitage looked up in slight puzzlement at the visitor, who was walking excitedly about the room.

'Chinese Dragon is the win I'm after – you'll hardly believe this, dulling, but a clairvoyant read my hand wince and told me that if I can build an array of Chinese Dragon – is that what they call it? – and get it to come out – then, dullings, she said I shall be virry, virry lucky – have my heart's desire!'

'Oh – isn't that interesting!' said Mrs Armitage politely. 'I must admit, I have never yet managed to make the Chinese Dragon come out – it needs three packs, you know, and you must have a large table – and it takes hours and hours—'

'Niver mind that! I'm sure that whin you have taught me – you with your cliver, cliver know-how – I shall master it in no time!' cried Lady Havergal-Nightwood eagerly. 'Can you show me now?'

'I'm afraid not just now – I'm due for a meeting of the Village Institute,' said Mrs Armitage hastily. 'Another time – very soon—' And she made her escape.

So did the Queen of the Wood, leaving Harriet and her father to wash up the tea things.

'Oh bother!' growled Harriet. 'I should have asked the lady if she kept dogs and needed any dog-walking done.'

'Are you still saving to buy a Himalayan bear?'

'Only twenty pounds to go now. As long as they don't put the price up.'

'So how many dogs are you walking at present?'

'Seven. The two Labradors, Mrs Smith's Jack Russell, Betty Grove's spaniel, a Russian greyhound that belongs to PC Walker, and Phil Turner's two pekes. If Lady Whatsit-Nightwood has a dog, I could pick it up as I cross the corner of Nightwood Park, that's the way I mostly walk the dogs, there's a public right-of-way where I can let them off their leads – that would bring my takings up to £8 *a walk*!'

The back door shot open and Lady Havergal-Nightwood popped her head back round it.

'Dulling child, did I hear you say that you exercise dogs? – The virry thing! Can you add my sweet Bobbie-Dob to your string? How virry, virry kind! Tomorrow, then – three o'clock at Nightwood Park Hall!'

'Yes – yes, of course,' said Harriet, a little taken aback. 'What kind of dog is, er, Bobbie-Dob?'

'A Pit Bull–Mastiff cross, dulling.'

'Oh. Er – is he good tempered?'

'He *can* be a little titchy, I must confiss! But I am sure you and he will git on splindidly! Your fee? Oh, bay the bay, I did not have time to inform your dulling mum that I am able to grant *wishes* – as a reward—'

'Wishes?'

'Just like in the fairy books, you know. Because I was born under Libra, so I am caring and giving.'

'But in that case,' Harriet could not help asking, 'if you

can grant wishes, why not give one to yourself? Instead of bothering about the Chinese Dragon patience to grant your heart's desire – whatever that is?'

'Ah, dulling, I can only grant wishes to other pipple. Not to my own self, do you see?'

'Yes I see,' said Harriet thoughtfully. 'I expect Ma would wish to be able to reverse the car into a parking space – she was saying the other day that the one thing she really wanted—'

'Will, will, anything, anything she fancies! And you, too, dulling. Tomorrow, when you come to the Hall, we can fix a time for her to show me the Dragon – can we not?'

Beaming, Lady Havergal-Nightwood withdrew her head round the edge of the door. As she did so the excitable robin hurtled through the narrow gap, shot across the kitchen, and steered a headlong course for the sitting-room, where it knocked over a vase and spilled water over two packs of patience cards.

'That bird has a death-wish,' snapped Mr Armitage, snatching up the Queen of Spades. 'I almost wish your brother were at home playing his oboe – one thing Mark's noise does seem to do is subdue wildlife—'

'Oh, thank you, Father, that's given me a good idea,' said Harriet. 'I am not mad about the sound of dulling Bobbie-Dob. I'll ask Mark to come along with me to Park Hall and bring his oboe.'

Nimbly she lassoed the robin in a teacloth, and tenderly escorted it to the very back end of the garden.

*

Mark was not very keen on the sound of Lady Havergal-Nightwood – 'I bet the wishes she grants aren't up to much; probably the sort of feeble thing you find in fortune cookies and Christmas crackers' – but he was curious to have a look at Nightwood Park Hall, which had stood empty for fifteen years.

'There might be a colony of bats. Yes, I'll bring my oboe. Bats enjoy oboe music.'

This was just what Harriet had hoped. Mark had oboe lessons from Professor Johansen who as well as teaching music ran a holiday home for dogs with owners overseas, and knew exactly the kind of airs and harmonies to please the canine taste. Harriet was not too easy in her mind about Bobbie-Dob; a Pit Bull–Mastiff cross might, she thought, be rather a tough proposition.

Nightwood Park lay about half a mile downhill from the Armitage house and was partly wooded, partly open grassy land. A gravelled track ran as far as the house, and beyond that a muddy footpath and right-of-way cut through the woods to a heathery common.

Since nobody had occupied the house for fifteen years it was in a very run-down condition, with ivy creeping up the walls, tiles missing from the roof, and several broken windows. The woods, too, were a tangle of brambles and undergrowth, a paradise for birds, badgers, and foxes. Otters had established a colony in the fast-flowing little river that crossed the path.

Harriet had expected that the Hall would be a scene of activity, with builders bustling about, but this was not the case. A builder's skip stood outside the front door, filled with rubble and odds and ends. At some distance round the circular, weed-grown gravel sweep an aged Morris car was parked. Harriet could not decide whether there was a person sitting in the car, or was it simply a blanket folded over the driver's seat? No one else was to be seen, but when Mark and Harriet and her seven satellite dogs reached the rusty wrought-iron gates that separated the sweep from the approach road, a deep, threatening bark could be heard from inside the house.

Harriet's troupe of dogs bristled, and several of them set up a hostile chorus of counter-barks.

'I'll just tie them up here,' said Harriet, looping the lead handles over the latch of the gate, leaving the dogs on the outside. 'No sense walking into trouble.'

She and Mark approached the house slowly and with caution, not wishing to run foul of Bobbie-Dob. Nightwood Park Hall was large and grey, with six pillars set across its front façade and twelve large windows on each storey. There were three storeys.

'Rather a big house for Lady Havergal-N and her Jimbo,' said Harriet. 'Unless they have dozens of children.'

The barking inside grew more and more menacing.

'How about playing a tune?' suggested Harriet. She wished that Lady Havergal-Nightwood would appear. There was a brass bell handle at the side of the two large double doors (from which the paint was peeling; a mess of crumbled paint lay on the cobbles inset on the steps that led up to the door).

Mark took his oboe from its case and played 'Oh Where Is My Little Dog Gone?'

There was a startled silence from inside the house.

Harriet gave another couple of vigorous tugs to the bell handle.

After two or three more minutes one of the double doors opened. Lady Havergal-Nightwood stood there. On a short, tight leash she held one of the most disagreeable-looking dogs that Harriet thought she had ever seen. It was the size of a large mastiff, brindled, with very large feet and a low-slung tail, and it had the squashed face of a pit bulldog. The face wore a thoroughly mean and hostile expression and the dog tugged at its leash as if it yearned to leap out and make mincemeat of these troublesome callers.

Mark played his little tune again.

Bobbie-Dob suddenly sat down as if he had booked a seat for a musical recital, showed his ticket at the door, found his place, and now wanted nothing more than to sit, listen, and enjoy himself.

'Gid hivens, dulling,' said Lady Havergal-Nightwood, 'you mist be a bit of a genius if you can charm my old Bobbie so cliverly! Will it last?'

'Oh, I shouldn't think so, not for more than five minutes. I'll have to keep playing while my sister walks the dogs.'

'Jist like the Pied Piper!' said Lady Havergal-Nightwood gaily. 'Here's the leash, dulling. And I'd keep him on it. There are roe deer in the woods, I believe, and – and – and he'd be after them in no time if you let him go.'

'This is going to be a well-earned wish,' thought Harriet,

as, controlling Bobbie-Dob with all the strength of her right hand, she returned to the gate and collected her seven other customers. Mark meanwhile kept up a series of mellifluous tunes on the oboe, which attracted the interest of several birds, wood-doves, peckers, and warblers as they walked along the muddy cart-track between the trees.

Harriet let the other clients off their leads as soon as they were well into the wood; the dogs were used to the path and trotted along rather soberly – it was plain that they were justifiably nervous of Bobbie-Dob and not at all anxious to provoke him in any way. He wandered along like a dog in a trance, only flicking up his ears, jerking up his head, and letting out a displeased growl if the music stopped for more than a moment.

His growl was particularly impatient when Mark broke off playing to say, 'Can you hear a car coming along this track?'

'Yes I can,' said Harriet. 'Whoever is driving along here surely must be crazy.'

'Well, I suppose it's the only way to get to the house if they are coming from the east side of the park. Otherwise they'd have to go all the way round, which would be about ten miles. They do have a four-wheel drive,' he added, as the car came into view. It was a white wagon of massive stocky build.

'Good heavens, it's Chinese!' exclaimed Harriet. 'I've never seen a Chinese registration plate before. Do you think they are friends of the Havergal-Nightwoods paying a visit?'

'No, they are police,' said Mark. 'Chinese police.'

'What makes you think that?'

'Their faces. And their uniforms. And the sign on the door.'

The sign on the car may or may not have said POLICE in Chinese. The two men, with serious faces and dark blue uniforms, certainly looked like police.

The car stopped. The door nearest Mark and Harriet opened, and the blue-uniformed driver asked them, very politely,

'Is this the way to Nightwood Park Hall?' His careful, correct English was certainly that of a foreigner.

Mark stopped playing his oboe for a moment, which threw Bobbie-Dob into a frenzy. He hurled himself at the white car and Harriet just managed to jerk him back before he assaulted the driver.

'Oh my!' said the driver. 'Oh my! I discover that you possess a Chinese police dog. But he does not appear to be very well trained.'

'He's not trained at all,' said Harriet, hauling on the leash. Mark hurriedly began playing 'Oh Where And Oh Where'.

'Now, this is quite interesting,' said the driver, carefully observing the struggles and furious snarls of Bobbie-Dob. 'He is not your dog?'

'NO – thank goodness!' agreed Harriet.

'He has recently come to this country from China?'

'Has he? I mean – I don't really know anything about him. He belongs to Lady Havergal-Nightwood. I'm just here to take him for a walk. But if he has just come from

China – shouldn't he be in quarantine somewhere? For six months?'

The driver – his name on a bilingual badge was given as Captain Tim Thing – studied Bobbie-Dob carefully. As soon as the music had exerted its tranquillizing effect, he lifted the dog's massive front leg and displayed a tattooed number. 'See? Chinese police dog registration number. He is for sure one of ours. Purloined!'

'Gracious!' said Harriet. 'Why would anybody *want* to?'

'Aha! But such dogs are most useful – for guarding some prisoner perhaps. Human or animal.'

'Animal?' said Harriet. 'You mean – like a lion? Or something fierce?'

'Just so. We are come in pursuit of this stolen dog all the way from China.'

'You came after him? He's yours? But what about Lady Havergal-Nightwood? He's supposed to belong to her.'

'She resides up at the Hall yonder?' He pointed. The house could just be seen past the trees.

'Yes, she's there. But do you mean to say,' said Harriet, 'that she may be keeping some other creature – or person – up there in the house? Is that why she hasn't got any builders there working? She's using this dog to guard something – or somebody?'

'Perchance. It may be so. Or – maybe – her other captive is somewhere in these woods. Such a small forest as this might well be a place of security for the retention of, mayhap, a modest-sized dragon.'

'A *dragon*?' said Mark, growing interested. He stopped

playing for a moment and Bobbie-Dob let out a warning snarl.

'I pacify him,' said Captain Thing, and he took from the car glove compartment a small case which contained tiny darts. One of these he neatly jabbed into Bobbie-Dob's shoulder. The result was even more immediate than Mark's music – the great dog's eyes shut, and he sagged smoothly onto the muddy track.

'He's not dead?' said Harriet anxiously.

'No, no. Asleep merely.'

'But what's this about a dragon?'

'We are missing a young one from our dragon sanctuary at Pa'ta'Chu. We know this lady and her husband were there. A fledgling dragon was stolen. We have followed them across Asia and Europe; we greatly hope they have our dragon-cub. Such are not easy to rear. I have with me Professor Tom Wrong – a great expert in the care of dragon broods and other offspring of winged reptiles.'

'Is so!' agreed Professor Wrong, vigorously nodding.

'(His English is not so good as mine.) But now,' Captain Thing pursued, 'it is most fortuitous, most opportune, that you have these other dogs with you. I ask your cooperation that we make use of them for half an hour to search this covert for our abducted tadpole-dragon. The weather in your land is not comforting. In this cold damp climate he may likely have taken a chill. We are concerned for him.'

'Shouldn't you go and ask at the house first? He may be there?'

'But as we are here – in the grove – with dogs—'

'Oh, very well!'

In truth, Harriet felt slightly uneasy at allowing the use of the dogs – who, after all, did not belong to her – for this unprogrammed purpose. Suppose the dragon was warlike? Irascible? Suppose some harm came to the dogs?

But Mark was definitely interested in the possibility of finding a dragon in Nightwood Copse.

'Let's go!' he said, parked his oboe in the Chinese police car, and relieved Harriet of four of her charges – she had hooked them onto their leads again while they were being approached by the car.

'I make a signal,' said Captain Thing, and he took from his pocket an elegant little metal triangle the size of a playing-card and struck it with a slender metal rod. The resulting ping! could only just be heard – but it *was* heard, for it was followed by an instant's total hush in the wood, and then by a soft and wondering chorus of chirrups, whistles, tweets, twitters, coos, croaks, carols, and warbles.

Captain Thing listened to these so attentively that Harriet wondered if in China the police ran Schools of Listening for their recruits. He repeated the signal – twice – and the third time, after the birds had finished their responses, held up a finger, and said, 'Hark!'

Harriet thought she heard a faint sound, between a croak and a bleat.

'Ah!' Captain Thing beamed in triumph. His colleague gave an emphatic nod. 'That is S'an Ch'in. But he sounds weak – not well – not in good order. It is well time we came.' He glanced at the group of dogs and his eye fell on the Jack Russell, who was straining at the leash and looking very alert and keen.

'Come. We follow him.'

The Jack Russell – whose name was Mickey – led the six other dogs and four humans along a difficult, bumpy, muddy, and tangled trail across the patch of brambly woodland to the river that divided it in half.

'Is there a bridge?' inquired Captain Thing.

'Only a fallen tree – but the river isn't deep,' Mark assured him. 'You can wade it.'

Captain Thing looked less than eager at this suggestion, and began to make his way upstream along the mossy and rocky bank. The river – hardly more than a brook – was clear and fast-running with small islands in it that were merely grass-grown rocks, and sandbanks that would be submerged when the stream was at its winter level but were now dry and clear.

On one of these lay a small dragon.

It would be plain, even to a person who had never seen a dragon before, that he was not in good health. His scales, which ought to have been crisp and shining green, were greyish in colour, damp and limp, like those of fish that have lain too long at the fishmonger's.

'S'an Ch'in!'

The little dragon bleated. It was a faint, pitiful sound. He opened one gummy eye. Then – as if he could hardly believe what he saw – he opened the other eye and feebly raised his head. A wispy flicker of pale flame spurted from his nostrils.

Simultaneous volleys of Chinese admonitions poured from Captain Thing and Professor Wrong. Plainly they were urging the dragonlet to save his strength, not to overexert himself. Professor Wrong pulled a little silver flask from his pocket, scrambled down the bank to where the dragon lay, and tipped its contents onto the long pale tongue and in among the curved razor-sharp fangs.

'Ginger cordial,' murmured Captain Thing. 'Best by far for sick dragon.'

The dogs, meanwhile, were evidently thunderstruck and wholly discomposed at the sight of this creature that had turned up in their accustomed playground. They stood in a row like a firing squad, panting, tongues lolling out, eyes trained on the dragon, as if they were waiting for a word of command. Harriet was thankful that Bobbie-Dob had been left in the police car.

Professor Wrong now unpacked from his knapsack a kind of canvas carry-all, and into this he and Captain Thing carefully and tenderly rolled the dragon, who was about the size of a well-grown twelve-year-old boy. He had been chained to some tree-roots on the bank; Captain Thing, with an expression of total disapproval, brought out a pair of metal-cutters and snipped through the chain.

'Who can have done that?' exclaimed Harriet. 'What a foul thing to do!'

'The Lady Havergal, no doubt,' said Captain Thing. 'Or her husband.'

'But why should they want to steal a dragon? And keep it tied up?'

'You want a Himalayan bear,' Mark pointed out. 'Some people want dragons.'

'And pay much money for them,' nodded Captain Thing. 'The lady may be a dealer in dragons.'

He and Professor Wrong now hoisted their reclaimed property up the bank, gave him another dose of ginger cordial, and carried him slowly, and with pauses to take breath, back to the car.

Here Mark and Harriet were amazed to see that Bobbie-Dob, who had just woken from his drug-induced nap, did not fly at the young dragon and tear him to shreds, but treated him with the utmost affection, licked him all over, and then lay down close beside him in the back section of the police car.

'He was a House Father in the dragon sanctuary. So it is often arranged if the dragon's own parent is not at hand. Dragons lay eggs, you know, and leave them buried, like crocodiles. – Now we leave you and return to China.'

'But – but aren't you going to go and see Lady Havergal-Nightwood – tell her off – arrest her?'

'What need? She will be her own punishment. That will soon overtake her. Our need was to recover our dragon – help him back to good health. I thank you for your assistance – most timely.'

Captain Thing got into the driver's seat, started his engine, and did a neat three-point turn.

'You're going to drive all the way to China? Won't that be a bit much for the dragon?'

'Ah! No! Him we send by plane – we radio for an ambulance plane for dragon and carer-dog.' Captain Thing raised his hand in salute, and the white car departed round a curve in the track.

'Oh dear,' said Harriet. 'Now we have to break the news to Lady Havergal-N that she has lost her dragon and dog. And that we know all about her wicked dealings.'

'I'll do that,' said Mark, who looked as if he quite relished the prospect. 'You had better take the dogs back to their owners – they'll be wondering where on earth you have got to.'

'That's true. I'll see you back at home.'

As it turned out, Harriet arrived home long before Mark.

'D'you know what,' he said, hungrily applying himself to a late supper when he came in. 'Sir James Havergal-Nightwood had been dead for *weeks*, sitting there in that old Morris car. The milkman spotted him in the end. Lady H left him there because of the inheritance quarrel. She wanted to be sure it was he and not the brother who got the house. But the brother turned up from some island in the Indian Ocean and was in a great rage about it.'

'Why did she want the house?'

'She wanted a house with a wood to keep the dragon in.'

'So she kept the dragon in the wood and her husband in the car. No wonder she didn't want builders about the place.'

'Oh dear,' said Mrs Armitage, 'I do hope we get some *nice* people in Nightwood Park Hall next time.'

The back-door bell rang and Lady Havergal-Nightwood popped her head round the door.

'Dulling Mrs Armitage! You were going to teach me the Chinese Dragon patience.'

Mrs Armitage was rather flustered.

'Oh! Dear me! So I was! But I thought you had left the village?'

'I moved into Mrs Hipkin's Bed and Breakfast. But now do, *do* teach me that game. I do *so* want my heart's desire!'

'And what is that?' asked Mrs Armitage, leading the way into the sitting-room with a slightly disapproving expression. She took three packs of patience cards from the games cupboard.

'Aha! I mustn't tell you that, dulling, or I shan't git it!'

'Well, I hope she doesn't get it!' whispered Harriet to Mark in the kitchen as they washed up the supper dishes. 'She doesn't deserve to. Look at all the trouble she's caused. And her husband dead all that time! What did he die of?'

'Fatigue and heart-failure, the police doctor said. After driving all the way back from China.'

'So she just left him in the car. What a pig! – Do call me Piggy!' Harriet giggled, wiping down the draining-board.

In the sitting-room they could hear Mrs Armitage saying patiently, 'No, the seven of spades may not be moved until the covering three cards are taken away . . . '

At half past nine she called: 'Children! Can you kindly make Lady Havergal-Nightwood and me some cocoa?'

At half past ten Mr Armitage came into the kitchen and hissed furiously: 'Isn't that perditioned female ever going to leave?'

At half past eleven he stomped into the kitchen again, carrying a brandy bottle.

'Why aren't you two in bed, may I ask?'

'We were just watching the end of the eleven o'clock news, Dad. A stolen dragon has been returned to a dragon sanctuary in north China. Isn't that good?'

At ten minutes to midnight Mrs Armitage called her husband excitedly. 'Gilbert, Gilbert! I believe it's going to come out!'

Rather sceptically, Mr Armitage and his two children left the warm kitchen and went into the sitting-room, where the large sewing-table was completely covered with cards in a complicated and curving pattern. The atmosphere in the room was tense, fraught, and breathless.

Mr Armitage looked over his wife's shoulder, said, 'Gad! There! I see how you can do it – take that nine across onto the eight – then that frees the Queen of Spades—'

'So it does! Cliver Mr Armitage!' Lady Havergal-Nightwood gave him a beaming smile and adjusted a couple of cards.

'That's it! You did it!'

'I have! I have! I have done it! Now I shall get my—'

A strange, puzzled expression came over Lady Havergal-Nightwood's face. Her hands, which had been up in the air, dropped to her sides. Her mouth fell open. Her eyes grew fixed. Then her knees buckled and she folded 'like a concertina', as Mark said afterwards, and fell to the floor.

'Oh dear, she has fainted from the excitement,' said Mrs

Armitage. 'I'll fetch the smelling-salts – if I can ever find them.'

She started for the door. But her husband, stooping over the unwelcome guest, said, 'Don't bother, salts won't help. Better phone the doctor. She's dead.'

'Oh goodness gracious me! Now she'll never have her heart's desire.'

And serves her richly right, thought Mark.

Something whizzed past his head.

'Oh, *no*!' cried his mother. 'Here's that dratted robin got in again! Where can it have come from? Open the window, Harriet, and shoo it out. We don't want the doctor to think we live in a madhouse—'

Harriet captured the robin in a rush fishbasket, opened a window, and cast it out.

'And don't come back!' she told it. 'If you are who I think you are!'

'Where did it come from?' said Mark. 'All the windows are shut.'

Harriet said: 'I've changed my mind. I don't want a Himalayan bear. Better it should stay on Mount Everest. – Oh *bother* it!'

'Now what?'

'That wretched woman never gave Mother and me our wishes!'

DON'T GO FISHING ON WITCHES' DAY

Mark whistled as he cycled along the narrow country road through the cool early morning air. The tune he whistled was well known in his village – 'Don't go a-fishing on witches' day, on witches' day, on witches' day, Don't you go fishing on witches' day unless you take me along, too . . .'

'But when is Witches' Day?' Mark wondered. 'Hallowe'en? St Wenceslas? St Swithin's? Midsummer? And who was the me in the song?'

'Harriet would be sure to know,' he thought. His sister Harriet was into all that kind of stuff. She did courses in curses, in philtre-making, potion-brewing, astrology, incantation and hoodoo; her ambition was to graduate into witchcraft like some old great-aunt on Dad's side of the family. Harriet would have come along with him this morning had it not been for a radio programme on BBC 13 about blessings and curses and ever-filled purses that she specially wanted to catch; the witchcraft programmes on BBC 13 were always at five o'clock in the morning. Mark was not normally up this early but he wanted to get to Herringbloom Ponds and cast an eye – and a fishing-line – over them before his father went and bid for them at an auction which was due to start at nine o'clock.

'Three beautifully situated carp ponds with adjacent ruined mansion,' said the estate agents' brochure, under a picture of a blue stretch of water reflecting the branches of green arching willow trees.

'Bless my soul!' Mr Armitage had exclaimed at breakfast the day before. 'Bless my soul, my dear, see here in the local paper, Herringbloom Ponds come up for sale at last. Great-aunt Marianna's curse must have run out at last. Or lifted, or whatever curses do when they die down.'

His family, munching toast, looked at him with interest. 'Great-aunt Marianna? Who was she?'

'My father's aunt. Lived with her cousin Victoria in Herringbloom Lane, beyond Froxfield. And there was some quarrel with Marianna's brother Wilfred – he was younger, but he claimed he should have inherited the ponds.'

'Why?' asked Harriet.

'Because he was a male. And because he said they were witches, not eligible to own aquatic properties. There was a great family feud about it. But Wilfred mysteriously vanished. And, after that, the old ladies' house burned down.'

'What happened to Marianna and Victoria?'

'Died in the fire. But Marianna was heard to say with her expiring breath that, because of Wilfred's unbrotherly behaviour, no man should ever cast a fly over the ponds without incurring doom and dole – or some such tarradiddle – she laid a curse on the water and foretold that anybody who fished in it should something-or-other—'

'Would what?'

'I really forget. Fish in peril of his life, perhaps.'

'And did the curse work?' asked Harriet eagerly.

'Well, I don't believe the ponds have changed hands more than a couple of times in the last fifty years,' Mr Armitage said. 'Old Miss Shelmerdene bought them from the estate, but she did nothing with them – I'm sure she never went fishing – she never lived in the house, it became more and more of a ruin – and then Sir Robert Pope-Nottingham bought the land – come to think, *he* hasn't been around for the last fifteen years—'

'So perhaps the curse is still working?' Harriet looked hopeful. 'Where exactly are Herringbloom Ponds, Father?'

'About fifteen miles from here, other side of Froxfield Green. I've a good mind to make an offer for them myself. The sale's tomorrow.'

'Oh, do. *Do*!' Harriet's eyes sparkled at the possibilities which opened before her.

Mark had not taken much part in this conversation, but he had listened hard. Mark was not particularly interested in curses, but just now he had a great passion for fishing, and he was keenly attracted by the thought of Herringbloom Ponds. If no one had fished them for fifty years, what treasures might those waters not hold? There was a local prize for the most uncommon catch brought in before St Swithin's Day, and Mark thought that Herringbloom Ponds might produce just what he needed to win it. But, on the point of urging his father to buy the ponds, he remembered that Mr Armitage was also a keen angler, so kept quiet.

And now here he was, out on Midsummer Morning when all the woods and fields were bathed in clear daylight at 4 a.m. and the sun was just readying itself to rise.

'In a minute,' thought Mark, as he pedalled along the road to Froxfield Green, 'all the trees will have long shadows stretching westwards.' The road was bordered by some young copper-beech trees, planted by Sir Robert Pope-Nottingham, owner of Froxfield Manor, before he failed to come home one evening and was never seen again.

Next minute the sun did rise, over Badger's Hill, and the shadows of the young beeches, and Mark on his bike, all cast themselves forward along the road. And, on either side of his own shadow, Mark noticed two others, tall gaunt skinny shadows, keeping pace with him on his bike.

He stopped pedalling, put a foot on the ground, and looked sharply behind him.

Nobody was there. And the shadows had disappeared. But as soon as he got back into the saddle and rode off, the shadows reappeared, keeping pace with him.

Harriet, meanwhile, was in her bedroom listening to BBC Radio 13. A paragraph of instructions in the *Radio Times* had said, 'Listeners will benefit by supplying themselves beforehand with three different recordings of J. S. Bach's *Chromatic Fantasy and Fugue*, BWV 903. These should be played at intervals of five minutes, overlapping, while the programme is going on.'

Fortunately Harriet's bedroom was an attic at the top of the house, for the noise made by three different recordings of Bach's *Chromatic Fantasy and Fugue*, all started at different times, was very complicated indeed. But Harriet had grown accustomed to it.

'Time is progress,' said the radio voice. 'A leaf grows, then withers. A flower opens, then fades. But the music that you are hearing now is not affected by time. It can be played at different speeds, on different instruments. It remains itself. Similarly, other activities can be undertaken without regard to time. Step outside the frame of time and you acquire power – power to move mountains, to plunge deep into the matter of existence, to cross immense divides of space, to go forward, backward, sideways.'

Harriet listened with great concentration. She was taping the talk so that she could play it again. 'Maybe I should make three different recordings of the talk and play them again at different speeds,' she thought.

'You have been listening to a talk by Regina Queenscape, Countess of Nearly Nowhere,' said the announcer. 'It is one in our series of programmes for student necromancers and beginners in auspication; the next in the series will be at the same time on August 1 . . .'

Harriet switched off the radio and went to look out of the window. The fine day had clouded over and large drops of rain were beginning to fall. 'I wonder if Mark has got to Herringbloom Ponds,' thought his sister. 'I wonder what is happening to him? It's lucky I made him cut his fingernails before he went off and put them in that little silver box . . .'

Mark did not appear at breakfast. Nor at lunch. This was not particularly unusual. But when his place was empty at supper time, his mother became a little perturbed.

'If he was going off for the day you'd think he would have taken something to eat with him. But nothing seems to be missing from the larder . . . And it's meat loaf for supper, his favourite.'

Harriet felt obliged to speak up. 'He asked me not to mention where he was going for twelve hours—'

'Why, for goodness' sake?'

'In case you were going to bid for the carp ponds, Father.'

'Well, I was,' said Mr Armitage triumphantly. 'And I did. And what's more, I bought them. Thought they ought to be back in the family.'

'Oh wow,' said Harriet.

'Darling! You bought those ponds? Whatever for?'

'Fishing, what else?' Mr Armitage helped himself to another slice of meat loaf. 'Always wanted my own fishing water.'

'But the curse?'

'Mark went off to Herringbloom? What time did he leave?'

'Four o'clock this morning. Or thereabouts,' Harriet said. 'He wanted to get there just after sunrise.'

'Why just at that time, may I ask?'

'Because I told him supernatural power is just at its lowest at dawn. And also he had an idea that you were going to bid for the ponds, Father.'

'Tough bidding it was, too, against old Lady Ullswater,'

Mr Armitage grumbled. 'I could have got those ponds for five hundred less if she hadn't hung on for so long, obstinate old besom. But why should Mark want to be there before I bought the place?'

'The owner of the ponds and his heirs are in the direct line of the curse. He felt it might be better to get there before you made that connection.'

'Troublesome young devil,' growled Mark's father. 'Now what are we supposed to do? What do you reckon has happened to him?'

'We had better go along there,' Harriet said ponderingly. 'If the curse has caught up with Mark there may be some way of unravelling or reversing it.'

'Yes, we'd better go.' Mr Armitage pushed back his chair. 'Anyway I'd like to take a look at the place before it grows dark. I'll get out the car.'

'Well, *I'm* not going,' Mrs Armitage said firmly. 'I always make the Christmas puddings on Midsummer Night, and I have got out all the ingredients and the pudding-basins – it would be shocking bad luck to alter that habit. If there is a curse you will have to unloose it without my help. Harriet had better take all her occult bits and bobs. Oh dear! I hope we haven't lost Mark for good. He *is* so careless! He was going to fix the oven door for me – he kept promising – thoughtless boy! And he's never done it . . . '

Her face crumpled, and Harriet gave her mother a hug.

'Don't worry, Ma; we'll bring him back somehow, even if it's in the shape of a goldfish. And perhaps after all he's just having a wonderful time fishing.'

'Selfish young tyke,' remarked his father.

Harriet ran off to collect three tape-recorders, a powerful magnet, a flute, Mark's fingernails, a tin of toast crumbs left over from the meat loaf, and a hand mirror, besides a few other odds and ends that might come in useful.

'What are the toast crumbs for?' said her father.

'To feed the fish! Have you brought your rod?'

'Of course.'

Harriet and her father were rather silent as they drove through Froxfield Green and on to Herringbloom. The trip took about twenty minutes. A beautiful golden glow lay over the midsummer countryside. The rain had stopped. Father and daughter were deep in thought. Mr Armitage was wondering what sort of bait to use; Harriet was wondering whether she had brought the right equipment to counteract a powerful curse.

Herringbloom Ponds lay linked by waterfalls in a shallow valley set about with alder and willow trees which dangled green and golden trailers over the still water. Each pond was oval in shape and about the size of a tennis court. By the middle pond grew a huge old willow whose gnarled and wrinkled trunk, wider than a church door, had Mark's bicycle propped against it.

'So he got here at least, silly young ruffian,' said Mr Armitage, and he threw his head back and shouted 'MARK!' at the top of his voice. His only answer was echoes, running up and down the side of the valley.

A few bubbles rose from the still surface of the pond. A couple of blackbirds chattered angrily in the trees.

'I don't think shouting is going to bring him,' said Harriet.

'Then I shall fish while you get on with whatever you think you ought to do.' Her father unpacked his rod and baited his hook. Then, with an expert twitch, he slung his line over the quiet water of the middle pond.

Harriet watched rather apprehensively. Suppose she were to lose both her father and her brother on the same day? How could she explain that to her mother?

She wondered how Mrs Armitage was getting on with the Christmas puddings. She hoped Mrs Armitage hadn't forgotten the lucky silver charms.

The tree behind Harriet whispered to her, '*Don't* let him do that! Don't let him cast!'

'Why?'

'It's a mockery of their power!'

'Power,' thought Harriet. 'Step out of the frame of time and you acquire power.'

'But who are *they*?' she asked the tree.

Instead of an answer, there was an explosion: a huge shape burst from the water, scattering spray all around. It was bigger than a hippopotamus, grey and white, shining, with a cruel, contemptuous mouth and two mean little eyes. Over the mouth hung a dank pair of black moustaches.

It snapped and swallowed Mr Armitage's rod and line as if they had been cheese straws, then sank below the water again, leaving arrowy ripples trailing from end to end of the pond.

'God bless my soul!' said Mr Armitage. 'A shark! A shark of the hammerhead species, if I am not mistaken.'

He stood looking perplexedly at the broken rod handle,

which he still held. Then he said, 'Do you suppose, Harriet, that the shark has swallowed Mark?'

'Well – I do hope not,' said Harriet. But her tone was rather shaky.

'I said they would be angry,' remarked the tree.

'What should I do now?'

'Answer three questions.'

'Yes?'

'What is sadder than a lost child? What remains when voices are gone? What dies every day and lives for ever?'

'The child's parents. Words remain when voices are gone. The sun dies daily and lasts for ever.'

'Look into your glass,' said the tree.

Harriet looked into the hand mirror and received a shock. Looking back at her was her own face as it would be if she lived to the age of a hundred. She shivered.

'Now you can remember,' said the tree.

'I remember their burying and my digging up a box with gold things in it.'

'So do that.'

Mr Armitage always carried a spade in the boot of the car. Harriet fetched it and began digging among the tree's bony and twisted roots.

Her father was sitting on the ground with his head in his hands.

'I don't understand!' he said tremulously. 'Talking trees – giant sharks – what *is* going on?'

'We are trying to find Mark.'

'But where is he?'

'Lost in the past, I believe,' said Harriet, digging away among the roots.

'The past? But why?'

'It's one of the commoner curses, specially among family feuds and disputes. If you think about it, worse than putting someone in prison. Women often used it to get rid of tiresome male relations. Ah!' said Harriet, and dug up a small, heavy metal box, rusted and crusted with earth. 'Can you open this, Father?'

Mr Armitage could, by dribbling on rust solvent (which, luckily, he also kept in the car boot). Inside were fragrant cedar shavings, a gold-backed set of false teeth, and a pair of gold-rimmed spectacles.

'*Give me the tooth, Sister*!' said Harriet.

'I beg your pardon?'

'It was what the weird sisters said. They shared an eye and a tooth between them.'

'I'm lost in all this,' said Mr Armitage gloomily. 'What about that shark?'

'The shark might be Marianna or Victoria. Or both of them using the same pair of teeth. But I'm not sure about that moustache,' Harriet said doubtfully.

A breeze shook the willow trees. Harriet had the impression that all the dangling fronds swung closer to listen.

She said cautiously, 'Or, of course, the shark might be Mark.'

'My own son? Turned into a shark?'

'You don't often find sharks in carp ponds,' Harriet pointed out.

'Outrageous impertinence!' Mr Armitage snorted. 'In *my* ponds! I bought them!'

'You bought the curse, too.'

'So how do we get rid of this infernal curse?' demanded her father.

'A curse is like a crease in material. You have to go back to the time before it was crumpled and iron it out flat.'

'Mark used to be a nice friendly little fellow,' quavered Mr Armitage, almost in tears. 'Liked me to take him for walks. Held my hand. Not the way he is now, always skiving off on his own to go fishing.'

Harriet, carefully hanging an Aeolian harp on a weeping willow tree, felt sad for parents who must always lose their children, stage by stage, into the harsh world.

The harp let out a soft sigh, as if agreeing.

A water-rat slipped from the bank and swam to the far side of the pond, leaving a wake of V-shaped ripples.

'Rats. Mark used to be afraid of rats,' recalled his father.

The surface of the pond cleared. As Harriet adjusted her equipment they could see a reflection of Mark, aged about nine, kneeling and looking into the water.

'Mark! Take care! You'll fall in!' shouted his father.

Mark paid no heed to the warning.

'He can't hear you,' Harriet said. 'He's in another time band.'

Mark's image in the water faded. The reflections of two ladies, dressed in white, with hats and plumy feather fans, appeared, upside down, sitting at a table under a parasol.

They seemed to be arguing. A man approached them and said something that annoyed them even more. They waved their fans furiously at the man, who slipped and staggered by the brink of the water.

The surface of the pond bulged as if the shark were about to explode from it again. Harriet had just fitted a tape into her battery player. Complicated music ran about the valley.

Now Harriet carefully scattered a handful of toast crumbs across the water. A whole school of small fish rose and snapped eagerly at the crumbs.

'Why, bless me!' said Mr Armitage. 'What became of the shark? The crazy pond seems to be alive with tiddlers. What became of the two ladies? *Where's Mark?*'

The reflection of Mark suddenly reappeared, aged about four, wearing brown canvas dungarees and a red shirt. He carried a seaside spade and bucket.

'Dear little feller he was at that age,' said his father fondly. 'But why can't you get him at the right age?'

'It takes a lot of practice. Where is the ruined mansion?' Harriet asked.

'Up by the top pond. I can remember being taken to tea with the great-aunts and being given home-made lemonade and ginger-snaps,' recollected Mr Armitage.

Harriet strolled upstream along the bank, leaving the tapes playing.

The ponds were connected by three cascades fringed with ferns and little daisy-like plants growing in cracks between the rocks. Above the topmost waterfall stood an aged house which was half-burned and ruinous. A green and juicy creeper climbed and dangled over the ruins. A wavering mist rose from the frothy pool at the foot of the fall, which was about the height of a two-storey house.

Harriet could see that it would not be possible to get into the mansion without fighting through a mass of vegetation which blocked the doors and window holes.

She stood by the lip of the waterfall, watching the smooth, shining water as it poured over, and thinking about Mark.

She remembered how, when they were six or seven, she had fallen into a stream and he had pulled her out; she remembered how he had given her his favourite shell because none of hers were as good as his; she remembered how he had cried when their cat Walrus was found dead of old age in the garden.

'Mark!' she whispered. 'Where are you? Come back . . .'

She dropped his fingernails into the waterfall.

The mist at the foot of the fall wavered. Then it began to form into a spiral. The sprays of green leaves dangling from the willows started to twirl. Clouds in the sky above darkened and writhed into corkscrew shapes. A whistling wind spun the long grass into funnels. Discs of rain scoured the surface of the pond. Then the whole pond rose into the air, as a cork is twisted out of a bottle. Harriet grabbed the trunk of a massive willow and wrapped her arms round it, or she would have been sucked up into the sky along with the pond water. She could feel the tree writhing as she hung on to it. 'What in the world can be happening to Father?' she wondered. 'And Mark?' She saw the two white-clad ladies, with their parasol, and the dark man, swirl briefly by; they vanished into a spiral of mist.

Then the landscape settled down; the pond sank back into its bed; only the dangling fronds of the willows and the long grasses remained tightly twisted and plaited.

Like the ribbons on a maypole, Harriet thought vaguely as she let go of the willow trunk and gave it a grateful pat.

She saw her father and Mark coming slowly towards her. Mr Armitage held Mark's arm. Mark looked rather dazed.

'A *tornado* in England in June, what next?' grumbled Mr Armitage. 'I shall certainly write to *The Times*. I hate to think what may have happened to my car . . .'

'Are you all right?' Harriet asked her brother.

'I think I must have gone to sleep.' He gave a great yawn. 'But my bike is a total write-off. And I can't find my fishing-rod. I'd have fallen into the pond if Dad hadn't grabbed me—'

The sun suddenly set.

'We had better go and see what's happened to the car,' said Mr Armitage, looking with disapproval at the slate-grey surface of the ponds, the dark, dangling, twisted willow tendrils. 'I'm almost sorry I bought this place,' he muttered.

'Oh, you'll see, it will be quite different from now on,' Harriet reassured him. 'Look, the old ladies are back at their table.' She pointed at the reflection in the first pond, where the upside-down ladies were offering a cup of tea to the dark man.

'He's getting his tea in a moustache cup!'

'What about all the things you brought?'

'Nothing left but bits and pieces.'

Harriet's mirror, tapes, Aeolian harp, magnet and flute lay shredded on the twisted grass. But she noticed one of the old ladies was wearing the false teeth and the other one had the gold-framed spectacles.

'We have got Mark back, that's the main thing.' Harriet gripped Mark's left hand; Mr Armitage still held on to the other.

'I never was away,' Mark argued.

But Harriet looked at the watch on his wrist, which showed date as well as time.

'According to your watch, you've been away for a year—'

'That's just nutty!'

'And where's the car?' demanded Mr Armitage.

Luckily the car was only a quarter of a mile down the road from where he had left it. And it seemed unharmed, but the boot, mysteriously, was full of shingle. A large dead shark lay on the grass verge. Mark would very much have liked to take it home, but fortunately it was far too big to put into the boot. It had a moustache.

'Good thing he's done for, anyhow,' remarked Mr Armitage. 'No hope of a peaceful day's angling so long as that feller was in the water.'

The house, when they reached it, after a rather silent drive, was full of the smell of Christmas pudding.

'Ah, you got Mark back, that's good,' said Mrs Armitage comfortably. 'If you had come back without him, I was going to suggest dropping one of my puddings into the pool.'

'Is that a remedy against curses?' asked Harriet, all professional interest.

'Oh yes, my dear, one of the best. Much more likely to work than all that BBC 13 mumbo-jumbo. You try it next time, you'll see. But the best thing to remember,' said Mrs Armitage, 'is, don't go fishing on witches' day . . . '

MILO'S NEW WORD

When Uncle Claud Armitage came back from the island of Eridu, he brought some problems for his niece and nephews. Climbing stiffly off the train (for Uncle Claud was quite an old man), he started the walk up Station Road to his brother's house. But he soon noticed that he was being followed. Pit-pat, pit-pat went the footsteps behind him in the dusk.

Uncle Claud stepped into a phone box and dialled his brother's number.

Outside the lighted box, in the shadows, something waited and listened.

'Hallo?' piped a little voice in Uncle Claud's ear.

'Hallo? Is that Mark or Harriet? Listen, quickly, there's no time to lose. I want to tell you a tremendously important mathematical secret – the greatest discovery since Euclid—'

He went on talking very fast. After a while he said: 'Did you get that?'

'Hallo?' said the little voice again.

Behind Uncle Claud, the door was softly opening. He

looked round – just too late. He felt the lightest possible touch on his arm. Next minute, his fingers curled up and turned black. They had become claws. His arms stretched out, flattened, and became leathery wings. Uncle Claud shrank. With a whir and a flit, he soared away into the dark-blue evening sky, where one star had just flashed out, ahead of all the others.

Uncle Claud had turned into a bat.

At the Armitage house, Mark was setting the table for supper, while Harriet made scrambled eggs. Their parents were out at a Village Green Improvement Society meeting in the church hall. Their young brother, Milo, was on the bottom stair, building a castle out of telephone directories.

'Who rang up?' Harriet asked, as Mark came back from the front hall.

'I dunno,' he said. 'I got there just too late. Milo had picked up the phone.'

'Milo!' called Harriet. 'You're a naughty boy! You know you aren't supposed to play with the phone.'

'Hallo!' said Milo. It was his word this week. Last week his word had been 'perhaps'. Milo used one word at a time.

'It's funny he's so fond of the phone,' said Mark. 'Seeing he's so slow at learning to talk.'

'Oh well,' said Harriet, 'I expect whoever it was will phone again.'

But the phone did not ring again, and soon Mr and Mrs Armitage came home, arguing about the village green.

'A ring of poplars would be nice.'

'A ring of poplars would be silly.'

When they were halfway through their scrambled eggs, the doorbell rang. 'Who can it be, so late?' said Mrs Armitage. 'See who it is, Harriet, there's a love.'

Harriet came back from the front hall, her eyes popping with excitement.

'It's a man who says he's from the Department of Security and Secrets.'

'I suppose I'd better go,' said her father, sighing.

The man at the front door had silver-rimmed glasses, a short black beard, a soft black hat, and a long black umbrella. He looked very cross.

'It's a matter of extreme secrecy,' he said. 'Half an hour ago a phone call was made to this house. It should not have been made. I must speak to whoever answered the phone.'

'Oh, that's all right,' Harriet told him. 'It was only our brother Milo.'

'I must see him at once!'

Harriet looked at her father, who shrugged, and said, 'Let the gentleman see Milo. Then he'll know there's nothing to worry about.' He explained to the caller, 'Milo's only two, and a backward talker. He's much too young to understand government secrets.'

Harriet went and fetched Milo. He was in his pyjamas, sucking a bedtime bottle of milk.

'You see,' said Mr Armitage to the visitor. 'There's absolutely no cause for—'

His words came to a sudden stop. For the man in the doorway had pointed his umbrella at Milo, who turned grey, sprouted a trunk and tiny tusks, and slipped from Harriet's limp grip onto the floor.

'No cause to worry now,' snapped the visitor, turned on his heel, and strode away into the dark.

Harriet said to Mark, who came out of the kitchen, 'That man has changed Milo into a baby elephant.'

'Oh dear,' said Mr Armitage. 'I'm afraid your mother won't be pleased.'

Next morning, Harriet and her father went to ask the advice of Mr Moondew, a retired alchemist who had lately come to live in the village, and was very friendly and useful in the Village Green Improvement Society.

Mark stayed at home, rigging up a harness for Milo. It had struck him that his brother, who seemed a very good-natured elephant, might be a great help in the garden.

Mrs Armitage stayed at home because she was upset. She had been knitting a new blue sweater for Milo, and could not decide whether to go on with it.

Crossing the village green, Harriet and her father were surprised to see six red phone boxes standing in a row under the big lime tree.

'British Telecom's selling 'em off,' explained Mr Pulley, the street-cleaner, leaning on his broom. 'A foreign gent, he made an offer for 'em. Going to convert them to fancy bathroom showers, I heard. Paid a fancy price for 'em. BT's going to put new plain-glass boxes in Station Road and Grove Lane and Mistletoe Crescent and Holly Ride and Copse Alley and Vicar's Way.'

'Shame,' said Harriet, who liked the red phone boxes.

'I'd no idea there were so many call boxes in the village,' said her father.

They found Mr Moondew clipping his front hedge. He was most interested to hear that Milo had been turned into an elephant. He asked a lot of questions.

'You say he had answered the telephone shortly before. You don't know who was calling?'

'No,' said Harriet, 'but the man from the Department of Secrets seemed very cross about it.'

'I'd like to come and take a look at your brother.'

Crossing the green again, they saw two men by the phone boxes. One was their visitor of last night. They could hear him saying angrily, 'Those boxes have got to be moved by Saturday.'

'Well, guv,' said the other man, who was Mr Miller, of Miller's Removals, 'sorry and all that, but my trucks are busy till then.'

'Sir!' said Harriet's father to the man from the DOS. 'You had no right to change my younger son into an elephant. I must insist that you reverse the process. At once!'

But the bearded man, without bothering to answer Mr Armitage, took his hat off and flung it on the ground. It turned into a Rolls Royce, and he jumped into it and drove off.

'How rude of him!' said Mr Armitage. But Mr Moondew said, 'You're lucky that he didn't change you into a toad. That man wasn't from any government department. I know him from college days. He is a powerful warlock from the ghost island of Eridu.'

'Why,' cried Harriet, 'that's where Uncle Claud was going for his holiday. He was supposed to come back yesterday.'

'Now things are becoming clear,' said Mr Moondew. 'Perhaps it was your Uncle Claud who rang last night? And our bearded friend (his name is Logroth) wanted to prevent him. What is your brother's profession?' he asked Mr Armitage.

'He's a professor of mathematics.'

'Aha! The ghost island of Eridu is full of runes, and mathematical secrets—'

'And now the only person who knows the secret is Milo,' said Harriet. 'And he certainly won't tell . . .'

'But the knowledge, the secret, is still there, stored inside his youthful mind,' said Mr Moondew. 'But this gives me an idea as to what can be done for him—'

They had reached the Armitage garden, where Milo, sturdy and good-natured, was pulling the big garden roller, encouraged by Mark, and watched anxiously by his mother, who was waiting to feed him a large dish-tub of bread-and-milk.

'Dear me, a most handsome small beast,' said Mr Moondew. 'You are quite certain you do not prefer to keep him like this?'

'Quite certain!' said Mrs Armitage indignantly.

'So. What you must do is this. Each day at dusk, when the star Hesperus first shines in the sky, you must place him in one of those red phone boxes. Each night a different one. For from one of them was the secret message sent, only to be heard by Milo. Hearing it a second time will change him back. But he must be in the box just at that instant when the star shines. For so must it have been last night.'

'Suppose it's raining.'

'Makes no difference if the time is correct. But I must warn you—'

'Yes, what?' said Mrs Armitage nervously, clasping Milo's little trunk, which had twined confidingly into her pocket.

'Standing in the right box, he will at once change back into your charming little son. But if it is not the right one, he will merely double in size.'

'Lucky he's not very big now,' said Mark thoughtfully.

'Yes – but suppose we keep getting the wrong one – and he doubles again – and again – oh well, we'll just have to hope for the best.' Mr Armitage measured the size of his son with a thoughtful eye. 'Anyhow, most obliging of you, Moondew.'

That evening, just at dusk, Mark and Harriet led their young brother out onto the village green. The sky was clear, and a pale duck-egg blue; their father had calculated that Hesperus was due to sparkle out in precisely four minutes' time. But when they came to within a few metres of the call box at the end of the row of six, a large flock of savage magpies dropped down from the lime tree above, pecking and squawking and flapping, dashing fiercely into their faces.

'Hmm, yes, thought we might get a bit of interference,' said Mark.

He slipped a handful of firework sparklers from his pocket, lit them, and tossed them to the ground, where they fizzed and spat and hopped about, and flung up showers of heat and glitter and puffs of yellow smoke. The magpies made off, screeching angrily.

'Now, quick, you hold open the door and I'll shove him in,' said Mark.

This done, they stood with their backs to the glass door and arms across their eyes, in case the magpies wanted to make a comeback. But the magpies had taken fright and were seen no more.

Sadly, it was not the right box. Hesperus flashed out in the sky, bright as the fireworks, the puzzled Milo was told that he could come out, but all that happened was that he had doubled in size. Now he was as big as a Shetland pony.

'Never mind, my duck. Better luck tomorrow, perhaps,' comforted Harriet, twining her arm into Milo's trunk. 'Come on home. Muselix and buns for supper.'

'He'll need quite a lot.' Mark looked anxiously from his brother to the row of phone booths, counting on his fingers. 'Monday today. By Saturday – if we keep choosing the wrong box – it'll be no joke squeezing him in . . .'

Next evening the interference was caused by snakes: large, thick, black ones as long as bean-poles, who appeared, hissing disagreeably, out of the village pond, and twined themselves all around the second phone box.

Elephants can't stand snakes. Milo trumpeted and reared, and seemed likely to panic and bolt into the next county. But Mark had been prepared for trouble. He had a large can of fixative, used for drawing classes at school. He sprayed the fixative over the snakes, who became quite stiff with disgust, and shot back into the pond.

'I'll never go near it again,' shuddered Harriet.

But – alas – today's box was still not the right one; Hesperus shone out, but Milo simply doubled in size, and could only just be dragged out of the booth, levered on each side by garden shovels.

Next evening, in front of the row of phone boxes, they found a dragon. But Harriet knew all about dragons; she ran to the village shop and returned dragging a laundry basket full of eggs. These the dragon was happy to eat, whipping them up one at a time with his long, forked tongue. He took no more notice of Mark, Harriet, or Milo.

They had brought a big flask of vegetable oil, and they poured it all over Milo before pushing him into the box. It made him very slippery.

'It's lucky he's so patient and good,' panted Harriet, wiping oil from her eyes, her arms, her hair, her jacket, her teeth, and her shoes, while the Evening Star came softly into the clear green sky.

That was their only luck. Milo did not change back into their young brother, but merely doubled in size, stretching and bending the phone box into a barrel shape.

'Having the box like this,' panted Mark, hauling on his brother's leg, 'at least makes it easier to slide him out.'

'I'm afraid the person who bought the boxes isn't going to be pleased. There, there, baby! All better now,' to Milo, who was a bit disgruntled.

On the fourth evening, rain poured down from a thick

and soggy sky; Mark and Harriet, having carefully checked Hesperus's coming-out time on their watches, were discouraged as they led the whimpering Milo across the green to see that the fourth phone box was all wrapped in cobwebs, and when they came up to it, a fat black spider, as big as a barrel, slid down on a line from the tree above, gnashed its teeth at them, pulled open the phone-box door with its pincers, and nipped inside.

'Oh dear. Now what'll we do? I hate spiders,' said Harriet, and Milo plainly shared her feelings, for he trumpeted dismally.

'But it's simple. There's no rule about which box we try,'

said Mark. 'The spider's welcome to that one, if he wants it. We'll put Milo in this one.'

And he poured oil over his brother and stuffed him (with difficulty) into the fifth phone box.

At that very moment, a black cloud on the horizon drifted away. Hesperus blazed out as if sponged clean, and a whole lot of things happened all together.

Milo changed back from a medium-sized elephant into a small boy in blue-striped pyjamas, clutching a bottle of milk and covered head to toe in salad oil.

The huge spider exploded, shattering the phone box it occupied, as well as the ones on either side, with a tremendous, echoing clap of sound. Something fell heavily on Harriet from above, and she let out a yell, thinking it must be another spider.

But it turned out to be her Uncle Claud, who was in a dazed state.

Soon quite a large crowd of people had gathered on the green, including Mr Moondew, Mr and Mrs Armitage, and the village policeman, Sergeant Frith.

'Milo! Milo! My own, precious, oily boy!' exclaimed Mrs Armitage, and hugged the slippery Milo, who was wailing with fright at all these happenings.

'A most successful result of your efforts,' Mr Moondew congratulated Mark and his sister.

'But where in the world did Uncle Claud come from?' wondered Harriet.

'That we shall perhaps know when your uncle recovers,' said Mr Moondew.

But Uncle Claud was no help. When he recovered his wits, he could remember nothing of his trip to Eridu, nothing he learned there, nothing of what happened after he got home.

When Sergeant Frith went, rather gingerly, to inspect the exploded spider, he found that it seemed to have turned into the man from the Department of Security and Secrets – or, more properly, Logroth, the warlock from the ghost island of Eridu. He had fainted. But while they were waiting for an ambulance, he sat up, pulled off his black beard, flung it on the ground, where it became a Rolls Royce, and he drove away in it at top speed.

He was never seen again – except, presumably, in the ghost island of Eridu.

On the following day, the six battered red telephone boxes were found to have changed overnight into poplar trees, a ring of them, growing in the centre of the village green.

Mr Armitage said they looked silly.

British Telecom announced that they were not prepared to replace all six phone boxes. A single plain glass one in Station Road would be quite sufficient, they said.

'But what about the secret mathematical message?' said Harriet to Mr Moondew, who had called in and was playing chess with Uncle Claud. 'What about the information, the important secret – whatever it was – that Uncle Claud brought back from the ghost island of Eridu?'

'We'll have to wait for that,' said Mr Moondew. 'That information is locked inside your young brother's head.

Sooner or later – when he has learned to speak and knows the use of letters and numbers and decimals and logarithms – he will be able to tell us what it was. Won't you, Milo?'

Milo looked up from the carpet, where he was building a nuclear power station with telephone directories, and grinned.

'Elephant,' he said.

It was his new word.